PRAISE FOR RICHA
THE MOON
Book One / A Moon Realm Novel

"*The Moon Coin* is a beautifully written fantasy novel, perfect for middle graders to pore over themselves or as a bedtime story for younger kids. The descriptions of everything, from Uncle Ebb's electronic fish-bird hybrids to the fanciful creatures Lily meets in the Moon Realm, are so rich that the action instantly comes alive for the reader. The story's tension builds slowly but the excitement is constant, with Lily asking the same questions puzzling the reader. *The Moon Coin* has all the elements of a great fantasy: a unique, complex world, a battle between good and evil, and creatures that are a mix of comical and terrifying."

—ForeWord Reviews

"Entrancing pictures, an engaging plot, and a great writing style combine to create a middle grade fantasy that readers of all ages will love."

—Danica Page

"The world created by Mr. Due is a wonderful mix of fantasy that will have middle grade readers and teens wanting more. The writing is as magical as the Moon Realm, with nicely shaped phrases that don't confuse the reader."

—Carabosse's Library

"So begins a beautifully descriptive, cleverly written, intricate story, full of adventure and captivating characters, who draw you into their very lives and worlds. The wider adult reading population will no doubt be entranced by the skill of the author, Richard Due. I just cannot believe that this maturity and skill with the written word comes from a debut author."

—Fiction Books

"*The Moon Coin* is middle-grade fantasy at its best! When I was a kid I would have annihilated this book, slept with it under my pillow, and carried it with me at school."

—Sizzling Reads

"*The Moon Coin*, fast, furious and immensely enjoyable, reminded me of what I love about fiction. There are surprises around every corner and by taking the more difficult theme of division, forcible annexation and the underlying currents of coloring up the truth, Mr. Due has made *The Moon Coin* into a story that is deeply layered and developed as much as it is entertaining and delightful. With a extremely wide cast of characters and a heroine we can appreciate, *The Moon Coin* just keeps giving."

—In the Closet with a Bibliophile

"The world of the Moon Realm is so wonderfully detailed and vivid that you have no trouble imagining everything that Lily is going through. Lily and Jasper's Uncle Ebb tells the kinds of tales that every little kid dreams about. For someone so young, she's incredibly brave and adventurous. Fantasy lovers will love escaping into this new world!"

—A Bookish Affair

"Carolyn Arcabascio's illustrations really bring the story to life. The worlds in this story are vivid and beautifully descriptive. If you have a young reader who enjoys Fantasy, loves to be lost in a good story, or just wants something new, give them this book."

—Hopelessly Devoted Bibliophile

"Mr. Due's world building is phenomenal. The idea of the Moon Realm, a place where nine moons orbit each other (though the natives of each moon insist that their world is a planet and the other moons orbit around it) and get close enough to touch, was completely original."

—Howling Turtle

"One of the things I particularly enjoyed about *The Moon Coin* was the way that Due does not talk down to his young readers. The book employs a rich vocabulary, giving its audience opportunities to learn new words in context. The intricately described universe of the Moon Realm is the highlight of the book."

—Agrippina Legit

To read more praise for *The Moon Coin*, visit http://TheMoonRealm.com

Richard Due

THE MOON COIN

Book One / A Moon Realm Novel

To Olivia,
Tales, unlike stories,
never lie.

153/250

Illustrated by
Carolyn Arcabascio

Gibbering Gnome Press
A Division of Ingenious Inventions Run Amok, Ink

Huntingtown

Gibbering Gnome Press, A Division of
Ingenious Inventions Run Amok, Ink
Huntingtown, Maryland

This book is a work of fiction. Names, characters, places, and
incidents are products of the author's overwrought imagination
or are used fictitiously. Any resemblance to actual events or
locales or persons, living or dead, is entirely coincidental.

http://TheMoonRealm.com

ISBN-13: 978-0-983-8867-2-3 (ebook)
ISBN-13: 978-0-983-8867-0-9 (ebook)
ISBN-13: 978-0-983-8867-1-6 (ebook)
ISBN-13: 978-0-983-8867-3-0 (pbk.)

First Gibbering Gnome Press, A Division of Ingenious Inventions Run
Amok, Ink™ ebook edition September 2011; print edition May 2012

To my river-nymph,
who shares with me her underwater kingdoms.

ACKNOWLEDGMENTS

I'd like to thank my editors, Liz Prouty and Emily Bakely, for tirelessly improving my prose and catching continuity errors. Thanks to all my readers, especially Janet Jiacinto and Jessi Wood (aka Twizbang and Snerliff). A special thanks to the early contributors in CL: Julia D'Anna, for lending me Hotel Julie; Jamie Casbon, for letting me raid her closet; Jimmy Humphries, for poking holes in magic systems; and Sharon Grummer, for sharing with me those things that might, on any given day, be found on a thirteen-year-old girl's bedroom floor. A special thanks to Carolyn Arcabascio, for giving me artwork that surpassed anything I could have imagined. Thanks to my two beautiful children, who inspired me to see this novel through to the end. A special thanks to Roger Zelazny, for teaching me how to dream while wide awake, and Kurt Vonnegut, Jr., for teaching me how to laugh unexpectly in a silent, crowded room.

And finally, my eternal thanks to the little one who kept elbowing me— you're not making sense, *Daddy!*—, without whose assistance I never would have snatched the Moon Realm from the precipice at the edge of my dreams.

CONTENTS

★
★ ★

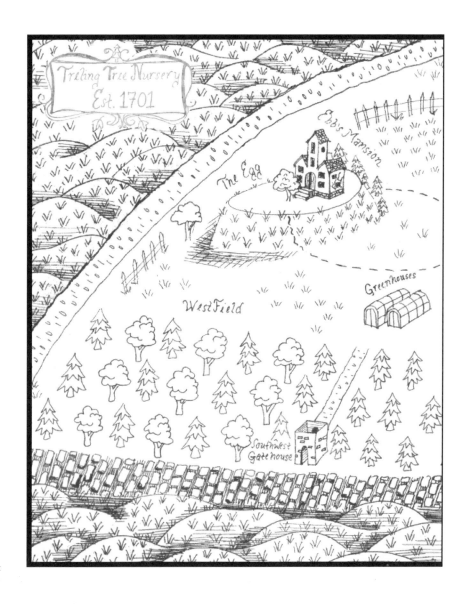

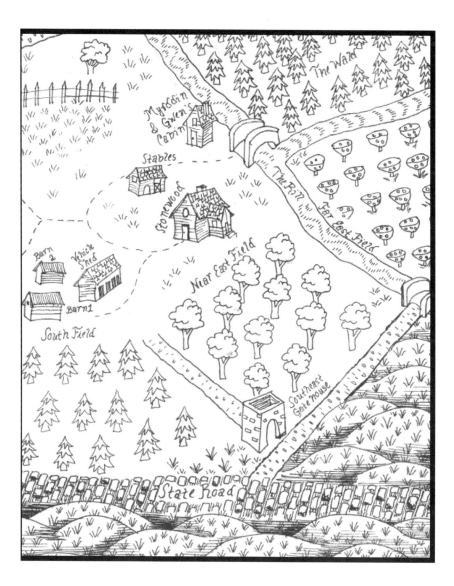

CHARACTERS

Earth

LILY VERVAIN WINTER, thirteen-year-old sister of JASPER, expert liar, trying to reform

JASPER MILFOIL WINTER, fourteen-year-old, would rather die than break a pinky-promise

TAY AND LINNEA WINTER, father and mother of LILY AND JASPER, owners of Treling Tree Nursery

EBB AUTUMN, LINNEA's brother, lives in the mansion on The Egg

BRUFORD, big black shaggy dog

TARZANNA, gray tabby, great mouser

HELLO KITTY, LILY's horse

GWEN MADSEN, geriatric botanist, works at Treling Tree Nursery, lives with her brother MYRDDIN in a cabin next to The Wald

MYRDDIN MADSEN, geriatric botanist, GWEN's older brother, good in a pinch

ISLA GORPMARCH, do not judge her by her size, LILY's best friend

THE ELECTRIMALS

OSCAR, bright red-plumed flying seahorse, unique among the birdfish

MR. PHIXIT, more than just two arms mounted to a tall dresser with exactly ninety-nine drawers

MR. CLIPPERS, eight-legged, solar-paneled lawnmower, lives on The Egg

FINDER, teddy bear-sized and -shaped, good at finding things

BOUNDER, larger, slower version of FINDER, good at carrying heavy objects

The Moon Realm

The Moon of Barreth

The Rinn

GREYDOR GOLDENCLIF, of the clan Foamchaser, Lord of the Valley Rinn

NIMLINN GOLDENCLIF, of the clan Broadpaw, Queen of the Valley Rinn

ROAN, warrior, head of his clutter

MOWRA, Court lunamancer

WYRRTWITCH, lunamancer, warden of Tower Clawforge

GENERAL LEWENHOOF, one of GREYDOR's top generals

The Wyflings

WITCOIL LIGHTFOOT, Lancespeed First Class, Royal Guard to the Queen
SNERLIFF, attendant to NIMLINN, stouthearted when not panicked
TWIZBANG, attendant to NIMLINN, a bit twitchy

The Moon of Taw

GRYGRACK, large green bird, currently royal messenger to the Valley Rinn
SQUARK, large yellow bird, currently royal translator to the Valley Rinn
CHERCHEER, large blue bird, currently royal translator to the Valley Rinn
ALERON, head of Heron Peck

The Moon of Dain

DUBB, Captain, Dragondain, master swordsman and tactician
LADY MAIRWEN, wife of DUBB and a Lady of the Court
TAVIN, Ex-Captain, Ex-Dragondain, cursed
EMBER, lunamancer, amateur Dain historian
QUIB, Dragondain, cook, man of many talents, wicked good with a whip
CORA, lunamancer, wife of QUIB, bakes a mean cherry muffin
KEEGAN HOARFROST, very old healer
RAEWYN, healer, daughter of KEEGAN,
MARRED, Dragondain, tracker, dragonologist, husband of RAEWYN
ANDROS, Dragondain, mountain of a man, bearer of Balherk's shield
JEMMA, Dragondain, wife of ANDROS
BOOTS, archer, rarely misses his mark, never stumbles, good with maps
ARRIC, lunamancer, good with wards, better with peerins
DARA, lunamancer
NIMA, healer, one of KEEGAN'S many granddaughters

Others

FAERATHIL, the Faerie Queen of Rel' Kah
MORGOROTH THE DEVOURER, Keeper of the Magic Flame, greatest dragon in all
the Moon Realm
WORNOT, mondo-huge talking bat
CURSE, nasty piece of work, inhabits a slag heap of a sword, likes to be oiled
regularly

PART ONE
THE RINN OF BARRETH

Nine Moons Make a Realm

Conjured Rinnjinn in Fangdelve keep,
*   the Rinn of Barreth making.*
Pearl of Dik Dek in oceans deep,
*   mer-made all for the taking.*
Kormor's work, hammer and anvil,
*   giants of Min Tar she forged.*
Terrible beauty Faerathil,
*   in Rel'Kah her dreams she poured.*
Three hearts bejewel the crown of Dain
*   Dragon, King, and Naramay.*
Lazy lives the long life in twain,
*   keying a lone memory.*
From grove to bird did language fly,
*   fluttering from Taw to Realm.*
Tinker's Secret? None to tell.

Darwyth's rising—a wellspring dell.

Bedtime Tales

Nine years earlier.

E BB Autumn stood tall and slender in his coat of many pockets. He was wearing his world-traveling clothes, and while the items in his many pockets normally remained private, tonight he had presents.

Lily and Jasper were bouncing on the bed when he knocked. A gentleman always knocks. Their uncle had a habit of arriving late or not at all, but when he showed up at bedtime, he always had a new story in need of telling—as if a thousand-year-old publishing factory resided in his head. And for this reason, as bedtime drew near on Lily's fourth and Jasper's fifth birthday, they were listening for him.

Ebb paused in the doorway, and a wave of concern passed over him. He'd missed their party. So many things to do. He brushed a long, silver-blond lock out of his eyes and stared with wonder, as if he were looking at the two most precious children ever born.

Jasper sat in plain sight, trying his best not to appear guilty by association, a situation he found himself in daily. Sometimes twice daily. Sometimes fifteen times. Next to him, beneath the covers, lay a Lily-sized lump.

A fearsome green dragon figurine rested on Jasper's lap. It was the last present he'd unwrapped that morning. His mother had gasped when she saw it, and his father had gone as still and silent as a statue. Jasper wasn't sure what that meant, but he knew immediately the dragon was special. Its emerald hide sparkled even in the dim light. Long whiskers drooped from its jowls, and the eyes in its spiked head gave the disturbing impression that they were staring back.

"Come to tell us a story, Uncle?" asked Jasper.

"Possibly," said Ebb. Striding into the room, he plopped down on the bed and rested his hand on the lump. "But where's your sister?" he pressed. "It wouldn't do to start without her."

Jasper knitted his brow. He had the look of someone who wanted to say something, but had been tasked with remaining silent . . . under threat of penalties . . . painful, awful, unrepeatable penalties.

Ebb smiled his crooked smile, which a stranger undoubtedly would have said looked sinister, but Jasper knew better. "Gone on an adventure again, has she? Leaving you all alone to fend for yourself? Did she swear you to secrecy before she left?"

Jasper fingered the tip of the dragon's long tail. "Nooooooo," he said, swallowing hard.

Ebb took a long look at his nephew. He was growing much too fast. Ebb observed Jasper's increasing mental prowess with both dread and fascination, but he felt only pride as Jasper screwed his courage to the sticking-place and gestured with his eyes to the lump under the covers. Ebb was pleased that Jasper's need to tell the truth was stronger than his desire to participate in Lily's schemes.

"Did you enjoy your fifth birthday?" Ebb asked enthusiastically.

Ebb was no stranger to enthusiasm. In fact, he had an unnatural talent for infecting others with the stuff. It was one of his gifts.

No longer burdened with the secret of Lily's whereabouts, Jasper's eyes lit up. "Yes!" he shouted. "Thank you very, very much for the dragon!"

"You're most welcome, my good man!" Ebb twiddled the tips of his long fingers atop the lump beneath the covers. "It's too bad about your sister, though. I was going to give each of you one more present." The lump stirred, but now it appeared as if Ebb's hand was holding it in place. "But I suppose . . . since Lily isn't here . . . I *could* give both of them . . . to you."

"You will not!" said the lump in a muffled voice.

Ebb leaned forward, as if listening intently. "What did you say, Jasper?" Jasper looked worried again. "Threatened you, did she?" he whispered conspiratorially. Jasper nodded, now looking a little sad. "Well then," said Ebb in a louder voice. "No Lily, no present. It's just as simple as that."

The lump shook violently. "My goodness," cried Ebb, "what's this?" The instant he lifted his hand, out popped Lily, like a towheaded jane-in-the-box.

"Presents!" she said.

"Why, there you are! You had me worried. Tell me, did you make any new friends today?" Lily tugged a winged figurine from under the covers and drew it up to her chest. A smile spread across her face, absorbing eyes, nose, and ears before it was finished. "Have you named her?"

Lily nodded, flinging hair into and out of her eyes. "I named her Blossom!"

Ebb's fingers flew to cover his lips. One of his fits had seized him. They always reminded Lily and Jasper of laughter, but this one was so severe Ebb was bouncing, ever so lightly. "Oh, dear me," he said under his breath. "Do do me a favor, won't you?" He paused, temporarily overcome. "If—no!—*when* you meet her—" Ebb slid his hand over his eyes, covering most of his face. Lily had just begun to wonder if something was wrong, when Ebb slowly withdrew his hand. "Don't"—he said in a forbidding voice—"*ever* tell her that."

Lily frowned. "Why not?"

Ebb's smile returned, his demeanor lightened. "Because that's not her real name, of course."

Lily gave her uncle a cold look. "Her *name* is *Blossom*," she said with a frighteningly steely edge for one so young.

"It's . . . a lovely choice," said Ebb. "For when your parents are around."

Blossom stood regally on Lily's knees. Graceful wings draped over her shoulders and hung down her body like a long, gray-feathered cloak. When Lily pulled Blossom's arms wide, her wings unfolded and spread with all the complexity of a living creature's. Underneath the feathers, she wore a dusky dark blue leotard, tattooed with a black pattern that blended so perfectly with her arms and legs that it was difficult to tell where the fabric ended and her bare skin began. Her wild black hair stuck out in all directions like striking snakes, and her face was a thing at once both terrible and beautiful.

Lily peered around the wings and eyed her uncle suspiciously. "So, what's her *other* name?"

"Can you keep a secret?"

"I *like* secrets," said Lily. She turned slightly and gave Jasper a superior smile.

"You can't ever speak her name outside this room, or to anyone other than your brother or me. You have to promise."

"I promise," said Lily quickly.

"It has to be a *real* promise."

"Real promise," echoed Lily.

"Same goes for you," Ebb said to Jasper. "Are you in?"

Jasper stared, paralyzed by the blatant subversive tactics being used by his sister and uncle. Lily and Ebb both knew that an actual, verbal *yes* was out of the question. But as the silence dragged on, and the opportunity for Jasper to decisively say *no* began to fade, Ebb held up his pinky. "Good," he said. "Then it's a pact." Lily hooked her pinky in Ebb's and stared at her brother. Jasper licked his lips.

"Come on," hissed Lily. "It's just a name."

Jasper held out his pinky and reached halfway. Lily pulled hers and Ebb's closer, but Ebb stopped Lily just shy of hooking their pinkies into Jasper's.

"It's your decision to make," said Ebb.

Jasper looked at them both by turns, took a deep breath, and hooked his pinky into theirs to seal the deal.

"Her name," Ebb breathed, "is Faerathil." Lily's face softened, as if she'd just heard a magic word. "The Faerie Queen."

"Faerie Queen," whispered Lily, spellbound.

"Yes. Oh, yes, most certainly—yes! And she can fly, just like— Well . . . throw her into the air and you'll see."

Lily hugged the figurine tightly. "She won't!"

"But I tell you she will. I designed her myself."

Jasper looked at his dragon. It had wings, too.

"She's too big and heavy!" exclaimed Lily. "She'll crash!"

Ebb crossed his legs, clasped his knee with both hands, and sat a little straighter. "Ah, I see. Well, as you grow older, you'll discover a curious thing about the truth—it plays by its own rules. It cares not one whit about your or anyone else's beliefs. The truth just *is*. There is no stopping or changing it. Further, I would counsel you to prepare yourselves, as the truth can be quite far removed from one's . . . expectations. Now, go ahead—give her a good toss. Do it over the bed if you must, and good luck catching her on the way down."

Lily loosened her grip and looked at her beautiful figurine. "You'll fix her when she breaks?"

"She won't break."

"Promise?"

"I promise."

Grimacing, Lily hurled Faerathil into the air. Once free of Lily's grip, once free in the air—free! like a jinni out of its bottle—she spread her long wings, dipped precariously, then swooped up and away from the bed. Lily let out a little scream—Faerathil was beating her wings and circling the room.

Ebb playfully fell backward onto the bed and pointed to the ceiling. "Launch your dragon, my good man!" he commanded.

Jasper threw his figurine as hard as he could at Faerathil. The instant the dragon left his fingers, its enormous wings snapped open and gave a single great beat, shooting it upward. As if on purpose, it deftly dipped one wing, maneuvered past a tall bedpost, then veered back toward its intended target.

"Oh, my," said Uncle Ebb.

Lily and Jasper flopped down on either side of their uncle.

"How long will they stay up there, Uncle?" asked Jasper.

Ebb laughed, pointing to Faerathil as she tactfully avoided a midair collision with the dragon. "I—I don't really know." The dragon banked hard, flying as if it could sense Faerathil's flight path. "Did you see that?" asked Ebb, pointing at the dragon and sounding astonished.

Lily let loose with a belly laugh. "My Faerathil's faster than your dragon!" she yelled.

"Does my dragon have a name too?" asked Jasper.

"Yes," said Ebb dreamily. "Morgoroth. Morgoroth the Devourer, Keeper of the Magic Flame, the greatest dragon in all the Moon Realm. Or so Faerathil would tell you. It was she, after all, who created him."

After a merry chase, and several near misses, the figurines spiraled downward—Faerathil landing on Lily, Morgoroth on Jasper.

Even at the age of four, Lily didn't miss much. "Moon what?"

Ebb sat bolt upright, looking very surprised—both at himself and at his niece. Lily had long been the more mischievous, but now her curiosity had made her dangerously observant; in watching Jasper's development so closely, Ebb had somehow overlooked this trait in

Lily. Jasper was going to have to work hard to keep up with his sister, at least until they were older. And how would Lily react when her brother was no longer so easily manipulated? Ebb didn't want to know.

"I . . . I have presents for you," he said, recovering. "In my pockets."

The children fell on their uncle like ravenous raccoons. Lily pulled out a small pencil worn to a nub. Jasper found a small pad of paper. Then Lily pulled out a second pad, and Jasper a third. During the assault, the top button of Ebb's collar popped open and Lily spied the glint of metal at his neck. Quick as a dragon bite, she took hold of a thick, golden chain.

"What a pretty necklace," she said. Ebb's hand shot up and enclosed her small one. "Can I see it?" she asked.

"No," said Ebb firmly.

"Please?" she pleaded. Lily patted a lump on Ebb's chest, just under his shirt. "What's—"

Ebb grabbed up both of Lily's hands and looked her squarely in the eyes. "No means no!" he said in a voice that would have sounded harsh to anyone else. It was a phrase Ebb used only when no amount of begging would change his mind, and Lily had heard it plenty.

Lily went back to searching pockets, but something strange had happened.

"They're all empty now," she said.

"Nonsense," replied Ebb. He produced a handkerchief from the pocket Lily had just searched, brushed off some unseen offense from his tan canvas trousers, and then returned it to the same pocket.

Lily dove after it, but again the pocket was empty.

"It's empty. You lied," said Lily.

"Are you sure?" said Ebb. "Lying is a pretty big accusation, you know."

Lily folded her arms. "Grown-ups aren't supposed to lie."

"But I didn't."

"Did too."

"Try this one," offered Ebb, indicating one in a row of pockets sewn down his sleeve.

"No!" said Lily.

"Suit yourself." Ebb offered the pocket to Jasper.

Jasper dipped in his fingers and closed them around something cold and hard. With a tug, he pulled out a golden disk the size of a drink coaster. Jasper shot Lily a look as though they'd just witnessed real magic.

"My turn," shouted Lily, thrusting her hand into a random empty pocket. She drew out her hand very slowly, looking disappointed.

"I think it's hiding from you," said Ebb. "Try the next one over. That one there."

Lily reached in tentatively and pulled out a beautiful shell the size of a grape.

"It's so pretty!" she gasped. "What kind is it?"

"The name doesn't translate well, I'm afraid," said Ebb, his voice suddenly sounding far away. "I picked that one up while strolling down a beach . . . while in the company of a most singular woman."

"Did you give it to her?" asked Lily.

Ebb arched his eyebrows. "Yes," he said. "I certainly did. If you look carefully, you can still see the small hole where she ran a chain through it."

"Where's the chain now?" asked Lily.

A shadow passed over Ebb's face. "With her," he said.

"What's this, Uncle?" asked Jasper, waving the golden disk.

"That's a dragon scale," said Ebb, snapping back to the present. "From a very special dragon, named Fendragon."

"A real one?" asked Jasper, astonished. "It's not very big." Ebb smiled.

"Dragon scales come in all sizes, many even smaller than that one."

"Are you going to tell us a story, Uncle?" asked Jasper.

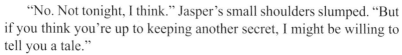
"No. Not tonight, I think." Jasper's small shoulders slumped. "But if you think you're up to keeping another secret, I might be willing to tell you a tale."

"There's a difference?" asked Lily.

"Oh, yes, yes, yes. You see, a story can be made up as easily as you please, or not. But a tale, now that's a moon of a different color. A tale is an account of things in their due order, often divulged secretly, or as gossip. Would you like to hear one?"

"Yes, please," said Jasper.

"What's gossip?" asked Lily.

Ebb eyed his niece and nephew shrewdly.

"We'll be quiet," offered Lily, crawling under the covers—standard practice for bedtime stories.

Ebb tucked them in. "What I'm about to say, I don't say lightly. And if I am truly to tell you a tale, then it must stay here"—Ebb tapped the tip of his finger to Lily's temple—"and here"—followed by a tap to Jasper's temple—"in the little black boxes that live behind your eyes. You must never breathe a word of it, especially to your mother and father. Do you understand?"

Jasper made the dragon pretend to sniff the golden scale. "I won't say anything," he said.

Lily held the shell to the Faerie Queen's ear. "Me either," she said.

"You won't find the tales I bear in any books. Well, at least not any books around here. My tales are from the Moon Realm."

"Where's that?" asked Lily.

"Sshh!" said Jasper.

"The Moon Realm is a place where nine moons, or worlds—depending on one's cosmogony—swirl around one another like—"

"What's cosmogogonanny?" asked Jasper.

"Sshh!" said Lily.

"It's complicated," explained Ebb. "Let's just say . . . the locals each have their own ideas about who's in charge and leave it at that, shall we?" They nodded. "Good. *Very* good. Now, the surprising thing about the moons in the Moon Realm is that they circle their sun as a group, bunched up together, as if caught inside a big, ball-shaped net."

"But don't they smash into each other?" asked Jasper.

"No," said Ebb. "But neither do they stray far. They do, however, at very special times, come so close that the tops of the tallest trees of one moon can brush up against the treetops of another."

"That's close!" said Lily.

"Why don't they smash into each other?" asked Jasper.

"Because they don't. Now, less talking and more listening. On the moon Dain, high on a hill, in the beautiful city of Perianth, lived three very special souls: King Mondain, Queen Naramay, and Fendragon, the Dragon King. They lived in peace, harmony, and friendship: the king and queen in their castle, and Fendragon, along with all his dragon kin, high in their perch-towers, looking down on the city and people they so dearly loved."

Lily raised her hand. "Do tales have talking squirrels?" she asked softly.

"No," said Ebb. "Those are only in stories."

Lily and Jasper exchanged a dubious look. "Some people are just sad when there aren't talking squirrels," said Lily. Jasper nodded.

"I think you will find there are other . . . *beings* . . . who are every bit as interesting as talking squirrels."

"Like what?" asked Jasper.

"Well . . . let me think," Ebb's gaze wandered around the room, as if looking for inspiration. "The Rinn," he said finally. "They live on a moon named Barreth. . . . They're cats, of a fashion."

"Cats," said Lily, clearly unimpressed.

"Yes . . . more like lions, actually, with wider faces." Ebb continued. "A full grown Rinn is a little larger than one of Ms. Jenny's Clydesdales."

Lily's eyes opened wide. "Can you ride 'em?"

"Oh, yes. The men and women of Dain who have that privilege are called Dainriders. You have to be kind of . . . born into it, of course."

"What else?" said Jasper, now clearly on the hook.

Ebb thought. "On Min Tar, there are giants—eighteen feet tall! They use their forges to fold magic into things."

"There's magic?" asked Lily.

"More magic than you can wave a wand at. Of course, the Tinkers use steam and arcane knowledge to make things you would *think* use magic, but don't. They're so secretive, they won't even tell the name of their moon! And Dik Dek, which is one giant ocean, is alive with coral cities, filled with merfolk, seahorse dragons, and pearls and gardens the likes of which you would have to see to believe."

"Your pictures!" said Jasper.

Ebb looked down at his hands. "Yes . . . all of my paintings are of the Moon Realm. And they will mean much more to you after you know the tales that go along with them. So . . . now . . . may I start?"

Lily and Jasper leaned back into their pillows, looking very pleased.

Nine years and hundreds of tales later . . . Ebb went missing.

Oscar Knows Things

L ILY eyed the piece of bark up close and compared it to the picture in her book. They didn't match. They *never* matched. She scowled.

Dark shadows drifted across Ebb's bright green lawn. A breeze kicked up, carrying with it the ringing sound of Mr. Clippers' shears, snipping and snapping at errant strands of grass. The vast network of branches above Lily's head sighed, and a great shifting sea of bright amber leaves waved at her . . . mockingly, she thought.

Lily slammed the book shut, tucked it under her arm, and slowly turned to face her brother, who was inspecting leaves on the same tree. "You wanna go in the house?"

"Of course I want to go into the house. But Dad told us to wait." Jasper glanced at his sister. "You heard him. He's in a mood." Jasper opened his own book and held it close to his face. None of the pictures matched the leaf in his hand. They never matched.

"What kind of tree," complained Lily, "has a broad amber leaf, never changes color, and never sheds a leaf all year?"

"Ebb's amazing mysterious never-evergreen?" said Jasper. They'd been over this before.

"Maybe it's a mutant," said Lily. "Like a unicorn."

"It wouldn't be like Ebb to give us a problem that couldn't be solved."

"Agreed," Lily sighed. "But . . . but did he really give us this task?"

"Of course he . . ." Jasper stared off into the branches above. "I mean . . . he gave us that feltleaf willow. And . . . that Tasmanian mountain ash . . . a couple years ago. And that juniper thingy out back beside the . . . pool . . ." Jasper turned to Lily, shock dawning on his face.

Lily crossed her arms and nodded. "We did this to ourselves," she confirmed.

"No!" said Jasper.

Jasper shot a glance at the many-windowed, sun-drenched brick of his uncle's mansion. The house, its gardens, and the lone tree in front, stood on a curious hill known as "The Egg." A large, geographical oddity, the hill was shaped exactly like an egg with one notable exception: after a steep twenty-foot rise, it was tabletop flat.

"Why's Mom so worried?" asked Lily.

"I wish I knew, Lil." Jasper sighed.

"I mean, it's not like Ebb hasn't been on long trips before."

Jasper got down on his hands and knees and combed the grass with his fingers, looking for anything that might have dropped from the tree. "No cones, no flowers, no catkins, not so much as a grain of pollen! How does this tree ever bear fruit?"

"She's freaking out. Why is she freaking out?"

Jasper thought for a moment. "He vanished."

"He's vanished before," said Lily.

"Never for this long."

"He's a grown man," countered Lily.

Jasper raised his eyebrows. "Time of year? We move a ton of trees and shrubs in the spring. She wants him at Treling."

Lily tilted her head, rolling this idea around. "I like it. He's needed here, he hasn't checked in, and she hasn't been able to reach him."

Jasper gazed past the tree's enormous trunk to the narrow end of the egg, across the long, oval-shaped swath of green, to where the trail vanished over the edge. "Mom and Dad should be here by now."

"Maybe Mom stopped to take cuttings," suggested Lily. "It's a beautiful day. Hey, I know." She made an effort to sound casual. "Let's go up to the porch and wait for them there."

Jasper laughed. "You're not getting inside. I know what you want to do."

"You do not," said Lily quickly, but she suspected he did.

Jasper continued to stare across the egg.

"Don't waste your time looking for them," Lily advised. "Dad'll let Bruford off the leash when they're close. The instant he sees us he'll start barking his fool head off."

"If he doesn't have it out with Mr. Clippers first. What is it with those two?"

As if on cue, a dog barked. Jasper took several quick steps away from the tree's trunk. Lily turned silently toward the mansion and set off at a full run.

Bruford, black and shaggy, bounded over the edge of the egg and onto the perfectly manicured grass. He ran straight for them and then veered off, making a beeline for Mr. Clippers. Barking madly, the dog began moving in a strange loping hop. Mr. Clippers, who was the size of a push lawn mower and just as low to the ground, raised his two long metallic arms and began snipping his shears like castanets. Using his eight shiny legs, he pivoted in time with Bruford's every lunge, waving his shears to protect his gleaming black solar-paneled carapace.

"Yep, just as I suspected. The lure of Mr. Clippers was just too—" Jasper, turning, discovered Lily was gone. "Lily?" he said, his voice rising, and he took off after her.

She was sprinting toward the center section of the mansion, which rose four stories tall and was flanked on either side by a long two-story wing. Dark green ivy clung to the lower brickwork. Near the second floor, the first patches of red brick appeared, and by the third floor, the ivy was only tendrils, lacing upwards like green lightning. Lily streaked toward the double doors.

Jasper overtook his sister faster than she would have liked. He arrived at the doormat a dozen steps before her, landing on it with an impressive *thwomp*. Gasping for air, Jasper straightened up and lifted his face to a large bronze door knocker, shaped like a lion's head but wider, with deep black sockets where its eyes should have been. It was a Rinn, straight out of the bedtime tales. Of course, when their parents were around, they pretended it was just an ordinary lion's head.

"Wake up, Rinnjinn!" he cried, as though addressing a living thing.

In response, the knocker's bronze eyelids snapped shut with a clank. When they reopened, a moment later, the sockets held a huge pair of bright blue eyes. The knocker emitted a sound like a throat being cleared, or maybe a yawn. The eyes scanned aimlessly, first right, then left. Jasper coughed. The pupils narrowed to slits and lowered themselves as if to glare at him. As Uncle Ebb's creations went, Rinnjinn was unimpressive. He always woke in the same way: first he looked side to side, then he canted his eyes down. If Jasper wanted to look straight into them, he had to plant his feet in just the right place so they'd make solid eye contact.

"Who goes there?" boomed Rinnjinn.

"Jasper Milfoil Winter," he said, hoping the hidden microphone would identify him on the first go. He waved his palms around like giant paddles. "Ninja Master!" he added.

He was rewarded with a loud *click*. "Enter, young master," said Rinnjinn, his voice trailing off, his pupils growing wide, and his eye sockets once again going dark.

Jasper excelled in physical contests. But Lily had not quit trying to keep up with him, or taking him by surprise. In a rush, she squeezed past her brother and pushed open one of the doors, planting her left foot just across the threshold and her right firmly on the doormat. Now barring the way, she held the thick door sandwiched between her open palms, smiling as she panted. A bead of sweat trickled down her brow, several locks of blonde hair plastered wetly against her flushed cheeks. The siblings looked so much alike they could have been twins.

Jasper could see it was dark in the great hall. He felt its coolness leaking out past his bare legs.

"Dad *told* us to *wait!*"

Lily smiled. The effect was at first wolf-like, and wicked. And then she was just Lily, smiling. She ducked her head into the darkened hall, then back out.

"Lily!" said Jasper.

She bit her lip. "I just want to see if his coat's inside." Jasper knew better than to believe her.

Bruford's bark sounded louder. The enormous black dog had given up on Mr. Clippers and was now streaking in their direction.

"Well, looks like he still has his nose," said Jasper, but when he turned back, Lily was gone. Again.

Jasper pushed wide the thick door. He stepped quickly across the landing past the two tall bookcases that flanked the entrance. The wedge of daylight streaming in shrank as the door behind him swung shut. Not wanting to get caught on the stairs in the dark, Jasper paused just for a second to look for Ebb's coat, the one with all the pockets, among the various cloaks, coats, and hats on the pegs that lined the walls. The narrowing wedge of daylight was nearly gone. Jasper glanced at the remaining steps. They were cut to resemble scalloped

waves and would be hard to manage in the dark.

"It's not there," called Lily tauntingly.

Jasper raced down the last few steps, reaching the hall just as the door clicked shut.

Lily laughed.

"Lily," Jasper called, "we shouldn't be in here."

Jasper followed the sound of her footsteps, ahead and to his left. She was making for the foot of the mansion's main staircase, where the old bridge telegraph was located. As he got closer, and his eyes adjusted to the darkness, the telegraph's round, softly glowing faceplate appeared. It was divided into sections like a pie filled with wedge-shaped text; he could make out the words FULL, HALF, SLOW, DEAD SLOW, STAND BY, and STOP. A dark arrow hovered over the word STOP.

Having reached the telegraph first, Lily grasped its big brass lever and gave it a pull. Still making his way across the hall, Jasper saw the arrow sweep across its face, a small bell dinging as the arrow passed from one setting to the next. It passed all the wedges, hovered over the word FULL, then pulled back and came to rest on the word HALF.

The high-pitched whine of an electric turbine sounded from below. The smooth marble floor gave a momentary shudder before settling down to a low, murmuring pulse. She'd done it now. The Tesla generator was roaring to life somewhere underneath them, charging hundreds of banks of capacitors with electricity. A powerful electromagnetic field now coursed through every room of the mansion, extending even to the grounds, supplying electric power through the air to any device designed to make use of it.

A wash of sea-green light began to fill the hall, as though it were shining down onto the mansion's walls. But the source of the light was one of Uncle Ebb's many illusions, and Lily and Jasper were convinced that the light was coming from inside the walls themselves. However, these were not normal walls. Instead, they were fantastic coral reefs, full of colors, encrusted in shells, sea fans, and anemones.

The light on them played in ripples, suggesting warm rays of sunlight cast through rolling waves. Caught in the hypnotic effect, Jasper's annoyance with Lily evaporated. He drifted toward the reef, transfixed as always by his uncle's creations.

The bottom two feet of the walls were paneled in dark wood, intricately carved with scenes of swimming seahorses and mercreatures, and vast undersea castles half-hidden in forests of leafy kelp. But it was the coral walls that enchanted the eye. Tucked among the coral crags, brightly colored sea anemones lifted slender tendrils and began testing the air, which smelled more and more like the sea with every passing second. Pale pink shells, large and small, slowly opened and closed. Purple, pink, and yellow sea fans began to twist and sway, as though being gently buffeted by slow-moving ocean currents.

Lily crossed the hall and joined Jasper. She cupped her hands on his shoulder, leaning her head against his arm. Directly in front of them was a strange-looking seahorse, its tail tightly clutching a small golden perch embedded in the reef.

Covered in varying shades of bright red plumage, he couldn't have measured more then ten inches fully stretched out. All along the reef were mounted more of the small golden perches, each occupied by equally strange-looking creatures, though the rest were more bird-like—or *were* they fish? It was hard to tell. Their wings were short for wings, and their fins were long for fins. And their mouths, though wide like fishes' mouths, were hard like birds' beaks. And now, with the Tesla generator supplying electricity, they had begun to twitch, their heads jerking in little jolts as the airborne electric current pulsed through their bodies.

The red seahorse untucked his head. Still quivering, he stretched out his stubby wings and began testing them in short, rapid bursts.

All along the reef wall, birdfish were testing their wings. Some sat still, moving only their flamboyant crests up and down; others spread their fins wide, like brightly colored sails. The seahorse, whose name was Oscar, began opening and closing his eyes in a way that always made Jasper think he was running some kind of internal systems check. Presently, Oscar opened his beak and let out a loud burble-squawk.

Lily grinned at him. "Well, hello, Oscar!" Lily had been five when she named him. He was the only birdfish to have an official name and the only seahorse. Oscar was a favorite.

With an explosive flapping of wings, Oscar popped upward a foot or more before settling down and once again clasping the golden perch with his long tail. He shook his head, ruffled his feathers, and opened his eyes wide to take stock of his surroundings, eventually settling his blinking gaze on Lily and Jasper. This appearance of wise scrutiny was completely at odds with his birdbrained nature. And yet. . . .

Lily nudged Jasper. "Oscar knows things," she whispered.

And it was true. In fact, of the many electrimals that lived in and on the grounds of Uncle Ebb's mansion, Oscar was one of the very few who remembered things from one day to the next.

Suddenly, all the birdfish began flitting and popping above their perches, each species making its own strange gurgle-chirp or glub-whistle. There were at least a dozen different species in all, each modeled on what appeared to be a blend of brightly colored tropical bird and fish. There were canary-yellow ones, which Lily called flit-doodles because of how easily they were spooked, and shimmering green ones, which Jasper called cloy-twins because of their habit of snuggling up together. Some had intricate patterns. Some sported deep blues, fuchsias, or oranges. Others were streaked with white or sparkling silver over velvet black.

Oscar gave a sharp cry and launched himself from his perch. Taking their cue from him, all the other birdfish lifted off and began darting in, out, and around the coral reef wall, quickly forming into a flowing, prismatic flocskool. Oscar cut a frantic path, and they were hard-pressed to keep up with him. Occasionally, smaller flocskools would split off and surge in different directions before eventually realizing their error and racing back to the main skool.

Lily and Jasper exchanged puzzled looks. "How odd," he said.

"What's wrong with them?" said Lily, her smile fading. "They're not quieting down. Why aren't they quieting down?"

Normally the birdfish would have settled into a slow and majestic swim, their little wings beating like hummingbirds', as they wound their way in and out of the coral's dark crevices, pretending to look for food.

But not today—not if Oscar had anything to say about it, which he most certainly did. Poking his head out of the larger holes, he would call out shrilly, pausing for a second as though listening, then call out again—only much louder. Occasionally, he would stop and hover, whipping his head back and forth. This activity positively panicked the other birdfish, and they engulfed him in a blur of bright wings as they looked about in confusion. Then Oscar was off like a shot, zipping down the reef and disappearing into one of the entryways that led into the rooms flanking the hall, leaving the others to flock behind him as best they could.

"I think he's looking for something," said Jasper slowly.

"Or someone," said Lily. "Do you think he could be calling for Uncle Ebb?"

"I don't know. I've never seen him so *frantic*," replied Jasper. "How would Oscar even know how long it's been since he last saw Ebb? Do you suppose he has some kind of internal clock that runs when the generator's off?"

"You mean like a little watch battery that keeps the day and date?" asked Lily.

Jasper nodded. "I don't see why not."

Oscar's plumed head popped through a hole in the coral directly in front of them, unfurling his crest to its full height. He looked wild-eyed at each of them before blasting out a gurgle-chirp. As the utterance trailed off, it rose in pitch, as if Oscar were asking a question.

Now *this* was something new.

Lily and Jasper shared a brief glance, each wondering if the other was thinking the same thing.

"Oscar?" said Lily, leaning closer. "What is it?"

Oscar wormed his way through the narrow hole and wound his tail about a bit of protruding coral, tucking his stubby wings. He leaned toward Lily, staring brightly at her through his jeweled, coral-pink eye as his plumed crest slowly furled and unfurled. From the other side of the wall, sounds of panicked birdfish erupted, no doubt due to the disappearance of their leader.

As Oscar stared Lily down, the flocskool streamed back into the great hall, pouring around doorways and through larger openings in the reef. It was as if they were in a race to reach him first. Oscar gave the merest nod to Lily and then Jasper and then did a very strange thing: he launched himself *away* from the wall and *out* into the center of the hall.

Taken by surprise, Jasper jumped back, angling sideways. Not even Oscar had ever shown such boldness before. Hadn't Ebb programmed the birdfish to keep to the reefs? When it came to crossing a room, they *always* took the circuitous, wall-hugging route. Lily knew this very well, having as a young girl made many unsuccessful attempts to tease or trick them away from their walls with treats—or threats.

The flocskool crashed together where, just moments before, Oscar had perched. Two long-tailed, orange bob-jabs squeezed out of the pile-up. They shot out in pursuit of Oscar, exchanging looks of terror, as if neither could believe what the other was attempting. The remaining birdfish surged down the hall, taking the long, sensible way around to the staircase.

They resembled a brightly colored, screaming roller coaster—careening down the hall, rising and dipping. At the end of the hall, while squeezing above the double French doors, the flocskool caused a noisy traffic jam. Occasionally, birdfish would pop loose and, like salmon shooting the rapids, spurt ahead before wriggling back into the rest of the flocskool.

Lily and Jasper followed Oscar's path across the hall to the staircase. The first of the birdfish to arrive were none too happy to find only Lily, Jasper, and two alarmed looking bob-jabs. Where was Oscar? they seemed to want to know. As the rest of the birdfish gathered, a dizzying hysteria built.

A neon-blue grib-peck mounted himself imperiously on the stair rail's towering newel post, which was carved to look like a family of merfolk rising through a column of water. As the little blue puff-ball glared down at Jasper, its eyes growing ever darker and more baleful, it issued a loud glub-whistle of protest or possibly outrage—you could never be certain with those grib-pecks; they were always on about something. Ears ringing, Jasper winced and pointed up the staircase. Two more grib-pecks settled on the newel post, one on a merman's arm, the other on a mermaid's head, and began mimicking the first.

Jasper covered one ear and pointed up the stairs. "He went up there, you birdbrained fish!"

The three grib-pecks stared blankly up the stairs and, clearly unimpressed, turned back to Jasper, glub-whistling more loudly than before.

Just then, from the second floor, came the distinct sound of Oscar's whistle. Taking flight as one, the birdfish vanished up the staircase in a bright mass of swirling, flapping colors.

All was quiet.

Lily and Jasper leaned forward, peering up after them.

An instant later, a thunderous clack echoed through the great hall. Startled, they turned to see their red-faced father gathering up his wooden walking stick to smite once more the stone landing of Ebb's great hall.

A Coin of the Realm

Lʏ ᴵ ɪʟʏ and Jasper wheeled to face their father. Tay Winter stood in the open doorway, framed by the bright light of the outdoors. His face was flushed, as though he had run the last portion across the egg.

"I thought I told you to wait for us," he said indignantly.

Jasper felt a sudden stab of guilt and failure, whereas Lily, wondering what might happen next, felt a dark thrill. Neither of them, though, wasted any time before pointing fingers and blurting out accusations.

"She went inside! She turned them on!"

Lily's mouth and eyes opened wide. She looked, very much to her credit, genuinely shocked. "*You* were the one who opened the door!"

she said pointedly.

Now it was Jasper's turn to look shocked—although unlike Lily, he was. Stung by the sudden and unexpected shard of truth, he winced. There was no denying it: he *had* awakened Rinnjinn; he *had* unlocked the doors.

"But—" began Jasper, "but—*you* were the one who went in!" he retorted hotly. "And *you* turned on the birdfish!"

Lily met her father's gaze fearlessly. "Daddy," she pleaded, sounding very earnest, "we waited until Bruford was in plain sight. And we never left the great hall. We didn't so much as *look* into another room."

"It's true," said Jasper, taking up the case just as their mother walked onto the landing.

Jasper froze, cursing his timing, and wondered if Lily had somehow planned that.

Lily couldn't read the look on her mother's face. Her brother Ebb's long absence was making her moods unpredictable. It had been nearly a month now—a very long time for Ebb to be away and unaccounted for.

Tay cast his eyes down and sighed. Lily knew her father couldn't stay angry for long, a trait she exploited often and with great abandon. And had there been any real harm? All they did was open the door and step inside! They had waited, after all, until they saw Bruford.

Still, he'd told them not to enter the house.

Lily watched her father wrestling with what to do. Jasper, unable to meet his mother's glare, hung his head, heat rushing to his cheeks. Their mother began to speak, but Tay put a restraining hand on her forearm. "Linnea," he said mildly. Lily suddenly realized she hadn't properly reckoned on what her mother might say.

But before she could say anything, Oscar's loud whistle broke the silence. He barrel-rolled down the staircase, a streak of fuchsia, the entire flocskool of birdfish glued to his tail. They made a terrible racket, swarming Tay and Linnea, who instinctively raised their hands in defense. But the birdfish meant no harm, and after Oscar led them in

a half-dozen tight turns around the Winters, he peeled off, disappearing with the flocskool up the staircase.

"What was that about?" cried Linnea in alarm, still waving one arm at nothing in particular.

The whistle sounded a second time and down came Oscar as before, again with his whole flock, encircling the confused parents, swirling around and between them in tight figure eights, only to vanish back up the stairwell.

Tay, holding a protective hand near his head, pointed to the bridge telegraph. "Jasper," he bellowed, "turn that thing off!"

Instantly, Oscar and his flocskool came down once more. This time they descended like a soft, silent rain, landing and perching as still as statues on whatever object came first to talon. In the silence, Oscar slanted his eyes back and forth between the children and their parents. He looked positively chastened.

The entire family gazed at the frozen birdfish. Lily's mother shook her head.

"Crazy little things," she muttered.

Lily's father gave them a long look, sighed, and then hooked his cap on one of the nearby pegs. He tossed his walking stick a bit too forcefully into a bin filled with umbrellas and walking sticks.

"Jasper, Lily," he said, looking distracted. "Your mother and I will need some time *alone* in Uncle Ebb's study. You may putter about as you wish." He hooked his wife's arm in his own, and they descended the stairs without another word, disappearing through the first doorway on their right.

Lily turned to her brother. "Mom is worried."

Jasper nodded, then held up a hand to shush Lily. Their mother was speaking.

"You don't really think they're involved, do you, Tay?" she said, her voice fading.

"It's always been a possibility," said their father. "They've been nothing but trouble since the day they were born."

"But surely they—" and the rest trailed off too softly for Lily and Jasper to understand.

Lily frowned, her lip sticking out slightly. "You don't think . . . you don't think they could mean *us*, do you?" she said uncertainly.

But before Jasper could answer, Oscar let out an ear-piercing burble-squawk and launched himself directly at them, the flocskool in tow. They rounded Jasper sharply and then twisted around Lily, quickly forming into a fast-moving figure eight of fluttery bright colors.

They were traveling so fast and so close that Lily was afraid to move. At last, her arms pinned to her sides, she began to laugh.

"The feathers!" she giggled. "They tickle!"

"I'm afraid to move my arms!" yelled Jasper.

"I know! Me too!"

Then Oscar broke free and flitted up the stairs, lighting on the old grandfather clock that towered on the landing. The flocskool followed him noisily, settling all over the clock and the coral reef behind it. The birdfish were loud, but Lily and Jasper could still make out Oscar's plaintive whistling over the din.

"Lily—" said Jasper, his eyes growing wide. "Oscar knows something . . . and he's trying to tell us what it is."

Jasper raced up the stairs two at a time, Lily right on his heels, and with every step, the coral walls brightened. Light purled across their surface as if it were shining through only a few feet of water.

The second floor ran perpendicular to the great hall for the full length of the mansion's long wings; the corridors vanishing in each direction were called the North Hall and South Hall. As Jasper peered down the twin halls, an uneasy feeling crept over him, like he was being watched. But there wasn't an electrimal in sight.

Suddenly he was engulfed by a colorful tornado of wings descending from the third floor. Jasper twisted around, trying to spot Oscar. That's when he saw it—or thought he saw it. About twenty feet up North Hall, just for a second, something—or someone—ducked through an open doorway and out of sight.

"Uncle Ebb?" yelled Jasper. There was no reply.

A moment later Lily stepped into the swirling flocskool, now thinning rapidly as the birdfish diverted down South Hall.

Lily eyed her brother, still staring at the doorway where he thought he had seen something.

"What is it?" asked Lily. "Did you see him? Did you see Ebb?"

"I don't know—I saw something. It could have been—but Uncle would have answered, right?"

"You probably saw Finder," offered Lily, as she stared down the hall at the departing birdfish. "He never answers when he's on a job for Mr. Phixit," she said quickly, grabbing Jasper by the elbow and giving him a hard tug. "Come on, they're getting away!"

The second floor of Uncle Ebb's home was like a museum, albeit one with glowing coral reefs for walls. Tall glass curio cabinets stood every few feet, and piled between them was just about anything you could imagine: busts, telescopes, sculptures, shields, saddles, whole looms still threaded and in working order, piles of books, barnacled anchors, and fully garbed mannequins, some in splendid gowns or cloaks, some in full suits of armor.

Between the cabinets, the reef walls were covered with dozens of small shelves, pictures, and brass hooks. From the hooks hung daggers, short swords, and belts.

Ebb's paintings peppered the walls. Portraits of merfolk mounted on seahorse dragons; hammer-wielding giants striking anvils before glowing forges; groomed Rinn, sphinx-like on their thrones; lavish interiors; castles; pitched battles; glowing horizons immense with overlapping moons—all were well known to Lily and Jasper through the forbidden bedtime tales. Long had they studied these paintings, matching snippets of tales and pieces of maps, searching for new clues or insights into the twists and turns of Uncle Ebb's ingenious mind. It was a long-played game, one they still played today, but there was no time for that now.

The birdfish doubled back and fluttered about, brushing against their arms and cheeks and using Jasper and Lily's bodies like moving islands to crisscross the hall.

Oscar darted out a doorway, whistled loudly, and ducked back in. The birdfish took off after him, and Lily and Jasper sprinted to catch up. The room they entered was large enough that the birdfish returned to their habit of hugging the walls on both sides, dipping around the furniture and picture frames as they spread out, their servos and motors silent. Lily and Jasper slowed to a walk.

They passed through several rooms in this fashion, the flock rejoining and splitting at each new doorway. When there was more than one doorway, Jasper and Lily would wait mid-room until it became apparent which way Oscar was taking them.

The journey ended in a darkly paneled room. The birdfish circled aimlessly before becoming strangely calm and alighting wherever they could find purchase. Dust motes hung in the air. And though it was one of the chief jobs of the birdfish to collect and transport dust to the dustbins, they simply perched and stared.

Directly opposite the entrance was an enormous nine-sided window. Through it shone the distorted crown of an immense tree. Liquid, golden, it glowed like the surface of a great sphere. Two long-tailed orange bob-jabs clung precariously to a grille in the middle of the window, their long tail feathers pressed like fans against the wavy glass.

Jasper compared their position to his woefully incomplete mental map of the mansion. He knew exactly where they were now: just under the eaves of the mansion's second story. Oscar had delivered them into one of Uncle Ebb's personal rooms. Jasper jumped back nervously.

"Lily! We're not allowed to be in—"

"Hush," whispered Lily, stepping further into the room. "They brought us here for a reason."

On either side of the door, rows of brass hooks held cloaks, coats, and jackets. Half the floor was taken up by two large, haphazard piles of clothes, many of which needed laundering. Shallow shelves overflowed with hurriedly piled hats, ties, belts, keychains, wallets, gloves, and every other accessory you could imagine.

Lily picked up a glove from a nearby shelf. "Odd place for a cloakroom."

Jasper stood in the doorway, holding fast to the doorjambs as if afraid of being sucked into the room.

"Lily!" he hissed, "Dad will have a fit if he catches us here."

Lily continued to glance about, looking for Oscar. "We'll just be a minute. Calm yourself." She beckoned to Jasper, tossing her blonde hair. "Come on in. Even the birdfish don't seem to mind it—and there's not a speck of coral reef in sight." Lily smiled in that strange way that Jasper always thought made her seem so much older. She seemed to save it for very disturbing times . . . like now.

Jasper looked at the birdfish dotting the walls; what Lily had said was true. "They must be malfunctioning. They've strayed too far from the generator or something."

"That's ridiculous. They're fine. The reason is obvious," said Lily, laying the glove back down and picking up a red velvet ring box. Prying it open, she frowned at its emptiness.

"Obvious?" said Jasper, sounding put out. "Obvious how?"

Lily smiled, put the box back where she'd found it, and picked up another. This one was covered in green velvet. "They do it," said Lily imperiously, "because Uncle has programmed them to do it. Simple as that."

The green box had three trees embossed in gold on the lid. When Lily opened this one, she gasped. Inside was a ring, set with a large round piece of polished bone wreathed by tiny golden wings.

"Lily!" Jasper took a step into the room and snatched the box from Lily's hand, closing it and returning it to the shelf. "These are his private things. We're not . . . to . . . ."

A glint from something in the umbrella stand caught Jasper's eye. He pushed aside the walking sticks, frilly parasols, and dark umbrellas, revealing the hilts and scabbards of several swords. He fished out a jewel-encrusted one and gave the hilt a yank, partially freeing the blade. It was bright silver, with a long line of runes engraved down its center. The light from the window caught the blade oddly, making it difficult for Jasper to focus. At the grip jutted two cross-guards, each studded with a moon, one full, the other crescent. When Jasper subtly pronated his wrist, the moons shone iridescent, like mother-of-pearl.

Oscar burble-squawked, and instinctively Jasper dropped the blade and scabbard back into the umbrella stand. The scabbard hit the bottom of the metal container with a hollow bang, and the blade re-sheathed itself, hidden once again among the swords, walking sticks, and umbrellas.

"Oscar!" exclaimed Lily, holding a hand to her heart. "Was that really necessary?"

Oscar dove between them, spread his wings, and glided to a row of coats hanging on the wall. He looped his tail around a big brass hook shaped like a praying mantis. With an impressive tug of his beak, he deposited one of the coats unceremoniously onto the floor.

Lily knelt down to pick up the coat. "Really, Oscar? Seriously? This place is messy enough without you—" This time Oscar dropped an outsized topcoat on Lily's head. "Hey!" Lily batted at the coat. Oscar added a gray wool hunting cloak, a black dress cape, and a houndstooth waistcoat. "Help!"

Jasper bent over to help, and Oscar cut loose a heavy cavalry-man's greatcoat. It looked like something from the Napoleonic Wars. The sudden weight unbalanced him, and he toppled onto Lily.

Oscar emptied half the rack before they could untangle them-selves. Jasper was the first to free himself and see it.

"Oh, no!"

"What is it?" asked Lily, her voice muffled from the pile of coats.

Jasper jumped up and began replacing the coats as fast as he could. "Nothing. Nothing at all."

But Oscar kept unhooking the coats as fast as Jasper could replace them. With a mighty heave, Lily popped free of the pile and spotted it.

"Jasper! We have to solve it!"

Oscar let out a low whistle and nodded his head.

"No we don't," said Jasper, replacing the black dress cape, which Oscar promptly unhooked and let fall to the floor. "We have to get out of here. We're in Uncle's private quarters! What if we get caught?"

"No, Jasper. This is why Oscar brought us here. First he tried to tell Mom and Dad, but they didn't understand. Now he's telling us."

Jasper dropped the cavalryman's greatcoat and turned to face the wall. Carved deeply into the wood was one of Uncle Ebb's bestiary puzzles. This was the seventh they'd encountered. Each of the previous ones had unlocked a secret: a drawer full of candies, a shortcut to another room or the outside, a secret playroom filled with stuffed animals. One puzzle led to a maze they still hadn't solved.

Anyone could look at the carvings and admire the artist's handiwork. But if you knew a little Moon Realm lore, and you knew the basic structure, you could solve the puzzle. All the principal denizens of the Moon Realm were represented—all but one. The missing one left you the clues you'd need to solve the puzzle.

"I see Rinn," Lily said, pointing to one of the enormous cat-like creatures, who lay on his back, belly-fur exposed, laughing ridiculously.

They both held out a finger, an unconscious gesture unchanged from childhood.

"That accounts for Barreth," said Jasper. "One moon down. Hey, aren't those Tinkers tickling the Rinn's belly?"

"Those little guys, yeah." Two fingers. "Can you imagine a real Rinn putting up with that?"

Lily and Jasper looked at each other.

"They'd eat 'em," they said in unison.

"Well, that takes care of the Secret moon," said Lily. "Look here. Where is this long coil headed? It looks like part of a dragon, and what are those two people doing along the edge?"

Jasper pushed aside a coat. "Um . . . giving a dragon a manicure?"

"'Three hearts bejewel the crown,'" said Lily, quoting from Ebb's

poem. "So that accounts for Dain. Three moons down."

Three fingers.

"This foot is obviously connected to a giant, although it's silly big."

"And I see plenty of birds. That accounts for Min Tar and Taw." Fourth and fifth fingers. "Hold on. I don't see any merfolk," said Lily. "Not a one."

Jasper removed the last of the coats at the edges of the panel. "You're right." Lily and Jasper moved closer, examining every inch. "Well then, that's our clue. So what have they left behind?"

"The emery board that woman is using on the dragon's nails is a starfish," Lily blurted.

"Good one," said Jasper.

They stared longer. "As puzzles go, this one is just absurd. There's no narrative."

"It's like a nursery rhyme," Lily agreed. "Maybe the starfish is the only clue."

"No. Good things come in groups of threes," he said.

"'And better things come in *three* groups of threes,'" said Lily, repeating one of Ebb's sayings. "There! On the Rinn's tongue. A pearl."

"You sure? Could be a piercing." Jasper nudged Lily with his elbow.

"On a Rinn? Not likely, idiot. That's two. But where's the third?"

With a sudden burst of his wings, Oscar dropped down and landed on Jasper's bicep, where his purchase was precarious at best. Jasper raised his arm, and Oscar inched his way down until he was pecking forcefully at Jasper's index finger.

"He wants you to point," said Lily.

Oscar's crest rose and fell, and he made a low whistle that sounded very impatient.

"That'll be enough from you, my little friend," said Jasper. "And staring at me like that isn't going to help one bit."

Jasper pointed his finger and Oscar nipped the knuckle of Jasper's thumb.

"I think he wants you to go in that dir—"

"And that'll be enough out of you, too." Jasper moved his hand to the right. Oscar held out his wings.

"I think he wants you to—"

"Shut it." Jasper raised his finger until he was pointing to a group of trails meeting in the far background of the scenery.

"Trails," stated Lily. "Paths. Roads. I don't get it. How does that fit with an ocean-covered moon?" asked Lily.

"The shape! They form a trident!" said Jasper. As he spoke, he pressed all three of the clues at once, using an elbow to reach the star-fish. A loud creak sounded in the opposite corner of the room.

Behind them, a floor-to-ceiling gap opened where the walls met.

Lily approached slowly and gave the walls a push, revealing a darkened passageway. She stepped back and gave her brother a quick smile. "After you, oh ninja master."

Jasper deposited Oscar on a pair of red leather dress gloves and gave Lily a cordial nod. "To the brave go the spoils," he said, striding past her into the darkness.

Lily's face fell. "Wait . . . spoils? What spoils?" She darted after her brother so fast she bumped into his back. Shuffling from side to side, she tried to find enough room to squeeze past him, but the passage was too narrow.

"What do you see?" she said, making little jumps to try and see over his shoulder. "Is that light? Tell me what you see."

Within ten feet, the passage opened into a long, narrow room that ran under the eaves. An inch-wide skylight ran the length of the room, and underneath rested nine enormous glass globes. Each one sat on a squat bronze base atop a low pedestal.

"They're terrariums," said Jasper, tapping the closest one.

Lily bent down low. "Look, there's writing," she said. Foreign scripts, each strikingly different from the next, were etched into the bases.

Jasper studied the writing. He paused before the only globe completely filled with liquid. "I've seen this one, in one of the paintings."

"The one of the merfolk library?"

"Yes!"

Lily started. Something had moved in the globe. The narrow band of light from the ceiling created a veil within the globe. In its center was a colorful lump of living coral, crags swirling with the frenetic movement of minute crustaceans and slowly undulating anemones.

Jasper pushed his forehead against the glass and cupped his hands around his eyes. "They're alive. Unless . . . you don't think they could be electrimals, do you? I mean . . . they're so small."

"Never underestimate the ingenuity of Mr. Phixit," said Lily, repeating one of Ebb's mantras.

Jasper smiled. "I suppose—"

Lily gasped and ran to the far side of the room. "Jasper! Come look!"

In the far corner, covered in dust, stood an old dress mannequin made of yellowed canvas, empty of clothes. Draped around its neck was a necklace with an elaborate pendant.

Jasper's mouth dropped open. "Ebb's necklace!"

Lily and Jasper had seen it many times, always around Uncle Ebb's neck, but they had never seen what dangled from it. *That* had always remained hidden, no more than a lump under his clothing.

Lily delicately fingered the necklace's thick chain.

"Why is it here?" asked Jasper.

Lily lifted it off the mannequin's shoulders and examined it in the light. The pendant was made of an outer ring and an inner disk. Connecting the two were a dozen thin tines, evenly spaced like the spokes of a wheel or the hours on a clock.

"What's that? In the center?"

Lily flipped over the pendant, examining both sides as best she could in the thin veil of light. The tines grasped only the very edge of the coin, allowing both sides to be easily viewed.

"I think it's a coin, a gold coin."

Lily fitted the pendant into the palm of her hand. There was a fob on the outer ring, perfectly placed for her thumb to open or close it. Mounted on either side of the outer ring was a crab-claw-shaped set of pincers made to clamp down on the coin front and back.

"Why would it need these pincers?" Lily said. "When it's already held in place by these tines?"

"Don't fool with it," warned Jasper.

Opposite the fob was a long, curved lever, shaped to look as though it were part of the outer ring of the pendant itself. It had a neat little catch, such as you might find on a bracelet to keep it from opening by accident.

Without thinking, Lily undid the little catch and pulled the lever. It swung open easily, and the tines retracted into the outer ring with a neat click. Now the pincers alone were holding the coin in place.

"What are you doing?" hissed Jasper.

Lily swung the lever back, and the silver tines shot back out of the outer ring and re-clasped the coin, much to Jasper's relief.

"Why is Ebb without his necklace?" mused Lily.

Jasper shrugged.

His sister's eyes brightened. "Let's take it home!"

Jasper took half a step backward, his palms upraised before him. "No way! Lily, Mom and Dad will want to see that."

Lily pressed the necklace tight against her chest. "Oh, come on. Just for a few days. Please? We can show it to them later. We can give it to them—tomorrow!"

"I—no—" Jasper hesitated, "Dad will want to see it. I'm sure of it. It might be important."

Lily knew he was right. Still . . . Mom or Dad would *take* it.

"What if I just drew it? Please? Let me draw it! I'll do it in one night. We can give it to them in the morning—first thing! Please?"

"You'll show it to them in the morning?" asked Jasper, dubious. His sister nodded fervently. "First thing?"

"Promise! Real promise!" Lily began carefully coiling the necklace.

"I . . . I don't know, Lily."

"Just *one* night." She stuffed it into her jacket pocket. "Uncle Ebb's been gone for so very, very long. What difference could one night make?"

"Just one night?" Jasper relented.

Lily smiled. "Just one." Then she pointed to the nearest globe. "So, what do you make of these?"

"I was thinking . . . there are nine of them," said Jasper.

"Nine moons make a realm," Lily whispered.

"Exactly." Jasper grinned and tapped the glass of the center globe. *"'Pearl of Dik Dek in oceans deep.'"*

"'*Mer-made all for the taking,'*" said Lily, completing the line.

"Dik Dek is all ocean!" said Jasper.

Jasper and Lily peered at the script. There were two short words that might have been *Dik Dek* at the very top, with smaller writing below.

"We should search *all* the paintings for more script," said Lily, "see what tales they're connected to. It might give us a clue."

"I agree, but why would Ebb make these terrariums?" Jasper wondered aloud. "And why would he hide them away like this?"

"I don't know, but I don't think terrarium is the best word for them."

Jasper gave Lily a quizzical look.

"What then?"

"They're for moons. How about . . . lunariums?"

"Lunariums!" laughed Jasper. "That's perfect. That's exactly what they are."

They peered through all the lunariums, looking for any kind of clue but finding none. Eventually, Jasper rose. "Mom and Dad won't be busy forever. And we still need to visit Mr. Phixit."

"You more than me," said Lily, smirking at her brother's anxious face.

Jasper took a deep breath. "Do you think he's fixed it?"

"He better have, or Dad's going to kill you."

Mr. Phixit

U NCLE Ebb's workshop, which occupied the entire third floor, was a giant windowless room filled with aisles of parts, cannibalized and half-finished inventions, and junk—lots and lots of junk. The staircase emptied right into the middle of it. The walls gave off a dark blue light, as though these reefs were deep under the sea. The electrimals that lived here were also different: large-mouthed, bulbous-eyed, with long dangling spines. They moved slowly, gliding along the walls like miniature deep-sea dirigibles.

Mr. Phixit sat directly in front of the landing. He consisted of two arms mounted to the sides of what looked like a tall dresser with exactly ninety-nine drawers. A sizable worktable was attached to the front of the dresser, and Mr. Phixit could raise and lower it to reach all his drawers. The worktable was ringed by all manner of tools that Mr. Phixit could easily grasp and use. At one time or another, Lily had looked through most of the drawers, which held nuts and bolts, wire, solder, batteries, screwdrivers, wrenches, and many other items for which she had no name.

On the corner of the worktable was an old, beaten-up keyboard with a tiny black-and-white video screen. By default, Mr. Phixit kept his table in a lowered position, so that a person standing in front of him could easily use the keyboard and read the tiny screen.

Jasper tapped the keyboard's space bar, and it fell off, clattering to the floor.

Lines of text rapidly scrolled across the video screen, stopping to display *Job 247ab6 in progress* and *Parts Needed,* followed by a long list of odd parts. The message *Parts Missing* blinked at them.

In the center of the worktable sat Job 247ab6.

"What do you suppose it is?" asked Lily.

Jasper reattached the space bar to Mr. Phixit's keyboard and began rummaging through several low-rimmed boxes labeled *Fixable, Unfixable,* and *Finished.*

"I can assure you I have no idea."

Jasper fished something shiny out of the *Finished* box.

"Yes! Dad's pocket watch!" he yelled, pumping a fist high into the air.

Lily laughed. "You're lucky he hasn't noticed it missing."

"It was an accident!" said Jasper, his face turning a deep shade of red.

Lily emptied the contents of her pockets onto the edge of the worktable. Cupping her hands, she pushed the little pile next to Job 247ab6 and typed *Parts arrival for Job 247ab6.* The space bar fell off again, along with the letters R and J.

Little spotlights on Mr. Phixit's two arms winked to life. His arms swung down noisily, and four tiny video cameras, mounted in pairs on each arm, scanned the worktable and the items from Lily's pockets. He poked and prodded the pile with his thin metal fingers. One by one, the items under the heading *Parts Needed* vanished from the tiny video screen. A second after the last item winked off the screen, Mr. Phixit began opening and closing drawers, pulling out various objects, and laying them on the worktable. He rearranged the items Lily had brought and set to work on the strange object that was Job 247ab6.

"Poor Mr. Phixit. It would be so much easier if we could just talk to him."

Jasper raised his eyebrows. "I wouldn't hold your breath on that one, Lil."

Lily picked up the space bar and carefully tapped it into place, followed by the letters R and J. That done, she gingerly typed: "New Job: replace keyboard with upgrade."

Jasper laughed. "That ought to confuse him."

Lily tenderly patted one of Mr. Phixit's arms. "Shut up, Jasper. Mr. Phixit has been very good to us. It's only fair that we try and take care of *him* every once in a while."

Jasper shrugged. "Okay, but you're paying for the new keyboard out of *your* pocket. I don't see why you don't just tell him to glue his keys back on better."

"I'll get whatever parts he wants. As long as they don't cost *too* much," she added, sounding unsure.

They both knew that Mr. Phixit wouldn't look at the keyboard job until he'd finished as much of Job 247ab6 as he could, given the parts he currently had on hand. Once he'd reached a roadblock, or finished, he'd get started on whatever was next on his internal docket.

"He might not even want a new keyboard. He'll just tell us what he needs . . . and we'll get it for him. Just like always."

"All right," said Jasper, glancing at his dad's watch. "We better check in with Mom and Dad."

Seemingly oblivious, Mr. Phixit continued his work as Lily and Jasper descended the stairwell, headed for the study off the great hall.

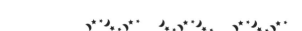

Their parents' mood was unchanged.

"Get into trouble, you two?" asked their father. Jasper was sure Tay knew they'd been up to no good, if not what they were up to in particular. Lily, however, could tell that her father was fishing, and before Jasper could stammer an answer, she stepped in.

"We didn't break anything, if that's what you mean." She gave her father a playful nudge as she walked out the door.

On the walk home, Lily couldn't stop thinking about drawing the necklace. After almost a mile of silence, Linnea draped her arm over Lily's shoulder and squeezed. "How's your work for the website coming along?" she asked.

Lily pulled her eyes away from her brother. "The web designers keep trying to jazz it up, and I keep telling them it should look as much like the print catalog as possible."

"Well, maybe it's time for Treling to move into the modern era," said Linnea. Lily and Tay rolled their eyes.

"But the fonts and layout are already super-hip-archaic old-school."

"What about the sketches?" asked Linnea.

"The old artwork is fine!"

"Yours are better. I want to see finished product by the end of the week."

"So," began Jasper, "this summer . . . do I get to work on the bigger equipment and work in the Wa—"

"No!" interrupted both parents at the same moment.

Treling was a substantial tree farm with orderly nursery rows and greenhouses, but on its northern border lay a great expanse of forest known simply as The Wald. Jasper and Lily never worked within The Wald, where the big trees grew. The rill, a meandering and unpredictable stream, separated farm from forest. The only easy way in or out was the old stone bridge next to Gwen and Myrddin's small cabin, a spirited walk north from Stonewood, the farmhouse where Lily and Jasper lived.

"But with the website coming online, we'll be busier than ever before. And with Ebb not—" Linnea shot Jasper a hard look. He changed his approach. "Gwen and Myrddin are old. How can the four of you expect to run Treling without more help from *us*?"

"Ebb will be back," said Linnea. "Until then, I'll teach you more about how the machinery works."

"But I already know how it works. And I have some ideas for improvements. If I spent more time with Mr. Phixit, I could make some smaller-scale prototypes to test—"

"Mr. Phixit has enough to do without you making up tasks for him," said Tay.

"Like what?"

Giving Jasper a knowing look, Tay tapped his wrist and patted his pocket.

The rest of the walk proceeded in silence, all the way to the kitchen door, the highest-traffic spot in any farmhouse.

Stonewood wasn't on the National Register of Historic Places in Pennsylvania, and it wasn't the first house built on the property—that honor went to Gwen and Myrddin's cabin. Nor was it the largest house, which was Ebb's mansion, but it *was* an old farmhouse, built at a time when settlers hewed wood in much the same way as ancient Egyptians carved stone. Part of the home had once been an attached barn, a feature that in seventeenth-century Pennsylvania allowed for easier care of the livestock during hard winters. But the old barn, which included a stone foundation and huge, exposed wooden beams overhead, had long ago been converted to living space for the family.

After dinner there were dishes to wash, followed by make-up homework that Lily hoped would boost her borderline grade in algebra. And then there was Treling's website. Lily's mother had given her the job of overseeing its design, but not the power to make the final decisions. Where Lily wanted flipping pages, the original woodblock artwork, and all the original handset fonts, Linnea wanted something . . . different. But what that different was, Lily had yet to decipher or concede to.

Lily trudged up to her room, sat down at her desk, and called her friend Isla Gorpmarch. Isla had been Lily's best friend since kindergarten, and she was brilliant. Lily wanted to run some ideas past her. But Isla didn't answer. Lily waited until the beep, held the phone in both hands in front of her face, and screamed as if she were being murdered. She shrieked, "Website! Website! It's killing me!"

Lily tossed the phone onto the litter that was her desk. She picked up her current sketchbook and hesitated. She slid her hand into her pocket, letting her fingers tangle in the cool metal links of Uncle Ebb's necklace. But the necklace would have to wait.

She opened to the sketchbook's first page. She had drawn Stonewood at an angle to show off the old barn. Above the house was a large rectangle around the words: *Treling Tree Nursery.* Under that it said: *Est. 1701.*

Below the house, she had written in a flowing hand:

Treling (pronounced "trelling") is proud to present its 304th catalog. Inside you will find an extensive line of shrubs, plants, and flowers, all renowned for their extreme hardiness. In addition, Treling offers a full selection of mature trees: trees to be delivered and planted on time, as specified, and always at the price originally quoted. If called upon, we at Treling can—in a single night—

transform a flat, barren field, where previously the largest structure had been an impoverished ant colony, into a park of towering majestic trees, complete with birds. Hardy trees. Trees to last many lifetimes.

Lily's eyes drifted to her phone. No Isla to save her this night. Resigned, Lily picked up a pencil and turned to her sketches for the website's index page, where a person could browse by tree or shrub size, by color, or by season. Even if she did manage to please her mother, there was nothing she could add that would make her father like it. The passage of time had little to no effect on his tastes.

Flipping back to the first page, she added more details and shading to the house. She spent about an hour crafting a spiderweb on the porch railing that no one would ever notice. But that was okay: she would know it was there.

At the earliest respectable hour, Lily went downstairs to find her parents and say good night. Returning to her room, she locked the door.

Once back in her chair, she placed the necklace on a stack of books, then turned on a small lamp and tilted it very low. From a box on a shelf she withdrew a pad of her best paper, then sharpened six pencils to varying degrees of sharpness. Starting in the upper right corner of the pad, she drew a sampling of links from the necklace. Below it, she outlined a square and inside drew two links very large to capture the micro fish-scale pattern that adorned each one. Once that was done, she sketched in the rest of the chain without much detail until she got to where it attached to the pendant. She flipped to a new page and sketched the outer ring, copying the smallest details that wound and tangled on its surface, mostly plant and sea animal motifs.

The coin had been minted with daring precision and bore even more detail than the outer ring that held it. Twice Lily added more books to the pile to move the coin closer to her eye. Tilting the top book helped some with glare, but the coin tended to slip off at unexpected moments. In the end, she wound the chain around her left forearm from elbow to wrist and held the coin nearly to her face as she sketched every detail she could make out. Lily was used to sketching small details of plants, leaves, and seeds; she was well-practiced, fast, and precise. Still, there was an impossible amount of detail impressed upon every surface of the necklace, pendant, and coin.

The rim of the coin was covered with an intricate vine and leaf motif, reminiscent of Celtic patterns, but it was not a design she recognized. Then came an inner ring of evenly spaced circles, each with a corresponding symbol. Holding the coin at just the right angle revealed the shapes of continents and oceans. Lily picked up the magnifying glass she used for plant specimens.

They were *worlds*, and there was enough detail in them to fill a separate page for each. Far too much detail to draw in one night. Lily knew she would have to make choices. She put down the magnifying glass and sketched only the barest details of each individual world's geography.

If the symbols were letters, they were in a language Lily didn't know. And yet, as she drew them, as she concentrated on them, they began to look familiar. There were ten little worlds, all the same size, and the crab-claw pincers pinched right down on top of one of them, making it impossible for Lily to see its surface.

The very center of the coin showed a fruit, something like a pear, which took her no time to draw. The back of the coin was completely filled with the silhouette of a tree. Around it was a wide circular walk on which stood nine thick pillars, evenly spaced, and between the pillars stood people who looked so tall and rigid that they might have been statues.

Lily tripped the fob with her thumb and the pincers popped open.

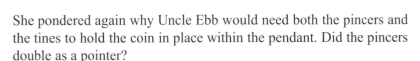

She pondered again why Uncle Ebb would need both the pincers and the tines to hold the coin in place within the pendant. Did the pincers double as a pointer?

Then Lily noticed something odd. The little worlds on the coin were changing to a silver white. Lily sat upright and pushed the lamp away. The circles were giving off their own soft light.

Using her pencil's eraser, Lily tentatively touched one of the glowing circles. Something moved. Lily drew away the pencil and examined the coin closely. The pattern of vine and leaf were the same, as was the piece of fruit in the center. But now the inner ring of little worlds was slightly off center. A quick comparison to her drawing convinced Lily that the entire ring had moved, just a tiny bit, clockwise. Lily put down the pencil, and with her index finger, she slowly spun the inner ring around. As each little world passed under the pincer—or pointer—a tiny click sounded. She turned it several times around, then flipped the fob closed with her thumb. Immediately, the little lights winked out, the surface of the coin once again gold. With the pincers back in place, Lily tried to spin the inner ring, but it held fast.

Well, she thought, *mystery solved.*

To Barreth

THE lamp on Lily's desk flickered twice before plunging her room into darkness. A sound like ocean waves rushed around her, and she sensed herself being buoyed upwards. She filled her lungs to scream, but before she could take a full breath, she felt herself torn from her room like a small piece of paper whisked away in a storm. The air felt thick, like water, and she was afraid to breathe. She tumbled over and over with increasing speed, rocketing faster than she could have imagined.

How many minutes passed this way Lily could not guess. Time and again she tried to right herself against the currents and regain some control. She was just beginning to think she was having some effect on her spinning—by pulling in her arms and legs—when it ended as abruptly as it had started. She tumbled and bounced on what felt like soft earth, taking a hard kick to the chest. Her own knees, maybe?

Lily rolled onto her stomach, dizzy and unable to breathe. Her fingers found earth and dug in. She tried to fill her lungs, but they would not cooperate. When she finally did inhale, the air was smoky and acrid, irritating her throat.

Slowly, the world around Lily revealed itself. There were sounds: something like birds, and something far off—something low, hoarse, and rumbling. Lily rubbed her eyes, but they refused to clear. She tried to sit up, but the woozy feeling churned into something worse and forced her to fall back again.

As she concentrated on her breathing, the coughing fits settled. The light grew brighter, and the scene gained shape and focus. She was in tall grass, maybe wheat, only the heads were short and thick like barley. It was a variety she was sure she'd never seen. Without even thinking, she pulled down a piece, broke off the head, and stuffed it in her pants pocket. More carefully this time, she pulled herself to a sitting position. The grain was tall enough that she would have to at least kneel before she could get some idea of where she was.

A blurred bit of movement passed overhead. As Lily stared into the sky, her distance vision resolved. It was a strange sensation, like someone was playing with a focus knob behind her eyes. The blotchy shapes streaming above became wings and tails, but the sky behind them remained gray and indistinct. With great concentration, Lily willed her eyes to focus. Colors emerged, and she saw that some of the birds were quite large, or perhaps some were just much closer. Dozens of them streamed by above, but something about the sky still seemed wrong. A slight breeze stirred the grass, and the terrible acrid smell worsened.

Trying to stand, Lily fell forward onto her hands, the necklace slipping down her arm and dropping away. She probed the earth where she thought it should have been, but found only loose dirt. Frantically,

Lily widened her search, digging her fingers into the roots of the tall grass. Then, far off, she heard the sound of voices, and froze.

Her vision had cleared, but when she looked up again, the scene made very little sense. It was as if someone had replaced the entire sky with an upside down forest of dead trees. A sickening wave of vertigo passed through her. Digging her fingers into the loose soil, she fought off an irrational fear of plunging down into it. Once the feeling passed, she dared to look again. The forest floor was suspended above like a high ceiling. Mist swirled around the trees' roots and boles, flowing over crags of rock and disappearing into dark canyons. Lily tried to pry her eyes away, but she found she could not stop staring. It was *all* dead.

The ground shook, and the grass swayed around her. Then she heard more sounds, disturbingly animal-like, mixed with the striking of metal on metal.

She crouched on all fours and renewed her frantic search for the necklace. How could it have gotten so far? Lily raked her fingers through the grass in places she was sure it couldn't be. At last, her hand brushed the cool links of the gold chain. She snatched it up and quickly put it on. Seizing the coin, she gave the little worlds a hard look. The glow had left them. Lily tripped the fob and gave the inner ring a quick spin; it made soft clicking sounds as each world passed the pointer. She closed and opened the pincers. Nothing. She spun the ring again. Again, nothing.

Lily tucked the pendant under her shirt, poked her head above the grass, and surveyed her immediate surroundings. Not ten feet from her hiding place ran a wide footpath. To her left, it traveled up a short but steep hill, sparsely covered with short-limbed, scraggly trees. Lily stood, resisting a bout of dizziness. She took deep, calming breaths, trying not to look directly above, where the strange world filled every bit of the open sky.

The ground rumbled again. Instinctively turning to discover the source, she confronted a scene very difficult to take in all at once.

In this direction the land fell away into a great valley that traveled to the horizon, rimmed on either side by distant mountains. Maybe a mile distant, Lily judged, stood a tall stone tower, standing in stark, defiant contrast to the flat valley floor. The tower rose to such a height, and the world above hung so low, that at first it looked as though the two were in danger of colliding.

Then Lily noticed something chilling. Dangling down in great arcs from the dead forest above were thin black lines that connected to the pinnacle of the tower. Dark forms emerged from the trees, crawling across the thin webs like spiders to their prey. Their numbers seemed endless. The top of the tower was black with them, and they trickled down the sides in dark ropy lines, like black wax dripping down a white candlestick. They climbed over themselves and clung to one another in a way that made Lily think of bugs—very large bugs.

Past the tower, deeper in the valley, the dead world arced downward until, perhaps a dozen miles distant, the two worlds came so close that—at first—they appeared to touch. There, thick black masses oozed and spilled down from the world above to the world below, like great clingy globs of molasses. In the valley, the dark masses spilled over themselves like swarming ants. Whatever they were, there were thousands upon thousands of them.

A large bird broke from the others and swooped down, veering rapidly toward Lily. Had it seen her? Her first impulse was to hide, but where?

Close by, a hail of arrows launched upward toward the descending bird, barely missing their mark. Lily gasped. The arrows made a terrible whizzing sound, and out of instinct, she ducked, but they arced far away from where she stood. Meanwhile, the bird continued its perilous descent. It was larger than she had first thought, and bright green. As it flashed overhead, she saw it angling its great head in her direction.

Lily tried to think of something to do but found herself rooted to the spot. The bird beat its powerful wings and banked sharply, making a second, even closer pass. Lily bent her knees as if to run, but instead locked eyes with the bird's, which flashed pale blue. It shrieked a strangely muffled cry, and the moon coin pulsed against her chest. In her mind a voice screamed, "Run!" Another volley of arrows whizzed across the field, close enough this time for Lily to see their yellow fletching.

Abruptly, the air split with a terrifying roar, and Lily felt all the blood drain out of her face and limbs, leaving her shaking and numb. Doubled over by a fear she didn't understand, fingers shaking, Lily fumbled for the moon coin and closed the fob. Quickly, she gave the moons a spin and closed the fob with a snap. Nothing happened. She would have to find her own way out of this place.

"Think!" Lily muttered aloud.

The coin pulsed again, this time both in her hand and her head. "Little one!" she heard in her mind.

Lily spun around until she saw it: the green bird, now perched on a low limb of one of the hillside trees.

"This way!" it cried, leaping from the limb and beating its great wings. "Now!" Again, Lily's ears perceived the bird's muffled squawk, and even the direction it came from, but it was only in her head that she understood the squawks as words.

She sprang out onto the road and ran up the hill, whether from panic or bravery she didn't know or care. The only thing she knew for certain was that she had no desire to meet whatever had produced that fearsome roar.

Ahead of her, the bird gathered speed slowly, then shot up and over the hill. Lily, following closely, crested the hill but lost her footing in the loose dirt and stumbled, falling hard on her chest. In her head, she heard the bird screaming, "Run! Run! No time to waste!"

The cacophony issuing from the valley grew louder. Lifting her head, she licked dirt off her lips and teeth, and spat. The hill she was on continued around in both directions, curving like the lip of a massive crater. Thirty feet in height, maybe a hundred feet thick, the strange hill had no ramparts or stairs, and its circumference was vast, stretching many miles around in a great circle.

Lily scrambled to her feet. From the center of the vast crater rose a tall mesa, crowned with a fortified city. The dead world hovered over everything, yawning into the distance, casting dark and angry shadows over the land and a distant sea. Between the two curving horizons, the sky was black as night, filled with glittering stars.

Lily's eyes widened in recognition.

"Sea Denn. City of the Rinn!" she exclaimed breathlessly. "I'm in the Moon Realm?" But how could that be? The Moon Realm, as Lily knew full well, was a dreamland—summoned from her uncle's imagination . . . a place out of tales, *bedtime* tales.

Just then, a dark line of helmeted men crested the rim of the hill not more than a few hundred yards from where Lily stood. They wore a beetle-green armor that shimmered eerily in the odd light. Carrying glinting spears and crossbows, each one bore multiple quivers strapped to its shiny armored back.

Fearing discovery, Lily squatted down, looking back into the valley. The Valley of the Rinn, she reminded herself. The undulating mass continued to drip from the world above. The globs in the valley had ordered themselves into rank-and-file formations.

Dusty clouds hung at the edge of these formations, where horse-sized animals struggled against their helmeted attackers. Lily watched helplessly as one of the great beasts, which she now suspected were Rinn, was overrun by an engulfing mass of the armored men, their ghastly beetle-green armor shimmering through the haze. A group of Rinn reversed their retreat and galloped back to help, only to be overrun themselves. Lily watched in horror as, one by one, they went down under the surging weight of the swarming army, not to rise again. Lily placed a hand over her mouth and felt tears well up. Moving quickly and strangely on their long, thin limbs, the Rinn's attackers flowed outward like a great warring mass of man-sized ants.

A sudden noise from inside the crater made Lily spin around, her heart nearly leaping out of her throat. A patch of scrubby brush exploded, and out shot two strange beasts, one riding the other. The mount was the size of a large boarhound. It leaped into the clear, trailing bits of brush and leaf matter, its six taloned claws raking air. Its large bridled head snapped wildly from side to side, showing off row upon row of pointed teeth. The rider, though short-legged, was a long-bodied creature covered with fur, looking very much like a child-sized otter or weasel. As the pair descended, the rider's evident excitement turned to panic.

The mount pinwheeled its legs right up to the moment of impact. When its sharp claws dug into the hillside, the two animals shot off, the poor rider on top bouncing like a limp doll tied to a paint shaker. Beast and rider bounded up the remainder of the hillside and, before Lily could do much more than cringe, scrambled to a dusty halt so close she could have reached out and touched the beast's bridled snout. The small rider pulled savagely on the reins. The six-legged beast shuffled and strained at the bit, refusing to remain still, wagging its thick neck, opening and snapping shut its powerful jaws. Its breath was putrid.

The little rider's eyes were were small, black, and deeply burrowed in its furry face. It regarded Lily with shock and surprise, as though she were something it had never seen before. Lily stared likewise. Its pelt was dusty-brown and thick under its clothes, and it wore a small metal cap on its head, looped under the chin by a leather strap. A jerkin of stiff leather completed its armor. Tied at its neck, flapping like a cape in the breeze, was a small cloak, which Lily thought made it look like some kind of otter superhero.

A rumbling from the valley interrupted their meeting, and the little rider's head spun to face it. When its eyes flicked to the engulfed tower and the many black lines dripping down from the forest canopy hanging above, it let out a loud, alarmed yelp.

"The tower is lost!" it shrieked. The coin pulsed on Lily's chest, and she heard the creature's barking and hissing translated in her head, just as with the green bird.

Lily also turned to the tower. This time she recognized it.

"Fangdelve!" she said in alarm, and then turned to look again at Sea Denn. "I must be dreaming."

"Would that we were all dreaming," said the rider softly, staring into the valley.

Lily tried to place the rider or his mount in one of Uncle Ebb's tales, but couldn't. "What are you? What is that *thing* you're riding on?" As she said this, Lily placed a hand to her throat, realizing that she had just spoken in hisses and barks that pained her.

The small rider whipped around to consider her.

"We are overrun!" it squeaked, speaking very quickly and visibly quaking with fear. "We must attempt to reach the city, young Dain cub. I will go for help, but by the rate of their advancement, I see, quite frankly, very little hope for any of us. Quickly, we must be on—" and then it yelped anew, nearly popping out of its saddle. It pointed a twitching finger, leaning forward, gaping at the necklace and gulping noticeably.

"By the moons!" it cried. "We are doomed! He will have a great prize this day! There will be no stopping him! Quickly, cub, hand it over to me before all is lost!" And it reached out its little leather-gauntleted paw for the necklace.

Lily clasped the pendant protectively.

"No. It's mine!" she hissed loudly.

Stung, it pulled back its hand. "No. Of course," it said. The creature scanned the valley, the tower, and then Lily, as though searching for something. And then, with no more than a twitch of its whiskers, its countenance flashed from fear and awe to determination and, Lily thought, bravery.

"Allow me to introduce myself: Witcoil Lightfoot, Lancespeed First Class, Royal Guard to Her Majesty the Queen," he said, with an air of calm command. "You have been sent? He gave you this?" he asked, nodding to the necklace.

Lily fingered the pendant. "Not exactly. I don't think I'm supposed to be here."

Witcoil bowed his head. "That is most unfortunate, but if we are to gain your safety, we must act swiftly!" Witcoil pointed down the hill in the direction of Sea Denn. "You see the break in the brush." It wasn't a question. "Keep to the right whenever possible, but don't lose sight of Sea Denn. That will give you the best chance to evade the scaramann advancing toward the city."

"Scaramann?" repeated Lily, and she pointed to a group of ar- mored men cresting lip of the crater less than three hundred feet from where they stood. "Is that what they're called?"

Witcoil gave the advancing men a look of contempt. Pulling him- self high in the saddle, he squared his small shoulders and addressed her.

"I will summon aid. Now be off! Keep to the brush—stay low."

And with a click of his tongue he wheeled his mount and vanished back into the brush, cutting a line straight for the city—and danger- ously close to the advancing men.

Lily set off faster than she meant to, but as she became more used to the terrain, she allowed herself to scan for any evidence of scara- mann.

She knew Sea Denn would be her only chance for safety. This much was obvious. But the city was on top of the mesa. First, she would have to climb the zigzagging switchbacks to reach the Ridge- gate, halfway up, where a fortified rampart circled the entire mesa. From there, she would need to climb the palace tower up to the city.

Running, listening to her breath labor, she found that she had, for the first time since vanishing from her bedroom, time to think. She knew all about the moon she was on. The Rinn reigned over all the valleys, mountains, forests, and even the open seas of Barreth. Sea Denn was its capital, and inside would be real Rinn. Larger than the largest draft horses on Earth, they were shaped more like lions with wider heads and eyes as big as dinner-plates. Surely they would help her.

Half a mile into her run, the lines of birds connecting Fangdelve and the top of the Ridgegate, which had been neat and orderly, suddenly scattered, as if on some signal. Lily couldn't imagine Rinnjinn, the real Rinnjinn, cutting his lines of communications to Fangdelve unless the tower was truly lost. Lily pictured Rinnjinn pacing the top of the Ridgegate, looking down at the valley of the Rinn, his generals and advisors close at hand, as he planned his defense of Sea Denn. The little rider couldn't have been right about this day being lost. Surely Rinnjinn would retake Fangdelve, and vanquish this army.

Several times, off in the distance, Lily thought she could hear the clanging of armaments. Each time, she corrected her course, always to the right, to lead her farther from the engagement. But always she would return to her course for Sea Denn, for the Ridgegate, toward her only chance of safety.

She was thirsty but told herself she had been through worse. So she hunkered down, ignoring her thirst, and maintained her long-distance pace. As the gentle grade leveled, the terrain changed. The occasional dry gullies she'd encountered were growing wider, and there were more of them. Crossing became more difficult, requiring small jumps, then leaps. Eventually, the gullies grew so wide she had to run through them. She had taken the first of these slowly, fearing mud at the bottom. But they were dry and sandy, so much so that she had to run hard and use her momentum to gain the opposite embankment.

Lily wondered if maybe running down the middle of the gullies could work to her advantage but decided they were just too twisty to be of any use. She dashed down into another one to cross it and found it swarming with scaramann. Her speed was far too great to consider stopping, so she planted her foot firmly on the back of one and hurtled over it. It clicked and hissed at her. A dozen others raised their heads. They weren't wearing helmets. They weren't men. What she had mistaken for helmets were large carapaces, like giant beetles' heads. Long, sharp spikes ringed their edges, and intricate green lines shone upon them. Their eyes were bugs' eyes, and their mouths were surrounded by flexing finger-sized mandibles.

"Seize it!" she heard in her head.

But before they could do anything, Lily was through the gully and up the other side. The wild grasses were taller and thicker here. Their roots gave a firmness to the ground that allowed Lily to risk accelerating her pace. Now clear of the dreadful scaramann, Lily felt a sudden wave of prickly revulsion wash over her. She wondered how fast could they run, stealing glances over her shoulder when she felt she could afford to. But the bug-men didn't follow. Why didn't they follow? Did they know something about the terrain she didn't? Had they deemed her unimportant? Were they on a more pressing mission?

Having no desire to run into another gully, Lily made instead for a small rise, where the grass was even taller, and the higher ground gave a better view. From here she could see that she had reached a middle ground of sorts. Behind her the land rose in a gentle grade back to the hill where she had started. Ahead, toward the Ridgegate, the land rose more steeply, becoming rockier. But in this in-between, where the rainfall gathered, the gullies snaked through everywhere. And in the bottoms of all those gullies—*they* were everywhere, too.

Beetle-green and black, the scaramann scurried through the gullies, surging toward her from every direction.

Lily dropped to the ground, her stomach flip-flopping as she imagined what would happen after her capture. Far too many of those scenarios ended with her being lunch. Lily fought down the tears and panic welling up inside. Never had she been more frightened in all her life. Panting, waiting for the courage to run again, she heard them clicking and snapping. There were so many! And they were getting louder.

Suddenly, she recognized the sound of powerful wings beating hard on the air. A flash of green darted overhead as a great plumed bird cut a tight arc over her. As it passed, she caught—if only for the briefest second—its intelligent eye tracking her. Several bolts whizzed toward the bird's great wings, but all flew shy of their mark.

The bird soared upward and screamed in a high pitch that carried far on the still air. In her head, Lily heard the words.

"Here, Roan! She is here, just below me!"

A rumbling began, but not a far off one, like she had heard earlier in the valley. This one was increasing in intensity—and rapidly.

Lily took the moon coin into her grasp. *This brought me here*, she thought. *This can take me away!*

The face of the coin, with its moons and odd designs, began to shake and blur as the ground below her quaked and rocked. She released the fob. With the tip of her finger, she spun the inner circle of moons. As it spun, she could hear in her head the faint clicking sounds as each moon passed by the fob's pointer. Picking a moon at random, she centered the pointer and snapped the pincers closed, just as she had done in her bedroom. But unlike the time in her room, the little moons remained gold, and she went nowhere.

The ground was now shaking so much that Lily had begun to lightly bounce, as if she were kneeling on a trampoline. What could make the earth shake so? Several times she tried to brace herself, as she was sure that whatever was coming must be upon her, but each time the shaking only increased.

Lily looked up at the dead moon.

Now what? thought Lily.

Roan's Charge

THERE were more scaramann within the ring than Witcoil had realized. He regretted leaving the Dain cub behind, but what else could he have done? Fought by her side until they were overrun by the scaramann? Accompanied her? No. The sound of his wirtle would have attracted their attention even faster. The cub's only chance was to remain undetected for as long as possible. But would it be long enough?

Witcoil jumped his wirtle over a pile of boulders, and several poorly aimed arrows whizzed past. Once firmly back on the ground, he leaned forward, every part of his body fluttering and shaking like a flag in a hurricane. From the moment he'd seen the necklace around the Dain cub's neck, he'd had only one thought: Roan. Only a few minutes before, on his way to see Fangdelve and the valley for himself, he'd passed Roan and his clutter. They'd been making their way cautiously back toward the switchbacks while trying to avoid the scaramann. But where was Roan now? Had he changed his course? Increased his speed? Then, just up ahead, Witcoil saw dust. A clutter of Rinn wouldn't leave a cloud of dust that big, unless they were really moving.

Witcoil leaned even lower and whispered a racing word in his wirtle's ear—a word he normally reserved for the home stretch of the Royal wirtle races—and held on for dear life. The boulders and shrub flew past, but Witcoil kept his nerve, guiding his mount through the rough terrain with a grace that would have made a rodeo star swallow his plug of tobacco without even realizing what he'd done.

"Roan!" cried Witcoil, expertly jumping a patch of dense scrub. "There's a Dain cub! Within the ring!"

Roan was certain he'd misheard, although his ears didn't usually play tricks. But with his clutter thundering in tight formation, surely he'd misheard at least two of the words.

"A Dain cub?"

"Yes, a female Dain cub."

A boulder too high to jump appeared out of nowhere. Witcoil swung his left leg off the saddle just as the boulder grazed the side of his mount. Jumping back into the saddle, he speared his foot into the jangling stirrup, gave the wirtle a kick of his spurs, and shot though a small opening in the Rinn formation.

"Roan!" he shouted. Roan flicked an ear back, and Witcoil leaned dangerously far out of his saddle, cupping one furry paw to his mouth. "She carries Ebbram's necklace!"

Roan misplaced a step and nearly fell, recovering just in time. He knew Witcoil. The wyfling was well-regarded by his wyfling commanders and brave to the point of being foolish. And Roan had seen Witcoil in the company of Ebbram the Wanderer more than once.

"She's all alone," said Witcoil. "In the gullies, where the rain gathers."

Without another thought, Roan radically altered his course, scattering his clutter and leaving them in utter confusion. Extending his claws for better leverage, Roan ripped out great clods of earth as he hurtled toward the gullies. Witcoil shadowed him expertly. But Witcoil had never run with a Rinn who had seemingly abandoned all caution in favor of speed.

"Are you . . . absolutely . . . certain?" grunted Roan.

Buzzing around like a hummingbird pursuing an eagle, Witcoil worked hard to keep his wirtle out of harm's way while remaining as close as possible to the charging Rinn.

"I have talked to her myself, while on the ring, not ten minutes ago."

Roan fought to increase his pace, hoping that sheer speed would carry the day.

"The scaramann . . . are everywhere," gasped Roan. "It will be . . . a miracle . . . to find her."

An enormous green bird dove down from the sky, barely evading a volley of arrows. "Save your miracles for another day," said Witcoil. "Follow Grygrack. She knows the way. I will inform Her Majesty of this news. She will want you to bring the cub to the Great Hall. Good luck, my friend." Witcoil peeled off, heading back toward the switchbacks.

Grygrack swooped lower, screaming over the heads of unsuspecting scaramann and vanishing from sight before they could react. She beat her great wings and began to outdistance Roan. "This way! Faster!" she screeched in the common tongue.

Roan caught his first clear glimpse of Lily while leaping across a small gully blackened by belly-crawling scaramann. She ran quickly for her kind, Roan thought, but she might as well have been moving in slow motion, given the danger she was in. He judged her either fearless or completely unaware of the enemy surrounding her.

Ebbram had always made it clear that if he failed in his task, he would send another in his stead, and the emissary would be known by the necklace. But a cub? At a time like this? Ebbram, though mysterious, had always made cautious plans—too cautious, by Roan's reckoning. This was no cautious plan.

Roan watched Lily dash into a gully full of scaramann.

"No!" he roared.

Amazed, Roan watched the cub plant its foot atop one of the scaramann and vault over it, running up the other side of the gully and making for high ground in a small field of grass. The scaramann had her surrounded now—they were ready to swarm. And then Roan heard them: the thundering feet of his clutter, running and leaping over the gullies. He would not be alone. Springing into the air, Roan roared the battle cry of the Rinn, and for a brief instant, the bugs cowered in surprise.

As Lily looked up, a new image obscured the sky: two outstretched paws thick as telephone poles sailed into view, followed by an enormous face lit by the two largest and most brilliant emerald green eyes that Lily had ever seen. The dead world was eclipsed by two massive shoulders, covered in long fur. A long underbelly came next, then rear haunches, followed at last by a long, thick tail.

Lily tracked the enormous creature's passage as it sailed over her. When it landed, the ground shook still more, and Lily fell forward. When she looked up again at the Rinn (for it could be nothing else), it was already on the move, reeling about with a cat-like grace that seemed impossible for an animal so large. And all the while, as it reeled and then closed in on her, more Rinn appeared, landing on all sides.

"Surround her!" roared Roan. "Surround her! Do not allow a single arrow through!" He dove toward Lily and lashed out his paw in a violent stroke toward her head.

Before she could even scream, Roan's massive paw flicked scant inches from her face, the wind of it ruffling her hair. The Rinn had swatted down an arrow that just a moment before was hurtling toward her.

"Brace yourselves!" he roared. "They are upon us!"

An instant later, the horizon vanished as a dark mass of the terrible bugs swarmed up from all sides. The Rinn rose to meet them, the big cats' powerful claws a blur as they furiously repelled the scaramann attack. The sound was horrific. A terrible crunching mixed with the snarling screams of the Rinn. The dismembered limbs of bugs flew in all directions. Goo splattered and soaked the Rinn's long-furred coats. But not a single live bug breached their protective circle. With each new wave of surging bugs, the Rinn reared up, tightening their circle, protecting Lily. Their twisting tails, as thick as fire hoses, made it difficult for her to stand, but she fought to remain upright to avoid being stepped on by their giant paws.

Roan turned to face Lily, his eyes alighting for an instant on the moon coin dangling about her neck.

"Come, little one," he said. "We must be off. Their numbers will only increase, and we are already overtaken. Keep that necklace from sight."

The memory of standing on the earth mound, seeing the enormous Rinn falling to the swarming black masses, flashed through Lily's mind. She knew this Rinn was right, that they needed to move. She knew, too, that she should try to speak, and she did try to speak. She tried to move, too, but mostly she just cringed.

An arrow streaked past and thudded into the loose soil, buried to its fletching.

"Roan!" roared a Rinn. "Swarm!"

The enormous Rinn spun away from Lily just in time to meet another wave of the bugs. This surge lasted much longer, and when it was over, she heard one of the Rinn behind her say, "We will not last long here!"

Lily watched with awe as the Rinn swatted away another incoming volley of arrows and then fought off another rising swarm of bugs. She shuddered, as the roar of the Rinn's battle cries mixed with the sound of the bugs being rendered into bits. She felt frozen with fear. It was too ghastly to bear.

"We will call down the darkness," said Roan. "We have just enough of us to cover this field. It will buy us time. Sheen, Wizcurs, Keenscent, Shadopads, protect us as best you can. You others, join me in the calling."

Half the Rinn in the circle lowered their huge heads, and a moment later, a rumbling sound began to emanate from deep inside their throats. The remaining Rinn, with heads high and eyes alert, kept a lookout for the telltale streaks of incoming arrows. After a while, Lily realized that the rumbling had a chant-like quality to it, but what few bits and pieces of words the moon coin translated meant nothing to her.

The incoming arrows kept the defending Rinn busy, and they couldn't reach a paw to every arrow. When the volleys were heavy, Lily watched the Rinn purposely lean into the arrows' paths in order to shield those who were chanting.

Suddenly, Lily noticed something strange in the air, like a dark string, thickening not two feet from where she stood. And then, next to it, another appeared. A black string formed right in front of her face. She tried to touch it, but her hand passed through it as if through thin air. The dark strings widened, sucking in all the light around them, growing thicker and blacker as they did. Finally, all at once, like a wave across a seashore, the day gave way to deep night. Lily looked up at the dead moon just as it faded into inky blackness.

Lily found the false night so complete that she could no longer see her hands before her face, and certainly not the Rinn whose tails she was trying to avoid. The whistling sound of the crossbow bolts stopped.

"It will not be enough," muttered one of the Rinn. "They will soon have numbers to swarm over us, darkness or no." And from the lilt of the translated voice, Lily was surprised she could discern a feminine quality.

Lily groped around her neck, suddenly afraid of losing the coin a second time. Clutching it tightly in her hand, she thought, *More darkness! Wouldn't that be good!*

And then, feeling with all her being that no need could be greater, she thought the words again. Only this time, in addition to just thinking them, she uttered the words out loud. . . .

The Ridgegate

HIGH atop the Ridgegate, Greydor, Pride of the Rinn, paced the gate's edge anxiously as he and his generals watched the developing battle below. Greydor had led Rinn into battle well beyond his prime, but it had been decades now since he had personally taken to the field. His long black fur was shot through with streaks of silver, yet there was still a sleekness in his step and a look of great strength to his limbs.

"We will lose this day," he growled, more to himself than to those about him. "And when we do, they will take our valley. They will destroy everything that lives in it." Greydor paced to the end of his line, turned. "They will cut off our food supply for the coming winter.

They will wait us out as we weaken and starve. And at every crossing, they will bring new forces to bear down upon us. The fields and pastures will become a roiling, twitching sea of bugs. In the spring, they will spread into the mountain footholds, to the forests, the deserts, the marshlands. They will take our whole world—just as they did the moon Dain!"

Greydor lifted his eyes to the dead moon that filled the skies above, wondering which of Barreth's moons were close enough to see this invasion. Would the people of Dain watch the destruction of Barreth, just as the Rinn had watched the destruction of Dain all those years ago?

Lewenhoof, Greydor's second-in-command, spat on the stone. "Dain!" he said with disgust. "That was a *good* day for us."

"Oh?" said Greydor. "Can you really be so certain?" Greydor wheeled about, looking hard into Lewenhoof's steel-blue eyes. Lewenhoof stared back without flinching, a feat few Rinn could have managed. "I am no longer so certain as you. And tell me, Lewenhoof, after we fall, who will be next?"

Lewenhoof stepped back affronted, looking up and down at Greydor as if he had lost his mind. "We will never fall!" he roared.

Greydor pointed to the earth mound. "Look at them, Lewenhoof. This is but their advance guard." He gestured toward the valley. "Their real army lies there! In our valley! Look at them! You've heard the birds' reports. You know what we're up against. They have chosen to attack in daylight when they can see us clearly. They outnumber us a hundred to one. No, Lewenhoof, my friend, no. This day is theirs!"

Then Greydor made the decision they had all been dreading.

"We will abandon Sea Denn—immediately. We will cross the mountains to join our kin, the clan BroadPaw. There, we will defend Rihnwood and bedevil Rengtiscura for as long as one Rinn stands!"

Stealthnight, a jet-black Rinn and one of Greydor's best field commanders, leapt to Greydor's side. "If we give them Sea Denn now, we will be giving it to them forever. If we leave, there will be no coming back."

Brighteye, another of Greydor's field commanders, pounced. "Is it not better to defend here, with our battlements to protect us?"

Greydor smiled grimly. "Defend at all costs?" he said dryly. "At all costs. . . . Yes, my young friends. That is precisely what he wants. Rengtiscura has brought to our doorstep the scaramann. Bugs. Poorly armored, it is true, but he has compensated for that by bringing us a black ocean of them. They are filling our valley as we speak. They have taken Fangdelve, and once they have secured it, they will surround Sea Denn. They will need only *one* night to dig in! They will go underground! Never to be cleared from our valley! Then, when our food has run out, when we are weak, they will break upon our walls. Climbing from every side, they will enter our fair city through every crack and crevice. We will mow them down in great numbers—of that I have no doubt!—but they will keep coming, relentless, like the sea. In the end, we *will* be overrun. Sea Denn *will* be our tomb. No, my friends, today you stand witness to the fall of Barreth. And there is nothing we can do to stop it." Greydor stood taller on his haunches. "Send word. Recall what forces we have in the field. We will make a run for Rihnwood. May our escape be swift."

Brighteye and Stealthnight looked to the faces of the older generals, but it was obvious they agreed with Greydor. There was nothing to do but run.

Looking nervous at all this talk of starving Rinn and short food supplies, Generals Twirltarn and Whirlyfur, wyflings both, stepped forward. Twirltarn tugged his thick leather jerkin stiffly, as Whirlyfur adjusted the leather strap that held his metal helmet in place. Walking upright, covered in short, thick fur, the two wyflings looked like battle-hardened, child-sized otters.

"His Majesty is right," asserted General Twirltarn. "To wait in Sea Denn with no ready supply of food would mean a slow and certain death."

General Lewenhoof licked his lips and stared down icily at the

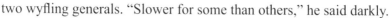

two wyfling generals. "Slower for some than others," he said darkly.

"That will be enough, General Lewenhoof!" barked Greydor. "Send the word. Recall our forces. Now, General!"

Lewenhoof grumbled as he crossed to the steps. But just as he was about to descend, they heard a clattering of claws on the stone steps. A Rinn scout, long and lean, bounded up the last of the steps and landed at Greydor's paws.

"Your Majesty!" said the Rinn scout, panting. "Roan has taken his clutter behind the scaramann advance line. He is surrounded and in need of reinforcements!"

"Roan!" bellowed Greydor. "The fool! What can he be thinking!"

The scout ran to Greydor's side at the edge of the Ridgegate and pointed to an area not far from the start of the switchbacks. And yet, far enough. "See them! They stand yet! And they have surrounded a Dain cub!"

"A Dain cub!" shouted General Lewenhoof. "What could a Dain cub be doing down there? You must be mistaken!"

Greydor hesitated, but only a second. "It is a great pity to lose a Rinn so bold," said Greydor quietly, "but there is nothing we can do for them now."

"Greydor," implored Stealthnight, "we cannot leave Roan to the bugs!"

"He is pinned, Commander, look for yourself. Meanwhile, the main force of the scaramann advances; soon they will breach the mound. We must be on the move before that happens. We will lose too much time trying to save him." Greydor turned to General Lewenhoof. "Time. Could that be his thought? A diversion to speed our retreat?"

"Retreat?" said the scout. "But then Roan will be lost."

"Much will be lost this day," sighed Greydor gravely. "Scout, to the valley—signal our retreat."

At the exact moment Greydor gave his command, a light flashed brightly, then faded to a shimmer in the center of Roan's circle. Even as far as the Ridgegate, the onlookers winced at the bright flare, but immediately the quality of the light around Roan grew clearer and more distinct to all the Rinn. The odd effect flowed outward from Roan's circle, slowly at first, and then more quickly. It engulfed the small field before halting. Several birds passing nearby altered their courses to skirt the disturbance.

The scout looked at Greydor. "They have called down the darkness. We could still send a small force to them. They are not so far from the switchbacks. The bugs will be helpless within the field—Roan and his clutter could still fight their way back. I volunteer myself!"

"No!" commanded Greydor. "There is no time! They knew their risk."

General Lewenhoof stepped to Greydor's side.

"They will hold out longer in the darkness. If the scaramann take the bait, Roan could occupy them for some time in this way."

Greydor, his keen eyes enhanced by the clarity that to any non-Rinn was anything but clear, cast a doubtful look at the shimmering field below. He could easily make out the Rinn, crouched in a tight circle, but in the very center . . . was there really something standing there?

"Curious . . ." muttered Greydor. Then, a second later, "Scout! Signal the retre—"

But Greydor did not finish his sentence. He was, instead, watching something impossible happen. The field around Roan had already filled with the spell of darkness, yet somehow the darkness was expanding—engulfing the surprised scaramann who had crawled to its edge.

"By all that is round," hissed Greydor.

General Lewenhoof gasped. "Greydor! In times of old, in times of great need, it is said a Rinn can double, even triple, his power!"

"Bah!" scoffed Greydor. "You speak of legends!"

The scout pointed to the expanding clarity. "Look! They have halved the gap to the switchbacks!"

Greydor craned back his head to look at Mowra, his court lunamancer. She stood tall on two legs, her paws folded in her long robes. Her expression of awe as she stared slack-jawed told him everything he needed to know.

Greydor stepped to the very edge of the Ridgegate, dug his claws deep into the stone, and leaned his great head as far out as he dared. "There *is* something small down there," he said quietly, "standing in the center of them." And then, more loudly, "It does not matter how Roan has managed this. He has brought to us something the enemy cannot ignore. We will not allow his sacrifice to be in vain. Scout! Sound the call! RETRE—"

Greydor's eyes grew wide with disbelief. A single strand of sparkling clarity had formed not two inches from his whiskers.

"For the love of moonlight!" he hissed.

A second strand quickly followed the first, and then another, and another, until shimmering strands danced everywhere about them. A heartbeat later, the clarity sped outward and enveloped all of Sea Denn. As it raced beyond the earth mound, it appeared to pick up speed, blanketing the valley, climbing up the mountains, racing over the sea. And though the darkness brought with it an enhanced clarity to every Rinn's eyes, it brought to all others inescapable, impenetrable night.

Greydor blew a gasp of air that set his muffs to waggling. The great scales of balance had unexpectedly shifted, and he weighed his decision during a single beat of his heart. Taking a great breath into his lungs, he bellowed down from high atop the Ridgegate in a voice that carried to the upper city, to the lower battlements, and far beyond.

"Rout them! Rout them! Rout them!"

Below, the massive doors of the Ridgegate clanked open, and the Rinn, in all their colors and patterns, streamed through the gate and poured down the long, twisting switchbacks.

Greydor pounced on the scout.

"To the Wornot! Wake him! Wake him!" Greydor pushed the scout to the steps and ran again to the edge of the Ridgegate to look upon the confusion spreading among the scaramann. "Wake his bats!" he roared. "We will want to know where the bugs cower."

Greydor then leapt to the corner of the Ridgegate, where two large birds had been translating the reports from the field. Squark, the large yellow bird, had already tucked her head under her wing, but Chercheer, the large blue one, fought to keep her eyes open.

"Chercheer, wake up!" commanded Greydor.

Both birds' eyes snapped open.

"You must fly straight to Clawforge and seek out Wyrrtwitch. If the Rinnwalk has not been conjured, tell Wyrrtwitch to gather all within the tower at the lower gate, where she is to wait. They are not to enter the field without a full escort!" Greydor leaned close to Chercheer, whose eyes were growing droopy again, "Chercheer, if the Rinnwalk *has* been summoned, you are to report back immediately. We cannot afford to waste a single Rinn's time this day!"

Chercheer fought off a yawn. "I will make it very clear," she chirped, tucking her head under her wing.

Frowning at the bird, Greydor shouted for Mowra. "Mowra, give Chercheer the sight! Immediately!"

Mowra towered over the two sleeping birds. "And what of the other?" she asked.

"Yes! Yes! Give them both the sight. But be quick about it. I will need you after."

A savage gleam lit Greydor's fierce eyes as he rounded on his commanders.

"Brighteye, send out the word. Empty Sea Denn of every whelp that can swing a paw."

Greydor lowered his head to face his two wyfling generals.

"Twirltarn, Whirlyfur, round up every wirtle you can set a paw to, arm yourselves with lances, and prepare for the true night. Roan's darkness will not last forever. Be ready for when your eyesight will once again be sharp."

The two wyflings, blind in Roan's darkness, squinted in Greydor's approximate direction and saluted no one in particular. Groping at the air with his paws, General Whirlyfur took two steps forward and unknowingly pinched Greydor's nose. Whirlyfur quickly realized his mistake, snapping to attention again and saluting Greydor a second time.

"Please accept my apologies, Your Majesty!" he yelped.

General Lewenhoof was not amused.

"Think nothing of it, General Whirlyfur," Greydor chuckled, "you will have your sight soon enough." He bounded away to an ancient-looking Rinn.

"Don't say it!" the old Rinn complained.

Greydor laid a massive paw on the old Rinn's shoulder. "Rasp, my old friend, rouse those too old for battle—"

"Too old!" interrupted Rasp. "Too! Do you think me so old that I cannot rake down helpless bugs? Because I can assure you—"

Greydor lowered his voice. "I need you to organize the old-paws. The larders must be emptied. The warriors will need plenty of food and drink. We will need many wagonloads."

"So, I'm to be a caterer now, am I? Is that what becomes of—"

"Listen to me, my friend. The wagons *must* be full. The bats will show you where to place them. There will be no sleep for the Rinn this night, and our forces will need something hardier than bugs to carry them till dawn."

"But Greydor, it will take forever to get all the wagons together. We'll miss the fight!"

Greydor smiled and leaned in close to Rasp's tattered ear. "I don't know how long Roan's darkness will last, but surely it will not stand the night, the true night, and when it fails, the bugs will regain their sight. That is when the *true* battle for Barreth will begin. *That* is when you will have all the bugs you can set a claw to—and then some. And Rasp, I promise you, they will be fierce!"

The old-paw grinned, showing his many missing teeth. "But not as fierce as the Rinn," he said, holding up his graying paw and un-sheathing his two and a half remaining claws.

Greydor nodded. "Go! May you cast no shadows."

Greydor leapt to Squark and Chercheer, who now looked as physically alert as Mowra looked depleted.

"Squark, there must be many Rinn stranded in the field. Tell all you see to assemble at the foot of Sea Denn. And warn everyone away from Fangdelve. Go!"

Two fresh scouts arrived at the top of the Ridgegate. "Find me Roan!" Greydor roared. "Tell him to cut loose his warriors!" And then, in a voice just loud enough for the scout to hear, he said, "Tell Roan I want to talk to this Dain cub in the Great Hall. Tell him if I am not there, then he is to take his orders from Nimlinn."

Their orders received, the scouts vanished down the Ridgegate steps.

"Mowra," bellowed Greydor, "come with me. We must make contact with the clan Broadpaw."

Mowra's shoulders drooped. "It is a long way to Rihnwood."

"Are you too tired?"

"No, but they will never get here in time."

"Not for this battle, but we will need them to retake Fangdelve. The scaramann were wise to attack it first. I dare not leave them there indefinitely. I am sure those bugs are planning more than mischief."

"But Greydor, in time, Fangdelve will surely become their tomb."

Greydor paused and narrowed his eyes at Mowra. "Need I remind you that Fangdelve is older than Sea Denn itself? It goes deep, Mowra, deep into the roots of Barreth. He's *wanted* that tower before. He's *had* that tower before."

Mowra smiled. "And not even the fabled Rinnjinn could get him out? Is that it, Greydor? We are believing in myths now?"

"Perhaps, Mowra, perhaps. Nonetheless, we will want every able paw before we attempt to retake it. We would do well to have the bows of our forest kin at our sides."

Before leaving the Ridgegate, Greydor turned to address his remaining commanders. "Rally your forces!" he roared. "Strike fast!

Strike hard! Do not let them taunt you into any traps. When tired, resort to stealth. Use the wagons as often as possible. Stay fresh. Stay rested. Be ready for the true night. I will join you soon enough."

Roan's Darkness

From his first words, Roan noticed something different at the center of things—something like a lodestone, only stronger. Immediately, he built this strange force into the enchantment; by anchoring himself to it, he would be able to increase the area of darkness, perhaps enough to cover half the way to the switchbacks.

When the darkness first extended beyond the fields, the other Rinn thought that Roan had sacrificed himself to increase the enchantment. But Roan's mind was safely intact, thanks to the lodestone. Sealing the enchantment would be the trick. While contemplating the spell, Roan became aware of possibilities he'd never imagined. He didn't hesitate. For this chance, he was prepared to give his life, even if it meant taking half his clutter with him.

Anchored to the lodestone, Roan threw wide the gates of their enchantment. And then, as the flood of magic poured forth, he clung to the lodestone for dear life. As the caster, Roan alone bore the brunt of this force, but he clung to the lodestone. Only when Roan was certain Sea Denn was safe did he seal the enchantment, as though closing some great door. But to Roan's great surprise, the darkness continued beyond Sea Denn, washing throughout the valley and across the land.

"Roan," said Sheen, in a hushed and reverent voice. "How?"

The darkness was racing for the mountains now, for the very horizons.

Roan's eyes touched on Lily, who, now enveloped in the darkness, could see nothing.

"I do not know," he said softly. "But this is no time to dwell on mysteries. You have the protection of darkness. Move quickly. Make for Fangdelve. Warn off all you encounter, but keep your distance from the tower—there's no telling what evil they have unleashed. The only way to re-take the tower now will be by siege. Send everyone you meet to the foot of the switchbacks."

"Roan, what of the bugs?" asked Wizcurs, licking his lips.

"Keep focused on your task! Even blinded they will try to trap and overrun you. Do not fall prey to their taunts. Go! Now!"

Roan's clutter leapt from the circle as one, leaving them alone in the darkness.

Lily heard the Rinn shift his enormous weight, and a sudden blast of warm breath blew into her face. She imagined his great emerald eyes inches before her own.

"I must take you to a safer place," said the Rinn. "Do you understand what I'm saying?"

"I can't see *anything*," she said.

"That is a result of an enchantment we have cast. I, however, can see perfectly well. Do not be afraid."

Lily tried to stand a little taller. "What do you want me to do?"

Lily felt Roan lower his body to the ground.

"You must . . . ride me," said Roan, the last two words nearly catching in his throat.

Lily had photos of herself in diapers, sitting bareback on old Thor, her father's hands holding her in place. Her mother was fond of saying she'd learned to ride before she could walk. Which wasn't really true, but it was close.

It's just like riding Hello Kitty, she told herself. *Only if she were a cat, and bigger, and could talk.*

Lily reached up and shoved her hands into Roan's thick fur. His flesh was very warm and wet with sweat. She felt for the ridge of his spine and twined two huge handfuls of hair about her fists. Roan's skin shivered reflexively, like a cat whose fur has been brushed the wrong way.

"Does that hurt?" said Lily, suddenly alarmed.

Roan made a low, deep sound that Lily didn't realize was laughter.

"Quickly, little cub," he said. "This is not the time nor place for jests."

Lily hauled herself into a sitting position. Once upright, she grabbed and twined new handfuls of hair.

"Hold tight!" commanded Roan, rising lightly to his feet. His back was wider than her horse's, and his skin wrinkled and twitched as she adjusted her position.

From her perch, even in the darkness, Lily realized she could anticipate Roan's course by reading slight movements of his body. First to the right, then straight. As he picked up speed, a rush of air filled her ears, tossing her hair.

Lily squinted against the wind. "Are you sure you can you see all right in this?" she shouted.

Roan laughed. "For me, it is like the clearest day, little cub."

"Please, call me Lily." And then, after a moment's hesitation, "What should I call you?"

After careful consideration, Roan said, "You, Lily, may call me

Roan."

"Where are we going, Roan?" she shouted.

From high above rang the voice of Greydor. "Rout them! Rout them! Rout them!"

Roan slowed some.

"Who was that?" asked Lily.

"That is my king, Greydor, Pride of the Rinn. He is emptying the city. He has chosen to fight."

Lily bent her attention to the sounds around her. Even far off, the Rinn descending from the Ridgegate sounded like a herd of charging buffalo. A short time later Roan stopped.

"What's the matter?" asked Lily.

"They are gathering at the foot of the switchbacks."

"Is that a problem?"

"I'd rather we not be seen. There is a narrow path that ascends next to the switchbacks. It is much steeper and used by runners. I don't see anyone on it at the moment."

"Why don't you want to be seen?" asked Lily. "If you don't mind my asking."

Roan didn't answer.

There was a nearly constant ringing sound, like steel striking stone. The Rinn descending the switchbacks came close at times, and several hailed Roan as he climbed the steep path, but he ignored them. Lily was amazed by Roan's stamina; a horse would have tired long ago from such a labor.

"Lily, we are coming to the Ridgegate. If you would, please say nothing."

She strained to hear. The noise from the switchbacks had faded. Now that they were at the Ridgegate itself, she could hear hardly anything, until, from a distance, a voice rang out.

"Roan! You made it! We feared the worst." It was an old-sounding Rinn. "So! It's true! It was out with the bugs? By the moons! What is it doing on your back?"

"I picked her up within the ring, but I can't stop to explain. Listen, old-paw, is that cub with you from Dewlicks' litter?"

"Yes, that's the scent! Very good, Roan, you do have an excellent nose. You should come visit and see my Dewlicks. She's all on her own now, you know."

"Yes, my condolences."

"Head of her own clutter."

"I've heard, and very good at it, I understand, but listen—"

"This little one, Swatfur, was number six. He's helping me make my rounds. I'm gathering the wagons. It's going to be a long night." Then the old Rinn's voice turned nostalgic, "We've been told it will be a lovely night for bug swatting."

Lily felt Roan lower his head to look at Swatfur.

"Is this your first hunt?" Roan asked.

"Eat bugs!" shouted the enthusiastic cub.

"Good!" laughed Roan. "Very good!" He continued. "Old-paw, I may have need of a runner who knows the way from the palace tower to the Ridgegate. I wouldn't need him for long—do you know of anyone I could borrow?"

"Hmm, I don't know . . . would it be important?"

"If, as I suspect, I do need such a runner, he would be delivering a message for Greydor—"

Lily heard the small Rinn gasp.

"I know the way to the Ridgegate! Old-paw! I know the way!"

"Are you sure?" asked the old Rinn. "You wouldn't get lost?"

"I'm sure!"

The old Rinn chuckled. "Then maybe it's a runner you'll grow up to be."

"No, old-paw, I want to be a warrior Rinn, like you and Mama."

"Thank you, old-paw," said Roan. "I'll send him to you shortly. Where will you be?"

"Gathering the wagons on the west ridge, but navigating them down the switchbacks will be tiring, and if you'll only be a short time, we'll be resting at the bottom before journeying on."

"I'll keep that in mind. Swatfur, we must be on the move. There is more to do this night than I have time to do it."

And with that, Roan took off at a fast pace, only this time on level ground. Lily's arms ached from holding on, but, unable to see, she dared not adjust her grip. From time to time, She heard the smaller, softer padding of Swatfur, keeping pace a little behind and to the left of them. Swatfur's breathing and pawsteps were very fast compared to Roan's steady gait and deep breaths.

Before long they were hailed again.

"Roan! What news have you? How did you do it? I saw it come from your circle. I saw it with my own eyes!" There was a pause, and when the Rinn spoke again, his voice was tinged with awe. "A Dain cub. So it's true—but how?"

"Do you have word for me, gatekeep?" said Roan gruffly.

"Why—yes! Yes, of course! You must meet Greydor in the Great Hall. And if he is not present, then you are to take your orders from Nimlinn. But I fear I have taken too much of your time already."

"It is all right. Matless fur requires no combing."

Roan increased his pace, and Lily was sure that Swatfur would be lost, but every so often she heard the quick pads of his paws keeping up.

Lily shouted to be heard as they rushed on.

"Who is Nimlinn, Roan?"

"Nimlinn is Greydor's mate and Queen. She is most powerful and very wise. When we meet with her, it would be best if you were to speak only when spoken to and not before."

"Will do," shouted Lily.

"And, Lily, you need not scream so loudly. I have excellent hearing. In fact, if you were to whisper, I would still hear you perfectly."

"Oh!" Lily said too loudly. Then, feeling a bit stupid, she said, less loudly, "I mean, oh."

They rounded a sweeping curve, Lily leaning to one side. A few seconds later, she heard Roan make a chuckling sound.

"Roan, what is it?" she whispered, testing Roan's ears.

"Ha! There are two wyflings on wirtles just inside the palace tower. They are peering into the darkness—at us—but they see nothing. They will be very surprised by our entrance. Hold tight, Lily. Your vision will clear once we are within the palace keep, and we are almost there."

Lily felt Roan bunch up his haunches. As they flew through the gate, two high-pitched screams sounded like sirens. The wyflings, each mounted atop one of the horrible-looking six-legged creatures, didn't even have the presence of mind to duck for cover.

The corridor they were in now was lit by tremendous lanterns, suspended from the tall ceiling by great loops of black iron chain. Red decorations were painted high along the sandstone walls. Now that Lily could see, her horse-riding skills took over, and she immediately sat in a more upright and commanding position. Roan's head and ears were fantastically larger than a horse's, but he kept his head low as they streaked down the corridor, and Lily couldn't help but notice, with some wonder, that Roan's long eyebrow whiskers rose nearly half as high as his ears.

Behind them, Swatfur, who Lily judged to be the size of a grizzly bear, ran as fast as his legs could carry him. Behind Swatfur, Lily could just make out the retreating black archway through which they had come.

Ahead, the passage widened enough for many Rinn to walk side by side, and the ceiling, made of beautifully carved stone, rose taller still. The lanterns here were larger, too, casting a warm yellow light throughout.

Roan seemed to know exactly where he was going, and he kept his pace quick. Lily wanted to take in everything, but it was going by too fast for that. In many places, the walls were draped with rich tapestries, which Lily was certain told tales she wanted to know.

Many of the hallways they passed led to rooms, but several led into what looked like cavernous halls. Soon, they began climbing a curved stairway that hugged the outer walls of the great keep. From time to time, they passed a window, but Lily could see nothing outside but inky darkness. Roan, however, glanced out of each one as they sped past.

"What is it, Roan? What do you see?"

"I see an entire valley full of scaramann, and someone is up to mischief in Fangdelve."

Lily didn't like the sound of that. "Mischief?"

"I know not what, but I assure you, great evil will come of it." They rushed through many floors of the tower, leaving one room behind while emerging through the floor of another. On and on Roan climbed. How tall could this tower possibly be, Lily began to wonder.

"How much farther, Roan?"

But he didn't answer.

And then, finally, they emerged into the Great Hall of the Rinn. A single room ringed with massive pillars, it was as big around as the tower was wide. Lily gasped.

"What is it?" asked Roan, and he spoke more quietly than she thought possible for a creature so large.

"It's just, well . . . it's complicated. I've never seen my Uncle's actual painting . . . just a photo."

"A photo?"

"It's like a painting, only a lot smaller. But still breathtaking. And now to finally *see* it in person . . . I just—I just thought I'd see the painting first, you know. I mean, not that I ever thought I'd see it . . . in person."

"Your . . . uncle?" said Roan. He swiveled his massive head as far as he could, and Lily loosened her hold on his fur, lest she be pulled off his back. The great Rinn settled a single narrowed emerald eye on her. "Ah, now I catch the scent."

Greydor's Decision

A WARM daytime breeze wafted through the hall, but the dim lighting, combined with Roan's darkness outside, infused the room with the feeling of deepest night. The archways between the pillars were black, unlike in Uncle Ebb's painting. She knew the image so well that she could almost see what would have been between the pillars: the tree-lined streets of Sea Denn, the nearby Tower of Clawforge, the sparkling ocean; on the other side, the valley and the distant Tower of Fangdelve. Then, without even trying, the images in her mind changed: a dead moon appeared; black ropes looped down to ensnare Fangdelve; a black army of scaramann blotted the floor of the valley.

Turning back to where the sea should be, Lily tried to push the image of the dead moon and scaramann out of her mind. She imagined what it would have been like to walk out on the balcony on the day in Ebb's painting. She'd see if the sea town of Foam was actually visible from the Great Hall of the Rinn, thereby settling a old bet with Jasper. Ebb had a wonderful painting of Foam's docks in his kitchen, with the gigantic wooden ships of the Rinn being loaded and unloaded. But the bet would have to wait for another day.

The hall's floor was cut from several types of stone whose names Lily did not know (although she wanted to), polished and shot through with thin veins of what looked like gold, silver, and copper. The shallow-domed ceiling was painted with scenes of majestic mountains, broad plains, valleys, tall forests, and oceans along its outer rim. In the center of the room lay a massive bronze brazier, twenty-five feet across. The air about the coals was wavy with heat, but Lily could see several figures waiting on the opposite side.

Roan padded around the brazier, delivering Lily to a raised dais, where a majestic orange-colored Rinn reclined like a sphinx. This Rinn's fur was no thicker than Roan's, but it had a luster and depth that suggested many hours of combing and grooming. A wyfling stood to either side of the Rinn, who Lily suspected was Nimlinn. The wyflings looked nearly identical, and if not for the different colored vests they wore, Lily would have been hard-pressed to tell them apart. Behind the dais, another staircase rose through the floor, and unlike the one they had come up, it continued up along the curve of the wall and through the ceiling.

Roan lowered his great bulk before the dais, allowing Lily to slide off his back. For a few futile moments, Lily tried to straighten and re-fluff Roan's fur, where her sweaty hands, twisting and pulling, had ruined it. But she knew it would need a good combing to get it right again. Roan moved off to one side, leaving Lily alone before Nimlinn's calm gaze.

Lily heard a soft snoring behind her. She turned, and instantly, her hand shot to her mouth. She let out a little shriek as she realized that a pile of wirtles were sleeping together on this side of the warm brazier, not ten feet from where she stood. They were a jumble of legs, fur, lolling tongues, tails, claws, teeth, and many pairs of bulging eyes, now closed. At her shriek, a dozen long ears lazily popped to attention and pointed in every direction. Seconds later, they flopped down again, one by one. A single pair of eyes opened to slits, then closed with a muffled sigh. It was not easy for Lily to turn away from them, but she felt it would be disrespectful to remain with her back to Nimlinn, so she summoned her strength and looked at Roan, thinking, *it's okay, he's got my back.*

Nimlinn stared long at Lily and narrowed her enormous eyes. Lily thought she detected what passed for a tight-lipped smile forming on Nimlinn's face. It was an oddly approving look. At least, Lily hoped it was. Lily wondered if maybe the expressions of the Rinn were not all that different from humans, just larger and covered with lots of fur.

"What is your name, cub?" asked Nimlinn.

"Lily, your . . . highness?" said Lily meekly.

"What is your full name—what is your clan?"

"My name is Lily Vervain Winter."

"Lily Vervain . . . of the clan Winter," said Nimlinn, smiling graciously. "I am Nimlinn Goldenclif, of the clan Broadpaw. My husband is Greydor Goldenclif, of the clan Foamchaser, Lord of the Valley Rinn," said Nimlinn. "But you may simply address me as Nimlinn."

A distant boom sounded, and Nimlinn's gaze momentarily shifted to one of the open archways. "Now, tell me, how is it that you speak our language so well? It is an uncommon gift for a Dain cub, is it not?" Nimlinn's tail swished from one side to the other. "And, more importantly, how came you to be the bearer of Ebbram the Wanderer's moon coin?"

"'The Wanderer?'" Lily mouthed silently, her fingers protectively encircling the pendant.

"I—I don't—" Lily tried hard to think of what to say next, but no words came. *Start at the beginning*, she thought. "This . . . ah, this is my uncle's necklace, but that isn't his name . . . though it is similar."

"How did you come by it?" said Nimlinn quickly, leaning forward a tiny bit.

"I—I found it." Lily thought of Uncle Ebb's house, running with Oscar and Jasper through the hallways, laughing—earlier that very day, right?

"You *found* it?" said Nimlinn.

"Well, yes," said Lily. "You see . . . he's missing."

Nimlinn's great, amber eyes flicked to Roan, then back again.

"But you have been instructed in its use, yes? You are *here*, after all."

Lily looked down at the pendant, suddenly feeling very stupid.

"Well, I remember part of what I did to get here . . . but not exactly." She looked up at Nimlinn. Lily felt like a child again, trying to explain to her parents about the freak accident in the barn that caused her to end up bareback . . . on her pony . . . wearing faerie wings and a tutu. *Faerie business is serious business!* "For example, I don't know how to get back home."

Nimlinn's eyes widened in surprise. "Lily," she said, suddenly sounding more concerned, "have you ever been to Barreth before?"

"No."

"Have you ever been anywhere within our realm?"

"No."

"I see. I thought as much. Well, Lily, I have very little knowledge of that device in your hand, and most of what I've learned I know by observation. However, I suspect time is not on our side. Lily, I want you to think very carefully about what I'm going to ask you next. All right?"

"Yes, of course."

"Have you turned the circle of moons since you arrived here?"

"Yes!" said Lily excitedly, happy to finally answer one of Nimlinn's questions with a *yes*. "Shortly after I arrived, I tried to use it to get back, but the moons wouldn't light up and it just spun around and around."

Nimlinn made a face that Lily didn't understand.

"Step closer, and let me see the face of the coin."

Lily hesitated. She could see no harm in allowing Nimlinn to look at the coin. As it was, the Rinn were so large and powerful that any one of them could have already taken the necklace if they'd wanted it. And they hadn't shown any desire to take it so far, so what was there to lose? Lily strode forward and, without allowing it to leave her neck, raised the coin high.

Nimlinn's nose wrinkled, and she gave the pendant a quick sniff. Lily watched herself in the twin reflections of Nimlinn's huge amber eyes, whose tall pupils narrowed to slits as she focused on the coin.

"Why is Barreth undistinguished from her moons," she said quietly, as though speaking to herself. "Lily, which of these designs brought you to our world?"

Lily blushed, feeling stupider, as if that were somehow possible. "I—I wasn't really paying attention."

"Do you know the language of these markings?"

"No. I—"

"Then we have a problem. You see, I have often suspected that Ebbram's moon coin required some fixed amount of time to replenish its power, as he would often need considerable time after arriving before he could vanish again. But he is a clever one, and so I have always assumed that, whenever possible, he would linger in hiding before making his presence known on Barreth. In this way, he could create an illusion of being able to come and go at will. However, on the occasion of his last visit, he had questions that could not wait. Likewise, after he got the answers, he had no time to stay. But stay he did. I could smell his haste. He wanted to run off and hide himself. I'm sure of it. Instead, he busied himself deep in the bowels of Fangdelve, where there are passageways too small for Rinn."

"If the passageways are so small, how do you know when he

left?" asked Lily.

"He didn't go down alone. He took wyflings with him, and lanterns."

"Did he find anything?"

"The wyflings didn't think so. But there were times when they thought he appeared to be reading things . . . on the walls . . . things they could not see. He made many notes in his little notebooks. All told, he lingered for nearly a full day."

Lily lowered the coin, a look of understanding spreading across her face.

"So, what you're saying is that when the coin's recharged—in a full day's time—that I'll be able to use it again. But unless it happens to be set on Barreth, I'll be sent to whichever moon the coin's pointer is currently set on, whether I want to go there or not."

"That is what I am thinking, Lily. However, it is just a guess. There is no lack of mystery surrounding that little coin. For example, why are there ten bodies on it, when Barreth has only eight moons?"

"By the nine moons . . ." Lily whispered, repeating a phrase her uncle used to express surprise or wonder. Now Lily understood why all the Rinn thought she was a Dain Cub. They didn't know about Earth, and apparently Lily resembled a child of Dain. So to Nimlinn, the moon coin had an extra moon—Earth. *She must believe Uncle Ebb is from Dain, too,* Lily thought.

Nimlinn began looking at Lily in a different way, as though sizing her up. Lily squirmed, certain the Rinn Queen thought her an idiot.

Nimlinn's ears suddenly swept back, and Lily feared she was angry. But Nimlinn's expression was merely one of alertness: a moment later, two Rinn appeared, descending the staircase behind the dais. The Rinn in front was black-furred, shot through with streaks of silver. Lily decided this must be Greydor. He was large, and his eyes were a bright emerald color, like Roan's. The second Rinn was much thinner and walked upright on its rear legs. It wore a beautiful orange and black robe that began at its chin and flowed all the way to the floor.

The robes were covered with delicate patterns that reminded Lily of smoke and light, and the huge buttons, which looked like polished stone, had deeply-cut runes on their faces. This was a lunamancer Rinn, who towered over everyone else in the room.

When Greydor reached the dais, he took his place beside Nimlinn, giving her a lick and nuzzle behind her ear before reposing sphinx-like beside her. At first, it was as though Lily were not even in the room.

"I have spoken with your father," he said to Nimlinn, "and he has promised many Rinn. But he is concerned about the Blight Marsh, as well he should be. There is no telling what Rengtiscura has planned for us. As for your kin, we can expect the first of them in two days, maybe three. They will be using the old paths. We must last this night, and the next. Retaking Fangdelve will not be an option until we have their bows, and in great number."

"Two days," said Nimlinn, sounding alarmed. "Can we risk waiting that long?"

"I don't see that we have a choice. Clearing the valley will occupy all of our time before then."

"Greydor, if we leave them in Fangdelve . . . we may find ourselves with considerably more to take care of."

Greydor shifted uncomfortably at this thought.

"I agree, Nimlinn. But to retake Fangdelve now, we would have to attack and defend at the same time, splitting our already thin forces. Without your kin to supply cover, we will not be able to open the gate."

Nimlinn nodded, but Lily could tell she was still of two minds. With a swish of her tail, she changed the topic. "Any news of my brother?" she asked quickly.

"He is still missing. And there is still no sign of—"

Greydor's great head turned to Lily, his emerald eyes focusing on her for the first time.

"This," said Nimlinn, "is Lily Vervain of the clan Winter. She is the niece of Ebbram the Wanderer."

"Indeed," said Greydor, sounding intrigued.

Greydor's strong gaze shone on Lily like a heat lamp. It felt as though he were somehow looking into her very thoughts and memories. She couldn't return his gaze for more than a few seconds at a time.

Nimlinn continued to explain, speaking quickly and precisely. "As you can see, she possesses the moon coin. But she is not its master. I fear that, due to her mishandling of the coin, she will be randomly sent to one of our moons, unless we can decipher the coin's markings and set it back to Barreth."

Greydor took no time to think.

"Mowra, come look at this coin. Tell me what you can make of these markings."

The robed Rinn walked upright over to Lily and leaned down to look at the coin. Lily stood on her tippy-toes trying to hold it as high as she could.

"It is a very old script. I have seen it, but only rarely. Sadly, I have never had reason to further my understanding of it." When she heard the lunamancer's voice, Lily got the distinct impression that Mowra was female.

"Who might have knowledge of this language, Mowra?" asked Greydor.

Mowra drew herself up and brought a huge paw to her chin. She looked cautiously at Roan.

"You may speak freely before Roan—you know that."

Mowra seemed dubious.

"Some of the larger birds on Taw may know. They are marvels of language. And their lines of communication are quick."

"Who else?" asked Greydor.

Mowra stepped closer to Greydor and whispered, "Ember. I'm certain she has traveled to many of our moons, and she continues to share everything we have ever asked of her. Her eyes and ears are sharp—she forgets nothing."

"Dain," said Greydor, his voice dripping with distaste.

"Well then," continued Mowra, "it would be reasonable to think that one of Rille's scholars on Dik Dek could read it. Smugglers still use the Embaseas during crossovers, even if they are officially dormant. And you can be sure that they do so with Rille's approval. As to others—"

"Mowra," interrupted Nimlinn, "which moons will we cross over with next, and where will the crossovers take place?"

"This cluster is strong. There will be three more crossovers within the next two days. First will be Taw, then Min Tar, then Dik Dek."

"And where will this crossover with Taw take place?" said Nimlinn eagerly.

But before Mowra could answer, the sudden sound of thunderous wing-beats filled the air. Roan was the first to act. In a single bound, he placed himself between his king and queen and the sound coming through the arch. Lily wondered again at the grace of the enormous Rinn.

Roan leaned through the archway. To Lily's eye, half his body disappeared into the darkness.

"It's the Wornot," he shouted. A second later, Lily screamed as a bat, easily twice the height of a grown man, emerged from the darkened archway, landing with a powerful thud on an enormous perch just inside the hall. Long, leathery wings folded tight to its glistening, hairy chest. Its head was like an enormous rat's, and its gaping mouth gasped for air, exposing ancient, pointed teeth.

"Greydor!" it screeched to the ceiling, its huge lungs alternately raking in and heaving out great gouts of air.

Greydor, too, had now leapt from the dais.

"Wornot!" he said. "What have you seen?"

The great bat, still staring blankly at the ceiling, hideous mouth gaping, lungs heaving, managed to spit out its message. "My watchers . . . are loose . . . and the enemy is . . . everywhere. . . . They cover the . . . valley floor. . . . They cannot see . . . yet not . . . so helpless. Still deadly . . . digging in . . . laying traps. . . . Your Rinn are . . . foolhardy . . . easily tricked. . . . There is chaos!"

Greydor glanced at Roan, "Where are your Rinn?" He showed no hint of alarm.

Lily noticed that more Rinn, both robed and walking on all fours, were now filing into the Great Hall.

"I sent them to warn off any direct attack on Fangdelve," said Roan. "Their orders are to gather what Rinn they can and bring them back to the foot of the switchbacks. They will not be easily taunted into any traps."

"Excellent, Roan. Now, if we are to survive this night, then we must bring order to this chaos. If the bugs are digging in, we will need to bring the lunamancers directly to bear on their burrows."

"Greydor," interrupted Nimlinn, "what about Lily? She needs our help. We cannot risk her being lost to a dangerous moon!"

Greydor glanced briefly at Lily, then to Nimlinn. "You are right, of course—"

"Greydor!" shouted a lunamancer Rinn, who was looking through a darkened arch that faced the tower Clawforge. "Wyrrtwitch has raised the Rinnwalk! The lunamancers are crossing to the city."

"Have them amass at the Ridgegate!" shouted Greydor. "Roan, recall the guards sent to Clawforge's base. We will need every Rinn in the field tonight!"

Roan nodded, then leaned down to the small Rinn, Swatfur, who had been trying to hide within Roan's shadow, unable to take his eyes off Greydor.

Greydor issued orders to the Wornot, who quickly turned and launched himself back into the false night.

"Swatfur," said Roan, raising his voice calmly despite the growing confusion, "now is your time. Run to the Ridgegate and make sure they know the Rinnwalk has been raised. Tell them to send a runner to tell the lunamancers' guard that they will not be needed at Clawforge's base. They are to enter the field of battle, but must avoid Fangdelve."

But Lily heard no more after another bat, half the size of the Wornot, entered through the same archway and began shouting frantically about a queen bug having been spotted within the valley. At this news, a great shout went up, and total chaos swept over the room.

Now, for the first and for what Lily would later remember as the only time, she saw something other than calm flash across Greydor's face.

"Greydor!" exclaimed Nimlinn. "Greydor! We must help the Dain cub!"

Lily watched Greydor wrench his mind away from the commotion in the room in order to face Nimlinn, who was frankly alarmed.

"What if the coin is set to Darwyth!" hissed Nimlinn.

Greydor grimaced and closed his eyes. When he reopened them, Lily could tell that he had made his decision. As Rinn shouted for his attention, he faced Nimlinn and looked deep into her eyes.

"My love," he sighed, "if there is even to *be* a tomorrow for the Rinn, then this must wait."

Greydor broke his gaze from Nimlinn and begin raining orders like lightning-bolts in a thunderstorm. Runners streamed in and out of the room; lunamancers nodded. The moon coin, which had been able to amplify the speech of anyone Lily concentrated on, became overwhelmed with the task of translating so much shouting at once.

As the din became a roar, Lily felt herself cut loose, like a kite whose string had broken. Her fate had been cast to the winds. She was all on her own now, on a strange world that she knew only in bedtime tales and dreams.

Numbly, she watched new bats land, one after the other, through the darkened archways. Mowra shouted to Roan. Nimlinn yelled instructions to the small wyflings by her side. The wirtles ran about the room in confusion, snapping and biting at each other.

A Rinn's leg bumped into Lily and nearly knocked her down. It was as thick as a tree and hard as stone. Lily looked around for an area where there was less commotion, but the best she could manage was weaving between one huge body and another, trying her best not to be stepped on.

She felt a tapping on her shoulder. Lily spun around, suddenly nose to nose with one of the otter-faced wyflings. It spoke very fast in a clear voice.

"Greetings. It is my great pleasure to make your acquaintance. My name is Snerliff." Lily stared as he produced a well-manicured paw. After a moment, Snerliff gently took Lily's right hand in his. She barely felt any claws at all, and his pads were quite cool. The fur between his fingers was velvety and supple. Lily continued to stare, shaking his paw.

Snerliff, unfazed by her odd behavior, smiled brightly, showing his many small white teeth.

"Nimlinn requires your presence," he said, pressing on. Lily kept shaking his paw. Snerliff pressed his lips together, gave her an understanding look, and patted her hand. "Nimlinn is not one to be kept waiting. Twizbang and I will accompany you," he said calmly. Snerliff made a graceful pivot, interlocking Lily's elbow with his own, and guided her toward the stairwell behind the dais, where the other wyfling waited. The main steps were Rinn-sized, but along the far edge, hugging the wall, was a narrow set of wyfling-sized stairs.

As Lily stepped down them, she gazed back into the chaos of the Great Hall of the Rinn. Just before she descended below the level of the floor, she caught Roan's piercing eyes briefly alighting on her own. Instantly, his eyes darted off to other parts of the room, in a decidedly frantic fashion.

The Tomb of the Fallen

L ILY couldn't recall if there'd been smaller wyfling steps carved alongside the ones she and Roan had taken to the Great Hall, and that bothered her. They had been moving quickly, but not so quickly that she would have missed a detail like that. Of course, without the smaller steps, how would the wyflings move anywhere within Sea Denn?

Lily counted six wyfling steps for every Rinn step. Maybe, she finally allowed, Roan *had* been moving too quickly for her to get a good look.

This stairwell was very different. It had walls on both sides. The craftsmanship of the carvings and tapestries was magnificent beyond anything she'd ever seen. Descending, they passed many open landings, beyond which Lily spied spacious, dimly lit rooms filled with more tapestries, gigantic paintings, and Rinn-sized furniture, touched with lustrous glints of gold and pearl. But they never paused, heading downward with no end in sight.

Snerliff and Twizbang talked quickly the entire time, their speeding words overlapping and interrupting their already complicated conversation. And still the stairs continued. Ten minutes? Twenty? Lily could not recall.

For Lily, the idea of being sent to a moon, especially a dead moon spewing scaramann, was becoming less imaginary with every passing minute. Why had she never wondered about the impossibly detailed nature of Uncle Ebb's bedtime tales? He never had to think about what came next. Shouldn't that have been a clue?

On the nights when Uncle Ebb visited, she and Jasper would beg him for new tales. And although he took great delight in telling his tales, their parents were very much against the activity. Now *that* should have been a clue. Why would their parents care about—come to think of it, the only times Lily had heard Uncle Ebb call them stories was when he talked to their mother.

Lily drifted back into memory, seeing Ebb through her child's eyes—although no longer with a child's perspective. The memory she settled on seemed ghostly now, unsettled, incomplete. She and her brother were very young. Had it been their birthday? Uncle was late.

"Are you going to tell us a story, Uncle?" Jasper had said, in the little boy voice she loved so dearly.

"No. Not tonight, I think," Uncle had replied. Jasper had looked like he might begin to cry. "But if you think you're up to keeping another secret . . . I might be willing to tell you a tale."

Jasper had smiled then, happy in the knowledge that he and Lily would get their story, but completely unaware of the subtle distinction being made. But Lily didn't miss it, no.

The memory flared, burning bright in her mind. She could feel the soft covers as he tucked them in, smell the dust of the travels in his clothes: smoky spices, cinnamon, the stuff of moon dust.

"A tale is an account of things in their due order, often divulged secretly, or as gossip," he'd said. "You won't find the tales I bear in any books. . . . My tales are from the Moon Realm."

But when Mom and Dad got wind of what was going on, they argued with him. Ebb stopped for a time, out of respect for their parents' wishes. Bit by bit, though, Lily and Jasper broke him down. They started by arguing for tales he'd already told. Where was the harm in that? They knew all those by heart. They just wanted *him* to tell them because he told them *better*. Of course, there would *have* to be questions. New questions. Uncle didn't catch himself until he was in he middle of it.

"Now how did we get started talking about the giants of Min Tar?" he said, over their giggles. "You've tricked me, haven't you?"

Sadly, it took only one careless slip in front of their mother or father to halt the bedtime tales again. Their mother would get so furious. Then there would be no more tales for a long time, no matter how hard they pleaded.

"They're just *stories*, Linnea," Uncle Ebb would say to Mom. But then she would fix him with her steely gaze and say . . . what would she say? Something strange. . . .

Lily concentrated, trying to pull the exact words from her memories. But it was stuck, like a splinter in her flesh.

"Just be certain," she would say. No. That wasn't right. What was it? "Just make sure—" Yes, that was it. "Just make sure . . . you *keep* them that way."

And Uncle Ebb, in a very sad voice, a voice Lily rarely heard, would say, "How could they ever be otherwise, Linnea?" And she would shush him.

But now they *were* otherwise. Uncle Ebb was missing, and no longer in possession of the moon coin. Lily wanted to find him, but she knew she couldn't do it alone. She'd need Jasper. That meant getting home—but how?

Lily surfaced from these memories, like a whale coming up for air, and realized her present was going on without her. How many landings had they passed? She vaguely remembered reaching a portion of wall that had been opened somehow, followed by more stairs.

Snerliff and Twizbang had argued there. They'd been expecting to see their mistress waiting for them and they were shocked to find the door open and unattended. They'd argued about what to do. But what *did* they do? Lily couldn't remember, although she suspected Snerliff had prevailed in the end.

The stairwell looked so different now. When did that happen? And why had they stopped? Her hand no longer rested on Snerliff's arm. Where was he?

Lily turned and looked up the stairwell. The two wyflings were a dozen steps higher, staring at an open door. They were arguing about whether and how to close it. *We must have just passed through that,* Lily thought.

She spoke up, for the first time since they had begun their long descent. "Your mistress must have felt she had no time to wait and left it open for you. And if it's a secret door, not to be opened, then you should stop arguing and close it *right* now before someone sees it."

The two wyflings stared dumbfounded at Lily, like she was some kind of great oracle.

Then Snerliff narrowed his eyes and poked Twizbang in his furry chest.

"See, I told you so," he said. They stared at Lily some more.

"So close it!" she shouted.

Startled, they jumped at her command. After a brief shoving match, they heaved the door shut. It sealed with a deep grinding sound, leaving only the smoothness of stone wall where, just moments before, there had been a door. Twizbang yelped and leapt spread-eagled at the now solid wall.

"We're trapped!" he squeaked. "What if we guessed wrong? What if our mistress isn't on our side of the stairwell? How will we ever get out? We'll starve!"

"Don't be silly," Lily retorted. "She'll just open it up again."

The two wyflings slowly turned to Lily, wearing faces like they'd been had.

"These doors," said Twizbang, in a shaky voice. "*These . . . doors . . .* are very hard to make appear. It could be days before she could try and open them again!"

"Oh," said Lily, wrinkling her brow and pursing her lips. "Well . . . you didn't tell me that."

"We thought you knew," they said in unison.

"How would I know? Besides, that's that." And suddenly, for some reason Lily could not explain, she felt much better, her spirit of adventure flooding back. "So, which way are we headed?" she asked cheerfully. "Down here?"

The stairwell beyond the secret door danced with shadows. Only a few of the lanterns here were lit, and those guttered as if the next moment might be their last. These stairs were in disrepair, narrow, and more crudely carved—the wyfling stairs especially so, as though they had been hewn from the rock in great haste by trembling paws. The only artworks adorning the walls were those left by spiders who, judging by the size of the webs, were much larger than the ones Lily was used to back home.

Lily skipped down a few steps, stopped, and turned. Snerliff and Twizbang, hugging themselves, hadn't budged.

"Come on, or you'll be all alone," Lily scolded.

Twizbang's teeth began to chatter.

Snerliff pried his arms loose and stepped down a few stairs. Twizbang pawed the open air before stuffing his paws in his mouth.

"Where do these stairs go?" asked Lily.

Snerliff's eyes widened. "This stairway leads to . . . The Tomb of the Fallen," he whispered, his voice cracking on the word "fallen."

"Have you ever been down there?"

Snerliff paused mid-step, saying nothing, Twizbang slowly swiveled his head to the left and then the right.

Lily decided the wyflings, though furrier, weren't all that different from the kids she babysat back home. Reaching up for Snerliff's paw, she said, "Come on then. Let's go and see."

Snerliff, who had been so composed in the Great Hall, grudgingly gave his trembling paw to Lily, and, slowly, they started down the stairs. Twizbang's soft sobs grew fainter. A moment later, he bumped into them. From that point on, all three stayed together, descending the never-ending stairs.

Lily comforted Snerliff, patting his arm.

"Your mistress will be with us," Lily assured him. She glanced over her shoulder to Twizbang. His teeth were still chattering. "We'll be safe with Nimlinn," she said encouragingly.

Snerliff's face calmed, then became steadfast, as had Witcoil's back on the crest of the hill following Lily's arrival on Barreth.

"Yes," said Snerliff, grateful to be reminded of something that he knew, deep down, to be true. "Of course! You are right."

Lily's legs began to ache. She was thinking of taking a break when suddenly she detected a widening of the passage. The stairwell was straightening out and the ceiling was disappearing into shadowy darkness. In another hundred steps, when the stairs were wide enough, Twizbang nosed between them. The steps widened further, and a railing cut from the stone wall appeared, followed by pillars and statuary. Far below, Lily could see the bottom of the stairs bathed in colored light.

As they got closer, the Tomb came into view, not twenty feet from the bottom step. Its beautiful stone doors were swung wide, resting against the face of the Tomb, and warm yellow light from inside spilled onto the foot of the steps.

But that wasn't the only source of light. The doors themselves held great panels of stained glass, illuminated from behind by what Lily rightly guessed were recessed lanterns. Through the stained glass, the light flickered in deep hues, projecting magnified images in reverse across the bottom of the staircase and up the nearby rock walls. The image in the left panel depicted an orange sun setting—or rising—over a lush forest, with a river running through its center. The panel on the right showed a twilit sky, crowded with moons of varying sizes, over a wide valley. They looked more like windows in a cathedral than the doors to an old secret tomb.

They had begun surveying the tomb when Nimlinn's huge paws came into view. She was waiting just inside the doorway, once again posed like a sphinx. The instant they saw her, Snerliff and Twizbang darted into the room and posted themselves on either side of her great bulk.

The tomb was crowded with thick pillars, immense lamps, and nine stone slabs, each topped with a reclining figure carved in marble. The low ceiling was comprised of shallow vaults, making it hard to judge the room's size. On display, just inside the doorway, rested the largest saddle Lily had ever seen. It was inlaid with gilt and silver, and its leather looked as soft and supple as the day it was crafted. Standing around it like sentinels were four short pedestals, whose tops fanned out to create wide, circular tabletops. In the center of each were objects that accompanied the saddle. On one pedestal were large metal discs, as big as hubcaps, but with curved blades sharpened to a razor's edge. Lily remembered them from Ebb's tales. They had a special name that, for the moment, eluded her. Suddenly, she wished Jasper were here. He had an encyclopedic memory of all the armaments Ebb had ever described. "*Boys*," she muttered. The discs were fashioned with a grip in the center so a Dainrider could hoist one from its pouch and hand it off to a Rinn without either of them being cut by the sharp blades—even when hoisting two at a time at a full gallop. On one of the other pedestals lay blankets; on the third, collars, stirrups, and saddle flaps. The last held open saddlebags turned on their sides, contents spilling out like cornucopias of tack and grooming tools.

Lily stepped farther into the center of the tomb, sidestepping one of the ornate cast-iron lanterns that hung from the ceiling nearly to the floor. In passing, she traced her fingertips across one of the lantern's tall yellow panes. It was warm.

"Nimlinn, how do these lanterns stay lit?"

"They brighten when the doors are opened, and dim when they are closed. I assume their source to be a magical one, but it is not of this world. Something older, I think. Something lost."

"Lost? Why do you say that?"

"For a Rinn to perform magic here, on Barreth, is difficult enough, even for one who is skilled. For a Rinn to perform magic on one of our moons, however, is nearly impossible. Only the most highly skilled would have a chance at attempting such a feat, and even then, the force of the enchantment would be but a tiny fraction of what it could have been had the caster been standing on her native world or moon."

Lily rifled through her memories. That wasn't right. In Ebb's stories, each moon had a distinct magic of its own, which did give it a strong home world advantage, but nothing so absolute as Nimlinn was saying. And magic was everywhere in the Moon Realm—at least, the way Uncle Ebb told it.

In the center of the tomb, one of the great burial slabs had been set all to itself. On it lay the stone figure of a powerfully built man, clad in full armor except for his helm, which he held at his waist. The features of his face were strong, and the skill of the artist's hand showed in the delicate rendering of the man's long, flowing hair. The edges of the slab fanned out—like the pedestals around the saddle, only wider—making for a museum-like display of what, presumably, this man had once carried.

Lily glanced around at the other slabs. Each figure was distinctive. There were men and women, some in armor, some in robes. But all of the slabs had wide sills, displaying each person's possessions. Swords, shields, bits of armor, robes, rings, helms, belts, jewelry, folded clothing, boots, and many other odd objects whose uses were obscure. Some of the items were rusted, or, as in the case of much of the clothing and leather, desiccated, cracked, or frayed. And yet, many more of the objects appeared untouched by time, as if they had been placed there just moments ago.

Painted on the walls were murals, accompanied by script.

Lily turned to Nimlinn.

"What is this place, and why have you brought me here?"

"Those are good questions, Lily. And I will answer them as best I can, but only after we are under way. You must understand that our enemy now is time; we have none to waste."

"Where are we going?" Lily asked.

"Barreth's next crossover is with Taw. We must reach it in hopes that Aleron, head of Heron Peck, can read the markings on your coin. Only in this way can we assure that you will not be sent someplace more dangerous."

Lily tried not to think about a valley full of scaramann, and what it must have been like to be in the Tower of Fangdelve when it fell. *More* dangerous?

And then it seeped in. Nimlinn was trying to save her. "Is this crossover far? How will we get there? What about the scaramann?"

Nimlinn closed her eyes to slits, and her tail flicked.

"If I am right, we have but one full day to get there. And, as for transportation, you will ride upon my back."

Lily thought about the ride on Roan and knew she would never last a day's ride holding onto Nimlinn's fur. Just the thought made her massage her forearms, which still ached.

"Nimlinn, I don't think I could hold on for one full hour, let alone a full day."

"You won't have to. Snerliff! Twizbang!"

The wyflings, already standing at attention, made little leaps into the air.

"Yes, mistress!"

"Laid out about that saddlebag are all of the grooming tools necessary to prepare me for saddle. Now, both of you get to work and be quick about it."

The two wyflings stared blankly at Nimlinn, as though they hadn't understood a single word she'd said.

"Quickly!" roared Nimlinn.

Stung by Nimlinn's voice, Twizbang and Snerliff rushed to the pedestal and seized the first tools that came to their paws. Not until after they had spun around and taken a few quick steps toward her did they seem to truly understand what had been asked of them.

Snerliff eyed the pair of clipping shears—in his own hand!— as though it were a poisonous snake. "You want us to do what?" he shrieked.

Nimlinn's eyes narrowed. "Groom me for saddle," she said, her voice simmering.

"But—" yelped Twizbang, "Greydor will *eat* us!"

"No!" bellowed Nimlinn. And then, speaking more quietly, "He may *want* to eat you, but I would never allow that."

Snerliff turned to Lily and gave her the pleading look of one headed for the gallows. Twizbang began to swoon, and Lily thought he was going to faint dead away when Nimlinn roared out so loudly the panes in the lanterns shook.

"Now!" bellowed Nimlinn.

Instantly, Snerliff and Twizbang bolted to Nimlinn's side, only to halt once more. After a few moments, Snerliff reached out a shaking paw, closed his eyes, and made a pitiful snip, cutting a single strand from Nimlinn's back. As the lone strand of fur drifted down to the floor, Snerliff pried one of his eyes open and viewed the damage, then smiled haplessly at Nimlinn.

"Our *time* is *short*," growled Nimlinn menacingly.

Twizbang shuffled forward and made a few tentative clips. After that, the pace of their snips increased, and the floor began to fill with Nimlinn's long, beautiful fur.

"Lily," said Nimlinn, finally satisfied by Snerliff and Twizbang's progress, "in this Tomb reside many objects of your people. If Ebbram

has been so foolish as to tell you nothing, if you are truly as completely unprepared as you seem to be, then you are in grave danger. I suggest you walk about this room and arm yourself with whatever you believe may aid you in your travels. But do not delay. We will not tarry for a moment longer than necessary."

Lily nodded. She made a quick pass through the entire tomb to get a better idea of what was available. At one of the slabs, she eyed a pair of golden vambraces, which would have fit nicely on the forearms of a good-sized man, but seemed a bit large even on her shins. She quickly tried on a helmet, but it was cavernous. The shields were also out of the question, and the swords she handled were much too long or heavy. There were bows, but they were nearly as high as her shoulder and she could barely budge the one she sampled.

At some point, her attention wandered to the murals on the walls. There was something familiar about them. From Ebb's paintings, she recognized the creatures of the Moon Realm. She had heard many tales about them. But not *these* tales.

The largest mural, which occupied the entire back wall, was eerie in that it clearly involved a titanic battle for Fangdelve, though there were no scaramann to be seen. Instead, the skies were filled with great winged insects, belching fire and mounted by archers.

The mural on the wall to the left was much smaller, as the room was twice as wide as it was deep. It told a story in successive panels. The first panel depicted a great tree, surrounded by a circular stone rampart on which rested nine thick pillars. Robed figures stood guard between them. From looking at the different panels, Lily deduced that a small band of people overcame the guards and destroyed the great tree.

The mural on the opposite wall was a jumble of engagements with no resolution. It showed many battles going on all at once. All the peoples of the moons appeared to be involved in some way or another: Rinn; giants; many types of bugs (large and small); great birds; misshapen, man-like creatures that Lily couldn't place; merfolk; winged dragons; and innumerable humans clad in clothing and armor of varying colors.

The last two murals, placed on either side of the doors, showed scenes of paradise. The one to the right showed the great tree again, with no rampart, pillars, or people, standing alone on an ocean shore. In the mural to the left, the tree stood within the stone rampart again with the pillars and robed guards.

Then Lily noticed there was something besides the murals here. Stowed in carved-out recesses framing the doors were four iron-tipped quarterstaffs, two to a side. But it was the mural of the tree all by itself that tugged at Lily's attention. Something about it seemed acutely familiar. She had taken only a few steps towards it, to examine the painting in greater detail, when Nimlinn called, "Lily! Surely you can find *something* here to aid you!"

Feeling foolish, Lily wandered back into the center of the room, where she busied herself by picking up items one after another, turning them over again and again with her fingertips before carefully placing them back down.

"Lily!" rumbled Nimlinn.

Hovering indecisively, feeling rushed, Lily picked up a modest ring with a half circle on it and held it up to show Nimlinn.

Nimlinn's whiskers drooped. "That? That tiny thing?"

Lily looked down at the ring. "Actually, it's kinda big. Maybe I could hang it from a necklace," she said, holding it up to her neck and smiling hopefully.

Nimlinn's face twitched, and Lily suspected she was fighting off a smile. "Oh, Lily, you are as impractical as any cub of mine. *That* I can fix. Bring it here."

Lily placed the slight ring in Nimlinn's huge paw. Nimlinn closed her eyes and began to make a deep rumbling noise in the back of her throat, only to stop abruptly a second later. She opened her eyes a crack and tilted her great head to one side, furrowing her brow and staring at the ring suspiciously.

"What's wrong?" asked Lily.

"Hold out your hand," Nimlinn commanded. Nimlinn dropped the ring into Lily's palm. "Put it on."

Lily stared at the oversized ring in her palm. It looked even bigger than she had thought. Not wanting to upset Nimlinn, however, she did as she was told. To Lily's surprise, the ring, once on her finger, shrank and became snug.

Lily looked up to see Nimlinn still eyeing the ring.

"What is it now?" asked Lily.

Nimlinn produced a single hooked claw from her paw and tapped the ring gently with it. "I don't know, but I think you could have done far worse in your choosing. That is no simple band of metal on your finger. There is far more to it than that."

Lily held up her hand and examined the ring more closely. It was silver, and very slim. It looked like a wedding ring, but it was crowned by that half circle, set with a small white stone.

"Finished!" barked Snerliff.

Snerliff and Twizbang, now buried waist-deep in Nimlinn's amber fur, appeared, at first, to be quite pleased with themselves.

Then Twizbang's face fell. "Greydor will eat us. I know it," he whined in a miserable-sounding voice.

"Nonsense," snorted Nimlinn, "a Rinn hasn't eaten a wyfling in over a hundred years." Neither Snerliff nor Twizbang seemed particularly comforted by this news. "Now, ready the saddle—and be quick about it!"

The wyflings ran to the pillars and quickly began filling the saddlebags with their original contents. Lily readied the blankets and draped them over Nimlinn's newly shorn back, but it took all three of them to lift the saddle and set it properly into place atop the blankets. Though the saddle itself was strangely light, its tremendous size nonetheless made for an awkward transfer. Tightening the belts also proved to be a difficult task, as Nimlinn complained continually that the straps were too tight, but the wyflings, who were expert in saddling wirtles, refused to modify the fit, simply saying, "Very snug, very snug."

Once saddled, Nimlinn shuffled—while still in the sphinx position—to the pedestal that displayed the huge metal discs. Snerliff and Twizbang, each standing on a pedestal, handed the discs one at a time to Lily, who was kneeling in the saddle. They must have weighed forty pounds apiece, and it took all of the wyflings' strength to manage the transfer, but once the discs were properly stowed in their thick protective cases, they seemed quite safe.

Finally, they attached all of the now-full saddle bags to their rightful positions on the saddle.

"Is it heavy, Nimlinn?" asked Lily, thinking the Rinn would be displeased by the added weight, especially as she had never worn a saddle before.

Nimlinn slunk back closer to the doors, where the ceiling was a little taller, and crouched. She shifted her weight.

"No, it's not," she said, sounding a little surprised. "And it's balanced perfectly." She cast an appreciative glance at the two beaming wyflings.

"Is that little ring all you can find, Lily?"

"Well . . ." said Lily, turning and looking doubtfully around the room.

Nimlinn sighed. "Lily, go to that one in the corner, the small one. I see a fine riding cloak there. You will want something to keep you warm. And see if those riding boots fit."

"Boots?" said Lily, perking up. "Riding boots?"

Lily strode into the far corner, weaving around the pillars and lanterns to a slab that showed the likeness of a young teen. He, or she (it was hard to tell), was the only youth in the room. Lily grabbed the cloak, which appeared to be in perfect condition, and draped it around her shoulders. She thought about grabbing the fine leather vest, too, but she didn't want to seem piggish. Still, she couldn't stop herself from fondling it lightly with her fingertips. It was perfect, with no signs of cracks or age.

And then, out of the corner of her eye, she saw them—the riding boots. They were a dark green and just as supple as if they'd been oiled that morning. "Mine," she breathed, snatching them up. She placed one sole-to-sole with her purple high-tops. A tad large in the toe, but Lily knew what to do there. They had beautiful lacing, and a slight rise to the heel. Lily frantically unlaced her high-tops and stood up with them in her hand, spinning around twice before deciding to place them on the slab in the exact place the riding boots had come from. They looked terribly out of place.

"You live *here* now," she said quietly to her favorite shoes.

Skidding in her fuzzy socks, Lily rushed back to Nimlinn and held the riding boots aloft as if displaying a great prize.

"Boots!" she exclaimed excitedly.

"Yes, I know. But now that I see them up close they *do* look a bit large. Don't you think?" asked Nimlinn, narrowing her eyes.

"No matter," said Lily, and she knelt down and quickly packed the toes with a bit of Nimlinn's fur before lacing them tightly about her ankles. Jumping up, she pointed a toe to the floor and swiveled right and left, showing them off to Snerliff and Twizbang. "What do you think?"

"Very lovely," said Snerliff, politely. He gave Twizbang a small kick.

"Yes, indeed," offered Twizbang. "A *fine* pair of boots."

"Nimlinn," began Lily, looking about the tomb, "how old do you think this place is?"

"I have often wondered that myself. It is ancient, to be sure, but knowledge of its existence has come to us only recently."

Pinching the lapel of her riding cloak, Lily said, "This material appears untouched by time, but there are other things here that look like they've been here for thousands of years. Why?"

"I imagine a powerful enchantment has been placed on this Tomb. And I suspect many of these items have magic of their own."

Lily pulled the riding cloak on. *Pretty good*, she thought with satisfaction. "Do you think the things will fall apart if they leave this room? I'd hate to destroy them."

"I had not considered that, but there's an easy way to find out." Nimlinn nodded to the open doors.

Lily walked solemnly to the edge of the doorway, pausing to glance back over her shoulder at the wyflings and Nimlinn, who were now watching her intently. Lily grimaced and pushed the toe of her boot over the threshold. Nothing happened. She lifted her foot and planted the boot fully outside of the tomb. Still nothing. Lily's face broke into a grin. "It's fine! It's okay!" she said, giggling in relief.

"Now," began Nimlinn, "there is one more—"

"Wait!" said Lily, emboldened.

Nimlinn's eyes widened, partly from curiosity and partly from the shock of having a mere cub speak to her this way.

Lily dashed back to where she had gotten the boots and quickly scanned the few remaining articles on the sills. The previous owner had traveled light. Lily tucked a small helm under her arm. "Now, what does Jasper call these metal thingies?" she muttered, as she picked up a pair of properly-sized vambraces. "Those are for my arms, and *these*," she paused to pick up a matching pair of greaves, "are for my shins."

Next, Lily ran to the great slab in the center. She had seen a strange wooden ball there, about the size of a baseball, covered with dark designs that had been burned into the wood. The weight of it surprised her; it was much heavier than she'd expected. Turning it, she noticed a hinge and a clasp. Unfastening it, Lily peered inside and saw a small, dark crystal sphere. She closed it quickly and fastened the lock. *Ooh, mysterious,* she thought. Lily placed it back on the slab, where it belonged.

"Finished?" asked Nimlinn.

Lily nodded, still staring at the wooden ball. So much writing. What if the writing was instructions? What if she could find someone who could read it?

"Good. Now, there is one more thing before we go."

Lily took a few steps toward Nimlinn, stopped, then doubled back to the slab, picked up the ball and tucked it into an inner pocket of her cloak.

"It won't do to have the three of you blind while we are out and about in Roan's darkness, so I will provide you with enough sight to last you through this day. Do not move until I say."

Nimlinn lowered her head, and a low rumbling from the back of her throat began to fill the room. The rumble continued for a full minute, then changed, slowly becoming chant-like. Suddenly, Nimlinn swept back her ears and grimaced.

Lily felt something strange happening, as when Roan and the others had been chanting. She fingered the moon coin and had a terrible thought. What if Nimlinn, in trying to give them the sight, undid Roan's enchantment? Lily clasped the coin with her fingers and thought to it:

Don't do anything! Don't do anything to Roan's spell!

Nimlinn lifted an eyelid just a crack. Her pupil was wide, a thin rim of amber surrounding it. She did not break her spell, but she took a good hard look at Lily before closing her eye.

"What is it, Your Majesty?" asked Snerliff, when Nimlinn finally finished.

Nimlinn took a deep breath, reviving visibly.

"It was like with Roan," said Lily, in a faraway voice.

"Lily," began Nimlinn, in a hushed tone, "what *exactly* happened when you were with Roan?"

"Nothing," said Lily quickly.

"Think, Lily. You must have done something."

"I—I remember seeing the darkness forming in the air. There were lots of arrows coming at us. The others were swatting them out of the air like flies, but there were so many. I remember thinking . . . darkness, what a great idea."

Nimlinn's and Lily's eyes locked. "And just now? What did you think about?"

"I was afraid you might undo Roan's darkness, so I told the coin to leave his spell alone."

"For a moment," Nimlinn paused, as though considering what she might say next, "I felt the presence of a bottomless power, Lily, before it was doused, like blacking cloth thrown over a lamp. I have cast many spells in the presence of Ebbram the Wanderer, and I never once felt anything like that.

"But we are wasting precious time. Climb aboard, Lily. It is time for us to begin our journey."

Twizbang and Snerliff helped push Lily up into the saddle and showed her how to strap in her legs.

Nimlinn looked down at the two wyflings. "You too, little fools," she said.

"Us?" squeaked Twizbang, in a barely audible voice.

"Climb aboard. You will make useful scouts, now that you can see. When we pass the wirtle pens at Clawforge, we will find you two steeds, and I will give them the same sight I've given you."

Lily pulled Snerliff into the saddle. Twizbang made little whimpering noises while clambering up but did not make Nimlinn wait.

Once all were in place, Nimlinn exited the tomb and padded over to where the stained glass doors reflected the sun on the rock wall. She produced a single claw and traced the outline of the orange sun, murmuring several words that Lily could not make out. The rock snapped apart where she traced.

Twizbang gasped.

A passage revealed itself, and the instant it became wide enough to accommodate her, Nimlinn bounded through. Within this passage, little to no light shone, but whether by scent, knowledge, or superior sight, she knew her way and proceeded rapidly.

Lily turned in the saddle to face Snerliff. "Can you see through this?" Lily whispered.

"A bit. There is a small amount of light being given off by the walls, perhaps from something growing on the rock, but it's not much."

"Why can't we see? Didn't she say we'd be able to see in Roan's darkness?"

"Ah," said Snerliff. "The darkness outside of the Palace Keep is magical in nature. But here, there is no light for the darkness to mask. Here, it is truly dark. If we were to light a torch or lantern, we would see just fine. But we have no need of such things, as a Rinn's eyesight in the dark is unparalleled. Indeed, with their whiskers alone they can tell much just by the temperature and direction of the air as it moves about them. Most remarkable creatures, the Rinn. We are very fortunate to have their friendship."

What little Lily could make out of this dark passage beneath Sea Denn led her to believe that it was more roughly-hewn than even the worst part of the staircase leading to the Tomb of the Fallen. During portions of their passage, the sound of Nimlinn's padding paws echoed as though through cavernous halls; other times Nimlinn would slow to a crawl, the sound so tight that Lily feared she might bump her head at the low point of some unseen ceiling. At times, she heard the trickling of water, or a gushing stream, and even, at one point, the sound of a roaring waterfall.

After what felt like half an hour, Nimlinn came to an abrupt halt.

"What is it, Nimlinn?" asked Lily.

"We have reached the door. On the other side lies the eastern slope of Sea Denn. The path beyond this wall is ancient, steep, and well-hidden. We will be safe from prying eyes until we leave the slope and head for the eastern gate, which lies in the shadow of the now-emptied Tower of Clawforge. And yet, we must be clear in our plan."

"Will there be guards at the eastern gate, Mistress?" asked Snerliff.

"No, Greydor has summoned every able body to the field. Not even the bats have reason to fly here now."

"Clawforge is defenseless?" moaned Twizbang.

"Don't worry. Greydor knows what he is doing. He has seized this sliver of opportunity, and he will leave nothing to chance. What we need to do now is get the two of you mounted on wirtleback. As soon as I can give them the sight, you will head for the eastern gate and make sure that it is indeed empty. We must leave nothing to chance. After we clear the gate, we'll make for the mountains, to the pass at Armashen. Once through the mountains, we'll follow the old sea road, along the edge of Rihnwood, and then through the great neck to the Blight Marsh. Are we all clear on this?"

Snerliff and Twizbang assented. Nimlinn began her chant.

The rock snapped, and a curved shaft of bright light cut into the dark tunnel. A round opening formed, and Nimlinn bounded out into a daylight clearer than Lily had ever known. By reflex, she threw up her hands to shield her eyes. But she realized very quickly that this strangely clear light did not hurt her eyes. So it wasn't until Lily lowered her hands and looked out onto the narrow path that she saw they were completely surrounded.

Race Against Time

No sooner had Nimlinn bounded through the opening than the rock behind them sealed shut. They were trapped. Snerliff and Twizbang screamed as though they'd been set on fire. A clutter of Rinn, panting and out of breath, perched atop the boulders half-hidden among the crags.

Lily glanced up. The dead moon was receding, but it still took up a third of the open sky. Around it were other moons, large and small, weaving among each other at different rates of speed.

Directly in front of them, blocking the path, stood Roan.

"Roan!" gasped Nimlinn. "But how?"

Roan tossed his head toward a disheveled Rinn, lying lazily atop one of the taller boulders. Lily had to look twice to see him, which she thought odd, given the clarity of her new sight. His fur was the color of sand, perfectly matching the rock he chose to rest on. Thick mats twined throughout his long fur.

"Tanglemane," sneered Nimlinn. "Just how is it *you* came to know this place?"

Instead of answering, the Rinn merely settled lower on his perch, rested his pointed chin on his huge outstretched paws, and closed his eyes as though to sleep.

Lily felt Nimlinn's scalp bristle.

Nimlinn turned to Roan. "Greydor ordered you to the field. You have disobeyed your King. Leave this place at once," she commanded.

"Stand fast!" barked Roan to his clutter. He gazed at his queen. "This is not a decision that I have made lightly, Your Majesty. It is far too dangerous for you to travel this day alone."

"You will do as I say!" roared Nimlinn. Roan didn't flinch.

"I will not leave you," he stated calmly.

Lily felt Nimlinn shudder with rage.

"You will leave," Nimlinn seethed, "or you will be banished, you and all your clutter."

Roan's reply was immediate. "Then I am banished," he said flatly. And then, to his clutter, "You are all relieved of my command. Do as you will."

The only signs of movement came from the wind stirring their long fur.

"Tell them to leave, Roan."

"I cannot. They are no longer mine to command, as I am no longer in the service of my King. Now, Nimlinn, where are we going? I assume we have little time to waste."

Nimlinn hissed.

"Fools!" she cried. "Greydor will have you all roasted on a spit!"

"Then I will bring the sauce," replied Roan, his voice rising, as though tired of all this talk.

"You are not needed, Roan. I am far from defenseless."

"Doubtless, but I will not willingly leave your side until you are safely back within Sea Denn."

Nimlinn made a sound Lily suspected was a Rinn expression of disgust, tempered with resignation. "It is more complicated than that," said Nimlinn, after a time. "I have a long way to travel. And during that time I will desire conversation with Lily—private conversation."

"We will remain out of earshot, out of sight," said Roan. "You need not worry—we will be discreet."

"A Rinn can hear a long way," said Nimlinn.

"Where are you going, and how fast do you intend to travel?" pressed Roan.

"It is not your place to question me!"

"Ah, then here we will wait." And he sat down in a casual fashion that Lily feared would only further infuriate Nimlinn. "As I am banished," he continued, letting out a small yawn, "I suddenly find myself in no particular hurry. This being, after all, my last chance to bask under the sheer cliffs of my beloved city."

Nimlinn gave a frustrated roar. Lily felt an involuntary shock of fear, and her nerves jangled. Nimlinn glanced at each Rinn in turn. None returned her gaze.

She spoke in steely, measured tones, as though she might lose control any second. "I don't want to see *any* of you." Roan quickly stood, giving Nimlinn his full attention. "And when we reach our destination, you will leave us and return to the field of battle, where you are *needed*."

"I will not," interrupted Roan. "I will not leave your side. Not until you are safely returned to Sea Denn."

Lily watched Nimlinn's eyebrow whiskers twitch. She was thankful to be on Nimlinn's back, rather than looking into her eyes.

"As I cannot stop you . . ." hissed Nimlinn, taking a deep breath, "we are headed for the pass at Armashen."

"If speed is an issue, I will send my fastest runners to the gates of

Armashen so they can make arrangements for food and supplies on your behalf," said Roan.

Lily heard Nimlinn grinding her teeth. "That would be . . . helpful. Once through the mountains, we will take the ocean road along the northern border of Rihnwood. We will then enter the Blight Marsh by way of the great neck. There is a crossover coming with Taw. We have one day's time to reach it."

"Very well." said Roan. "But I believe you will find that distance far too great, even for one such as you." Then, addressing his clutter, he commanded, "Move out!"

Instantly, they vanished.

Leaving only Tanglemane.

To Lily's eyes, he appeared overcome by slumber. He was nearly invisible. Slowly, silently, Nimlinn padded down the path, giving his rock a wide berth.

"You needn't be so hard on him, Nimlinn," yawned Tanglemane, his head still resting on his paws. Twizbang and Snerliff each let out a little yelp when he spoke.

Nimlinn halted, but did not turn to face him. Something in the way the moon coin translated Tanglemane's voice told Lily that he was not so old as he looked.

"You never answered my question," stated Nimlinn. "How do you know this place?"

Lily turned in the saddle, as did Snerliff and Twizbang. Tanglemane's eyes were still closed. He looked exhausted, spent.

"You know, Nimlinn . . . he was absolutely frantic when I found him. He had recalled all of his clutter from the field and placed them around Sea Denn. He knew you were on the move with the Dain cub, but he had no idea how you intended to make your escape."

"So, Greydor knows where I am as well—knows that I am on the move!"

"No," said Tanglemane, dismissively. "Roan knows perfectly well that's the last thing you would want. He has told no one." Tanglemane yawned widely, showing an impressive array of teeth and his wide pink tongue. "You know full well that he would do *anything* you asked of him."

"Except obey my orders!" snapped Nimlinn.

"Well . . . anything within reason," snorted Tanglemane.

"I'm being unreasonable now, am I?" said Nimlinn, her long fur and mane rising.

"He is young, Nimlinn. . . . He has little faith in what he has not seen with his own eyes. He honors you."

"Honors me? Is that what you call it?" asked Nimlinn.

"He feels you have no chance of making it to the Blight Marsh, and yet he intends to aid you on this impossible journey."

"Impossible? And do you share his thoughts?"

Tanglemane cracked his eyes to slits.

"My eyes, Nimlinn, see much that others do not." Then he nuzzled his nose into the fur of his legs and closed his eyes for good.

"So, where are you off to next?" asked Nimlinn. "The field of battle? Or do you intend to *honor* me also?"

"I intend neither," murmured Tanglemane, his voice muffled by the long fur of his paws. "I could sleep for a week." Then he began to snore.

As curious as Nimlinn was, she knew this was neither the time nor place for a protracted argument, especially as her fellow debater was asleep. She clucked her tongue with distaste, then gathered herself. Through clenched teeth, she said, "Hold tight, Lily," and sprang away.

The rocks that lined the narrow trail blurred, and the wind raked through Lily's hair. Behind them the cliffs shrank, and eventually, the twisting path opened wider. The sky seemed pale and unnatural to Lily. The retreating dead moon, still large and fat, ascended like a deadly spider, back into its swirling web of clouds, moons, and faint stars.

The base of the tower Clawforge was planted squarely within the hill ringing Sea Denn. Far above, connecting the upper tower's reaches and the city proper, Lily could see the thin shimmering line of the Rinnwalk. With her enhanced sight, Lily thought she could even make out a few small shapes moving along it toward the upper city of Sea Denn.

Nimlinn kept her pace quick, as fast as a horse at gallop. In very little time, they reached the stables, where Snerliff and Twizbang had no trouble finding and saddling two wirtles. After Nimlinn gave the hideous beasts—all leaping legs and snapping teeth—the power of sight, they barked with joy.

"Snerliff," hissed Nimlinn. "The gate."

Snerliff and Twizbang clicked their teeth, whirling their beasts around with expert precision. The wirtles shot away like water bugs jetting across a pond, Snerliff and Twizbang blurring upon their backs. Leaning forward, noses first, their bodies bounced like rag dolls while their heads remained remarkably level. No sooner had they left than they were back.

"The gate is open, and the way is clear!" cried Twizbang, and he rounded his wirtle with such speed that, for a moment, it appeared he would be torn from the saddle. But his twitchy reflexes saved him, and he remained firmly seated.

Nimlinn bounded after them, passing through the gate and down the old sea town road. From time to time, the wyflings would double back with reports of finding half-eaten scaramann, but not much else. Once clear of Clawforge, Nimlinn paid little attention to the wyflings' reports. Lily felt Nimlinn's cadence shift and suspected she was deep in thought. They traveled this way for more than an hour before Nimlinn spoke.

"Lily, the time has come. I promised to answer all that I could. Ask me what you would most like to know."

Suddenly embarrassed, Lily felt her face flush. In all this time, she hadn't worked out a single question for Nimlinn. Instead, she realized, she had been simply taking in her new surroundings, enjoying the beauty of the view. And yet, there were *so* many questions. She wanted to ask good ones. But where to start? What to say? And what *not* to say?

On the one hand, Lily didn't necessarily want to reveal how little she really knew—she didn't want to appear stupid. On the other hand, Uncle Ebb *had* told an awful lot of bedtime tales, and Jasper and Lily had memorized them all. Additionally, they were very familiar with the paintings, which filled Ebb's mansion and offered many clues to his unfinished tales. Complicating matters were a few paintings that Uncle Ebb never discussed, ones that seemed unrelated to the bedtime tales.

And then it struck her. Back at Ebb's, on their stroll to the strange cloakroom—she had seen paintings in those rooms! She could picture the birdfish ducking around them, but she couldn't remember their subject matter.

Faking her knowledge seemed like a bad idea. Wasn't Nimlinn trying to help her? And hadn't Lily confessed in the Great Hall of the Rinn that she'd never been to Barreth, or to any of the other moons in the Realm? That decided it. This was no time to be shy. But she knew she would still have to be careful, keeping track of all she revealed, and to whom.

The one thing Lily most wanted to know was why so much here differed from the Moon Realm of the bedtime tales. In those tales, magic was *everywhere*. And there was no dead moon, no wyflings, no scaramann, not even wirtles. However she started, she didn't wish to sound the total fool. So she decided to start with one of her favorite, and one of the most powerful, characters from the bedtime tales. Surely, she thought, meeting him would be a good place to start.

"Nimlinn, where is Rinnjinn?"

"Rinnjinn?" said Nimlinn, sounding surprised.

"Yes, I would like to see him. I'm sure he could help us."

"Help us?" Nimlinn chuckled. "Lily, Rinnjinn cannot help us."

Lily's spirits dampened. "Why? What has happened? He can't be dead. He is much too powerful. He built Fangdelve! He raised Sea

Denn!"

"Lily . . . Rinnjinn is . . . well . . . I suppose he is as alive as he ever was—"

"Then we must go see him!"

"You don't understand. He is alive, but only in story."

"They're not stories!" Lily blurted. "They're tales. There's a difference," she added softly. Then Lily's vexation returned with full force. "He slew the serpent of Naamian! He fought beside Meloric and saved Castle Relinngold! He saved them, Nimlinn—he saved them all!"

"I have heard the one about the serpent of Naamian. In fact, there is a lovely fountain in Sea Denn devoted to that story. I'll be happy to show it to you sometime. But this Meloric, I have never heard of her."

"Him! Meloric is a he! A giant, in fact—twenty feet tall! And *he's* real, too."

"The Rinnjinn stories I know, I heard when I was no more than a cub. I tell them the same way to my cubs. They're just bedtime stories, Lily."

Lily's new reality was blurring at the edges. *Just* bedtime stories. That hit too close to home. The possibility that some of Uncle Ebb's tales might not be real—here—had never occurred to Lily. So what was real?

For her next question, Lily asked one she was certain Nimlinn could answer.

"When did you last see my Uncle Ebb?"

Nimlinn thought for a time before answering.

"It's been a little over a year, but he was up to something. I suspect he's been on Barreth since I last saw him, though I have no solid proof."

"A year! Where has he been?"

"That is not mine to say, but I would tell you if I knew."

Lily felt a wave of hopelessness sweep over her. Nothing made any sense.

Lily stared off into the sky, and the dead moon gradually captured her attention. "Why are the scaramann attacking your moon?" she asked.

"Moon? Moon! Lily, *this* is no moon! This is the one true world of the Moon Realm. These here"—Nimlinn's paw swept the sky—"are moons! Moons of Barreth."

"Um, I didn't mean offense."

"As to the scaramann, they are attacking us because they have been ordered to do so."

"Ordered? By whom?"

Nimlinn's pace slowed, becoming erratic just before stuttering to a halt. With a great turn of her head, she locked eyes with Lily.

Lily felt her pulse quicken. Nimlinn was sizing her up again, eyes boring into her. This was just the kind of thing she had wished to avoid. Lily tried hard to meet Nimlinn's gaze with strength, but as the seconds ticked off, the task became more and more difficult.

"You really don't know, do you?"

Lily tried to speak, but no intelligible words would come out.

Nimlinn turned away from Lily and set off again.

"He has many names, Lily," began Nimlinn, in a faraway voice. "I know only a few. On Taw they call him Werfryht, on Dik Dek . . . Wergmyrk. On Dain he is known as Wrengfoul. But here on Barreth, he is named Rengtiscura." When Nimlinn pronounced this last name, she rolled the first R and hissed the S.

"His dominion is the dead moon of Darwyth. I am told he resides there within a vast fortress of towers, surrounded by dead forests, perched on the rim of an empty, long-dead sea. If you were to take a single step on Darwyth, Lily, it would be your last. It is a place of death and despair. And as to these other moons, there are precious few that I would recommend. Here, of course, on Barreth, you will be safe . . . at least while you are a cub. No Rinn has ever killed another's cub. When you are older, you will need to be with one of us who knows you.

"Dik Dek may suit you, but be careful which Embaseas you visit. I recommend Dik Dek's own: The Palace Embasea. It's the largest and safest. I suppose the Embasea of Taw would be safe. In fact, the moon of Taw is probably the safest place you can be. Remember, Lily, that the forests of Taw are always safe! All but one, that is, but the birds would never let you venture there. They will take good care of you."

Lily found herself wanting to talk more of Taw and the Embaseas of Dik Dek—a beautiful painting of the Palace Embasea hung at the foot of the stairwell in Ebb's great hallway—but she didn't want to get off the subject of this many-named evil, Rengtiscura.

"Has he attacked before?" she asked.

"Not in recent times—not with this kind of strength. But I have begun to believe—with the counsel of your uncle—that once, very long ago, Barreth and our moons attacked him as one force, united. It was that battle and those that followed which nearly destroyed us all, including Rengtiscura himself. . . . But to my knowledge, he has forever been with us."

Werfryht, Wergmyrk, Wrengfoul, Rengtiscura. Lily was frustrated that she didn't know *any* of these names. Did he have another five names? One for each moon? Did she know one of those names from the bedtime tales? Lily itched for a pad of paper and pencil, and not for the last time, either. There was just too much to keep straight. She didn't want the facts to blur with the fantasy. She wanted the facts to remain clear and separate, and that would take a journal.

Ebb had told Lily and Jasper hundreds of bedtime tales. And yet, if all those tales were of *this* place, how could their uncle have missed such a central character? *He has forever been with us,* Nimlinn had said. But how could that be?

Which parts of Ebb's bedtime tales were real? Which were made up? In the Great Hall of the Rinn, someone had talked of scholars on Dik Dek and mentioned a name—what was the name? She had already forgotten. Was he a merman, or she a mermaid? Did the giants of Min Tar exist, or had Ebb made them up too? The dragons of Dain?

She had seen some of the great birds of Taw, hadn't she? Wasn't the big green bird that had helped her a bird from Taw? Lily felt a pang of regret that she hadn't even asked its name.

Nimlinn went on. "Rengtiscura meant to deliver to us today a battle of such force as to match that he dealt Dain."

"But wouldn't the dragons have just eaten them?"

"Being the Queen of the Rinn, Lily, I know a little more of Dain than most, but, mind you, my knowledge is woefully incomplete. The dragons of which you speak are monstrous eating machines, that is true, but they are wild and thoughtless, attacking anything they meet. They are senseless—unorganized. They would be useless in battle, for they would just as soon attack friend as foe."

Lily didn't like the sound of this. The dragons in Uncle Ebb's tales were intelligent, thoughtful, wise, and, for the most part, friendly.

"When did he attack Dain?"

"Let me think. It was . . . seventeen years ago. It was dreadful to behold. During our times of crossover with Dain, when we were so close we could hear their screams, we watched Rengtiscura's ever-expanding swath of desolation. For our own defense, we massed our armies during these crossovers, for fear that we might be next. We watched. We waited. We did nothing as Dain fell before our eyes to his dark armies. He has destroyed their moon, Lily. They are now a mere shadow of their former glory. Their largest cities lie in ruin. They cower in a few fortified areas, packed like vermin, barely able to feed themselves.

"I fear Barreth is not safe from this same fate, Lily. Greydor has much work to do. If my kin are late, it will be all the more difficult to re-take Fangdelve. And we will be desperate for their bows should any of the fire-breathing dragonflies return." Nimlinn's tone changed, became softer, "Greydor is a good king, Lily. And he would have cared more about your plight if not for all of Barreth being at stake today—"

"Fire . . . breathing . . . dragonflies?"

"Yes. And they are much larger than you might think. Wyrrtwitch believes—"

"Wait—who is Wyrrtwitch?"

"Forgive me, I'll explain. Wyrrtwitch is a lunamancer. She's in charge of the tower Clawforge, where the rest of the lunamancer Rinn live and study. She believes that these fire-breathing dragonflies were once much smaller, and that the original stock was taken from the place we now call the Blight Marsh. That is not really so hard to believe, as it is not uncommon for dragonflies there to be six or more feet in—"

"Six feet! How big are the fire-breathing ones?"

"No living Rinn has seen one, but the large ones are said to measure over thirty feet; saddled, they could easily carry four scaramann. Between the bowshot and their breaths of fire, they would be formidable enemies."

"Wait—I saw them in the murals, in The Tomb of the Fallen."

Nimlinn scanned the skies. "That was the last time he controlled the tower of Fangdelve."

"But Nimlinn—" said Lily, trying to absorb all these new names and places, "aren't *we* going to the Blight Marsh?"

"Yes. But we are talking about events from our dimmest history. Allow me to tell you what I know. I will be brief and accurate. According to our scholars, at the dawn of the Second Age, the Age of Destruction, Rengtiscura attacked all of the Moon Realm within one cycle of crossovers. On Barreth, he attacked us from the Blight Marsh. On that day, he forever fouled what had been a place of great beauty. And even though it has healed much since that time, it is still tainted. He attacked Barreth first because he desired to capture Rinnjinn—"

"Wait! I thought you said you didn't believe in Rinnjinn?"

"Well, I don't . . . not exactly, anyway. You must take into account that almost everything from the time I'm telling you about has been pieced together. The beginning of the Second Age was six millennia ago, and precious little has survived. And while your uncle can spout stories and dates like a living encyclopedia, I cannot bring myself to believe that all he has to say is true. I'm sure there was a Rinn, or maybe a group of Rinn, who did some of the things Rinnjinn is said to have done. But for Rinnjinn to have achieved all he is credited for is simply not possible. These remaining stories of Rinnjinn are tavern tales, Lily, told so many times they have grown big. They are myths— mere bedtime stories!

"But we are getting too far off point. Wherever Rengtiscura attacks, he likes to capture creatures to take back to Darwyth. There, his dwythbane warp them, changing them from their natural state into something he desires. The dwythbane breed them and train them to fight in Rengtiscura's armies. In this way, so Wyrrtwitch believes, the fire-breathing dragonflies were created."

"Are the dwythbane like bad lunamancers?"

"They wield magic, yes, but they are equally adept with weapons. I have never seen one, but I'm told they walk on two legs, just as you do. Furless, their skin peels like bark, and their paws are said to resemble clumps of roots."

Lily tried to let this sink in, but it was a lot of information, and she cursed the bits and pieces that she knew were getting by her. This wouldn't happen to Uncle Ebb, Lily thought. And an image of Uncle Ebb surfaced in Lily's mind. He was smiling, standing in the doorway of his home, flanked on either side by those tall bookcases, loading and unloading his coat pockets with handfuls of little books and newly-sharpened pencils. And then it hit her. Uncle Ebb could have been visiting the Moon Realm since before they were born, and those little books were full of the things he was learning there. The sneak! The smiling little sneak!

Lily knew she'd have an easier time remembering all these facts if they were answers to questions she made up herself. Reconciling the bedtime tales—sorting out what was real from what was not—seemed a good way to start.

"Nimlinn, wait, what happened between the Rinn and the Dain? Why do you hate each other? I thought you were friends."

"Now you are talking like your uncle. But it's not just the Dain from whom we are estranged, Lily. We have no formal contact with any of the moons within our Realm except Taw."

"What about Dik Dek?"

"Ah, very good. We have no *official* contact with them, but long have the seagoing Rinn traded there. Rille is as close as you will come to a leader of the merfolk on Dik Dek. I have only spoken to him through the birds, but Greydor has a way to contact him and can actually see him when they talk. There is a crossover—more than one, actually—where Barreth's oceans meet our Embasea on Dik Dek."

"Have you ever been to an Embasea?" asked Lily.

"I have never visited any of our moons, and I don't expect I ever will. But I haven't finished answering your question about Dain. The Rinn don't talk with the Dain, if we ever did. First, you must understand that almost all the Rinn harbor a great hatred for the Dain. They believe the people of Dain once enslaved us and rode us as dumb beasts to labor under their will."

Lily shifted uneasily in the saddle. She fingered the curving lines engraved in the design atop the saddle's pommel, tracing what appeared to be a single letter in foreign script. And yet, it seemed familiar, like she'd seen it somewhere before.

"Your uncle has worked tirelessly to refute the image of the Dain enslaving the Rinn. And to his credit, he has convinced a handful of powerful and important Rinn. But in general, among the populace"— she made the clicking sound with her tongue—"it would not be safe for a Dain to walk on Barreth without powerful protection."

Lily thought back to her meeting with Greydor. There had been a name . . . a name attached to a Dain.

"Nimlinn . . . that lunamancer . . . Mow—Mow—"

"Mowra," Nimlinn finished.

"Thank you. She talked about someone from Dain. It was as though Mowra had talked to her many times and thought she might know something about the necklace. Has this person been to Barreth?

Can she walk here safely?"

"You are speaking of Ember. It is true; she has been here on Barreth, but only very rarely. And on those occasions, she had to be secretly escorted and carefully hidden until delivered to Clawforge. There she has made a name for herself among the lunamancer Rinn. They have taken to her in a way that I would not have imagined possible. But on the streets of Sea Denn, or any other place on Barreth, she would most likely be torn limb from limb by the first group of Rinn to cross her path."

A chill passed through Lily. "So, when I'm not a cub," she said mechanically, "*I'll* be torn to pieces."

"Not as long as you are under the protection of those who know you," answered Nimlinn immediately. "You would not be forcibly removed or attacked if you were with me, Greydor, Roan, or any of his clutter."

"What if I was with Swatfur, or Twizbang, or Snerliff?"

"Swatfur?"

"A Rinn cub."

Nimlinn's silence was answer enough. Lily tried not to think about when the line between cub and whatever came after might begin to blur. Instead, she thought back to Tanglemane, lying sleepily on his rock. Was he dangerous? Nimlinn sure didn't trust him.

"What about Tanglemane, Nimlinn? Who is he?"

"He is Qaz. They have no true clan. They wander wherever valley meets mountain. They are good Rinn, Lily, but I believe Tanglemane has some mountain Rinn in his blood, and that makes him very . . . unpredictable."

"Mountain Rinn?"

"Feral beasts. They live deep in the mountains, near the high passes. They are very difficult to understand or deal with, though I understand the Qaz manage to coexist with them."

"Nimlinn, how many types of Rinn are there? And what did you mean by *good* Rinn? Are there *bad* Rinn?"

"There are sea, mountain, valley, forest, and the Qaz. And as to *bad* Rinn, Lily, let us just hope we do not meet any of them tonight . . . or any night, for that matter."

Lily's gaze swept across the brightly-lit landscape. Night, the real night, would come eventually. She wondered if that might somehow break Roan's strange spell.

"How long will Roan's spell last, Nimlinn?"

"I don't know. No one has ever cast darkness that widely before."

"How did he do it?"

Nimlinn laughed, tossing her head.

"You tell me; you are the one who caused it!"

Lily knew perfectly well that she had done nothing of the kind.

"I cast no spells!" she protested.

"No, I don't doubt that, but you have something about you—something I have never felt before. I felt it when I cast the sight upon you so you could see through this darkness."

Lily absentmindedly patted her shirt, making sure the hard lump of the pendant was there beneath the fabric.

"It wasn't me, Nimlinn. It was Uncle Ebb's necklace. It has strange powers, and I don't really know how to use them."

Nimlinn harrumphed.

"With this sight, will I be able to see in the real night, after Roan's spell fades?"

"No."

Lily looked off to the mountains, which were growing nearer with every stride of Nimlinn's powerful legs.

"For a spell called darkness, it sure isn't very dark."

"It is an old spell, Lily. Nearly all the Rinn can call it down, even those not well versed in magic."

Lily looked down at her hand, sure she had never had such an easy time making out the lines in her palm, or bugs on the ground, or leaves on far away trees.

"Tell me more about Dik Dek, Nimlinn?"

Nimlinn veered to the right, briefly jogging on three legs, and pointed her enormous paw toward a huge moon hanging low in the sky.

"That blue one there, that is Dik Dek. It is virtually all water. The only exception being the—"

"Embaseas," Lily interrupted.

"How much do you know of the Embaseas?"

"I've seen paintings of them—living coral castles that soar out of the sea. Along their walls and around their spires swim enchanted airborne fish, the brightest colors you can imagine. And on darkward nights, when no moon's light can reach their shell-and-anemone-covered walls, the whole Embasea glows in deep hues of phosphorescent purple, green, and sapphire, streaked with fiery reds and firefly sparks of yellow and gold." Lily felt a wash of emotion overtake her, and her eyes welled up as she recalled the bedtime tales she so desperately wanted to be true. "And in their pearled halls, where the merfolk surface from the pools and fountains with feasts harvested from their gardens, they sing songs, and tell bewitching tales, and drink until all the nighttime hours have evaporated. Finally, at dawn, they depart for the open sea through the labyrinth of passages that flow from all the lower courtyards and halls."

The road canted upward, and the mountains were getting closer. Lily could sense Nimlinn exerting herself more to keep up her pace.

"You sound like you've been there," said Nimlinn.

Now it was Lily's turn to harrumph.

"I've heard lots of tales, Nimlinn. And I mean *lots* of tales. When Uncle Ebb thought we were old enough to keep quiet, he'd tell us new ones. But if we slipped up in front of Mom or Dad, they got very angry with him."

The angle of the saddle pitched back. Lily instinctively grabbed the pommel with both hands, and glanced about her, surprised to see that they were now moving through rumpled hills and scrubby trees at a much faster rate than before.

Nimlinn bounded into the air, and Lily caught her breath as they soared over a hillock, then landed gracefully, still maintaining a full gallop.

"Lily, I am now certain that this saddle is even more magical than I had hoped. I advise you to watch what you think—and do—very carefully when sitting in it, as we do not know the extent of its powers. And not knowing the powers of a magical object, even a good one, can be very dangerous."

"What kind of powers are you talking about, Nimlinn?"

"Look ahead. In that gap in the mountains, directly before us, lies Armashen. It is a small, well-fortified city. It is meant to provide safe passage to Rihnwood. I'm sure, even with your eyes, that you can see the bridge arching across the river, to the right of the falls."

Lily squinted, "Yes, Nimlinn, I see it."

"Those falls mark the headwaters of the river Barradil, which cuts through a great canyon that runs along the mountain's edge to the sea. Roan is waiting for us on that bridge. I have now borne you nearly one hundred miles, and yet I feel as though I have barely begun. More importantly, I have felt no need for food. And that, I can tell you, is *very* unusual for a Rinn. But there is another thing I feel. . . ."

Nimlinn's course shifted slightly eastward then, down and away from the pass, away from the bridge. Lily followed the rest of the run to its terminus, where it rose abruptly and ended on a cliff high above the river.

"Lily, on your saddle, there should be straps for your legs."

"Yes," said Lily, suddenly listening intently. "Twizbang showed me how to hitch them."

"And you have them on now?"

"Yes," said Lily, trying to hide the tremor in her voice.

"Are they tight, Lily?" shouted Nimlinn, over the sound of rising wind. "*Really* tight?"

Lily nervously made a rapid check of the straps buckled around her legs, tightening them as much as she dared.

"I'm good, Nimlinn," she shouted back, her stomach now feeling uncomfortable.

"Good, Lily! Good!" Nimlinn made a sound that Lily feared was laughter.

She felt Nimlinn's body lower as she increased her pace, her paws raking in the earth below them, swallowing greater and greater distances with each stride.

Lily leaned forward in the saddle and found two great loops she had originally thought were for a rider's weapons, but the loops fit her hands so perfectly that she now thought she might have discovered their true purpose. As to where they were headed, Lily no longer needed her newly enhanced sight.

"Nimlinn?" Lily shouted to the wind. "Nimlinn! There's no bridge here!"

In the span of an instant, Nimlinn's great frame bounded up the last of the long rocky slope. Her front claws just kissed the cliff's edge, but with such force that they cut into the rock, shearing off slivers and blasting heated sparks. Her back coiled like a spring, pitching her body forward and giving Lily a brief and all too clear view of the chasm below, before her rear claws hammered into place alongside her front paws. And the great coil that was Nimlinn unwound with the force of a thousand bows, hurtling the two of them into nothingness.

Lily screamed.

Nimlinn must have miscalculated. The other side of the gorge was too far away. At least, Lily *was* thinking this before she realized that they were still ascending, as though momentarily on wings. As Nimlinn soared, she kept her paws fully extended. Lily had an instant to think *we might just make it* before they smashed into the ground on the other side. She had braced herself, fully expecting to be flattened against the saddle on impact, but the shock was nothing near as great as she'd expected, and Nimlinn made resuming a full run look like cub's play. With a quick glance, Lily looked back and saw they had cleared the gorge's edge by over thirty feet. Now, in the mountains,

Nimlinn's pace refused to slow, and she leapt just as often to a boulder as to a bit of path.

"You've been through here before?" yelled Lily, over the ringing sounds of Nimlinn's claws as they struck and ripped out paw-sized gouges of rock.

"No—" Nimlinn grunted, executing a particularly harrowing leap that caused Lily's stomach to drop away for a time before bouncing back, "but it does feel as though I can see the way. Or . . . as if it is being shown to me."

"Another power of the saddle?"

"That would be . . . my . . . guess."

Nimlinn raced across a narrowing sliver of rock before leaping at the very last second and just reaching an overhang. Her claws drove into the rocks like steel into ice. Lily marveled at Nimlinn's climbing ability. It quickly became obvious that all she needed was the purchase of a single paw to pull up her entire body, rider and all, to whatever ledge or rock awaited.

When Nimlinn explained, during a brief moment on what looked like the hint of a trail, that their conversation would have to wait until they were out of the mountains, Lily didn't argue.

Hours passed as Nimlinn hauled them up the mountainside, never slowing, never missing a step, always ready and able to make the next leap. It wasn't until they reached the final pinnacle that Nimlinn, breathing hard, paused to survey her achievement. It was like being at the top of the world. The valley was behind them, the great Rihnwood forest before, and always, the ocean to the right.

"There, Lily," she said, pointing leftward to a green canopy that started at the root of the mountain and stretched to the horizon's edge. "The great forest Rihnwood, home of the BroadPaw."

But before Lily could get out a word, Nimlinn dove down the other side of the mountain. In seconds they reached terrifying speeds. On the way up there had been gaps, ledges, and long stretches on narrow spines of rock, but going down was more like a barely controlled fall. Just when it seemed Nimlinn couldn't descend any faster, she dug in her heels and sent them plummeting with such force that Lily was sure there was no hope for them.

After enduring constant vertical descents, they entered the final stretch. A thin spine of mountain gradually gave way to a long arm that slowly curved around until it met the beach and the pounding surf. Nimlinn was now running so fast that Lily had difficulty making out her legs. They met a narrow road that Lily assumed was the way back to Armashen or onward to the Blight Marsh. Once on the road, Nimlinn slowed a bit. On their left rose the great forest of Rihnwood, and on their right crashed the sea. The roar of the waves created a strange, slow rhythm. And for the first time in a long time, Lily discovered she wasn't terrified.

Slowly, she relaxed the stiff muscles in her arms and shoulders. Lily wondered what time it must be on Earth. The last time she had seen her clock it had been a little past ten. How many hours had she spent on Barreth? How many since she left Sea Denn? In the mountains, down the mountains. Surely it must be morning on Earth. She'd missed a whole night's sleep. Her parents would be waking up soon. What would they think when she wasn't in her bed?

Lily knew she should be very tired, but she felt wide awake. How could that be? The saddle?

"Nimlinn?" Lily shouted to the wind and surf. "Nimlinn? Shouldn't I be more tired?"

Nimlinn slowed to a lope.

"Lily!—" she panted.

"I should be sleepy," Lily continued. "I haven't slept for a day. I really need some—"

"Lily, don't!—" roared Nimlinn.

But it was too late. Lily's eyes were already drooping down, her body falling forward limply onto Nimlinn's back.

"—sleep," Lily murmured, her head lightly bouncing to the rise and fall of Nimlinn's ceaseless stride.

The Blight Marsh

THERE was a sound of waves, and an endless blur of trees. And moons—too many moons. Occasionally, a name. But not much else.

Later there were more trees—huge trees on all sides, and darkness. By bits and pieces, the world revealed itself and then retreated, hidden from view, back to a restful, peaceful place that Lily had no desire to leave. But there was, sometimes, a name.

Muffled, faraway sounding: "—Lily."

And sometimes: "—Lily, you must wake up."

From what?

It could have been hours. It could have been days. Then finally something she could identify: the discomfort of a pommel that kept bumping.

"—Lily, you want to be awake. Say it. Think it."

Awake? What's that?

There was fur, like a pillow, and the smell of an animal. And that pommel, bumping and bruising.

Lily couldn't see. Her eyes would not open, and she sensed that something was not right.

And then she *could* see. A marsh stretched outward from a forest's edge. A dead moon hung above. Suspended upside down on its surface were row upon row of siege engines, hurling nets to the moon below. The leading edges of the nets, descending like curtains, slowed down strangely before crossing into Barreth's gravitational influence. But after picking up speed, the weighted spiked balls and trailing nets splashed and thudded into the black muck and pools of Barreth's marsh, creating a vast network of black spiderwebs connecting the two moons. The nets filled with dark creatures, moving quickly from the plains of the dead moon to the marsh. Tens of thousands of them, forming in ranks in the wet gloom. Then her vision turned dark, and her eyes still wouldn't open.

Lily could hear the sound of Nimlinn running, and a clanking of armor in the saddle with her. And a voice, also nearby, or perhaps inside her head. The voice of a woman, sleepy or confused: "*Is that you? Where are you? Are they there? Oh! Ride swiftly, my love.*"

Lily opened her eyes again. They were barreling down a long straight corridor through the forest—a tunnel of trees. The end of the tunnel was filled with light, and marked the entrance to the marsh. They raced to the edge of the forest without slowing.

Dark forces roared a single name. Over and over again, echoing across the water. The webs were growing taut now, as the spikes and balls were lifted by the departing moon, dripping through the dank air. At the bottom of one net was a lone figure, yelling something as he rose. Then, from his hands, a terrible light flashed. The waters of the marsh churned sickly green, and dull lights moved within the black waters. Dark shapes broke the surface. A nightmarish noise—shouts and screams and laughter—rose from the hideous army. Lily watched the lone figure, watched its head swivel to the forest's edge. She could feel its eyes in the darkness, seeing *her*, looking into *her*. And she thought, *I must wake up!*

Lily jerked upright in the saddle. She wiped the drool from her cheek with her sleeve and rubbed the sore spot on her side where the saddle's pommel had dug into her.

"Lily!" said Nimlinn. "Wish yourself alert!"

Without hesitation, Lily complied, and at once the whole world snapped into clear focus. She was still being swiftly borne by Nimlinn, hurtling toward the Blight Marsh. But the ocean was gone. They were on a wide path. Trees towered on both sides, crowding out the sky with their thick branches and foliage.

"What is this place?"

"We are in the tree tunnel, passing through the Northern Neck of Rihnwood, on our way to the Blight Marsh."

"Nimlinn!" Lily yelled desperately. "We must turn back. It's a trap!"

Nimlinn did not slow. But this news changed the way she ran. She lowered her body, and her head swept to all angles as she took in the dark surroundings.

"What are you talking about, Lily?"

Lily explained to Nimlinn about the nets and the army forming in the Blight Marsh, but when she got to the part about the woman's voice, she paused. A small light near the pommel had caught her eye. She moved her hands in a shooing motion, but the light followed her hand. Then she saw it. The light shone from the ring on her hand. Lily raised the slim silver band to her face. The half circle on it glowed a bright milky white. Had it been doing that before?

"A dream, Lily," said Nimlinn. "Nothing more. We are heading for a crossover with Taw. The moon Darwyth is now far away. No moon can cross over twice in such a short time. There is *no* way that what you've seen could be happening now. You must trust me."

Nimlinn's words did nothing to dispel Lily's dread, and the closer they drew to the Blight Marsh, the worse the feeling grew. The figure she had seen rising in the nets—those eyes! It must have been more than a dream.

And the woman's voice. . . . It was as if the woman had been talking to her, but *not* to her—like listening in on a phone line.

Shafts of bright green light shone through the treetops like stage lights on the path ahead, but no such shafts penetrated the deep forest to either side. The boles of the trees were wide and gnarled. Running through them would have been difficult. Lily wondered how the wide path had ever been cut in the first place. It must have been like blasting through stone.

"What is that light? And why is it so green?" asked Lily.

"It is from the reflection of Taw. It's green because Taw is all trees. This means Taw is descending, filling the sky. Lily, we still have a chance!"

Nimlinn labored to increase her speed, and the trees blurred.

"Nimlinn, you're exhausted."

"I'm fine. It's not much farther."

Lily felt like she was atop a train barreling down a green tunnel. As they rounded a bend, she saw the tree tunnel's exit looming into view, and through it, more of the intensely green light.

Her anxiety continued to increase.

"We should slow down, Nimlinn." Lily patted Nimlinn's neck heavily with her open hand. "We should sneak up to the edge. We don't want to do what *they* did." *In the dream.* Lily balled her hands into fists, pounding harder. "Nimlinn, listen to me. Listen to me! We *don't* want to be *seen*!" She screamed, her voice rising sharply.

"No! We must hurry!"

Lily groped at the straps holding her legs. The straps were tight, and her hands shook. Then Nimlinn burst through the forest's edge and into the Blight Marsh. It was a dead, festering landscape, and the smell of sulfur and rotting wood filled Lily's nostrils. Above their heads, now filling all the open sky, was a lush green world of trees. And it was descending quickly.

"You see, Lily!" panted Nimlinn. "It's Taw! Just as I said it would be."

Lily let go of the straps, her head swimming. Something terrible and loathsome, something in the very air, began leeching at Lily's mind. Thick mists hung over the stagnant pools; insects buzzed and swarmed over dark clumps of decaying wood and fetid grasses.

Nimlinn slowed, stopping at the edge of a dark pool. "This part will be a little trickier." Tentatively, she pressed her paw into the damp earth and the depression quickly filled with water. There was a sucking sound when she pulled away her paw and gave it a shake, flicking away the water.

"We're going in there?" asked Lily.

"Yes. I can see the way." Nimlinn crouched at the edge of a pool, then launched herself into the marsh, landing on a clump of soft, squishy peat.

"Ugh," she complained, flicking more water off her paws with every step. Slowly, carefully, Nimlinn took them deeper into the morass.

"Before we left Sea Denn, I gave the power of sight to the swiftest messenger I could find. She will have crossed over to Taw the instant the wind eddies died down enough to give her safe passage. I imagine Aleron mobilized a flock as soon as he saw Barreth shrouded by darkness. We will not have to wait long to find out if we have been successful."

"How will the others see through the darkness?"

"Roan's darkness faded during your rest. It has been almost a full day since we left."

Lily tried to fight the creeping uneasiness the Blight Marsh radiated, but it was hard. She shifted her gaze upward and watched Taw descend. Behind a few wispy clouds, she could see an endless canopy of trees, through which broke the occasional rocky cliff or waterfall. Watching a whole moon slowly fill the sky was awe-inspiring.

"How can they breathe when they fly between?"

"At a time of crossover, our atmosphere and that of the moon reach out to each other and join. The wind eddies created at that time are deadly, but they calm down before they reach the lower atmosphere. I have been told that the switch in gravity from one world to the next can be dizzying, but approaching with enough speed can lessen the effect. At least, if you happen to be flying. Lily! Hang on!"

Nimlinn stood up on her hind feet and waved her massive front paws, crossing and uncrossing them repeatedly.

"What is it, Nimlinn? Do you see them?"

"Yes. And it is Aleron! I can see the missing feathers on his right wing. Do you see, Lily?"

Lily, holding tightly to the pommel, strained her eyes until she could just make out a small flock of birds descending steeply through the clouds.

Nimlinn planted her front paws firmly. "Lily, get out your moon coin!"

Lily hastily grabbed the necklace and gave it a yank. The pendant popped out from under her shirt, and she snatched it up. The little golden moons were dull.

"You've done it, Nimlinn! You got us here in time!"

"Oh, Lily, don't say that! Not yet," Nimlinn cautioned. "Now, quickly, hold the face of the pendant up to the sky—Aleron's vision is like no other's."

Lily ripped off the necklace and wound the chain around her wrist. Her hand was so unsteady she had to grab her forearm with her other hand to hold it still as she held it high.

One of the birds tucked its wings, dropping like a stone before bursting into frenzied activity.

"He's seen it," said Nimlinn.

"But—"

"Hush now! Let me listen!" Nimlinn strained to hear.

Lily, holding the coin, willed it to focus on Aleron. And a moment later, she felt the now familiar pulse of the coin in her hand. In her head she heard the words: "No! Not there!"

Lily stopped breathing.

Aleron called out again. He was approaching very swiftly. Again the coin pulsed, and she heard his words in her head. He sounded more alarmed. "Release it! Release it! Now! No time to—"

Lily felt her last shred of hope rip away. With a terrible feeling in the pit of her stomach, she turned the pendant to face her, still holding it high. The little moons glowed a soft silvery white.

"Oh! Oh, no!" she gasped. Her fingers fumbled, and the pendant slipped through them, the necklace sliding down her arm to her shoulder. "No! No! No!" she repeated, grabbing at the thing, trying to right it in her hand, searching for the fob. Lily felt the world begin to fade, just like before, in her bedroom.

"Nimlinn!" she cried out.

"Oh, Lily!" said Nimlinn. "I'm so sorry."

As the world grew dark about her, she heard a final cry from above. Lily looked up to see a huge, bright bird swooping down, claws open, streaking toward her hands, toward the pendant. But the turbulent waves were snatching at her. As she felt herself slipping away, she heard three words: *Eel, Eight, Ear*. It sounded like Nimlinn's voice. And then she was gone, engulfed in the sound of crashing waves, spinning end over end. Only this time, she dared to breathe.

Dragon

L ILY had been through this once before, from her bedroom to Barreth, and she was confident she'd make it through this time, too.
She landed feet first on damp stone, but toppled, pitching over and
sliding a few feet before slamming to a stop. Her mind was dark and
dizzy, and her limbs felt weakened. Twitching, out of breath, she waited for her strength and wits to revive. The stone was cold and damp
against her cheek.

As soon as she felt able, she sat upright. She pulled herself to her
feet and gave her head a vigorous shake. Her mind seemed to be clearing more quickly this time, and yet her sight had still not returned.

She blinked her eyes a few times and attempted a survey of her new surroundings. There was a chill breeze, and she could make out the dim shapes of drifting clouds, and their shadows on the stones before her. So her eyes *were* working—it was just nighttime here.

Lily shivered and drew her cloak more firmly about her. Her stomach growled. When had she last eaten? She made mental notes for next time: food, water, flashlight. The thought of food sparked another image of Ebb, this time in his kitchen. He was rapidly manufacturing sandwiches at his big wooden cutting board and handing some to her and Jasper.

"For your walk home," he'd said, with that warm, crooked smile of his. But he had made for himself more than a dozen, wrapped them all in wax paper, and stuffed them into his coat of many pockets. Lily concentrated. What kind of shoes had he been wearing? Was there a hat? Had he let slip any clues? In retrospect, it was obvious he'd been preparing for a journey.

Lily plumbed the depths of her memories. Had he been wearing his farm boots? She couldn't remember, and she was infuriated—not just at the poorness of her memory, but at Ebb's living a double life right under their noses. And she hadn't suspected a thing!

Lily let the memory go. It wasn't going to give up any more than it already had. But there would be other memories, things Ebb had said or done that seemed to mean one thing but turned out to mean another. She would have to rethink everything and sift her memories for clues. And she'd really have to be on her guard around her parents.

A noise of rolling rocks brought Lily back to the present in an instant. Insects chirped. Frogs, very large frogs from the sound of it, croaked in the distance. Her eyes had adjusted. More quickly this time? It was hard to tell, given the night.

Dense clouds filled the sky, with few openings to show the moons and stars. The landscape was bleak and rolling, covered in layered blankets of wispy ground fog. Lily studied a small break in the clouds. She could see part of a greenish-blue moon. "Taw," she said aloud.

As she lingered, and the break in the clouds shifted, she saw part of an orangish-brown-and-blue one next to it. "And Barreth."

They were still in crossover. This was bad news; if she could see them in the sky, then that meant she wasn't on either of them. And Taw had sounded pretty good, too—but she didn't allow this information to sink her spirits. Not yet.

A pain shot through her hand, and Lily suddenly became aware of how tightly she was grasping the pendant. The moon coin's face was dark again—no ring of little glowing moons. Taking great care, she made sure the fob was closed before slipping the necklace back on and tucking the pendant beneath her shirt.

Slowly, she gave her surroundings a once-over. She was halfway up a steep slope, on what might have been, at some better time, a well-kept flight of stone stairs. The air was dank and pungent, but she thought she also smelled a hint of woodsmoke. Looking around, though, she could detect no firelight to account for it.

At the foot of the slope was a bottomland. Punctuated by rocky mounds, it continued into the distance until it disappeared into the night mists. Among the mounds were a few stunted trees and piles of rubble, chiefly stone, covered in what looked like damp moss. While taking this all in, she heard a new sound, like that of a long hollow log being dragged across stone, echoing upward from below. The insects and frogs went silent for a time before slowly resuming.

Lily wondered if she might be on Dain or worse, on Darwyth. Neither would be good; Nimlinn had said so. She looked up again and noticed a thin line of smoke amidst the cloud cover. Had that been there before? Craning her neck, Lily followed it back to its source, somewhere higher up the steps. A fire? The one she'd smelled earlier?

The sound rose again, closer this time: a long hollow log being dragged across stone. Not wanting to wait around, Lily made her way up the tall broken steps, navigating as best she could over bits of stone and debris. At the top, the stairs emptied into a wide, dilapidated thoroughfare, in the center of which was a fountain, its once-commanding structure collapsing into cobblestones. In the scant moonlight, Lily could just make out the toppled form of the smashed and disintegrating dragon that had once been the fountain's centerpiece.

The edges of the thoroughfare were marked by bone-white stonework, chest-high and laced with dark moss and lichen. The street ran to the remains of a circular keep, now no more than twenty or thirty feet at its highest point. A few scrubby trees grew out of the stone, their gnarled roots exposed, their twisted, leafless branches looking poisoned. An occasional stone arch, still intact, marked doorways that now led nowhere.

And then she saw it, on one of the taller walls of the ruined keep: a slight flicker of firelight high up on the stonework.

All of a sudden, Lily felt very exposed. Quickly, she made for the deepest shadows. Her stomach growled at the idea of food cooking on that fire. She crept along, wondering whose firelight she might be looking at. Did she really want to find out? But retreating didn't seem any better.

After several minutes, she decided a careful look might be best. So, as quietly as she could, she set out for the source of the light, keeping to the shadows, picking her way around fragments of stonework, and peering through the remains of shattered doorways. What survived of the walls and the fallen heaps of stone made a maze of the place. She passed a flight of stairs that led up two dozen steps before emptying into open air. Many of the old doorways were blocked, and many of the unblocked ones led to dead ends. Eventually, she found one that led through what were once long, rectangular rooms, their old walls no more than waist-high.

Rounding a corner, she froze at the sight of firelight spilling through a gap. She took a few breaths, waiting for her nerve. Then, cautiously, she chose a bit of wall to peer around. The adjoining rooms were like a courtyard. On the far side was a high archway, through which Lily could see the fire. It was large, and its logs wheezed and popped in the damp night air. Even from this distance she could sense its warmth. Lily leaned back into the shadows and listened for a *very* long time. She heard no voices or activity, just the sound of the fire. Obviously, it was a fire built for more than one person, but where were they now? Had they gone? She would have to get closer. Could they have taken refuge in what was left of the keep? Maybe the fire was just for turning back dangerous night beasts and warming up chilly teenagers from Pennsylvania. That seemed very possible . . . excepting the last part.

Lily gathered her courage and darted through the gap, hurrying as much as she dared. She approached the archway from an angle to stay out of the fire's dancing orange light. Once across the expanse of ruined room, she placed her back against the stone arch and listened. Still no sounds but the fire.

Lily took a deep breath and peered around the edge of the stone. Around the roaring blaze, she could clearly see the remains of a hastily abandoned camp. She could smell something sour now, like spoiled food. The fire was contained by sizable stones, surrounded by a ring of even larger stones and logs that must have served as seating. She noticed baggage and gear stowed away in the shadows. The fire flared up and spit. On the other side of the flames, Lily could see dark crags that looked like entrances into what was left of the ruined keep.

All of a sudden, a dirty face leaned forward from one of the dark crags, and squinted at her as though it couldn't believe what it was seeing. When it spoke, the pendant resting on her chest throbbed, and in her mind she heard, "By the moons! It's a girl."

Lily sprang backwards. Everything happened very quickly after that. Suddenly, there were people standing all around her in the dark. A man in strange armor stepped into the light that Lily had so studiously avoided. He dipped his sword and removed his helmet. He too wore a look of astonishment. She turned to bolt, and all at once became aware of someone standing directly behind her, blocking her flight. When she made to scream, a hand clamped down over her mouth. Before she could get her arms moving, they were pinned by a blanket wrapping rapidly around her body. And then she was lifted like a baby and carried into the encampment, where she was very carefully set down by the fire.

Now in the light, she could see that the man who had carried her was no taller than she was. His eyes were widely set. Tufts of short red hair stood out at odd angles atop his head, and the sides of his face were peppered with a scraggly beard. Men and women filed in from the shadows. There were more than a dozen of them. Lily couldn't even begin to imagine how some of them had sneaked in without her hearing them.

"What have you trapped us, Quib?" said the man who had removed his helmet. "Not much of a dragon here, boys," he chuckled, but he didn't sound all that amused.

The swordsman sheathed his blade as he approached. With his gloved hand, he grasped Lily's chin firmly and turned her face first to one side and then to the other, examining her in the light, as though searching for recognition.

Lily glared back at him, wresting her chin from his grip. His face was haggard and grimy, but Lily thought that, in a better light, it might be a handsome one.

Speaking lower now, the gloved man said, "Don't be afraid. We'll get you back to Bairne safe and sound."

Then the redhead, Quib, said, "How'd she make it all the way out 'ere? This is nae little wastrel, Dubb. Look at her cloak. Much too fine to be a farmer's child." Then, to Lily, he asked, "Are you alone?"

Lily nodded.

From out of the darkness staggered a great hulk of a man. Over his broad shoulders was draped a normal-sized man.

"I think we should feed him," the big fellow said to Dubb.

Dubb tore his gaze from Lily and looked up distractedly. "Not now, Andros. Later. Just put him down for now, will you?"

Andros straightened and flexed his shoulders, letting the man drop—rather roughly, Lily thought—on a threadbare blanket next to the fire.

"For the love of moonlight," wheezed Andros. "He grows heavier as the hour grows later, I swear it!"

The man beside the fire rolled onto his side and gave Lily an odd look, as though he wasn't quite seeing her. He too wore the strange armor, but his arms and legs were tightly bound; his mouth, gagged. But his eyes were full of expression, and whatever he was mumbling into his gag was beyond the moon coin's powers of translation. Lily took a better look at this mountain of a man, Andros. His skin was nearly white. He also wore the unusual armor, as did everyone except those in robes.

"You want me to ungag him?" Andros asked Dubb.

"No. Not tonight. Not until we're closer to home," he said, rubbing his eyes. Then, in a more commanding tone, he said, "Marred, why don't you go and have a look around?"

"Not me," answered Marred, stepping closer to the fire. He had a round boyish face, with short-cropped black hair and a dark complexion (or was that just grime?). "Listen, I'm telling you. That dragon *is* out there. And the last thing we want to be doing is looking for it in the night."

"Marred," said Dubb, looking pained, "you've been saying that for weeks. But if it *was* true, and if it *was* close, then how do you explain this girl? Wouldn't she have been an easy snack?"

Marred considered this last bit. "All right. I'll go take a look, but only if Andros goes with me and fires up that ring of his."

"Dragon hunting in the dark, lucky me," lamented Andros sarcastically. "Are our opportunities to die really so few that we need to go looking for more?"

Marred motioned to Andros's huge hand. "The dragon won't be able to see us with that ring going."

Andros eyed the ring with a sudden look of distaste. "And just how do you know what a dragon *can* and *can't* see?"

"You've used it around them before. I've watched their eyes. The one that almost got you was by sense of smell—"

Andros shivered. "How could you tell? It was looking right at me!" he exclaimed.

"But it was using its *nose*. I could tell. Trust me."

Andros turned to Dubb. "I need a rest first—no more than an hour."

"Sleep," said Marred, in a dreamy voice. "Ah, now you're talking. How about that, Dubb? Me and Andros here, we get a few winks, and then we go looking for the dragon."

Another man, wearing enormous boots, stepped silently out of the darkness and sat down on one of the stones by the fire, where the light was good. He had a tall bow lashed to his back. In one hand he held a long shaft of wood; in the other, a short knife. He looked down the shaft of wood very carefully, then whittled a thin strip off one side of the shaft. With his elbow, he motioned to the bound body.

"Maybe we should let Tavin here have a little walkabout. If there's really a dragon out there, I'm sure he'd be happy to volunteer."

The bound figure—Tavin—perked up, looking avidly from face to face while vigorously nodding and making muffled sounds through his gag.

The man with the bow smirked, and Lily heard several others chuckling.

"Maybe you should go, Boots," suggested one.

"N-o-o-o-o, not me!" rejoined the man with the bow.

Dubb seemed unfazed by this breakdown of his authority.

Lily considered the company before her. They looked asleep on their feet. And she thought it strange that the bound man was wearing a full suit of armor—stranger still that he was armed with long sword, daggers, and who knew what else, though his bindings appeared so thorough and tight that he didn't stand a chance of setting so much as a pinky to any of them. But why hadn't they taken away his weapons? It struck Lily as an unnecessary risk.

Dubb mumbled to himself. He removed his glove, revealing a heavily scarred hand, which he used to massage his mouth and chin.

"I think not. If you are correct about the dragon, Tavin on his own would be nothing more than a tasty snack." At that, Dubb pursed his lips, as if weighing the advantages and disadvantages. But he gave his head a violent shake, clearing these thoughts. Stooping, he retrieved a log from the woodpile and tossed it on the fire.

"So, are you well? Can you talk?" asked Dubb, turning his attention to Lily.

She nodded.

Dubb motioned to Andros. "She looks a bit like your youngest, but fair-haired, no?"

The giant stepped closer to consider Lily's face. "Yes," he said, sounding amused, "and it appears she shares the same knack for getting into trouble." Then he smiled a warm smile, showing pink gums that stood out sharply against his ghostly skin and teeth.

Everyone laughed, then stopped, as if on cue. They all stared at Marred. His head was cocked to one side, and his face was screwed up with concentration. A moment later they heard a noise, very close, like a great hollow log being dragged over stones. Dubb made a silent hand gesture, and the group sprang into motion.

Blades leapt from scabbards, and shields appeared from behind cloaks. The man who had been whittling at the shaft of wood suddenly held a fully drawn bow, notched with arrow. Every head wore a helmet.

Dubb picked Lily up under one arm and made for a crevice in the rocks. Spying over Dubb's shoulder, she watched Andros step over the bound man, pointing a wicked looking dagger directly at him. She gasped, but she couldn't look away. Dubb and Andros locked eyes for an instant, and Lily thought she detected a small nod between them. Deftly, Andros raked the blade across Tavin's bound body. Lily would have screamed with her next breath had Dubb not clamped his hand over her mouth. "It's all right," Dubb hissed.

The ropes holding Tavin's limbs fell loose. Andros lifted him to his feet as if he were a child. Next, Andros made a fist and spoke a word. With a bright flash, an envelope of vivid detail bloomed around his whole body. He drew an enormous sword.

Darkness! thought Lily. *Andros has the moon ring of Barreth!*

Tavin pulled the gag down below his chin, revealing a wild, toothy grin.

"Dragon!" he breathed, his eyes darting about madly. Tavin took a moment to massage his wrists and forearms. He didn't seem the least bit hurried, nor the least bit afraid. Indeed, as he adjusted his armor and boots, he began to whistle. When all was in order, he strolled away from the fire and into an area that might once have served as a great hall. He stood facing a long curving wall made up of grand arches that the firelight refused to penetrate.

Tavin cupped his hands to his mouth. "Here, dragon-dragon-dragon!" he yelled.

Lily stared in amazement. *Well, that was bold*, she thought, *and* stupid.

Dubb whispered in Lily's ear, "I'm going to take my hand away. Can you keep from crying out?"

Lily nodded, and Dubb let his hand fall.

"What's wrong with him?" she whispered.

"Yoooooo hooooooo!" Tavin teased. "Here, dragon-dragon-dragon!"

"Listen—" began Dubb.

With a sound of ringing steel, Tavin unsheathed his sword and held it high above his head. Suddenly, the night's chill air filled with an equally chill metallic voice, high-pitched and full of glee.

"Kill it! Kill it! Kill the filthy beast!"

At first, Lily thought Tavin had changed his voice, because the sound came from where he stood. But Tavin was still calling the dragon as this second, unearthly voice rang out and shouted over him.

Dubb took Lily by the shoulders and shifted her behind him, pushing her deeper into the crevice. She could tell he was trying to be gentle, but his fingers were like vises. Dubb looked at her intently.

"That's my cue. Listen now, make sure you—"

His face froze. The blanket that Quib had wrapped so tightly around Lily's shoulders had loosened and slipped down enough to reveal a bit of the golden necklace. With the sudden speed of an animal, before Lily could react, Dubb snatched the bit of exposed necklace and pulled out the pendant.

"By the grace of the moons!" he gasped.

Lily recovered her wits quickly and snatched back the pendant.

"Well," said Dubb, "aren't we full of surprises."

A dragon bellowed then, and Lily felt her skin turn to goose flesh. Dubb's eyes darted to the campground, but returned to Lily. "Stay here until someone comes to get you," he commanded. And then, even more forcefully, "Do you understand me?"

Lily nodded.

"Good girl!" he said. "And keep that necklace out of sight."

As he stepped away from the crag, Lily watched his face break into a fierce and terrible smile. She would see it many more times—a look fierce, terrible, and . . . happy. It was the face they all wore when going into battle, or whenever they faced death. The sight of it never failed to make Lily take a step backward, as though sighting some dangerous and unpredictable animal.

Speaking through the smile, Dubb said, "Let us hope this dragon has not yet acquired its breath," and then he was gone, disappearing into the rocks and shadows.

Lily leaned forward to get a better look, but Dubb had vanished. Tavin, however, stood right out in the open, still calling for the dragon, whose thudding footsteps were loud and clear.

Across the way, not far from Tavin, Lily watched someone lean out of a shadow to toss him a large, heavy-looking shield. It was a good toss; Tavin needed only to reach out his free arm to catch it. But instead, as the shield neared him, he stepped aside and watched the shield drop into the dirt, looking at it as though he were uncertain as to its purpose.

"Pick it up!" urged a voice from the shadows.

Instead, Tavin took a step away from the shield and slowly began meandering, the sword extended before him shoulder-high, as though feeling out the dragon's location through the blade. His eyes were closed, and a playful smile graced his lips. While facing one of the dark arches he paused, but only for a second.

"It . . . is . . . there!" whined the metallic voice. "It has come to do battle with us!"

At these words, Boots, the man with the bow, stepped into the firelight and loosed an arrow toward where Tavin's sword pointed. The arrow whistled off and disappeared through the arch. THUNK! An instant later the ground shook, as though a great mass had landed heavily. The dragon bellowed, and loose dirt and rock shifted among the broken walls and boulders.

Tavin swung his head around to see where the arrow had come from. He looked very displeased.

"*My* dragon!" he cried, his eyes wild. "Mine!"

His back was still turned when the dragon's huge reptilian head sprang through the arch. Its face was wide, angular, and heavily armored with thick green scales. Its jaw stretched open, exposing tall yellow teeth and a lively red tongue. The blue fletching of Boots's arrow stood out brightly, embedded deep in the beast's snout. Old broken arrow shafts dotted its face.

Tavin sprang into motion, running recklessly at the dragon's open maw. Lily gasped and crept to the edge of her crevice. The dragon's long neck uncoiled like a spring, and for a moment, it looked as though Tavin would be swallowed whole. At the last possible second, however, he leapt sideways, landing lightly atop the ruins of an old wall running parallel to the dragon's outstretched neck. At full speed, with daring leaps and jumps, Tavin ran the length of the wall—some parts were more like narrow stairs—right to the opening through which the dragon's shoulders now strained. From here, Tavin buried his sword deep into the beast's neck. The dragon bellowed in pain, coiling its long neck around for a bite at its tormentor. Tavin ducked under a crumbling stone dragoyle, all that remained of the majestic pair that had once flanked the arch. The dragon smashed into the dragoyle, breaking off its remaining wing and snapping off its stone head and upraised foreclaw.

As if this had been his plan from the beginning, Tavin lunged from his hiding place and thrust his long sword deep into the surprised dragon's left eye. The howl that followed was the loudest and most terrible thing Lily had ever heard, even worse than the roar of a Rinn.

Out of the shadows poured Dubb's warriors, heaving nets, spears, and throwing axes. From their belts they produced iron hammers and spikes, and quickly secured the loose ends of the nets, hammering them into the earth or lashing them around nearby boulders.

Boots, who had not paused once since his first shot, moved in closer now, expertly loosing his arrows with deadly accuracy towards the dragon's one remaining good eye, which it kept shut tight—rendering it no less blind than if the eye had been lost. The dragon roared in pain, shaking its head, and attempted to retreat, but the nets held. Dubb shouted something, and his troops advanced with everything they had: spear, sword, and axe. The wounded dragon let out a long roar, and then began to inhale, making a sound at once both pitiful and terrible.

"Find cover!" ordered Dubb.

Everyone scattered.

All save one.

"Tasty dragon," said the metallic voice.

The dragon sucked in vast quantities of the cool night air. Tavin held his ground, staring dumbly at those who fled.

"Cowards!" he screamed, eyes flashing.

Andros leaned out of his hiding place, begging Tavin to take cover.

He looked blankly at Andros, who held out his hand imploringly. Others began shouting encouragement. For a second, Tavin lowered his swordpoint and took a step toward Andros.

Then came the shrill metallic voice.

"Kill it!" it hissed.

Tavin held up the sword and staggered backward, as though he were attempting to back away from it. The dragon continued to inhale. Tavin stepped on the edge of the shield in the dirt. He looked down at it, confused.

"Nooooooo!" screamed the metallic voice, "Rush it! Rush it now! I will show you where to bite!"

Dubb's men and women shouted to Tavin. "The shield! Pick up the shield!" and "Run! Get away!"

Tavin made as if to reach for the shield again, but the voice rang out.

"No! We must kill it! Now is the time!"

The dragon's lungs quieted, releasing Tavin from his indecision. He rushed to the dragon's forelegs and stooped low. Planting his feet wide, he placed the tip of his blade to where the dragon's scale-plating was weakest, at the pit of the joint between the chest and leg, and heaved upward with all his strength. At first, the tip of his long blade strained against the hide, and then, with a horrible sound, it pierced the dragon's scales and thrust upwards, aiming straight towards the heart.

The dragon jolted upright, snapping the nets like kite string. Its long neck uncoiled, stretching upwards and smashing through the arch as its head sought out the night sky. The blast of its breath formed a tall pillar of flame from which the mists and clouds shrank. The dragon's breath lasted far longer than Lily expected, briefly lighting up the entire camp like daylight. The opening around the fiery pillar grew, revealing stars and moons.

And then it was over. For a moment, all was black except for the light of the moons and stars that shone down on the dragon's face and body. Its neck twisted and swayed, jaws opening and closing, its surviving eye taking one last long look at the heavens. Its great frame gave a violent shudder, and it released one final cry. The moon coin resting on Lily's chest pulsed. Over the sound of the dragon's bellow, she heard two words in her head: *forgive me*. And then the beast collapsed, like a giant redwood felled.

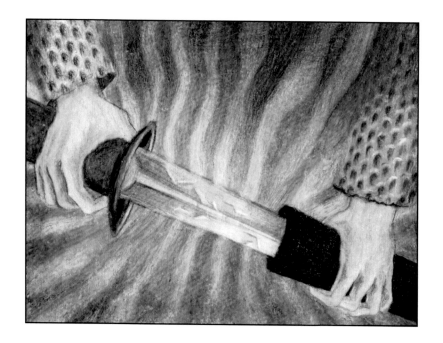

Harvest

Bathed in moonlight, Tavin stood alone under the shrinking hole burned into the clouds by the dragon's breath. Lily took a step forward. Had the dragon really spoken? Or had it been someone else? People were talking and shouting in voices she didn't know. *Forgive me.* The words could have come from anyone—even from the peculiar metallic voice.

What happened next surprised Lily nearly as much as the sight of the dragon.

Tavin spun around. The campsite slowly dimmed as the clouds closed up. The men and women had not stood down from their battle stances, though they had all exchanged their weapons for nets and ropes. Their quarry had shifted—to Tavin. And he knew it.

Two robed figures stationed themselves on either side of him.

Lunamancers? wondered Lily. They placed their hands before their chests, slowly spreading them apart.

"Peerins!" gasped Lily, stepping out from the crag. How many times had she and Jasper tried to make them: placing their palms together, fingers pointing to wrists, then slowly sliding them apart, spreading their fingers until only the tips of their index fingers and thumbs touched? How many times had they tried to peer through the rectangle they'd made in hopes of revealing the world of magic that lay beneath? Lily placed her palms together. How old had she been the last time she tried? Six? Seven?

The lunamancers chanted spells, for which the moon coin offered no translation. Suddenly, bright beams of light erupted from their palms and focused directly on Tavin's eyes.

"Run, you fool!" shrieked the metallic voice. "Get away!"

Lily ducked back into the deep shadows, flattening herself against the wall of the crag.

Tavin turned on his heel, but one of the lunamancers had anticipated this and was waiting to shine another beam into his eyes.

Quib moved into position, just out of Tavin's lunging range, and uncoiled a whip from his belt. He flicked his wrist, and the whip leapt up to Tavin's chest, encircling it like the living coils of a snake. Instantly, Tavin's arms were lashed to his sides. Only from the elbow down did his sword arm remain free. He tried to pivot, but the whip fought to hold him in place.

The metallic voice whined then. "Imbecile! Idiot! They will have us!"

Even with his elbow pinned to his side, Tavin struck at the whip, but it dodged his blows. Tavin made a rush for the whip's master, but Quib bore down, squeezing the coils still tighter. The lunamancers moved closer now, intensifying the light trained on Tavin's eyes.

Then Andros appeared. Moving with tremendous speed, he seized

Tavin's sword arm. The instant his big hand closed around Tavin's wrist, everyone jumped in, each grabbing some part of Tavin's forearm or scabbard in a vigorous struggle to sheathe his sword.

"Stop them!" screeched the horrible voice. "Stop them! I demand to be sharpened! I demand to be oiled! *I* am the *hero!*"

The second Tavin's blade tip aligned with his scabbard, Andros slammed the hilt home. Tavin groaned. Limbs limp, he collapsed to his knees.

"Bind him!" said a commanding voice that Lily recognized as Dubb's. "Marred! Quickly! Is the thing truly dead?"

But Marred needed no urging. While the others were struggling with Tavin, Marred had rolled a boulder to the dragon's mouth. Using a stout spear as a lever, he pried open its jaws and propped them open with a log.

"Marred—" cautioned Dubb.

Marred tossed off his helmet and quickly wiggled out of his strange armor, which Lily now thought looked suspiciously like dragon scales. He lit a small hand torch.

"Marred, is it—"

Holding the torch in front of him, Marred plunged into the dragon's mouth.

"—dead?" finished Dubb, just as the heels of Marred's boots vanished.

People around her murmured, and Lily heard someone say, "Not *again.*"

A second later, the dragon twitched. Its jaw muscles strained spasmodically. The log holding open the dragon's mouth burst into splinters. A puff of foul smoke came out of its nostrils, and its tail knocked someone to the ground.

Dubb's sword leapt from its scabbard. "Swords!" he cried, "Andros! Spike that tail!"

A "Why me?" look flashed across Andros's face, but he dove for the tail just the same, tackling it and dragging it to the ground.

The ones who hadn't drawn swords set to prying open the dragon's jaws again. Straining and tugging, they finally forced the jaws apart. There was Marred, face blackened, torch in hand, kneeling on the dragon's tongue. He wore a big grin on his face and slime in his hair. As he wormed his way out, carefully skirting the dragon's sharp teeth, Lily noticed that in his hand was a small lump of what looked like dragon flesh. He held up his prize triumphantly.

"The igniter organ!" he announced, looking very pleased. "You wanna talk spicy?" He rubbed his stomach for emphasis.

"I think I'm going to be sick," said Boots, placing a hand over his stomach and turning away from the sight. He wasn't the only one.

"They're best pickled," Marred explained to Lily, rummaging through a pack by the fire and pulling out an earthenware jar. The jar fizzed loudly when he opened it, and its odor caused all in the immediate vicinity to scatter. Quib, though, with a dreamy look in his eyes, smacked his lips hungrily.

Marred popped the organ into the liquid and recapped the jar.

"And, yes, if you're still wondering, it's *quite* dead." He sounded happy when he said it, although his face reflected a disappointment that Lily didn't understand.

Quib clapped his hands together. "All right! You heard the man! There's work to be done. It's dragon chili time!"

To Lily's horror, this brought smiles to everyone's faces (except Tavin's; he had slumped forward and fallen face first into the dirt). A cheer went up.

Lily chose this moment to step out of the darkness and into the firelight. "Just beans for me," she said brightly. Her stomach was empty, but not *that* empty.

An odd stare flitted across Quib's elfin features.

"No dragon chili?" he asked, clearly not understanding.

But it was impossible to keep Quib's spirits down for long. "Don't you worry, lassie," he said, a big grin filling his face. "We'll have this critter stripped to the bone in no time. As the youngest, you can have the first bowl of dragon's blood pudding. And that's a promise!"

Lily blanched.

"Of course," Quib went on, "the meat closest to the bone is the best."

Lily shook her head, confusing Quib.

"Plenty . . . to . . . go around?" he said.

"Just beans, if you don't mind."

"Well, suit yourself," he said, and he turned to those around him and began barking orders.

The dismantling of the dragon began in earnest then. Three wagons, pulled by half-starved horses and loaded with sacks, chests, barrels, and buckets of tools, were wheeled out from the center of the ruined keep. Men and women tossed their cloaks and helmets to the ground and rolled up their sleeves. Boots grabbed several tool-filled buckets from the wagons, selecting a wicked looking knife for himself, before he and the others descended on the fallen dragon. The lunamancers formed their peerins, chanting indistinctly. Lily could see they were casting spells on the tools, which glowed strangely. The men and women made small incisions behind the dragon's scales, peeling back the hide bit by bit. The work was laborious, and the magical glow barely lasted long enough for a cut or two.

Everywhere Lily looked, people were in motion: lighting fires under cauldrons, cutting long strips of meat, dragging out smoking racks from the shadows. The work reminded Lily of Native Americans stripping buffalo—nothing went to waste.

Lily helped move the packs and bedrolls into an adjacent wall-less room, and Andros plucked up Tavin's senseless body, tossing him heavily before the fire. Andros knelt down gingerly, as though his knee was in great pain, and propped Tavin up against a large rock. Tenderly, he brushed off some of the caked dirt on Tavin's shoulder, which Lily thought rather pointless, as all the men were covered in grime and filth.

"Ah," sighed Andros, pushing the hair out of Tavin's vacant eyes.

"You've outdone yourself this time. Now there's one less monster in this world." Andros turned to Dubb. "He won't even remember, will he?"

"Doubtful," said Dubb, in a quiet voice. "Thank you, Andros. If I'm not mistaken, I think you'll find Quib is very much in need of your services."

Andros nodded his big head and thudded off to the adjoining room. Now there were just the three of them: Dubb, Tavin, and Lily.

Stiff-legged, Dubb slid down into a sitting position, shoulder to shoulder with Tavin, who was blinking uncertainly. Dubb motioned to Lily and pointed to a stone opposite them. Lily was glad to finally be sitting, and the new fire was warm and comforting.

Dubb gave Tavin a hard nudge in the ribs and lightly slapped the sides of his face.

"Wake up, Tavin. Wake up. I have a surprise for you."

Tavin continued to blink his eyes. He didn't appear to know where he was, nor did he seem to care. He stared at Lily blankly.

After a time, he seemed to focus. "Where are we?" he asked, looking up at the night sky. "Bairne?"

"No, Tavin. We're still far from Bairne. We're at the ruins; we're at Perch."

The name Perch pricked at Lily's memory, but she couldn't recall anything specific.

Tavin looked at Lily more carefully. "Perch . . . we brought a maid with us to Perch?"

"No."

"Well . . . then where did she come from?"

"A fine question." Dubb turned his attention to Lily. "Would you be so good as to enlighten us?"

Lily bristled. Again, just as with Nimlinn, she found herself in the position of not having considered what she did and didn't want to tell. She had lots of questions, of course. Like, where she was, and if these people knew Uncle Ebb. True, she felt a budding trust in Dubb, but

Tavin's Jekyll and Hyde act had her a bit worried. And the two of them were obviously friends.

"Why don't you start with your name?" prompted Dubb.

"All right," she said. "It's Lily—Lily Winter."

Dubb glanced quickly at Tavin, but Lily's words had made no impact on him.

"Winter. Interesting. Does the name Autumn mean anything to you?" murmured Dubb.

This caught Lily off guard, and her face showed it.

"You see," continued Dubb, "the name of Autumn has long been connected with that necklace you wear. Odd names: Winter, Autumn—they almost sound as if someone just made them up."

"Yes," said Lily, trying to decide what else she wanted to say.

He made an effort to smile pleasantly at her. "A relative, perhaps?" he asked.

"Perhaps," said Lily, considering for the first time that maybe her uncle wasn't really her uncle.

The light from the fire was bright, and Lily realized this was the first good look she'd had at either Dubb or Tavin. Their armor was indeed made of dragon scales, mostly green, but with flecks of blue and red. And the scales seemed far smaller than the scales on Tavin's dragon. The breeze shifted, and Lily covered her nose.

Tavin leaned over to Dubb and said, half under his breath, "Would it be all right . . . could I . . . just sharpen it a little?"

Dubb shook his head no.

"Please?" he begged, in an even more pathetic tone.

"No," answered Dubb. He spoke out of the side of his mouth and nudged Tavin. Tavin nudged back.

This eccentric behavior made Lily uncomfortable. She decided she would need to collect more information before giving any away.

"I have some questions of my own," stated Lily.

Dubb turned to Lily and smiled in a way that made her think he was a little surprised and also pleased by her attempt to take charge of the conversation.

"By all means," he said cordially, giving Lily so much of his attention that she wondered if maybe he would deduce more from her questions than she would gain from his answers.

"This moon"—Dubb's eyebrows shot up, but he held his tongue—"there are bits and pieces of dragoyles all over the place; I saw the fountain. I'm on Dain, aren't I?"

"Moon?" said Dubb in an indignant, loud tone. Tavin laughed. Affronted, Dubb gave him a sideways glance, but then softened and began chuckling himself. "Yes, you are indeed right, Lily. Welcome to Dain. But moon?" Dubb shook his head. "No, no. Make no mistake. You have found the one true world of the Moon Realm."

"One true . . . Dain? But I thought—"

"You thought what?" asked Dubb pointedly.

"I thought, um, Barreth was the—"

"Barreth!" shouted Dubb.

Tavin blew air through his lips as though Lily had said something funny. Dubb's astonishment faded, and he too began to chuckle. Tavin began to laugh louder, and Dubb nudged him in the ribs—hard—which finally quieted him down. Lily thought they looked like two schoolboys sharing some personal joke at her expense. And she didn't like it.

"Barreth?" repeated Dubb. "The one true world?"

Their renewed laughter bordered on maniacal. Lily's eyes narrowed to slits.

"Ba-Ba-Barreth?" wheezed Tavin. "With those overgrown . . . overgrown . . ."

"—house cats?" supplied Dubb.

They held their sides, fighting to breathe. In fact, they were entirely useless for quite some time.

Lily crossed her arms. "I just came from Barreth," she said. "And their Queen was quite adamant about it."

This news caused Dubb to go completely silent, his face serious again. Tavin, on the other hand, thought it was hilarious. But Dubb shushed him, giving Lily his full attention.

"You're serious," he said.

"Yes. I was there for almost a full day. I arrived here only about thirty minutes ago."

Tavin quietly began his strange pleading again. Dubb tried to ignore him, but it was obvious that Tavin's pathetic display was beginning to take a toll on Dubb.

"Tavin, for the love of moonlight, would you please drop it?"

But Tavin continued. "Just a little . . . sharpen," he mumbled.

Dubb grimaced and struggled to his feet. He grabbed a stick out of the fire, hooked Tavin's sword hilt with it, and slid the blade out a few inches from its scabbard.

"Ooooooil meeeeee," crooned the sharp metallic voice. "Shaaaaarpen meeeeee," it continued beguilingly.

The edge of Tavin's blade vibrated minutely, like a tuning fork, with every syllable. The nails-on-a-chalkboard voice was enough to make Lily cover her ears. Dubb motioned to her that it was all right.

"Listen, *Curse*," said Dubb, speaking to the sword, "if you want a sharpening, you'll have to swear that you'll not attempt to free yourself or cause any mayhem—of any kind—*and* that you will allow yourself to be sheathed without struggle as soon as you have been serviced."

"I swear no oaths," it replied menacingly, "and certainly none to the likes of you."

"Suit yourself," said Dubb, and he began to slide the sword back into the scabbard.

Tavin's face contorted, and he struggled against his bindings, bunching and releasing his muscles.

"Wait!" said Curse. "Sweeten the pot."

Dubb's face darkened. He clenched his teeth. "No! Now swear it!" he hissed. "Swear upon your lifting!"

"Never!" it whined.

Dubb began to slide the hilt back into the scabbard again. But just at the last second, an awful whine began.

"Ahhhhh!" it screamed. "If I must!"

"Then swear upon it! Swear you will lift yourself from this pathetic, chipped slag of metal you inhabit, never to plague us again with your pestilence should you attempt to free yourself or cause any mayhem, and that you will allow yourself to be sheathed without a struggle as soon as you are serviced."

"Ahhhhhhhh!" it screamed. "Ahhh, ahhh, I swear it! I swear it! For this time, for this one time—I swear it."

Dubb relaxed visibly. He tossed the stick into the fire, and resumed his place next to Tavin. Almost casually, he untied Tavin's arms—just the arms, Lily noticed.

Tavin massaged his biceps and flexed his hands for a few seconds before fumbling with a pouch on his belt. His hands were shaking, but in time, he produced both a sharpening stone and a small bladder containing oil. Still trembling, Tavin removed the long blade from the scabbard and began scraping. With each scrape, he grew calmer.

Dubb put his hand on Tavin's shoulder, rubbing and patting as one would a dog. "We've been out here too long," said Dubb, sounding regretful. "We've got to get you back."

"What's wrong with him?" Lily whispered, horrified.

"There is nothing wrong . . . with him. It's the sword he bears. It's cursed. And when we're out of here, out of these wastes, he'll be the better for it. I don't know exactly why, but while we're out here, it feeds on him, and as Curse's strength grows, Tavin's fades."

"Why doesn't he just throw it away?"

"He is unable to do that willingly. And if it is removed by force, he will sink into madness. But please, tell us about your time on Barreth and how you escaped that horror."

"It wasn't a horror at all," said Lily defensively.

Tavin looked up at Lily as if this were the first time she had said anything about Barreth.

"You were on Barreth?" he said, sounding genuinely concerned.

"And the Rinn brought you here?"

"No."

"Then how did you get here?" asked Tavin.

Lily looked nervously at Dubb.

"Go ahead." Dubb nodded. "Show him."

Lily opened her riding cloak, pulling loose the gold chain from her garments. Tavin leaned forward as Lily revealed the pendant.

"By the moons!" he hissed. "Lord Autumn's moon coin!"

"*Lord* Autumn?" said Lily. "*Lord*?"

"Wait," interrupted Dubb. "One thing at a time. Lily, put that away again, and do not let anyone else see it. I trust everyone here, but tongues do wag."

Lily tucked the moon coin back beneath her shirt.

"Please, tell us more about Barreth," resumed Dubb.

Lily recounted much of what had happened on Barreth. But there were a few things she did not tell. She said nothing of the Tomb of the Fallen, nor what she had taken from there. She made no mention of Earth, Tanglemane, or anything about the strange dream she experienced during her approach to the Blight Marsh. But she gave a good account of the battle, the wirtles, the wyflings, Roan, and the meeting in the Great Hall before Greydor. Tavin expressed astonishment from beginning to end while Dubb seemed more subdued. The only exception was when Lily mentioned the name Ember—at that point Tavin grew subdued. They rarely interrupted and when they did, it was always for clarification of some small point, which Lily easily managed.

By the middle of the story, Tavin had finished with his cursed sword and sheathed it. His eyes seemed clearer after that, and he appeared to have less trouble following the story. Near the very end, Quib arrived, bearing three steaming bowls: two of his dragon chili and one, which he handed to Lily, of just beans. He took much pleasure in the presentation, and would not leave until the meal had been tasted and commented on. When he departed, he did so with a strange shuffling dance. He even sang a little song, though Lily could not make out the words. After Quib left, she concluded her story with the arrival of Aleron.

After a long silence, Dubb said, "Ember will be able to read those markings on the coin. She may even be able tell you something more about how it works."

Lily's heart lightened. And she marveled, not for the last time, at finding friendly people waiting where the moon coin sent her. "I'd like that very much," she said. "Maybe now you can answer some of my questions. Like, where exactly are we, and why did you have to kill that dragon, and why didn't it have any wings, and when can we meet Ember, and—"

Dubb raised a hand. "Wait . . . wait. I will answer all your questions, but not this night. We must harvest this dragon as quickly as possible, and we still have much to do. It is highly unlikely that anyone saw its breath, but we can't risk being raided. This dragon will pay many debts.

"I will, however, give you a few brief answers. These ruins are known by various names to those who draw maps. Most call it the Western Ruins, or just the Ruins, as almost no one ventures down the eastern road, where you will find another one quite like it. Others call it the Tower Ruins, but there are too many structures for it to have been *just* a tower. Personally, I think it was more than that. We call it, as our fathers before us called it, Perch. It sits on a high hill that marks the beginning of the fens and the end of the moors, which at one time held strategic importance.

"We are many hours from Bairne. And as for the dragon, we have killed eight of the foul beasts in the last twelve years—one a year the last four counting. And as for Ember, she is a gifted lunamancer, a knowledgeable historian, and our friend. I will arrange a meeting for you as soon as I can. But how it is that the cats of Barreth know her, I know not. I find this news quite disturbing, but that's her business."

Dubb glanced at Tavin, who cast his eyes downward. "We're partly here on Ember's business. She is worthy of your trust."

He stood up. "Why don't you get some sleep? Quib will need all the help I can give."

Tavin offered his wrists, and Dubb rebound them tightly.

"You go on ahead," said Tavin. "I'll just hang out here by the fire."

Dubb smirked at him and turned to leave.

"Wait!" cried Lily. "You're leaving me here?"

Dubb didn't get Lily's point. He scanned the area for hidden dangers, and it hit him all at once.

"Oh!" he said. "You mean Tavin?"

Dubb considered Tavin for a moment. "I wouldn't worry. He's harmless . . . for the most part."

Tavin's smile faded, as though offended at being called harmless.

"Aren't you?" Dubb asked.

Tavin licked his lips and seemed confused.

"Aren't you, Tavin . . . harmless," Dubb said more slowly.

And then, having gotten it, Tavin perked up.

"Harmless! Oh! Oh, goodness yes!" said Tavin, nodding his head. "Just like a little babe in the woods, I am."

Lily narrowed her eyes at Dubb, who realized this was going badly.

"Lily," said Dubb, waving a hand toward Tavin, "he's bound hand and foot. He's not going anywhere."

"He's . . . very heavily armed—and armored. He just slew a dragon nearly single-handedly—"

Tavin snorted, looking quite pleased with himself.

"I what?" he asked incredulously.

"And he suffers from multiple personalities," Lily continued, "one of which is quite unfriendly!"

Dubb stopped talking. It was just making matters worse. Instead, he produced a few moth-eaten blankets from a leather sack and tossed them down. Using his foot, he kicked the blanket next to Tavin into the rough form of a bed. Lily quickly picked up the rest of her blankets, hugging them as though they were a giant teddy bear. She sat back down on the stone.

"You *will* be safe," said Dubb, backing away slowly. "I'll have Arric place warding spells on all the entryways into this area. There are no more dragons about. You'll be safe."

"But it's not the things outside the . . . that worry . . ." But Dubb continued walking away.

And then it was just Lily and Tavin. Lily leaned her chin on her blankets and stared at him. He in turn squirmed around in an attempt to look more relaxed, or, at least, as though he weren't bound hand and foot. It didn't really work. Then he smiled, and Lily noticed he had really nice teeth and a boyish dimple in one cheek. She began to ask a question, then thought better of it.

After a short time, Arric came striding in and introduced himself. He was different from the rest. His eyes were almond shaped, and his skin was a shade or two darker. He was also better-kept. He wore no armor—just clothes, robes, and a fine pair of boots. "I won't be but a moment," he said confidently.

He stepped away and flicked his hand as though tossing something small, accompanying the movement with a few quick syllables. Lily thought she could hear a slight sound after each toss.

After the fourth toss, Arric frowned and looked down at his fingertips, as though something wasn't quite right. Lily didn't move.

He repeated the tossing motion, in another direction, again accompanied by the quick syllables. He paused, standing very straight. He took a step toward Lily. Lily didn't look up, but she sensed Arric's gaze hanging on her. Lily closed her eyes and tried to think of being small, invisible, insignificant. Arric tossed out another warding spell, followed by a few more.

"Everything all right, Arric?" asked Tavin.

"It's strange," said Arric. He formed a peerin and scanned the campsite, peering through the rectangular hole made by his fingers and thumbs. He examined Tavin, his sword, the fire, and Lily . . . Lily for a long time.

"Arric?" pressed Tavin.

Arric brought his palms together, collapsing his peerin. He shook his head, as though to clear it. "I . . . I guess I'm just tired, Tavin," he said sheepishly, before stumbling away.

Lily went back to staring at Tavin, and Tavin went back to trying to look comfortable.

"Why didn't that dragon have any wings?" she asked in a soft voice.

"Wings?" repeated Tavin, perplexed.

"Yes. The dragon in the fountain has wings. The stone dragoyles have wings." *The dragons in the bedtime tales have wings.*

"Ah! As in the faerie tales from Rel' Kah," said Tavin. His face brightened with old memories.

Rel' Kah! thought Lily. *Moon of the Faerie Queen: Faerathil.*

"Like Morgoroth the Devourer," continued Tavin, glints of firelight dancing in his eyes, "Keeper of the Magic Flame. Greatest dragon in all the Moon Realm, to hear Lord Autumn tell it. And were they not the stuff of stories, I'd risk all my gold on our own Fendragon. Lord Autumn has no end of stories. He certainly spent many an hour filling my head with them."

There it was again: what was true and what wasn't? Who was her uncle? Were her parents really her parents? Did they know about the Moon Realm? Or was that Ebb's secret? All the emotions swirling around inside made her dizzy, and not a little sad. "They aren't just stories," she said softly.

"Oh, but they are to me. And some of my favorites. Very exciting. I've repeated them to many a child. Never tired out one of 'em yet."

First Rinnjinn, thought Lily, *now Morgoroth and Fendragon.* It was just too sad to think about.

"So," Lily began, in an effort to change the subject, "just why *do* they have to tie you up all the time?"

"Ah—that. Well, you see, these days, I'm just a wee bit . . . cursed."

"You mean the *sword* is cursed."

Tavin glanced down at the hilt and scabbard attached to his belt. "Well, you can quibble about it all you want, but—cursed sword, cursed Tavin. We're a matching pair, I'm afraid."

And this time, when Tavin smiled, Lily decided that while Dubb was handsome, Tavin was charming.

"But it's not *all* bad. No need to make it sound worse than it is." He laughed jauntily. "Take right now, for example. Now that we've dealt with the dragon, now that it's gone, I'm as sane as you or I." *You or I?* Lily thought. "In fact," continued Tavin, "now that I'm all better, I could be *very* helpful."

"What do you mean?" asked Lily.

"Well, for one thing, there's the clutch. Oh, I understand they're busy and all with the dragon. They have their livelihood to think about, after all—"

"What clutch?"

"Dubb didn't tell you?" Tavin asked, his voice trailing off.

Lily shook her head slowly.

"This dragon . . ." Tavin nodded in its direction. "It's been a bad one. We've been hunting it off and on for two seasons now. It's eaten its fill on the outer farms, far beyond the city walls, where the poorest of the poor farm. Animals, men, women, children, some smaller than yourself. A dragon that big needs to eat often. But its clutch—ah, that is a far more dangerous thing. And it's out *there*." Tavin tilted his head to the darkness beyond the fire.

"How do you know?" asked Lily.

"We found it, day before yesterday. It's not very far from here, really. And they're ready to hatch."

"Why didn't you destroy them?"

"We could have. But Dubb had a better idea. He took one of them in order to lure the dragon here. If we'd destroyed the eggs, the dragon would have fled, and there would be another clutch next season. A clutch we didn't know the whereabouts of. No, we needed to destroy the dragon first. At all costs."

"You have a dragon's egg here—ready to hatch?"

Tavin nodded.

"What's going to happen to it?"

Tavin pursed his lips. "Hm. Well, I suppose Quib has some sort of stew that calls for a dragon's egg or two."

Lily made a face. "Why this place?"

"We wanted to fight the dragon on familiar ground. On *our* terms."

"And Dubb will destroy the clutch tomorrow?"

"If they don't hatch before then, we'll be okay. *That's* what they're betting on, but it's an awful risk. And unnecessary. I could easily reach them before morning. I'm quite good in the dark, really."

"But you—"

"Right! Yes, I know." And Tavin held up his bound wrists. "There is this one small problem."

"But you're saying you could be back before morning?" Lily heard herself saying.

"Oh, absolutely. Two hours—three, tops."

"And you would come back right away?"

Tavin laughed, leaned in. "Where else would I go? These are my only friends."

Lily couldn't see a flaw in his logic, and he seemed so honest.

"And you *promise* to come back right away?" asked Lily.

"Promise? Most certainly. I give you my word as a gentleman," said Tavin very earnestly.

"And you'll come straight back?"

"Of course! What we harvest from this dragon *must* get back to Bairne. We have debts to pay. *I* have debts to pay."

Lily dropped the blankets from her arms and felt her head. It was warm, and she felt a little dizzy.

Tavin presented his wrists and said, in a suddenly powerful voice, "Go on now, Lily, untie these ropes so I may save the children from the evil dragons. There were ten eggs in that clutch. Dubb will destroy the one we have, but I must destroy the other nine. Imagine, nine free

dragons . . . they would be more than we could bear."

"Nine dragons," Lily breathed. "Nine!"

"Eating little children, along with their mothers and fathers." Tavin's eyes flashed fiercely.

Slowly, Lily leaned forward and began pulling at Dubb's knots.

"Good, that's it! We don't want to let those little dragons get loose and grow up to be big ones!"

Lily picked at the ropes. The longer she took, the more agitated Tavin became.

"Hold on," said Lily, rethinking her strategy. "I think I see . . . wow, these are really tight."

Tavin turned his wrists upward.

"That one, Lily, start with that one."

"No, I don't think so. I think it's this one over here—"

"No, it's this one." And Tavin again turned his wrists to expose the dangling strand.

"Um . . . no . . . I'm pretty sure—"

"Listen, you useless maggot! Grab that end! Right there!"

Stung, Lily grabbed the suggested end and started working it clear, then she stopped.

"What did you just call me?" she asked, still feeling strange.

But now the ropes were uncoiling, like a snake struck dead uncoiling from its prey.

The glint of a dagger flashed in Tavin's hand, and he parted the ropes binding his knees and ankles with a single stroke.

"Stupid child," he sneered. "We could've been caught, with all the time you were taking."

A feeling of rising alarm pierced Lily's woozy thoughts. She turned her head in the direction Dubb had gone, taking a deep breath.

But Tavin had anticipated her thoughts. Before she could scream, he made a small hand gesture, uttering a strange sound. Instantly, Lily felt paralysis grip her body. She couldn't move, she couldn't breathe, she couldn't even blink. Using the edges of her vision, she watched helplessly as Tavin stole toward one of Arric's wards. His back was to her, so there was very little that she could make out, but by the placement of his elbows, it appeared he was holding his hands about stomach height. From the way his elbows moved, it seemed he was manipulating something in his hands. Then Lily noticed a reddish-purple light that must have been coming from whatever he was holding.

After that, the world darkened about the edges. Lily's fright had cleared her head sufficiently to realize that she had been duped. But she couldn't worry about that. She had more immediate problems— like breathing. Try as she might, she simply couldn't draw in a breath of air. All she could do was watch and listen.

Tavin paused at his work and muttered something in a language that the moon coin couldn't translate, followed by something that it could.

"Well, well, well, my little friend, look at all these fiendishly clever surprises you have left for me."

White sparkles filled the edges of Lily's vision, and a fuzziness descended on all her senses.

Breathe, she thought. *Breathe.*

Then there was nothing.

Egg-Hunt

L ILY woke to voices.

"He couldn't have—he's Dragondain."

Dragondain! thought Lily. *When did the King's guard arrive?*

"Your ward must have failed," said a voice Lily recognized as Dubb's.

"No," protested the first voice. *Arric?* "They're still in place! Dara helped me examine them—"

"It's true, Dubb," said a woman's voice.

Lily tried to open her eyes.

Why can't I see? Why can't I move?

"They're fully intact," Dara continued. "Any one of them would take me hours to deconstruct, if I didn't trip it first."

"Dara!" gasped Arric. "Form your peerin and train it on Lily."

Lily heard feet shuffling close by in the dirt. And then she felt a strange sensation, as if someone had opened her up like a window and shone bright beams of sunlight into her dusty corners.

"Why can't you wake her?" asked Dubb. "What's going on?"

"There's something . . . on her," said Arric.

"What do you mean?"

"Some kind of enchantment. Do you see it too, Dara?"

"Yes. But what is it?"

"I don't know."

"It's all over her," said Dara. "Could this be from a dark peerin?"

"*Dark* peerin!" said Dubb. "Are you saying a blackmage was here last night?"

"No," began Arric. "If this were something from a dark peerin, we wouldn't be able to see anything at all. More likely, it's something very old."

"Or very new," interrupted Dara. "Arric, what do you think this part is—here?"

"*That* is something *she* must have cast."

I cast? thought Lily. *Okay, now you have my full attention.*

"Are you saying Lily's a lunamancer?" asked Dubb.

"Not necessarily," said Arric. "It's not exactly an enchantment, although I don't like calling it a ward, either. I think it's something else altogether."

"So, you're saying that this thing that Lily cast could have been stored in something, like an amulet or a ring or—"

"Or a pendant," interrupted Dara. "Is that a necklace around her neck?"

"Yes. And that's stranger still. Look at the lines of power that have formed between the necklace and what's she's cast."

"I've never seen anything like it. How much longer do you think she can last?"

"She must be getting a little air somehow. She did make it through the night, after all. But I don't see how—"

"Arric, look at these places!"

"Where?"

"Around her throat . . . near her temples. The spell attacking her looks damaged here, as though it's unraveling. What if we tried to help it along here, here . . . and *here*—"

Lily felt the muscles of her chest constrict. She wanted to scream from the sudden jolt of pain, but she couldn't inflate her lungs.

"Don't touch that!" said Arric hastily.

Breathe, thought Lily.

"Well, now, there's something unexpected," said Arric.

"Did we do that?" asked Dara.

"No. That came from her. Lily, can you hear me? If you can hear me, do that again. But concentrate very, very hard on it."

Breathe!

"Arric! She's made a weak spot."

"No . . . I don't think so. I think that's another trap."

Though still unable to move the rest of her body, Lily felt a new strength. She blinked open her eyes for the first time since she had fallen unconscious. She lay on her side, in the dirt, frozen in place like a toppled statue. Dara and Arric were kneeling next to her, peerins drawn. Each was awash in a different colored light: Arric's face was lit by fiery reds, Dara's by blues. Behind the two of them stood Dubb, bent at the waist, hands on knees, his eyes focused intently on her face.

"Lily," said Arric, "wait for my signal." While holding his peerin, Arric twitched several of his fingertips; he spoke a phrase the moon coin couldn't translate. "Do you see my plan, Dara?"

"Yes."

"Are you ready?"

"Yes."

"On three. One, two—now, Lily. Fight!"

Breathe!

Lily's paralysis dissolved all at once. Suddenly overwhelmed by the weight of her limbs, she collapsed onto her stomach, as helpless as a beached jellyfish. Her first lungfuls of air came in uncontrollable spasms. The air was cool, piercing, and filled with dirt and dust.

Lily struggled to push herself upright, but her muscles, twitching and jangling, refused to obey. Dubb and Arric lifted her into a sitting position. Lily scuttled backwards until she bumped against a large stone, next to the smoldering remains of last night's fire. She blinked back the early morning light. The sky was full of moons and faint stars.

Half a dozen people had gathered, and Dubb knelt before her, his blue eyes twitching over every detail of her face.

"Lily," he said, with gentle urgency, "what do you remember? What happened here? Where is Tavin?" She could hear his alarm rising with each new question.

"He did it," said Lily, adjusting her collar to hide the little bit of necklace showing.

"Who?"

"He tricked me. He seemed so nice, so reasonable. Then he tried to kill me!"

Dubb looked puzzled. "Who? Who tried to kill you?"

"Tavin! Why did you leave me with him? He was kind at first, then he started talking about the dragon's eggs and how you brought one here to lure the mother dragon. He promised he'd come back. He gave me his word as a gentleman."

"Gentleman." Dubb blinked a few times, momentarily stunned. He turned away and looked imploringly at the faces of those standing near him, more confused than worried. "Gentleman?"

"Tavin?" said someone in the crowd.

"A gentleman?" said another.

Dubb turned his attention back to Lily. "Tavin's *no* gentleman."

"I know that *now*!" said Lily.

"And we've taken no eggs. We don't even know where the clutch is." Dubb became more agitated. "How did he leave this place? Who came here to get him? And who threw this spell on you?"

"He threw it. He did all of it. He tricked me—"

"Who? Who threw the spell?" shouted Dubb.

"Tavin!"

Dubb jumped up and backed away. "Tavin? But that's not possible! Tavin is Dragondain. He's incapable of using magic—even if he *wanted* to."

"Dragondain?" said Lily in a bewildered voice. "Dragondain are valiant and true! Tavin is no Dragondain!"

"Lily," began Dubb. "Listen to me. It is true the Crown has stripped Tavin from our ranks, but I swear to you: you will find no truer heart."

"He paralyzed me."

Dubb's face fell.

"He said something that I couldn't understand and flicked his wrist at me. Then he stood over *there*." Lily pointed to where Tavin had worked on Arric's ward. "He kept his back to me, but he was working something with his hands. He said something about a friend having left him fiendish little surprises. And then . . . and then . . . I don't remember any more after that."

"Dubb," said Arric, "it sounds like he was looking at my ward—with a peerin."

Dubb's face darkened with anger. "That's . . . not . . . possible!" he said.

"He called me a useless maggot," said Lily softly.

Dubb wheeled around, reached down, and gripped Lily's shoulders.

"Had he drawn it?" he asked, now sounding desperate. "When he called you *that*, had he drawn it?"

"Drawn what?"

"His *sword*!" Dubb's fingers dug in. "Had he drawn his blade from his scabbard?"

Lily thought back, but she already knew the answer. She remembered very well everything that had happened last night—right up to the point where she blacked out.

"No. I'm certain of it. His hands were still bound when he called me that."

Dubb sprang backward again. He spun around and scanned the horizon. "The moons are in motion," he hissed. And then, to Arric, "It's learned a new trick!" Dubb's face was red with fury.

"Dubb," said Dara, "we have to find him."

"He has quite the head start. Tracking Tavin will be like tracking a gust of wind. Boots, wake Marred. We'll need to travel light and fast. I'll take Andros. Maybe Quib."

"It won't be easy getting Quib to leave that dragon," said Andros. "He's barreling its organs. And you know how particular he is about—"

"Then he can stay, but we'll need to borrow his whip." Dubb raised his voice. "Listen up. I'll say this but once. I believe this girl before you is Lord Autumn's niece."

Everyone pivoted toward Lily, looking at her through new eyes.

"Trust me when I say: if she were to fall into Wrengfoul's hands, it would quicken the death of us all. Lily must reach the safety of Bairne. That is all that matters now. Do not let her out of your sight." Dubb locked eyes with Lily. "Should it become necessary, defend her to the expense of all your lives—she *must* not be taken."

Lily felt the strength drain from her limbs. "You can't be serious . . . to the expense—"

"I'll be back as soon as I can, but if I don't return by tomorrow, get her to Ember."

Dubb strode away, Andros right behind him. Lily could feel people staring, but she could think of nothing to make them stop. *All die,* she thought, *for me?*

Fires flickered throughout the camp, producing an oily black smoke that burned the eyes and clung thickly to the ground. Lily watched as the men and women stumbled about, dead on their feet, but struggling for one great purpose—to harvest the dragon.

At first, Arric would not let Lily wander. She spent the first hour following him around while he added wards around the entire camp. By his third casting, he had removed his robes, his face covered with a sheen of sweat. By the fifth, he had opened his shirt and rolled up his sleeves.

The other lunamancers prepared no wards, but they followed Arric on his rounds, worried expressions creasing their faces. At one point, they all gathered around him and did something like a laying on of hands. After that, he seemed better for a time, though they themselves looked much worse for the effort.

When Arric finished, he collapsed onto a pile of rags and fell into a fitful sleep. Boots, the bowman, took over Lily's care then. They climbed to the highest point in the camp, where he carefully laid out several quivers' worth of arrows. With one arrow notched in his bow but not drawn, he took up a keen watch.

Boots told Lily she could have the run of the camp as long as she remained within his sight, and the morning passed quickly. Lily was pleased to find she could help. There was much to do in this dragon-dismantling business. Not a single scrap was overlooked. The first and largest project was the hide, which dulled blades so quickly that a grinding wheel had been set up. The big stone wheel was cranked by hand in shifts and did not cease until nightfall.

They didn't use ordinary blades. The lunamancers took shifts standing next to the wheel, peerins drawn, working spell after spell into the dull blades until their tips glowed white hot, edged in blue. They cut from underneath, anywhere an opening had been made in the hide, but they could cut only a few inches at a time before returning to the grinding wheel for a new edge and more spells.

They cut the meat loose in great strips, and dried them over hastily erected drying racks in what had once been adjoining rooms. The floors there were black with ash and grease. Even the dripping fat was

periodically scraped up and barreled. Quib took special care overseeing the entire process. There were tendons to be harvested, and he
didn't want them damaged by the act of a hasty hand.

They cracked open the bare bones, removing and storing the mar-
row. They saved the claws and teeth; horns, tongue, and jaws; and the
spines that jutted out like cat whiskers. At one point, Lily discovered
Quib nearly crying at the state of the poor dragon's punctured eyes,
but even there he salvaged the tough secondary membranes, along
with every bit of colored iris he could find. All of the internal organs
were placed in barrels and topped with brine, or dried, pulverized,
and powdered. The blood was barreled, too. When they got to the
dragon's heart, Quib finally broke down into heaving sobs: Tavin's
cursed sword had cut it nearly in two. The emptied bones were buried in white hot embers until they were clean of tissue. Once cooled,
they were stacked onto one of the waiting wagons. Lily spent her time
serving bits of food and cups of water to the workers. She helped tend
the fires, which burned all day, creating great clouds of greasy black
smoke.

The afternoon passed quickly. Lunch was a small bowl of mil-
dewed beans. Lily had a terrible time explaining to Quib what it meant
to be a vegetarian. He kept saying things like, "Well, I could spare you
a bit o' brains. They're not meat, right?" and "At least let me ladle on
a good heapin' bit o' the grease, eh? No meat in that!" Twice, Lily had
to grab his ladle and push it away from her bowl. "But how will you
grow?" he asked.

Once the sun dipped below the horizon, smoking, guttering torch-
es marked the edges of the camp. Arric finally arose from his nap and
posted himself near the grinding wheel. He was deep in thought, but
now and again he would casually flick off a spell into one of the passing blades. Arric's blades, Lily noticed, held an edge for far longer
than the ones sharpened by the other lunamancers.

An hour after nightfall, Boots lit a torch and waved it in the air, instantly gaining everyone's attention. He tossed the torch out toward the camp's perimeter. It kicked up dust where it fell, but continued to crackle and burn.

"From that direction," called Boots, pointing past the torch. "Better hurry up, Arric—by the sound of it, they're moving fast."

Arric ran to his ward and formed his peerin. A small crowd gathered behind him. As Lily watched, she again noticed the reddish light that bathed Arric's torso, and though it seemed to be coming from his peerin, she could see no source—just the empty peerin.

After several minutes, they heard footsteps crashing through the brush. At what seemed like the very last second, Arric stepped aside as though he were opening an invisible door, and Andros, with Tavin on his back, thudded into the camp and collapsed. Tavin, bound in a cocoon of rope, flopped onto his belly and lifted his head to look at them with wild, uncomprehending eyes. Two pulsing veins stood out on his forehead. A dirty rag gagging his mouth muffled his screams. Andros let out a great groan and rolled onto his back, still trying to catch his breath.

A few seconds later, Dubb staggered into the camp, barked a few orders, and trudged off to the crumbling inner keep. People ran everywhere, doing his bidding.

Marred was the last to return, and he immediately called for Quib. Like Dubb, Marred was drenched in sweat.

"Take this . . . *thing*," he spat, holding out Quib's whip. "Right wicked, that is!"

Quib took the whip and held it to his waist. Like a living thing, it coiled around his belt and then went slack.

"What happened out there?" Quib asked quickly.

"I tracked him back to the clutch—"

"You found the eggs! Did you—"

"Yes, but . . . we were too late. He'd destroyed them all." Marred spoke quietly.

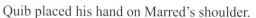

Quib placed his hand on Marred's shoulder.

"It had to be done," whispered Quib. "You *know* that."

Marred licked his lips and nodded, but it was clear that he felt differently.

"Was it a long way?" asked Quib.

"No, but it was very well hidden. Finding Tavin was what kept us."

"He left the clutch? Where did he go?" Quib asked in wonder.

"I tracked him. It wasn't hard. He kept as straight a line as he could, down from the moors and toward the fens. He was moving fast, all things considered. He was on the old high roads, where the water is shallowest."

"Into the fens? You mean to say he was—"

"Headed for Perianth? I think that's certain. When I first sighted him, he was already waist-deep. I don't know how he kept to the middle of the road, but he did. Ten feet to his left or right and he'd've been in the deep. It was like he didn't even know he was in the fens." Marred ran a dirty hand through his greasy hair. "When we got close, we fanned out as best we could. The water was up to our chests—well, all but Andros—and too black for us to see how well the edges of the road were holding up. But it turned out we didn't have to mind that so much."

"What do you mean?" asked Quib, his eyelids crinkling to slits.

"He was out of his head—raving mad."

"Wha—You sayin' he di'n't know you was there?"

"Quib," said Marred, "he wasn't playing any games. . . . He didn't even catch sight of us until we were right on him."

Quib's mouth swung open. "Di'n't notice you? Tavin? And it was no trick?"

"We took him—easy-like. He's wounded, too." Marred motioned to Tavin's leg. "The left one. An ugly cut of some kind. I'm not sure what from, but it's not healing as well as I'd expect, given that it's Tavin and all."

Quib bent down to take a look. The rope binding was caked with mud and powdered with road dirt, but the area just below Tavin's knee was matted with dried blood.

Lily was just beginning to worry that she'd lost track of Dubb when he strode through a crumbling arch, leading an old and mangy-looking horse by its bridle. He'd donned a dark riding cloak and was pulling on an old pair of leather gauntlets with the aid of his teeth.

"Quib, Marred, help me lash him behind the saddle, and don't worry about being gentle."

Quib grasped Tavin's legs, and Marred and Dubb each took a shoulder. Tavin twisted and tried to kick, but they lashed him down quickly. Dubb then burdened the poor beast with his own weight. Taking firm grip of the reins, he held out his other hand for Lily, who simply stared at it.

"Come now. There is no time to waste."

Lily eyed the poor old horse. It was already struggling, and it pained her to think of adding any more weight to its load. She glanced at Quib and Arric, who had just arrived.

"I can get you home," said Dubb.

Quib squatted, holding out his clasped hands like a stirrup. "You won't get a better offer than that," he said. "Your parents must be worryin' something awful about you, eh?"

Home! thought Lily. *How long have I been away?*

It had been well over a day now. What would her parents be thinking? They must be nearly out of their minds.

With a small apology to the horse, Lily placed her foot into Quib's hands and accepted Dubb's gloved hand. With very little effort, Dubb hoisted her into the saddle before him.

Quib took hold of the horse's bridle. "Dubb," he said, sounding very serious, "this horse won't take the kind of riding you just gave ol' Andros there. You'll never make it back to Bairne on this bag of bones."

Dubb adjusted his cloak. "Don't worry," he said to Quib, "we aren't going all the way to Bairne tonight."

"Then where *are* you going?" asked Quib, now sounding more concerned.

Marred swung a dirty oilskin pack from his shoulder. "Provisions," he said. Lily helped him lash the pack to the front of the saddle, between her and the nag's dirt-matted mane.

Dubb gave a tug on the reins, but Quib held tight to the bridle.

From her position in front, Lily couldn't see Dubb's face, but she thought she noticed Marred catch his eye, holding Dubb's gaze for a moment before giving a small nod.

"Dubb hasn't got time for this, Quib," said Marred, who suddenly yanked Quib's hands from the bridle.

Quib stepped back, startled.

"Yes, of course. You must go," he smiled grimly. "When you're safe, send us at least three more wagons—soon as you can!"

Dubb drew the sides of his cloak around Lily's shoulders. "Here," he said, "tie the ends of my cloak around the pack in front of you. It will keep off the worst of the road dust."

Lily tied the cloak in place, shielding her from chin to foot. As the poor horse stumbled out of camp, the last thing she saw was Quib, Marred, and Arric helping a pained Andros to his feet.

Unannounced Guests

THICK clouds blanketed the sky, obscuring the moons and stars. Dubb guided the horse down Perch's steep slope, into the bleak, rolling landscape. Soon the ruins behind them were swallowed up by layers of mist and darkness.

"Where is this place?" said Lily softly, but Dubb said nothing.

"Is all of Dain this desolate?"

Still nothing.

"Why did Tavin try to kill me?"

Lily felt Dubb shift uncomfortably in the saddle.

"It wasn't Tavin who tried to kill you," he answered after a time. "That was Curse's doing."

"Curse?"

"Yes, the voice you heard talking through the sword. The attempt on your life was its doing—you have to believe that. Tavin would *never* have tried to hurt you."

"Does Curse take him over like that often?"

"No. Never like—I mean, this was a first. I blame myself. I should have anticipated this. We should have headed back to Bairne weeks ago."

"Why is Perianth surrounded by fens? Why has Castle Fendragon been abandoned?"

Dubb took a deep breath and let it out slowly.

"Wrengfoul . . . he managed all of this, he and his foul minions. It was the year 2436, in the early spring. We were just a few years older than you are now."

Lily's heart raced. She knew the power of numbers. *Numbers can tell you things,* Ebb was fond of saying, *but only if you're listening.* Nimlinn had said Wrengfoul attacked Dain seventeen years before. That meant the present year in the Moon Realm was 2453. And if Dubb had been a few years older than she was now, he was in his early thirties. Lily was surprised. Dubb looked as old as Ebb, even though he was fifteen years his junior. Could a hard life age a man that much?

"Dain was nearly two and half millennia into an age of rebirth," continued Dubb. "Darwyth was dead, just as it's always been, but it seemed farther removed from us in those days. You'd hear the name Wrengfoul, but more often than not in a sad ballad, a story, or after someone stubbed a toe. In those days, the roads between the townships and coastal city of Warsh were well traveled. Dragons were sighted only rarely. And though they were just as dangerous as today, they kept mostly to the mountains.

"The city Perianth was a beautiful sight that daybreak. I know because I was there to see it, as were Tavin, Andros, Quib, Marred, and many others you've met. No one suspected a thing. We had no warning. The system of windmills and locks was one of the four wonders of the world then. Tinker-designed, they said, and Dain-built thousands of years before the start of the new calendar."

"You mean before the year zero."

"Correct. I knew the mills had been built to keep out the sea, but I didn't understand to what extent. I suspect few did. Even in the rainiest of seasons, the low roads never flooded. The fields and pastures were productive. Farms stretched outward in all directions from Perianth.

"Then *he* came back to us . . . Wrengfoul. I say 'back' because legend has it that before the new calendar began, there was an Age of Waste, a dark age much like the one we're in now. Ember could tell you more. In addition to her lunamancy studies, she is an accomplished collector of tales, constantly piecing together what's left of Dain's far-flung tapestry."

Lily thought back. In most of the bedtime tales, the magical city Perianth covered the slopes and top of a towering lone hill, and Castle Fendragon sat within its center like a crown jewel. The lowlands that surrounded Perianth were divided: first by the high roads—all of which led to Perianth—and then by the low roads, which crisscrossed and serviced the farms and communities. But she remembered tales where the fens were being drained, too. Ebb had called them old, but not ancient.

"I'd never imagined such a day, Lily. We were *so* young. Far away, on the coast, foul serpents slithered from the sea, destroying the great windmills and locks, and the sea roared through. I still don't know how he amassed such a large force so close to us without our getting wind of it. It was as if they came out of thin air, storming across the high roads from all directions. We met dread-knights that day, armed with their poisoned blades. There were thousands of them. And the blackmages." Dubb paused. "It's said a hundred of them roamed the fields of battle that day . . . a *hundred*." Lily could hear the awe in his voice. "There were plenty of scaramann to go around, pestilent bugs that they are. More than one could count. They covered the earth like a raging black sea, devouring everything in their path."

Lily, thinking of what she had seen in the Valley of the Rinn, shivered.

"Ah, but you've seen them, haven't you?"

She felt Dubb shift in the saddle and imagined he might be looking to the sky.

"I wonder how Barreth has fared this day? Not well, I would think."

"Greydor will save them," said Lily in a soft voice.

"I hope you're right, Lily. No one deserves that fate, not even the cats. When you were on Barreth, did you hear tell of any dwythbane?"

"No. What are they?"

"They're like blackmages, but worse, wielding sword as easily as spell."

"What do they look like?"

"A dwythbane's clothes look like something dug up from wet earth, but they wear like iron. His skin blisters and peels, like thin tree bark. Feathery tendrils and matted roots hang down before his eyes." Lily recalled the images of the misshapen creatures she'd seen in the Tomb of the Fallen. "When he speaks, his white tongue slithers and flicks around weathered teeth that look like something you'd find in a graveyard, not a living mouth. Rootlets grow on his hands, giving him a grip that can crumble stone.

"The dwythbane rarely leave Darwyth these days, and we believe they are few in number. At Wrengfoul's bidding, they harvest living creatures from Dain and our moons. Using dark magic, they alter the creatures' bodies and blacken their souls, twisting them until they are ready to join his horrible army."

"Like the scaramann?" said Lily.

"Exactly."

"What about the dragons?" Lily asked, now wondering whether or not the shrewd and resourceful dragons of her childhood had ever existed. "Were they mad when you were a boy?"

"When were they ever otherwise?" said Dubb wistfully.

Lily was certain important information could be mined from her old bedtime tales, but she doubted Dubb would take them seriously enough to give them a fair listen.

"So where are we going now?" she asked. "And why wouldn't you tell Quib?" she added, even before he could answer.

They rode in silence for a long time, and Lily had just about decided the conversation was over when Dubb spoke up.

"We're going to the homestead of a very powerful healer. We must see what can be done for Tavin's mind. Our horse can get real food there, and proper care. Then we'll travel to Bairne, where you can meet Ember."

Uncle Ebb had told many tales of Perianth, but Bairne was a name she didn't recognize.

"What is Bairne?"

"Bairne is where we cower, packed like two hatchling dragons in the same egg. It lies at the end of these moors, where the mountains begin. I suppose the location was chosen for protection, and for the rich valley that cuts into the mountains there. The old outer walls are all but gone, leaving the workers easy prey to the likes of dragons."

"Will Tavin come with us to Bairne?"

"Yes. And he'll improve with each step we take from these wastes. When he's back among the press of people, he'll be safe. And you'll be safe, too."

Lily wanted to believe Dubb, but she couldn't stop thinking about how he'd been fooled, how he'd left her with Tavin in the first place.

"In fact, Tavin should improve greatly as soon as we reach the lands the healers inhabit. They're scattered thinly, but they have a collective effect . . . over the land."

"If they live outside the city, why aren't they eaten by the dragons?"

"They live outside the city because they are not trusted by the Crown. And the dragons act as if they don't see them."

"Why aren't they trusted?"

"In the aftermath of Wrengfoul's devastation, a rumor began that a healer, a very important healer, helped heal a dying blackmage."

"And did he?"

Dubb shifted in his saddle. "Well . . . he did not deny it."

"So they banished him? For that?"

"Oh, no, Lily, no—they *killed* him for that. After that, things only got worse for the healers."

"And so they kicked all of them out?"

"No. Quite the opposite. A healer named Keegan Hoarfrost *led* them out. They took refuge in territory that no one would willingly travel—at least, not without dire need. They did things to the trees, hid themselves among them. Somehow, they changed the land where they settled—that, or the land changed around them. Out here, they've made themselves safe."

After what seemed like hours of riding, they came to a more densely wooded area with towering trees. Dubb steered the poor horse onto an even worse road where tree branches occasionally brushed against their faces. The horse stumbled more, over what Lily guessed were gnarled roots.

Gradually, though, the clumping of the old horse's hooves grew softer, and the sounds of night insects and frogs grew louder. Owls called to each other in the distance, and occasionally one took flight, disturbed by the trespassers.

Then, not far off the path, a light appeared, illuminating a pool of water and what looked like a mound.

"Dubb," whispered Lily, "what is that?"

"Shhhh!" hissed Dubb.

And the light winked out.

It was a long time before Lily saw another light, farther off this time. Awhile after that, more lights appeared. Some illuminated small open fields, while others revealed clumps of trees. This time Lily stayed quiet.

Some time later, she spotted something moving: something very short, but walking on two legs. Then it was gone, disappearing into the taller grass.

A sound startled Lily, as though a finger were tapping on the outside of Dubb's riding cloak. Lily drew her feet up as far as she could. When the sound resumed, she could tell it was coming from in front of her. At first she imagined a small bird, pecking at the outside of the cloak. But what if it wasn't a bird? What if it had little hairy arms and legs and had crawled up the horse from the road? What if it had sharp teeth? What if there were more than one of them?

Lily reached out and touched the pack that Marred had handed Dubb. Her fingers slipped over its smooth, oily surface. The tapping came again, only more forcefully this time. Now she was certain. Something was clinging to the outside of the riding cloak, maybe after some food in Marred's pack. She gave the pack a quick shove and listened. The tapping stopped.

Dubb shook Lily's shoulder and leaned down to speak in her ear. "Are you awake?" he said softly.

"Yes!" hissed Lily. "Like I would be asleep! Are you mental?"

"Good. We're on Keegan's ground, nearing his homestead. Tavin has finally gone slack and is, I hope, sleeping."

Lily had almost forgotten about Tavin, who was lashed to the back of the saddle. Hearing Dubb use Tavin's name brought back the memory of his face when he had called her a "useless maggot." Lily's stomach clenched at the thought of Tavin being cut free from his ropes.

The horse stopped.

"Don't be afraid," said Dubb quickly, just before a dozen lights flared up.

They had halted between two great tree trunks. Lily saw animals all about them. Most were sleeping, but a few turned their heads, squinting. A young girl holding two lanterns walked out of a nearby barn. She held one of the lanterns high, lighting her young face. She didn't look happy, and the closer she got, the angrier she became.

"Get off! Get off that horse!" she scolded, with a very forceful manner for one so young.

Lily hurriedly untied the riding cloak, and Dubb helped her down.

"He's expecting you," said the girl. Getting a good look at the poor horse, she gave Dubb an even darker look. "Two of you," she sneered. Dubb dismounted, and the young girl saw Tavin. "Three of you!" she shrieked. "And packs!"

Dubb unlashed the pack that Marred had given him and handed it to Lily. It was much heavier than she expected, and it took both arms and most of her strength to carry it. Dubb waved his hand. With a swishing sound the ropes binding Tavin to the horse parted. Only when Dubb stowed the short blade did Lily catch a glimpse of flickering steel. He eased Tavin off the horse and onto his shoulders.

"Come on," he grunted.

"You'll need a lantern," said the girl.

Dubb tried to free a hand, but bending down was difficult.

"Here," she said, hanging a lantern over one of Tavin's outstretched legs. "He's in the main house. Make sure you keep to the walkway."

Dubb made a face—part smile, part grimace—and thanked her.

The path wound alongside several structures that Lily had mistaken for giant trees or rock ledges. Shortly, they reached a stone house with a thatched roof. On top, smoke curled out of an opening that didn't look like any chimney Lily had ever seen.

They came to an open door. Dubb turned sideways and allowed the lantern hanging on Tavin's foot to lead the way into a long mudroom, where hooks and pegs lined the walls.

"You may wish to leave your cloak and armament here," said Dubb. "Don't worry. No one will take them."

Lily set down the heavy pack on a low bench that ran along one side of the room. Dubb loosened the chin strap of his helmet and bent down his head so Lily could take it off. "Just put it on one of the pegs."

"What about your sword?" asked Lily, a little too quickly.

"The sword, and my armor, stay with me tonight."

Lily hung her own helmet and cloak on pegs. Unstrapping her greaves and vambraces, she placed them on the floor underneath her cloak before turning back to Dubb, who strained under Tavin's weight.

"Bring that pack along, won't you?" He nodded to an open door at the opposite side of the mudroom. "Follow me."

Dubb, Tavin, and Lily emerged into a spacious room with a high ceiling and were met by an old man and a young woman. Small lamps hung below the beams, giving off a soft light. The old man held up a hand to shield his eyes from the bright light of the lantern. He had a terrible crook in his back and stood no taller than Lily. His face was covered in stubble, and his eyebrows protruded like ledges beyond the dark sockets of his eyes. He wore a fine vest over a coarsely woven wool robe. And his smile, though pained, was happy and affectionate.

"Come in," croaked the man, "come in. Is that you, Dubb?"

"What?" said Dubb, chuckling, "Couldn't you tell?"

The young woman, wearing a finely woven gown, lifted the lantern off Tavin's leg, doused its flame, and set it by the doorway. Lily guessed she was much younger than Dubb, easily in her twenties.

"Oh, well." The old man made a face. "All they told me was that the cursed one was coming, he and four others."

"Four others?" said Dubb impishly. "But we are only two. Are you expecting more tonight?"

Keegan's gaze grew serious. His eyes settled first on Dubb, then Lily, as though searching for some hidden clue that he'd rather not miss out on.

"Keegan," said Dubb, "allow me to introduce you to Lily Winter." He spoke her name slowly and deliberately.

Keegan smiled. "Miss Winter, yes, of course."

"Lily," continued Dubb, "this is Keegan Hoarfrost."

Lily didn't know if she should curtsy, bow, or offer her hand. In the end, she lowered her head and simply said, "Hello."

"And this," continued Dubb, "is Nima, one of Keegan's many granddaughters, each as beautiful as the next." Nima blushed, and offered her hand to Lily.

In the dim light, Lily thought Nima rather plain until she smiled. It was a small, pursed-lip smile, like she knew something that others didn't. Nima gave Lily a long appraising look that made her squirm, but it wasn't nearly as nerve-wracking as when, in the Great Hall of the Rinn, Greydor had borne down on her with his potent emerald eyes.

Keegan let go of Nima's arm and hobbled forward on his cane. He twisted his head to get a better look at Dubb. "You were at the top of my list as *one* of the others." Then the old man swiveled his gray head toward Lily. They were standing nose to nose. She could see his eyes, even in this dim light, tiny and sparkling below his frosted eyebrows. "*You*, however, my dear," he said softly, "most certainly were *not*."

Dubb and Lily exchanged puzzled glances, although each was wondering about something different.

Keegan hobbled back to Nima's proffered arm. "Come," he said briskly. They passed through the large room and turned down a short hallway, moving slowly.

"I imagine Tavin must be getting heavy by now," said Keegan.

"*Getting* heavy?" laughed Dubb, adjusting Tavin's weight on his shoulders as he walked. "Tell me, Keegan. Was that Pippa who took our horse?"

"Yes. Our resident personification of indignation and outrage," chuckled Keegan.

"She's grown so," said Dubb half under his breath.

"Yes. And she grows louder as she grows taller. Of course, if you visited more often . . ." murmured Keegan.

Nima opened a door to a small cool room with a lone window. With Nima's help, Dubb laid Tavin on the bed, which creaked under his fully armored weight. Nima gasped when she got a better look at him.

"For the love of moonlight! Must you bind him so tightly?" she exclaimed.

"Yes," Lily and Dubb answered together.

Nima slid open a drawer and withdrew a small pair of scissors, then set upon the ropes binding Tavin's arms.

"Are you sure you want to do that?" asked Dubb.

Nima shot Dubb a fierce look.

"Leave him to me," she said. Then, to her grandfather, "Bring me a tea of quarnel root and simpkin leaves. And not too heavy on the simpkin leaves, mind you. We don't want to make him daft."

"Yes, dear," answered Keegan politely. "Right away."

Keegan motioned to Dubb and Lily, leading them back to the big room that served as kitchen and dining room. The tables and cabinets against the walls were filled with bottles and jars. Keegan picked up a pitcher and filled it at one of several wooden sinks. Then he filled a large black kettle, and Dubb hoisted it onto a rack above banked, glowing embers. An open flue piped the smoke up through the roof.

Keegan opened one of the taller cabinets and began poking around, pulling out jars filled with roots and small boxes stuffed with bits of twig, moss, and leaves.

"We won't be staying long," said Dubb.

"I'm not surprised," said Keegan, now bent over a wooden drawer.

"I've brought you something."

"Most people do," murmured Keegan, and, still stooped, he turned his face to them. "So what do you have? An injured cat? A bird with a broken wing?"

"No. I have something for you to take to Raewyn—two some-things, actually." Dubb motioned to the pack that Lily had placed on the table. "Lily, open that up and get one out, will you?" he asked.

Lily walked over to the pack, loosened a knotted string and peeled back a flap of oilcloth. Inside she saw what looked like two large stones the size of volleyballs. Using both hands, she pulled one out. It was heavy.

Keegan's eyes grew large, and he cocked his head back in surprise. He stood up straighter, and the small spoon he was holding slipped onto the table with a clatter.

"Oh my!" he said. "Does Marred know?"

"Yes, he's the one who found them."

"Who else knows?" said Keegan, speaking quickly.

"Andros, you, and now Lily."

Lily pressed the stone against her cheek and peered around it with a big grin on her face.

"Well, your secret's safe with me," she said reassuringly. "I mean, it's a rock, right?"

"That's no rock you have there, Lily," said Keegan.

Lily looked at the stone. As she approached the table, light illuminated a dull pattern that Lily assumed had been painted on by someone, possibly Marred.

"Are you kidding? By the weight of it, it's either a stone, or the largest . . . egg—" The word stuck in her throat. Her smile froze in place, her brows knitting together. "Oh, my God! Is this a dragon's egg?" she said, finishing in a rush.

"Draca Fyrblume, by the looks of those markings. A more magnificent and cunning beast you'd be hard pressed to find," said Keegan, nodding thoughtfully.

As though on cue, or perhaps in answer to its name, Lily felt and heard the same tapping she'd heard on the horse. Only this time, there was no mistaking where the noise was coming from. Lily shifted her grip and held the egg as far away from her as she dared.

"Take it!" she ordered, thrusting the egg at Dubb. "Take it—take it—take it—take it!" But Dubb just smiled and made halfhearted shooing motions, as though she were playing some kind of game.

"You said Tavin destroyed them all! You lied!"

Dubb's eyebrows rose.

Suddenly, the egg in her hands shifted. With a sharp intake of breath, she tightened her grip. She couldn't stop imagining what might happen to her fingers if the egg suddenly cracked open and the hungry hatchling popped out. Taking small but rapid steps, Lily navigated back to the pack, replaced the egg, and leapt backward.

"Don't worry, my dear," said Keegan, "you couldn't crack that egg with a pickax."

Lily wasn't convinced. "Tavin didn't have any pickax!"

"No," said Dubb darkly. "He had something far more fierce. For all its faults, that cursed sword he carries can take a murderous bite . . . when it has a mind to."

"Marred must be happy; he's been promising to bring home one of those since before he married my Raewyn. How did you come by them?"

"We destroyed the dragon that's been preying on the western fields, near Fallowden's old farm."

"Did you now," said Keegan, placing a hand over his heart.

"Then Tavin escaped." Dubb glanced toward Lily, but she was ready and returned his gaze with admirable calm. "Marred tracked him to the clutch. The ground there showed the signs of a small battle. One of the young had hatched early and was protecting the clutch."

"They often do," interrupted Keegan, who was now working over some dried roots with a mortar and pestle.

"Yes. Well, Tavin took a bad bite or a claw to the leg. He bound it himself. I haven't gotten a good look to see just how bad it is, but it hadn't stopped bleeding by the time we found him. I'm not so worried about that, though; Tavin heals fast." Dubb's gaze wandered over to the hallway where they had taken Tavin. "I should tell Nima that, so she doesn't tax herself on the leg. It's his mind that needs help."

"Don't fret on that account. Tavin's in good hands. If I know my Nima, and I do, she won't rest this night. And she won't waste her energies on a leg that will heal on its own."

"Still, I may be of help. He's not himself, Keegan. I've never seen him this bad. I should warn her."

"I wouldn't think that wise." He gave Dubb a shrewd look. "You're exhausted. When did you last sleep?"

Dubb sighed and sagged a bit.

"Truth is, I'm afraid if I sit down, I may never get back up."

Keegan placed a delicately patterned china teapot on a serving tray and removed its tiny lid. He took a step toward the large black kettle on the fire, but Dubb swooped in and lifted it easily, filling the teapot before returning the big kettle to the fire. Keegan replaced the lid, added a matching tea cup, and motioned for Lily to pick it up. "Do be a dear and take this to Nima," he said, smiling.

Lily carried the serving tray very slowly through the main room. Glancing back, she noticed Keegan steering Dubb toward the big couch.

"I can't. I have two messages I must send," she heard Dubb say.

"Tell me what they are. I'll take care of them."

The door to the small room down the hall was ajar now. Greenish light from inside the room spilled across its threshold. If Lily tilted her head just so, she could see into the room. Nima was standing opposite the bed, facing her. She had formed a triangular healer's peerin, both palms out, and was examining Tavin's face through it. As with Arric, Dara, and Tavin, a light seemed to shine from the peerin. Nima's was an eerie pale green.

"Set the cup on the table and pour the tea," said Nima, her voice a low drone.

Lily pushed open the door, looking warily at Tavin. He was completely unbound, and though he was still dressed in his dragon armor, Nima had removed his gloves and boots. His eyes were closed, but his chest rose and fell irregularly, and sometimes his jaw twitched. What if he opened his eyes while she was pouring the tea?

"Is he awake?" asked Lily softly.

"Yes," answered Nima.

Lily didn't budge.

"And no."

"He tried to kill me."

Nima's brow creased. "Hmmmm."

A moment later she said, "I don't see that memory. I don't see much of anything these past few days. And yet . . . it's like he's hiding . . . or protecting . . . something. He's very strong, even now. But he's lost control. I don't understand it."

"Dubb said it was Curse that tried to kill me."

"Hmmm. Possibly."

Possibly? thought Lily.

"Please, Lily, the tea. And don't spill it."

Lily watched a look of pain cross Nima's face, as though she were fighting back something.

Lily glanced down again at the tea tray in her hands, then at the table. She licked her lips and nodded.

"All right," she said.

Lily took the last steps to the little table, thrust down the cup, and poured the tea as fast as she dared, then raced out, closing the door behind her. After a dozen quick steps, she slowed her pace, noticing for the first time just how organic and alive the architecture in Keegan's house was. The exposed wooden supports were still covered in bark. Sprouting here and there were sapling twigs in full leaf. And the stone portions had been so perfectly laid that they looked like the mason hadn't used any mortar.

Back in the main room, Dubb was sprawled on a couch, face down, and Keegan was holding a blanket, a bemused expression on his face.

"What is it, Keegan?" asked Lily.

Keegan glanced about helplessly. "I couldn't get him to take off his sword."

"I don't think they do," said Lily.

"Can't exactly blame them, out in the wastes, hunting dragons—not much time for leisure activity, I wouldn't think."

Dragons, thought Lily, and her eyes nervously searched out the pack with the two eggs.

"Keegan, what's going to happen with those eggs?"

He returned her worried look.

"Hard to say. Raewyn has plans, I know. But what will become of them . . ." he said, his voice trailing off. "They get so big so fast." Keegan's face suddenly cleared. "Raewyn! Yes! I have messages to send. I promised Dubb." Keegan settled his eyes on Lily once more. He was troubled.

"What is it now?" she asked.

"I have many questions for you. And I imagine you have a few for me. But it's very late, and I have tasks that cannot wait. I should show you to your room, where you *must* stay until Dubb arises."

Lily nodded.

Keegan shuffled around the couch and opened a narrow door. "It's not much."

She peered into a room with a dirt floor and walls full of shelves.

"It's a stillroom," Keegan explained. "Storage for winter. No window, I'm afraid, but quite dry."

"Um, okay."

"And it has a lock, but not inside . . . Dubb refused to sleep anywhere unless he was outside your door. He kept mumbling some kind of nonsense about Tavin being dangerous."

Keegan pulled a quilt off a nearby chair and handed it to Lily, who took it into the stillroom.

"It pains me not to set you up in a proper room, with a proper bed—"

"It's fine, Keegan," said Lily, managing a smile for him. "I'll see you in the morning."

Keegan looked chagrined. "I'm not accustomed to locking people up in my own house, Lily."

"Really, it's all right," said Lily, as she spread her quilt on the floor.

Keegan handed her a blanket and pillow before closing and locking the door.

Lily stood perfectly still, hugging the bedding tightly to her chest. The storeroom, from what she had been able to see, was long and narrow, with shelves packed with bottles and small wooden boxes.

Standing in the dark, Lily wondered: *How could I not have brought a flashlight, or a lighter, or even a pack of matches?*

While still contemplating the darkness, she heard the sound of a key turning the lock. The door swung open quickly. Keegan's face was full of determination this time.

"I'm not locking you up in my own house!" he said heatedly. "And I don't care what I promised Dubb! You're welcome to come with me. Maybe you can even be of some help."

Lily eyed Dubb on the couch. She wondered whether Keegan simply wanted her to help him get around better. Then she thought about Tavin.

"It's a very kind offer, but I think maybe I'd rather stay here."

"Nonsense! You're just worried that I want you to help me walk around and that maybe I can't handle Tavin."

"Ooh—"

"And I can see you're not the least bit tired," he continued. "Come on, now. Get out of there."

Lily felt her stomach flip.

"Really, I don't know—"

"You need not be concerned about your safety: a healer is never more powerful than when walking his own ground," said Keegan. His voice grew deeper and he seemed to straighten a little, making Lily realize he was much taller than she had first thought. "And this has been *my* ground for a *very* long time."

Lily liked the sound of that. "All right, then. I'm in." She tiptoed silently to Dubb's couch and set the pillows next to his head.

Much to their surprise, Dubb rolled into a sitting position and grabbed the pillows. Hunched over, he squinted, bleary-eyed, his face wrinkled from the fabric he'd been lying on. He gave the pair a look as though he judged them responsible for stealing all the happiness he would ever possess. Then he heaved a heavy sigh.

"All right," he croaked. "Have it your way." He struggled to his feet, grumbling, and shuffled down the hall toward Tavin's door, tow-

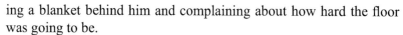

ing a blanket behind him and complaining about how hard the floor was going to be.

Keegan turned to Lily. "He does sleep, yes?"

"He must," said Lily, with false certainty, "but I have yet to see it with my own eyes."

Keegan's Ground

ONCE outside, every step Keegan took conjured a ghostly light in front of them while extinguishing one behind. The trails between the buildings were narrow, and everywhere nestled sleeping animals, noses tucked under each other. Every outbuilding appeared to be made for housing or tending animals. Lily kept a wary eye for Pippa, but she was nowhere to be seen.

"Keegan, why don't any of the fences have gates? How do you keep the animals from wandering off?"

Keegan gave Lily a cautious, sideward glance.

"My problem is quite the opposite. I must turn *back* animals every day. And those ready to go I must push out. It is the way of the land now. One of Wrengfoul's many gifts."

"How long has it been this way?"

Keegan pursed his lips. "It was this way once before, well before my time. But this most recent period began after Wrengfoul last attacked us."

"And that was when Perianth was flooded, and Castle Fendragon abandoned?"

"Precisely, but the fall of Perianth was just the beginning. After that, he spread his forces over the land and destroyed or poisoned as much as he could, leveling towns and crippling once-powerful cities."

"But he's gone now, right?" Lily pointed out. "So can't you rebuild the locks? Can't you drain the fens again?"

They crossed a small creek via a wooden bridge no more than five or six feet in span.

Keegan smiled. "Well, Lily, we're working towards it, of course. But it isn't something that can be changed quickly. At least, not by any means I can imagine. You see, the locks and the windmills were great works, and their original construction must have required thousands of people working diligently over decades. We're far fewer now, and the act of survival occupies most of our time. Many things need to be accomplished before the fens will ever be dry again. It will take the work of many generations to restore the windmills to their former glory, I can assure you."

"So, the windmills and locks are completely destroyed? They were so beautiful."

"You talk as if you've seen them."

"Only in a painting. But a very good one. It's looking down the shoreline. There must be twenty of the mills in view, their stone arches soaring into the air—tall as cathedrals! The sunlight is bright in the foreground, but everywhere else is dark because a storm is moving in. The sea is roiling against the seawalls, and you can just make out the crews in the closest windmills, reducing the amounts of canvas on the blades. It's a large painting, but even up close the people look like ants."

"I saw them once . . . as a boy. That was a sight, I can tell you. They bore the Tinker's mark. Can you imagine?" asked Keegan, his eyes twinkling. "Tinkers! Working on Dain! You can be sure no one from Dain ever saw *those* plans! For that matter, I doubt any one Tinker was privy to all of it—they're such a secretive bunch. And the Dain who stayed on to run them were a strange, secret lot themselves. So much that you would have thought they'd been infected with the Tinkers' arcanum."

"What's that?"

Keegan thought for a minute. "In your uncle's tales, the Tinkers are a taciturn but still productive race. They choose to communicate sparingly, but understand the benefits of trade with others in the Moon Realm. In times of need, they could even be described as . . . helpful."

Ebb's words came back to Lily. "'Given the proper tools and materials, a Tinker can build anything. They have no word for impossible.'"

"That I wouldn't know. You see, the Tinkers *I* know about are secretive to a fault, unable or unwilling to communicate, and incapable of sharing so much as their name. They all suffer from the same malady: the Tinkers' arcanum."

"Sounds like more of Wrengfoul's work."

"A distinct possibility."

On Jasper's seventh birthday, Uncle Ebb had given him three Tinker figurines. Jasper had named them Think, Thank, and Thunk. In the stories she and her brother invented, Think, Thank, and Thunk would have been appalled by the behavior Keegan described. In their stories, the three Tinkers would often save the day, using one of their wonderful devices to get the other figurines out of some troublesome spot at the last second.

"So . . . all the windmills are gone?" asked Lily.

"I haven't been since they were destroyed, but my understanding is that only the stone foundations—the arches and piers—still exist.

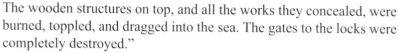

The wooden structures on top, and all the works they concealed, were burned, toppled, and dragged into the sea. The gates to the locks were completely destroyed."

"What happened to the people?"

"They moved east to the costal city of Warsh. They carved out their own place there and keep very much to themselves, even after all this time."

"Why didn't they ever come back?"

"Allegedly, the serpents responsible for destroying the windmills still survive. And in numbers great enough to attack again should any-one attempt to rebuild." Keegan stopped and pointed at a stand of tall trees. "These will do," he said, before cupping his hands and making a loud noise that sounded like a summoning. The moon coin failed to translate it.

After a long silence, Lily heard the approach of wingbeats. A dark shape entered one of the trees, rustling the limbs.

"Greetings, Keegan," spoke a deep voice. "What can I do for you this night?"

"Greetings, my friend." Keegan spread his arms wide. "I have a very important message for the Lady Ember of Bairne. Can you help?"

"You need only ask."

"Good. Tell her she is needed at Tavin's home by midnight tomor-row. It is of the utmost importance that she be there. Tell her Dubb sends for her."

"Easily done. Anything else?"

"Yes, but not for you. Go."

The branch of the tree dipped low, and the sound of flapping wings faded into the night.

Now the healer called again, and another messenger arrived. Keegan sent word to a Lady Mairwen of the Royal House duBair, explaining where and when Lord Nalren would arrive and that provi-sions were needed for stabling two very fine horses. Keegan leaned more heavily on Lily's arm. "Let's get back to the house, shall we?"

In the kitchen, Keegan poured two cups of tea, pulled out two chairs, and sat down heavily in one of them.

"Who's Lord Nalren?" asked Lily, taking the other seat.

"In time. First, I want to hear about Tavin. What spooked you and Dubb so?"

Lily stared down at her tea. A sudden suspicion arose in her: Nima was looking into Tavin's mind in the next room . . . using tea.

Keegan seemed to sense this, saying, "Sometimes, Lily, tea is just tea." He smiled politely.

Lily took a sip from her mug.

"He tried to kill me."

Keegan laughed at that, but as he looked into Lily's face, his mien slowly changed from indulgence to disbelief.

"Forgive me. I don't mean to laugh at you, but what you say makes *no* sense. I've known Tavin since he was—oh, much younger than you. He couldn't have tried to kill you. If he had, then you would most certainly be dead. Trust me."

Lily took another sip and stared at Keegan.

"I see no sword at your belt," continued Keegan. "You seem rather young to be a master swordswoman . . . and even if you were, you would not be *Tavin's* master with the blade—"

"He tried to kill me . . . with a spell."

Keegan's face registered his disbelief. He sat up a little straighter. "No, Lily, you *must* be mistaken. Tavin is—"

"Dragondain, yes, I know—whatever *that* means." Lily explained exactly what had occurred when Tavin escaped. Keegan looked more and more puzzled as she described Tavin's actions as he worked on Arric's ward. Several times he opened his mouth to speak, only to close it wordlessly a moment later. When Lily finished, the two sat in silence, sipping their tea.

"Curses don't throw spells, Lily. . . . *People* throw spells," murmured Keegan.

"I agree: it was Tavin." Keegan winced. "Who's Lord Nalren?"

Lily asked again.

Keegan smiled. "You know him as Dubb."

"He's a lord?"

"Of the Royal House duBair. A venerable family."

"And the Lady Mairwen?"

"His wife. They have two children: Darce, who is perhaps a year older than you, and Teague, who must be, oh, entering his eleventh year, or so."

"Does he . . . own a castle or something?"

"Or something, but his lands, as with all the lords, are now in the wastes, making it more of a title than anything. Oh, they get to live in the upper reaches of Bairne, and they *are* technically part of the court, but not the part currently in favor. Mind you, his time spent with his old friends from the Dragondain would be frowned upon, hence the alias Dubb."

"So it's a secret? That he was in the Dragondain?"

"Oh! By the moons, no. Lord Nalren's captaincy is renowned. It's the current company he keeps that is secret."

"You mean Tavin and the rest."

"Mostly just Tavin. But don't think less of Dubb for it. Publicly distancing yourself from a cursed person is a very wise decision."

"I'll say," Lily agreed.

"So," Keegan began, "Dubb tells me you're a relation of Lord Autumn? Is this true?"

"He's my uncle."

"You do bear a strong family resemblance."

"So you know my uncle?"

Keegan nodded. "Yes, all my life."

Lily narrowed her eyes at Keegan. "How—"

"My father and mother knew him very well." Keegan glanced up to the ceiling in a moment of thought. "My mother met him through her aunt's father-in-law, now that would have been . . ."

Lily shook her head. "You must have the wrong person, Keegan.

My uncle is, like, forty-something."

"And how old are you, Lily?" asked Keegan, as he examined a nail that he had been chewing a moment before.

"I'm thirteen."

Keegan wedged his fingernail between his teeth again, lost in thought.

"Hmmm," he said, after a time. "Interesting . . . so are you the younger one, or the older one?"

Having a brother so close in age, Lily was not unaccustomed to this question. But considering she'd made no mention of Jasper to anyone on Dain, it struck her as out of place.

She had a thought. "Uncle Ebb has talked about us?" she asked, nodding encouragingly.

Keegan's eyes remained on his nails.

"Terrible habit," he began, "biting one's fingernails." He made a weak smile.

"Keegan . . ."

Keegan cleared his throat, shifted in his chair, and then stood, using his cane.

"Time for bed, I think."

Lily stood, too. "He *has* talked about us, right? That's how you know I have a brother?"

"A brother? Very nice." Keegan motioned for Lily to follow. "I have a nice room for you down this hall, one I use for guests."

"My brother is twelve months older than I am," said Lily flatly.

Keegan turned and regarded her as she approached him. "Your uncle, in personal matters, is famously tight-lipped." Lily took Keegan's arm to steady him better. "Although quite the opposite in everything else, and never more so than in all things to do with tale telling." Keegan's face softened.

"You call them tales? Not stories?" asked Lily.

"Oh, yes," said Keegan, a mercurial glint in his eyes. "There's a difference, you know."

"Yes, I do. So, are you saying you believe they're true?"

"Every one. My favorite is one I heard secondhand—well, *over-*heard, really." Keegan leaned forward. "It was the one about . . . The Mermaid and the Sea Jewels."

"The Mermaid—" began Lily, suddenly very excited. "And the Sea Jewels. I've never heard that one!"

Keegan's face fell. "Pity. I was rather hoping you could tell it to me."

"I don't understand. Didn't you say you knew it?"

He tipped his head back in thought. "We were celebrating a rare, lunar alignment. There were many people here, of all ages. It was late, and I'd had a bit much to drink. I had just sat back to rest before the fire when I heard a familiar voice in the next room, a woman's voice. She was telling the tale to some children, I suppose. I—I just couldn't place the voice, but I remember very clearly, at the time, thinking it was one of the grandest tales I'd ever heard. Unfortunately, by the morning, I couldn't have told you half of it. I have never attempted to repeat it—retelling one of your Uncle's tales badly is nothing short of criminal. Sometimes, I wonder if I just slipped into the twilight of sleep. Could I have simply imagined it? Is that why no one else knows the tale?"

"If you could narrow down who was—"

"I know, I know. I've given the matter a great deal of thought, questioned the likely suspects the next morning, even talked to the children. But alas, some things in this life are just meant for the moment.

"At any rate, as regards *your* personal matters, I think you would do well to remain as tight-lipped as your uncle. At least, until you know whom you can trust, and just as importantly, whom you can't."

"I trust Dubb," said Lily.

"Ah! Yes, Dubb would be a good choice . . . if not for Tavin."

"What do you mean?"

"Dubb has known Tavin all his life, trusted Tavin all his life. They are like brothers. And there's the rub. If I'm not mistaken, all that has changed now, or is going to very soon. Even Dubb will have a difficult time reckoning it, Lily. They trust each other with their very lives, all of that bunch do. Oh, this is going to be bad, very bad. Dubb will need to find a balance."

"And the Lady Ember? Can I trust her?"

"Ember—" Keegan grimaced. "I'm afraid Ember has not trusted Tavin in a very long time. But she trusts Dubb . . . who . . . trusts Tavin." Keegan shrugged his shoulders. "Which makes this all very complicated. You will need to keep your wits about you."

Keegan opened the door to a small room not unlike the one Tavin and Nima were occupying. "This will be a good place for you to sleep until morning. Good night."

Leaning in, he added, "And Lily, I don't recall Lord Autumn ever mentioning any kin. I can only conclude that he never intended you to be here. Or possibly," he mused, "he didn't intend for you to be here *now*." And he closed the door.

Lily reached up and slid home the heavy iron bolt on her side of the door. She used the wash basin in the corner of the room, and dried her face with a coarse towel. She placed Ebb's necklace under her pillow and quickly undressed. Sliding into the sheets, she was happy to find they were not nearly as scratchy as they looked, but they were cold and took a long while to warm up. Shivering, Lily reviewed the day's events. Her biggest questions kept leading back home.

Where is Ebb? What do Mom and Dad know? Is Ebb really our uncle?

Lily's thoughts wandered back to Ebb's bedtime tales. *The Mermaid and the Sea Jewels.* He'd told tales to other children that he hadn't told to her or Jasper? Lily fought down a pang of jealousy. She willed herself back to her younger days, back to their shared room, back to where it all began. They would huddle together in one bed and hang on every word: pulling the covers over their heads during the scary parts, bounding about on their knees acting out scenes during the exciting parts. Lily concentrated hard, trying to imagine *all* the tales. She could see Ebb, sitting on the edge of the bed, wearing his coat of many pockets. For some tales, he produced the most amazing little props from those pockets—props that had, at the time, seemed like magic.

Of course, when they were older, after Ebb had told his tales and left for the night, they argued about the sleights of hand necessary to make Ebb's props work. Jasper wasn't always able to explain them away logically, and Lily clung to the possibility of magic. It wasn't until they were older still that they both admitted there was no such thing as magic—just sleight of hand.

But why, wondered Lily, were so many of the tales wrong? Why weren't the Rinn and the people of Dain friends? Why were the dragons crazed, bloodthirsty beasts? Where was their intellect? Why were there only land dragons? Where were all the winged ones? Who was this Wrengfoul? And what of Darwyth? Never had Ebb spoken of it as a dead world—quite the opposite.

These were the questions Lily thought about as she drifted off to sleep, but if her subconscious mind had any answers for her, it did not reveal them in her dreams.

ɣ˙ʾ⸲ˌɣ˙˙ ⸲ˌɣ˙ʾ⸲ˌ ɣ˙ʾ⸲ˌɣ˙˙

She woke to a soft knocking at her door. The room was even colder now.

She leapt out of bed, stiff-limbed, and pulled her cold clothes on, making sure to tuck the necklace under her shirt before approaching the door, to which she briefly placed her ear.

She opened her mouth to speak, but then an image of Tavin flashed before her eyes: Tavin, covered in gore.

"Lily?" came a muffled female voice.

Lily waited.

"Please open the door. It's Nima." The specter of gory Tavin vanished.

Lily shot the bolt and took a step back. Nima hurriedly entered, closing the door behind her. She looked exhausted and excited at the same time.

"Listen, Lily. We're about to wake Tavin, but there's something we want to know, and we need your help to figure it out."

"What?" asked Lily, shrinking.

Nima placed her hands on Lily's shoulders, looking her straight in the eye.

"Lily, I've quickened Curse's release of him, of that I'm certain. But I find nothing of you in Tavin's memories. We want to do a little test. Are you game?"

"For what?"

"At breakfast, we want you to sit at the table just as though you belonged—like you were one of us. All we want is to see his reaction to you. Will you do it?"

"Will Dubb be there?"

"Of course."

Lily hesitated.

"Lily," Nima continued, "if Tavin doesn't remember you, then you don't have *him* to fear—"

"—just Curse," said Lily.

"Yes! Just Curse," said Nima encouragingly.

"You know they're kind of a package deal, right?" asked Lily.

"Yes, but Curse can only take him in the wastes. Otherwise, he's fine. You're safe here, and you'll be safe in Bairne."

"All right, I'll do it," Lily mumbled, already regretting it.

The big wooden table from the night before was now set with serving plates piled high with fruits, sausages, eggs, and little flat cakes that looked a lot like pancakes. There were cups and silverware at every setting and big clay jugs at either end. Lily recognized some of the people at the table: Keegan; Pippa, the young girl who had greeted them on their arrival; Dubb. She guessed that the old woman next to Keegan must be his wife, but there were two others she didn't know.

Dubb stood at once on seeing them, motioning to the empty chair between him and Pippa. Everyone looked a bit nervous, except Dubb, whose freshly scrubbed face showed nothing but warmth and normality.

"Sit. Sit," said Keegan, speaking quickly. "Lily, this is my wife, Jessa; my granddaughter, Tam; and her husband, Aiden."

Lily tried to retain the names, but she had a hard time taking her eyes and attention off Nima as she disappeared down the hall to Tavin's room.

A moment later, Tavin's voice sounded loudly, and the table went silent. All eyes turned to the hall. Next came Nima's raised voice. Keegan and Dubb exchanged glances. It sounded like an argument. Dubb's hand dropped to the grip of his sword. Tavin burst out of the little room, limping heavily, but moving under a full head of steam. Lily saw Dubb tense in his chair, as if he were about to bolt out of it and leap over the table.

"No!" shouted Tavin. "The leg is fine!"

Dubb relaxed and suppressed a chuckle. He reached out a hand for one of the platters, and as if on some prearranged signal, everyone at the table started talking and passing around food.

Nima herded Tavin through the main room and toward the table.

"It's not fine," said Nima, sounding concerned. "It's a very bad cut, and you should let me have a better look at it!"

Lily thought she sounded genuinely angry, but when Tavin was taking in all the faces at Keegan's table, Nima caught Lily's eye and gave her a wink.

There were only two empty seats, both opposite Dubb, which meant that Nima would be sitting next to Tavin, a situation that did not appear to please him.

Keegan didn't stand. "Tavin, you're up!" he said merrily.

Tavin nodded and thanked him, but he seemed a bit lost and self-conscious as he pulled out his chair, wedging his stiff, injured leg under the table. He was wearing the dragon-scale breeches and a coarse, grimy shirt that might have once been white. There was a distinct line of demarcation just above his collar bones from where Nima had washed him the night before. His face and neck were clean; everywhere else he was covered in grunge. His sword, ever present, was belted to his side. Lily stiffened at the sight of it.

As Nima took her seat, she turned away from Tavin, placing her hand over her nose.

"For the love of moonlight, Tavin," she said, under her breath, "you could use a good washing."

"Nima!" snapped Keegan. "*After* he's eaten."

Tavin, barely raising his head from his chest, accepted a platter and began filling his plate. He said his thank yous softly and kept eye contact to a minimum, staring mostly into his breakfast.

"You could cut him some slack, Nima; after all, it's not every day you slay a dragon," said Keegan.

Tavin froze mid-chew, casting an alarmed glance at Dubb. Lily turned in Dubb's direction, ostensibly to grab a piece of fruit. But her real plan was to catch a glimpse of Dubb's face, which turned out to be too difficult to read.

"Well," began Dubb, splitting and buttering a roll, "it certainly began as a group effort. But it was Tavin who took the devil down with a single stroke."

Tavin choked on a piece of food. As he reached for his mug, Nima gave him a few good thumps on the back, then withdrew her hand, making a face. She threw in a few more thumps before giving up and setting to work on her dirtied palm with a napkin. Lily and Pippa laughed.

Nima glanced at them, gravely at first, and then she too started to laugh. Tavin paid no heed to their amusement. His face had gone pale at the turn in the conversation.

"Is that so, Tavin?" asked Jessa.

Tavin dabbed his napkin to his lips.

"Uh—" he began, glancing up at Dubb with large, appealing eyes. Dubb, for his part, let him hang.

"I, uh . . . well . . ." Tavin squirmed in his chair, fighting to remember something, anything.

Lily watched Dubb subtly touch his pinky finger to his heart while dabbing a napkin to his chin. It was a deft move. If she hadn't been watching him carefully, she was certain she would have missed it. Tavin blinked back a look of shock. He placed his open hand on his chest, subtly mouthing the word "me?" to Dubb, whose eyes flashed slightly larger in response.

Tavin, regaining some small amount of composure, said, "Really, Dubb is too kind. It was most certainly a *group* effort. And any one of us could have landed the . . . the—" Tavin glanced to Dubb, his voice becoming more uncertain, "—fatal blow to its heart?"

Dubb confirmed this to be the case, and grim congratulations issued from all directions. Tavin expressed gratitude to everyone in turn, sneaking glances of disbelief toward Dubb whenever possible.

After that, the conversation turned to other, more mundane topics, and Tavin began to look more at ease. He was taking a relaxed pull from his mug when Nima leaned forward and announced excitedly to the table, "And he singlehandedly destroyed an entire dragon clutch!"

Tavin spewed his drink onto his cuff and began choking again.

"That's how he injured his leg!" she added, nodding.

He continued coughing. This time, Nima grimaced and made an icky-waving gesture, unable to bring herself to thump his dirty back again.

Tavin pushed himself away from the table. He examined the injured leg, prodding the wound with newfound interest. Breathing through his mouth, shoulders bowed, he appeared anxious and confused. Lily glanced at Dubb and saw that he looked pained.

"Tavin?" said Keegan. "You're not going, are you? You haven't even finished your breakfast."

Tavin's eyes darted here and there as though looking for something.

"Not hungry, Keegan." He lifted himself from his chair and staggered away from the table toward the mud room, and then he was gone.

Nima, obviously conflicted about the play they had just put on, threw down her napkin and rose to follow.

"No," hissed Dubb, "let him go."

Keegan turned to Dubb. "What are you thinking?"

"I've seen that look before," said Dubb. "Tavin has no idea what's going on."

Keegan turned to Nima. "What say you, child?"

"If he has any memories of the past few days, then Curse has hidden them beyond my power."

Lily thought this made an impression on Dubb, who pushed himself from the table.

"Lily, after you finish your breakfast, make sure you're ready for travel."

"So soon?" said Keegan.

"He should spend the day here," said Nima.

Dubb nodded. "I agree. But he's unsettled, and when Tavin's unsettled he is . . . harder to predict. If he decides to leave in a hurry, there won't be any stopping him. I want to be ready."

"But where are you going?" asked Keegan. "You haven't finished, either."

"I think Tavin's gone to the creek to bathe."

"Thank the moons," said Nima, under her breath.

"I'm going to join him," Dubb continued. "I'll try to occupy his mind with other things. He'll have questions, but I fear my answers will only make him more restless. He'll want to be in Bairne. He knows he can think in Bairne."

"Dubb," said Nima, her voice now full of concern, "keep him there for a while, will you? Don't take him out into the wastes again so soon."

"That won't be hard. When Bairne learns a dragon's been slain, they'll want a celebration, and Tavin will want to lurk among the crowds. Somehow . . . it helps." Halting at the entrance to the mud room, Dubb glanced back to the table. "Cruel, isn't it? How the thing that heals him the most is the one thing he must hide from."

To Bairne

L ILY followed Dubb like a second shadow. The steps cut into the
hillside were large, making the descent swift. Lily could see Tavin
at the bottom of the hill, with two horses and a pile of gear. How he
had transported all the gear was a mystery. But as Lily was quickly
learning, mysteries had a way of popping up around Tavin, and as
with the severing of a hydra's head, solving one only meant two more
would take its place.

"I'll take good care of them, I promise," he was saying.

"Keegan did *not* give you permission to take Wax *or* Wane!"
shouted an angry Pippa.

Tavin's hair and hands were now noticeably cleaner. He had been saddling one of the horses when Pippa discovered him. He stood uneasily before her wrath, his dark, tangled locks already mopping up the dust on his dirty armor.

The steps ended, and Lily got her first good look at the horses. Unlike the poor animal they'd ridden from Perch, these two were magnificent. Dubb's eyes shone appreciatively as he ran his fingers through Wane's thick mane.

Tavin let a pack drop to his side and leaned toward Pippa, displaying one of his most charming smiles.

"Of course he did. Do I look like a horse thief to you?"

"He did *not* say, *take* Wax or *take* Wane!"

Tavin waved nonchalantly toward the main house.

"If you feel so strongly about it, go ask him yourself. Keegan will tell you."

"And have you run off? I think not!"

Tavin looked genuinely taken aback. Placing an open palm to his chest, he said, "I have no intention of running off. Besides, look at all this baggage that needs to be stowed." Tavin waved at the packs strewn about him. "I couldn't possibly prepare these horses before you get back."

Pippa eyed the baggage doubtfully. There *was* quite a lot of it.

"Dubb—" she began.

"Oh, no, Pippa," said Dubb, raising his hand defensively. "Don't get me involved in this,"

Pippa narrowed her eyes at Tavin, squared her little shoulders, and pointed a finger at him. "If you leave while I'm gone," she began, her blue eyes sparkling with cold vengeance, "you will live to regret it, dragonslayer." She spit out the last word like a curse.

Then Pippa turned on her heel and dashed up the steps, but not without looking back several times.

Speaking through clenched teeth to hide the fact that he was talking, Tavin said, "Do you think she'll double back on us?"

Dubb, who was also tracking Pippa, smiled through his own

clenched teeth. "Personally, I think you'd have an easier time stealing a faerie's shadow."

"I knew I could count on you," said Tavin.

The instant Pippa stepped out of sight, he leapt back to Wax's saddle and finished tightening the girth strap.

"Oh, so now *I'm* helping *you* steal the faerie's shadow?" asked Dubb.

He shot a look at Lily. "This is *always* how it starts." He snatched up a blanket and began saddling Wane. Their hands moved with an efficiency that Lily had previously thought possible only in highly-trained Indy 500 pit crews.

"The only way I'd be helping would be if we were stealing *back* the faerie's shadow from the one who stole it in the first place."

"A good deed?" grunted Tavin as he tied down another pack.

Dubb adjusted Wane's bridle. "Best kind."

"For a faerie?" added Tavin.

"No faster way to improve your luck."

"*I* could use some good luck."

"Don't I know it."

"Whoa!" said Lily. "What are you doing? Are you stealing these horses?"

Dubb turned to face Lily, but his hands continued their swift work.

"No, of course not," said Dubb. "What do you take us for— common horse thieves?" He looked at Tavin. "You at least *talked* to Keegan, right?"

"Yes, yes, yes," said Tavin, lacing down a saddlebag and motioning for Lily to hand him another. "No."

Dubb hissed through his teeth. "Damn your darkward soul, Tavin," he grumbled.

"Keegan did say he would take care of that nag we rode in. Although I must admit, even *I'm* having trouble reckoning how that entitles us to Wax and Wane."

Lily stopped handing Tavin baggage. "So you *are* stealing them!"

she accused indignantly.

Dubb hoisted another pack to Wane's saddle. "And if we can't get them back? Can you reckon that?"

"Can I reckon Keegan's punishment for us? . . .We'd make it up to him."

"You mean like . . . the last time?" asked Dubb flatly.

Tavin bit his lip. "Have you ever seen a finer-looking horse?" he asked, patting Wax's flank.

Dubb ignored him, but Lily cast an appraising eye as she stepped closer. "Wow. They really are magnificent, aren't they?"

Suddenly she shook her head, as if trying to break a spell. "No. This is wrong."

Tavin fit his last bag into place and pulled himself into the saddle as best he could with his wounded leg. He'd had a head start, and a little help from Lily, but Dubb had been no slouch, finishing just seconds behind Tavin.

Tavin turned Wax northeast and was about to apply his spurs when he noticed that, although Dubb had mounted his horse, he was stalling.

"Come on, man! The moons don't wait!" urged Tavin.

Dubb held out his hand to Lily. "Come on."

Lily crossed her arms. "I will *not* be part of horse stealing."

Tavin brought Wax closer. "What's going on?" he asked, astonished. "What? Is this a passenger service now?"

His face darkened, his demeanor changing. "You don't expect her to ferry these horses back alone, do you? Healer or no, she's just a girl! What if she wandered into a hive of leech beetles, or met up with a full-grown eetle?"

Lily gave Tavin a hard look. His sudden concern for her safety meant nothing to her.

"You two were fast, but Pippa's sure to be back any second. She'll see you," said Lily.

"Good point," said Dubb. "I'm a bit surprised myself that she's not back already."

Tavin glanced to the main house. "Perhaps Keegan is . . . stalling for us," he suggested, somehow managing to keep a straight face.

"Ha! And why would he do something like that?" asked Lily in irritation.

"Why, Tavin, I do believe you've stumbled onto something," remarked Dubb.

"You can't be serious!" Lily threw up her hands in frustration.

"On the contrary," said Dubb gravely. "I think from Pippa's delay, we can easily derive Keegan's tacit approval."

Lily threw up her hands in frustration. And with that, Dubb wheeled Wane in a tight circle, reached out his hand, and plucked Lily up by the forearm.

"No!" she screamed, but as Wane continued to come about, Dubb locked Lily in place with an arm that may as well have been a bar of iron, while applying his spurs to Wane's flanks. Before Lily could say or do another thing, they bolted away, and unlike the ride on Nimlinn, this one was bumpy.

Dubb and Tavin ran out Wax and Wane for far longer than Lily thought they should, testing and measuring the horses' strength and prowess. They took turns chasing each other as though they were boys at play rather than grown men. Lily scowled her disapproval even as she sensed that Wax and Wane were enjoying the romp more than anyone. They truly were magnificent animals, and Lily felt chagrined that she wanted a turn at the reins herself.

After an hour or so, they slowed. Tavin moved up from behind, and they took the road—or what passed for one—two abreast.

"Not trying to lose me, are you?" Tavin chuckled.

Dubb was silent. Lily, still angry at the both of them, stared off into the distance. She had not spoken a single word since they left. When Tavin offered her water from a skin, she refused, even though she was thirsty.

The two men dismounted and walked the horses down the trail in silence for some time before Tavin finally spoke.

"Dubb? I've got to tell you something. Something you probably already know, but certainly not to what degree."

Dubb eyed his friend, but said nothing.

Tavin took a deep breath. "I don't remember anything about fighting a dragon."

Dubb snorted. "Tell me, Tavin, what *is* the last thing you remember?"

"That's hard to say. I remember bits and pieces, but placing them . . ." He shook his head. "I remember being in old rooms. Old Wizard Mingan's place?"

"Is that a guess?"

"I remember riding there. Ember had sent us to take rubbings, but . . . I don't remember leaving. At least, not well. What I mean is, I remember some things that must have happened after we left, but just small moments. Did we get what Ember wanted?"

"Yes, but we can talk about that later. We have more pressing needs."

Lily listened to Dubb tell, in remarkable detail, everything that had happened to them from the day his band had left Old Wizard Mingan's until the night Lily showed up. To her surprise, Dubb allowed Tavin to interrupt freely. When Tavin learned he'd paralyzed Lily, he grew agitated, and he was further shaken when Dubb described how easily Tavin had passed through Arric's ward.

After another long period of silence, they remounted their horses, setting a pace Lily felt was faster than necessary, especially considering the horses were on *loan*. She was relieved when they exchanged Wax and Wane for fresh horses at the home of another healer. The horses they received in trade were nothing like Wax and Wane, but they were far better than the nag they had ridden from the ruins of Perch to Keegan's.

Once they left the healer's, the terrain opened up into hilly moors, and Lily caught sight of mountains each time they crested a hill. A swiftly moving stream crisscrossed their path. They forded it where the water was not so deep, but twice crossed crumbling bridges that looked far too large for the wispy trails that led to and from them.

Eventually, the moors gave way to an ascending plain, with the mountains a constant backdrop. As the shadows of the horses stretched longer, the character of the mountains changed. Their dull slate faces turned orange in the day's waning light. Dubb pointed out to Lily the remnants of Bairne's outermost walls, scattered here and there like great broken teeth. He explained how the walls had once protected the fertile valley beyond, which cut deeply into the mountains, providing a rich pocket of soil for fields and pastures.

The stream was now a constant companion, and as the sun slipped under the horizon, the moons, which had been clearly visible in the daytime sky, brightened markedly. The moons created deep shadows, and Dubb and Tavin urged the horses to a quicker pace as they entered the valley. In less than an hour, they were skirting the tall remnants of what must have been at one time a strongly fortified wall. In the moonlight, Lily judged the valley to be several miles wide, surprisingly flat, and filled with fields.

As the valley narrowed, the view of moons and stars became more constrained. Black shadows swallowed large portions of the landscape. Lily could smell burning wood. Smoke hung over the fields. As they progressed, she noticed more complete walls forming on either side of the valley.

Tavin raised a hand, bringing both horses to a stop. After several minutes passed, he quietly led them off the road and into a field. The walls to their right vanished in the haze. Light spilled through gaps in the wall head, stretching toward them across the flat fields, and Lily began to make better sense of the landscape.

Tavin steered them through the deepest parts of the shadows, keeping well away from the light. Behind the walls, Lily could see lamps hanging from the upper stories of houses. As they got closer, she could see that where the breaks in the walls were widest, even the houses shied away, as though the buildings themselves were afraid of the open gaps. Dubb tapped Lily on the shoulder.

"Here begins the walled city of Bairne," he whispered. "These walls, such as they are, run along both sides of the valley, their repair improving as they go. At the end of the valley lies the city proper, where the streets are wide and well-lit."

"So this is where the poor live?" asked Lily.

"Yes."

Lily eyed the long broken wall stretching into the distance. "Why so many?"

"They came from Perianth with all they could carry on their backs. The original builders of Bairne never expected to house the fleeing population of Perianth. Tavin will part company with us here, where there are no eyes of royal importance."

Above the rooftops, Lily could see the ghostly lights of houses built right into the mountainside, looming in tiers. These higher homes were of stone, and even from this distance, Lily could tell they were in far better repair than the lower ones.

Thirty feet from the wall, Tavin slid off his horse and walked it over to Dubb, reins held high. Lily sensed a routine and imagined they had performed this handoff hundreds of times.

"Where is he going?" asked Lily.

"Shh!" hissed Dubb.

But Lily felt anxious at the idea of not knowing where Tavin was. "Where is he—"

Tavin held a finger to his lips. "We can't afford to be seen together."

As Dubb removed a gauntlet, Lily leapt down from the saddle and snatched Tavin's reigns. She held up her left foot. "Help me up," she commanded.

Tavin's eyes widened. "Do you even know how to ride a horse?" he said softly.

"Yes," she whispered.

Frowning, Tavin glanced from Lily to Dubb.

"Do you ride . . . well?" asked Tavin delicately

"As well as you," she snapped. "Now help me up."

He gave one last look at Dubb, who shrugged. Tavin quickly side-stepped Lily's upraised foot, catching her about the waist and lifting her into the saddle as though she were a five pound bag of flour. If he had moved more slowly, or given her time to think, Lily would have screamed. But in a trice, Tavin had cut loose a small pack from the back of the saddle and disappeared into the shadows.

Dubb slowly brought his horse about, motioning for Lily to do the same. It did not take the horses long to find the road again.

Lily pulled alongside Dubb.

"In a mile or so lies Bryd's Gate, where respectable people enter the city of Bairne," said Dubb in a voice just loud enough for Lily to hear.

"And is that where *we* will enter?" said Lily dubiously.

"No, we will enter at the Gate of Guard, shortly before Bryd's."

"Where the despised and ridiculed enter the city," said Lily.

Dubb chuckled, and Lily saw his teeth flash white in the darkness. "Yes, something like that."

As they drew closer, Lily discerned two great lamps hanging high on either side of a gate barred by an enormous portcullis. Bryd's Gate was an imposing sight.

About a hundred yards shy of the gate, Dubb dismounted and led his horse to a section of wall that lay in shadow. They passed through an opening barely wide enough for the horses and so low that Lily could have touched the ceiling if she'd reached up. Black as pitch inside, the passage wound upward and to the left, and the horses' hooves echoed loudly on the stone flooring. Eventually, Dubb halted.

"Time to dismount. Can you remove your saddlebag?"

"Yes," said Lily, hoping this was true.

"Fasten your cloak about you and pull up your hood." His voice sounded loud in the confined corridor.

After some shuffling, Dubb pounded something heavy on what

she supposed was a wooden door. A small, face-high slat slid aside, and warm light spilled into the passageway. A young boy, rubbing sleep from his eyes, peered out. His eyes opened wide when he saw them. Hurriedly, he slammed the slat shut, and a few seconds later, a door creaked open. The boy stepped into the passage, taking both sets of reins.

"Take these horses to the stables of the Dragondain; send the baggage to the house of the guard," Dubb said gruffly.

"Yes, sir, and who shall I say has sent them?" the young boy asked, still rubbing his eyes.

Dubb leaned forward, his riding cloak hiding his face.

"Tell him it was a moon-wraith, riding in from the wastes."

Startled, the boy took several quick steps backward, pulling the horses along with him.

"This way," said Dubb, extending his arm to Lily. He guided her through the open doorway and down a long narrow corridor to an iron door.

Dubb rapped on the door and spoke through a small hole. Lily heard the sound of bolts being released, and a little square opened. She saw only an eye, briefly, before the square closed again. Larger bolts scraped, and the door swung inward, revealing an old man in worn leather armor.

"What you doin' out this late at night?" he said, sounding both gruff and surprised.

Dubb ignored him and swiftly ushered Lily through several small rooms and passages, finally exiting into the night. They ran down a short flight of narrow steps, moving quickly into a street where few lanterns burned. The buildings here hung over themselves, giving little room for fresh air or moonlight. Many of the upper stories appeared to be connected by short walkways or supports—Lily wasn't sure which.

Dubb swept Lily behind him and drew his blade. "Quickly now," he urged.

The streets were twisted and narrow, and between one lantern and the next, Lily had to listen keenly to keep up with Dubb. He only slowed when approaching darkened alleyways or low overhangs. His sword arm reacted constantly—pointing one way or the other—to the changing dangers and terrain. They moved this way for so long that Lily began to lose her breath.

In a darkened courtyard, they halted at the edge of a gurgling fountain before walking down the first wide street Lily had seen since entering Bairne. The buildings on the left were several stories tall, with the ground floors showing darkened shop windows. To the right ran a row of small houses about ten feet apart. All were built in exactly the same manner out of large stone block.

"These houses were built for the Dragondain—the real Dragondain—a *very* long time ago." Dubb pointed to the fifth one on the right. "That one answers to Tavin."

It was only one room wide and two rooms deep, with the rear room slightly taller. This made for two squat roofs, with the rear one overhanging the front. A long rectangular window occupied the narrow band of wall between the roofs, and a smoking chimney poked up from the very back. Set off to the left was the front door, a great wooden thing, round-arched and bound in iron. The door was illuminated by two niches carved in the stone that framed it. Their shape, and the way they flickered, made them look like two great eyes. Lily wondered if their source of illumination was magical, like the lanterns in the Tomb of the Fallen.

She was still staring at them when Tavin came around the corner and into the pale light, sheathing what looked like a long dagger or short sword. Dubb rammed his own blade into his scabbard, and the three assembled on the doorstep.

"Did you just get here?" asked Dubb.

"No, I stopped in at Cora's and let her know that Quib and all were well."

Dubb tilted his head toward the house. "It looks like Ember is already here."

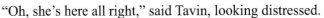

"Oh, she's here all right," said Tavin, looking distressed.

"How do you know it's Ember?" asked Lily.

"The smoke—" Tavin and Dubb said as one, but only Dubb finished, "coming out of the chimney."

"That, and she *also* stopped to see Cora . . . about three hours ago. It must be her."

"So Ember told Cora she was coming here?" asked Lily.

"No," said Tavin softly.

"Then it doesn't *have* to be Ember inside," said Lily. "It could be anybody."

"Not likely," said Tavin.

Lily frowned. "How did she get in?"

"Yes, Tavin," said Dubb, his voice beginning to sound more relaxed, even playful, "tell us how she got in?"

Tavin eyed his house suspiciously. "That's a very good question," he said gravely. "And one for which I have no answer."

"But she's a powerful lunamancer, right?" asked Lily. "Couldn't she force her way in?"

"The problem, Lily," began Tavin in a low voice, "is that this is no ordinary door. This is a house belonging to a descendent of the Dragondain—me—and it is protected by an ancient magic. And ancient magic is not a plaything, even to those as powerful as Ember."

"Maybe she has a key?" offered Lily.

An amused look flashed across Dubb's face.

Tavin smiled and stepped closer to the door. "The only key that can *easily* open this door"—he removed a gauntlet and showed Lily his empty palm—"is this." Tavin grasped the knob. A soft click sounded and the door swung open effortlessly.

Ember

Lily thought the size of the door ridiculous, and the wide entryway beyond it equally so. She could easily have ridden one of the farm tractors through it and not even worried about ducking her head. From the back room, firelight flickered down the hall. Lily peeked in an arched entrance, as big as the street door, leading to the front room. Except for a small cot just inside, the entire room was packed from floor to ceiling with furniture, draped with moth-eaten blankets.

Lily's curiosity spiked. Why was Tavin storing all this in his front room? Was it a lifetime of bounty from their raids in the wastes? Was this his treasure room? Were the drawers and chests stuffed with gold goblets and priceless gemstones, or were they dark and ordinary, full of what the moths ate? What kind of wood was that dresser leg made out of? How old was it all? *A good piece of wood can tell you many secrets, Lily,* Ebb would say, *but only if you know how to listen.*

She wanted to investigate, or, as Jasper would have put it, insnoopigate. But Dubb kept walking, and she felt safe having him between her and Tavin, so she stuck close. The rear room was as wide as the house, but awfully small as Tavin's sole living space. Mismatched furniture lined the room: a long, low dresser; a large, disheveled bed; two wooden chests. Drawn up to the fire was a comfortable chair, and Lily saw another in the corner, where Tavin was using it as a poor man's valet.

As Dubb and Ember greeted each other warmly, Tavin busied himself picking up piles of clothing and stuffing them into the chests. Feeling like an outsider, Lily tried to stay out of sight.

"Did you succeed?" Ember asked Dubb.

Dubb pulled a thick parcel of folded papers from his pack and began unfolding them. "I have them right here."

Ember pushed the papers aside. "By the eight moons! You *know* what I'm talking about. Did you succeed?" she asked more forcefully.

"No, we didn't," said Tavin softly. "The fault is mine."

With a sweep of his arm, Dubb cleared off the top of the low dresser, and placed the unfolded rubbings on it. There were at least a dozen pages, each full with dark script and designs.

The moment Dubb stepped aside, Ember saw Lily and let out a small gasp.

"And what have we here?" she asked.

"Ember," continued Tavin, his voice strained, "I killed it."

Ember's face collapsed. "You killed her?" she echoed tonelessly. "Oh, Tavin, how could you?"

Dubb kept on talking about the smoothed-out papers. "We found them right where you thought they'd be. It was as if you'd been there. I hope they're some help to you. This is your bailiwick, not ours."

Ignoring Dubb, Ember took a step toward Tavin, her eyes glinting with fury. Tavin met Ember's gaze bravely, Lily thought, though he did wince.

"I'm sorry," he said.

"Have you any idea what you've done?"

Tavin began to say something, but then thought better of it, or worse—it was hard to tell.

Ember sank into the chair by the fire and buried her face in her hands. "Such a loss." There was a catch in her voice. When she finally looked up, she settled her eyes on Lily.

"Why is this girl here?" she demanded.

Dubb whipped around and looked at Lily as though he had forgotten she was there.

"Oh, right," he said offhandedly. "Ember, this is Lily, Lord Autumn's niece."

Ember stared at Dubb, puzzled.

"Don't be shy, Lily," said Dubb, "show her."

Lily watched Ember's eyes, which were wide to begin with, grow still wider as Lily carefully pulled out the necklace and revealed the dangling pendant.

"Lily, is it?" said Ember, looking very tense.

"Yes, my . . . lady?"

"Lily, where is your uncle?" she asked sharply.

Lily looked down at the moon coin as though it might hold the answer.

"I don't know. I'm trying to find that out myself," she said.

"But he gave you the moon coin, yes? He showed you how to use it? You and your brother . . . you have been prepared?" she said doubtfully.

"Prepared?" said Lily, nettled. "Wait, you know about my brother?" She held the moon coin farther from her body, as though it were something she no longer wanted on her person.

"I . . . just . . . found it," she said.

Ember's face contorted to something between fascination and

horror.

"You know . . . *nothing?*"

Lily felt her pride rise at the suggestion, even though she knew what Ember was really trying to say.

"Almost, I guess. I mean . . . I've figured out a little of how it works." Lily palmed the pendant and moved her thumb to the fob.

"Wait!" hissed Ember. She jumped up from her chair, but seeing that Lily had stayed her hand, suppressed her initial alarm. By the time Ember crossed the room, her countenance had changed.

"Dubb," she said, "I need to be alone with Lily for a few minutes. Is there something you and Tavin could do for a little while?"

Dubb and Tavin nearly fell over each other trying to get through the hall and out the front door.

After the door shut, Ember turned to face Lily. Lily was tall for her age, and they stood nearly eye to eye. Ember's hair was a beautiful shade of amber that didn't look quite natural. She had wide green eyes, a slender nose, and a face that, below her cheekbones, quickly narrowed to a smallish, attractive mouth. Lily guessed her to be in her early thirties. She looked strong and capable. The gown she wore was gorgeous, made of a purple satin-like material. Lily had seen nothing like it in the Moon Realm so far. It was tailored like something out of a Jane Austen novel, or possibly an earlier style.

"Lily," said Ember in a hushed voice, "you must not show this pendant to *anyone.* Do you understand?"

"Yes."

"Even more importantly," Ember continued, her eyes narrowing with emphasis, "do not *tell* anyone how to operate it. Am I making myself perfectly clear?"

Lily nodded.

"Very well. Now let me explain a few things. But first, you must tell me how you knew to come here. Did Lord Autumn give you instructions?"

A feeling of dread came over Lily, and she wondered if Ember could sense it.

"Lily?"

It seemed unfair that Lily should have to pick and choose whom to trust with so little to go on. She would have preferred having more time. But time was short, and she *needed* to know how to operate the moon coin. She *needed* to get home. Nimlinn trusted Ember. And Lily already trusted Nimlinn with her life. That would have to do—at least for now.

Lily took a deep breath. "Ember," she began, not wanting to finish her sentence, "I . . . I just spun the moons around—"

Ember reeled. Her eyes suddenly dark and wild, she pounced on Lily.

"Lily! You could have been sent *anywhere!* You could have been sent to *Darwyth!* You could have been sent straight into the arms of Wrengfoul!"

Ember's reaction frightened Lily, but she knew that if she didn't tell all of it—now—she might not have the nerve to tell her later.

"Ember, this isn't exactly the *first* place I've been."

A vein popped out at Ember's temple.

"Where did it send you?" she screamed. "Where have you been?"

"Barreth. I've been to Barreth. I met Nimlinn and Greydor and Roan—I met wyflings and wirtles, and I saw the Wornot, and scaramann."

"Scaramann!" moaned Ember. "So it's true—Wrengfoul has moved against Barreth!"

Lily knew exactly how Ember felt. Fear and empathy bubbled up from some locked place deep inside. Finally she was safe, here with Ember, in of all places, Tavin's guardhouse. Now she could finally panic. "They've taken Fangdelve!" she blurted, tears welling up in her eyes. "I saw it happening! I saw the scaramann filling the valley like a black ocean. Nimlinn tried to help me. She tried to get me to someplace safe, but the coin brought me here before Aleron could reach us!"

Ember sat on the edge of the bed. Not knowing what else to do or say, Lily sat beside her and waited. The fire sputtered and wheezed.

Holding the moon coin before her, Lily stared at it forlornly. "I spun it around the second time, too," she added. "When I was on Barreth."

Unable to look at Lily, and still unable to speak, Ember reached out and covered the moon coin with her palm.

Lily's words tumbled out uncontrollably. "I didn't know what else to do. The little moons wouldn't light up. They just stayed golden. At first I thought I might just have to close it again and start over, but after I opened it—"

Ember silently raised her hand from the moon coin and placed it over Lily's mouth.

"*Mumph*," said Lily.

"Shush, child," said Ember, still not ready to meet Lily's eyes.

Without moving her head, Lily allowed her eyes to wander the room. A soft light leaked though the high, rectangular window she had seen from outside. Its panes were so sooty that had it not been propped ajar, she wouldn't have been able to see out at all. Outside, the clouds glowed eerily through the haze of smoke. Lily wondered which moon or moons were hiding behind the gloom.

When Ember finished composing her thoughts, she lowered her hand and spoke calmly.

"The moon coin, when properly replenished, will take you to any of the moons in the Moon Realm, or back to your own."

"You know of my . . . ?" Lily trailed off, suddenly unsure what to say or not say.

"Yes. Now listen. When you're here, it takes less time for the coin to replenish itself if you're traveling to another moon within the Realm. When going back to *your* moon, however, the coin needs much longer." Lily smiled inwardly at the idea of Earth being a moon. "On your world, the coin replenishes fastest of all. I don't understand why—maybe due to an abundance of magic native to your moon."

Lily pressed her lips together tightly. It felt strange trying to hide a grin when she felt so anxious to get home. *Abundant magic? On Earth?*

"Listen carefully—this is a bit tricky. When you leave a moon, the coin will remember the last place you were. Meaning, if you were to leave from this house right now, you would come back *here* when you next returned to Dain. If instead you left from some other location, you would return to that place." Ember touched Lily's chin, making sure she was paying attention. "Do you understand?"

Lily nodded. "So you're saying that if I went back to Barreth, I would return to the Blight Marsh."

"You left from the Blight Marsh?" said Ember, her shoulders sagging.

"That's where the crossover with Taw was."

"How very unfortunate. Then that option for returning to Barreth is closed to you. The Blight Marsh is far too dangerous."

"Then how *can* I return?" Lily asked, but her quick mind had already jumped to the answer.

"You can return by way of crossover, but only if you choose a safer location and make arrangements for friendly Rinn to meet you there."

"Like you do," said Lily.

Ember looked her in the eye. "And what makes you think that?"

"You've visited Clawforge. You'd have been risking your life unless the Rinn thought you were a cub. And you're no cub."

Ember smiled. "You learn quickly. This is good."

"I need to get back to Barreth. Can I go back with you?"

"We'll see."

"How will I contact you?" asked Lily.

"Dubb, or any of the others, can reach me easily. Just make sure that when you leave Dain, you leave from someplace you feel safe coming back to—like home."

"Return *here*?" said Lily, clearly appalled at the thought.

Ember had no idea what was disturbing Lily. "You'll be safe," she explained reassuringly. "I can't think of anyplace safer, or as well hidden. Tavin is rarely here."

Lily wondered if now was the time to mention that Tavin had tried to kill her. But while she debated, Ember continued, "Enough talk. Now let me show you some things."

Ember took Lily's hand, the one holding the moon coin, and pointed one by one to the ten small circles. "This one is yours." Earth's was slightly larger than the others, and next to it was a tiny dot that Lily hadn't noticed before. Annoyance flooded through her. How had she missed Earth's moon when she was sketching the coin? Had it been obscured by the pincer?

Closer to the center was the ring of symbols, each next to its corresponding moon. Ember pointed to each in turn. "Earth, Barreth, Dain, Darwyth, Dik Dek, The Lazy Moon, Min Tar, Rel' Kah, The Secret Moon, Taw. But you already know all of their names. Don't you?"

Lily licked her lips and repeated the rhyme her uncle had taught her and Jasper so long ago:

Conjured Rinnjinn in Fangdelve keep,
 the Rinn of Barreth making.
Pearl of Dik Dek in oceans deep,
 mer-made all for the taking.
Kormor's work, hammer and anvil,
 giants of Min Tar she forged.
Terrible beauty Faerathil,
 in Rel' Kah her dreams she poured.
Three hearts bejewel the crown of Dain
 Dragon, King, and Naramay.
Lazy lives the long life in twain,
 keying a lone memory.

From grove to bird did language fly,
　　fluttering from Taw to Realm.
Tinker's Secret? None to tell.

Darwyth's rising—a wellspring dell.

"'A wellspring dell?'" repeated Ember, tilting her head quizzically. "On Dain, we say, 'Dead moon rising—a paradise fell.'"

"I like ours better," said Lily quietly.

Ember gave Lily a pained smile. "Me too."

"Uncle Ebb rarely spoke of Darwyth. But when he did, he talked of beautiful forests and great oceans." A warmth spread over her as she remembered his face, which was so much like her mother's, and heard his voice in her mind. "He loved the oceans most of all." She gazed up at the open window. "Of course, a lot of things are different in the Moon Realm."

Lily noticed Ember looking at her appraisingly.

"Lily, do you know what your uncle has been up to here?"

"No. Until I arrived on Barreth, I never suspected the Moon Realm was real. All I know I learned from—"

"—bedtime stories," Ember finished.

"Tales," said Lily softly. "Bedtime *tales*."

Ember nodded knowingly. "Tales, yes. I misspoke."

Ember seemed to know so much! It disturbed Lily, and she felt even worse that she was having trouble hiding it, but she composed herself. Hiding things from Ember was going to be even harder than hiding things from her mother. And then it hit her: what did she really know about her mother? Lily fought to remain calm.

"You seem to know quite a bit about my family," Lily continued, "and about me . . . even my brother."

"Your uncle has been working here, in the Moon Realm, for longer than you know."

"Keegan thinks he's been around for over a hundred years," said Lily quickly. "But that can't be. I mean, sure, he's old—like in his 40s—but a hundred? No way."

"I see," said Ember, her eyes filling with mirth. "Well, I can assure you he's far older than forty. And while it's true that I know many things that you don't, I suspect you know the most about your uncle. He only talked about you and your brother once. He said certain things would come to pass long after I was dead."

Ember walked to the dresser and began to examine the rubbings idly.

"Even the wisest predictions fail," she said, almost as though talking to herself. "Would you like to know what I think?"

"Yes, of course."

"I don't think you're *supposed* to be here, not now anyway. And I fear that all your uncle's hard work may be unraveling."

"His work?"

"Yes. His life's work: to see the Moon Realm united. He's been desperate for it, yet very patient and obsessively careful. His disappearance, I think, is a bad omen."

Lily thought about the bedtime tales. Many of them involved the inhabitants of one moon helping another. But was this just Ebb's dream? Was he just making up fanciful stories of how things could be? Or was he telling tales of a past so long ago that no one remembered, a past known only through myths . . . and bedtime tales?

"But you *must* unite!" cried Lily.

"That's your uncle talking," said Ember, distracted by something she saw in the rubbings.

Lily stood, her eyes shining fiercely in the firelight. "You must! You must join together to fight Wrengfoul. You must defeat him and restore the Moon Realm to its proper order."

"And what is its proper order, Lily?" asked Ember quickly. Lily had the sense that Ember was repeating a question she'd asked before,

perhaps even debated. With Ebb? Her father? Her mother? It was a good question. *What is the proper order?* Lily felt an answer forming in her, but she could not articulate it. She hesitated.

Ember peered at Lily from the corner of her eye. "It's not as easy as all that," she said.

"Why? Why don't you all just *do* it? It would be eight moons to one. How could you lose?"

Ember shook her head. "Because we don't trust each other. The only alliance that exists among Dain and her moons is in your and your uncle's heads—and perhaps as bits of myth, uttered long ago and remembered by few. Meanwhile, Wrengfoul is powerful. Having conquered Dain, he has set his sights on Barreth. Even as we speak, his scaramann are overrunning Sea Denn. Barreth has fallen under some foul darkness, and it will last no longer than we did."

"That's not true! *Roan* called down that darkness."

"Roan?" Ember looked puzzled.

"And Greydor himself emptied Sea Denn to fight the scaramann while they cannot see."

Ember considered this, but concluded, "It will not be enough. Wrengfoul will have planned for this possibility. He has foreseen every outcome, and he will win in the end. When he attacked Dain, Lily, he crushed us in a single day. I know. . . . I was there."

"Yes, but you don't believe Dain is truly lost, do you Ember?"

A small spark kindled in Ember's eye, and she looked at Lily with interest. "Time will tell," she mused. "Dain was once a beautiful land—and not so very long ago. She is smoldering now.

"There is goodness here yet," she continued. "But what we need, Lily, is a hero. Someone to bring us together—someone to bring us hope. We *must* drain the fens—we *must* regain Perianth. We must find a way . . . to cure the dragons."

The dragon! thought Lily, remembering how Tavin had heaped all the blame on himself for killing it. She considered telling Ember how things had actually happened: that the dragon had been on the attack, that Curse had taken hold of Tavin, that Curse had delivered the fatal blow. But then Lily remembered something else that had been puzzling her.

"Ember, I saw Andros burst into darkness."

"Did you now," said Ember with interest.

"Yes. And I heard Marred mention something about a ring. I thought the Dragondain couldn't use magic."

"The Dragondain can't perform magic, but they can wield it. The ring Andros bears is one of the nine ambassadorial moon rings—Barreth's, to be precise. But the shield he carries is far more powerful, or was. A frightening thing to behold when fully awakened, but it's been sleepy of—"

"How did he get it? The ring, I mean."

"That's a story for him to tell, if he wishes it. In the meantime, you would do well not to mention it to anyone."

The door opened, and Dubb hurried in, his eyes taking in the room in an instant.

"What's the matter?" asked Ember.

"Tavin hasn't come back?" he replied.

"I thought he was with you."

"No. We split up. We have much to do," Dubb explained. He dismissed his worry. "But I'm sure he's fine. I just . . . thought he would be back by now."

He motioned to the rubbings. "Are these what you were hoping for?"

"Yes," said Ember, shifting her attention. "They may explain a few things."

"Ah!" Dubb exclaimed. "I almost forgot." He dug into a pocket, pulling forth a wad of oiled paper, tied with cord.

Ember peered at the paper wrappings suspiciously. "And what is this?"

"I don't know. It was in a hidden room off Mingan's bedchamber. Arric found the way in, but he was so drained, we had to carry him out.

I actually thought he was going to leave us."

Ember's face showed her consternation. "He shouldn't take risks like that. What could be worth such foolishness?" Pulling loose the string, she unfolded the paper and froze when she saw the small book inside.

"This is Balherk's!" she gasped. "I knew that old wizard would have something special hidden away, but I never would have dreamed . . . did Arric find anything else?"

"No. But we were not the first to search that house. It had been torn apart. Dara took a good look around, but she was worried she might be missing something. And Arric was in no shape to hide the room again. Before we left, he made us burn the place to the ground."

Though pained, Ember nodded. "I'm afraid that was best," she agreed.

Dubb nodded at the book in her lap. "Maybe you can find something in there to repair Andros's shield . . . if indeed Balherk was the one who forged it."

"Dubb," said Ember, as though remembering something. "Speaking of repair . . . I may have made a discovery concerning your sword."

Dubb reached down to his belt and began to unbuckle his scabbard.

"No—not that one. The old one. I'd like to have a look at it when possible."

Dubb straightened, his face unreadable.

"You could see it now, if you wished."

"You mean it's here?"

He nodded. "Can you think of a safer place? The stink of Tavin's curse alone would keep any thief from even *thinking* of breaking in. But what's your idea?"

"I may have found a way to mend it."

Dubb hesitated.

"I won't have you risk yourself unnecessarily. I don't *need* that sword."

"Dain's greatest swordsman deserves Dain's greatest blade."

"I am not Dain's greatest swordsman, not by any means."

"Oh? Then who?"

"I can think of many I would not wish to cross blades with."

"That's only because you are so cautious."

"The Dragondain do not draw blades idly."

"I know that," she allowed. "But if I'm right, there should be no risk."

"And if you're wrong?"

"Then no harm done."

"All right, then," he said, after a time. "I'll get it for you."

Dubb stepped closer to the fireplace and took hold of a long iron poker. He plunged its tip into the red-hot coals, probing for something. With a sudden jerk, the poker jumped forward a few inches and locked into place. Dubb unscrewed its handle a few turns, revealing a small hinge. He bent the handle to make a right angle, fashioning a crank. Slowly, but with great force, Dubb turned the crank. After several full turns, a muffled click sounded underfoot. Adjusting his grip, Dubb moved the poker like a lever from one side of the fire to the other, and a floorboard rose beside the hearth.

"Quick, pull that board upright," he said, his voice straining with effort.

Lily and Ember grabbed the edges of the board, pulling until it locked into place. Dubb let go the poker, which held its position. Kneeling by the raised board, he reached in, retrieving a long bundle of dusty rags that he deposited on the edge of the bed.

Dubb parted the rags, revealing a beautiful scabbard, intricately inlaid in silver and gold. Each of the sword hilt's cross-guards was tipped with a moon: one at three-quarters full and gibbous; the other one-third full and crescent.

Dubb yanked the blade free from the scabbard, laid it back down on the rags, and stepped aside. Unlike the scabbard and hilt, the blade was a wreck. A dark twisting crack, starting near the hilt, ran halfway down the length of the blade, marring inlaid silver and gold runes as it went. Even the blade's edge appeared lifeless and dull.

Lily thought the sword oddly familiar. She had seen many swords since arriving on Dain, but none so finely wrought. Had she seen one like it in the Tomb of the Fallen? She made a mental note to check if she ever got back there again.

Ember formed her peerin.

"I don't understand," Dubb commented. "I thought peerins couldn't show the magic underlying the moon swords or the rings."

"It's true that no one has seen into them with a peerin before," she acknowledged, "but things change. I'm always learning. One can never be certain. However, I'm not planning to use my peerin. I'm just being thorough."

"So if not your peerin, then what?"

"I've learned something very old. And I need something old to test it on. You see, I'm now certain that the moon swords were forged much earlier than commonly thought, and the reason we can't see the underlying magic is that no one knows it anymore. Which would make sense—if no one knows it, who would teach it?"

"You haven't been *experimenting*, have you?" said Dubb warily.

"All lunamancers experiment. It's not dangerous to rearrange the things you understand, trying to build new things . . . usually, anyway. But as I say, I have no intention of using my peerin."

"Then what are you going to do?"

"You'll see soon enough, though I must warn you: it could damage the blade further—although I don't think it will come to that," she added quickly.

Dubb rubbed his chin. "Well," he sighed, "it's useless the way it is now. And the fire that forged it has long been lost. Even if you turned it to dust—what would it matter?"

Ember closed her peerin, and her look changed to what Jasper would later term "Ember's working face." It was deeply contemplative, and not easily distracted.

Ember had studied the damage to Dubb's moon sword before, but she had never attempted to do anything about it. She had learned a great deal since she first pondered mending it. First, she was certain that she had uncovered the sword's true name and, just as importantly, its origin. And there was a third thing—something ancient.

What Ember now contemplated was far different from anything she had ever done before. Despite what she'd told Dubb, there *was* a risk. But she was firmly committed to the attempt. Whether out of guilt for all the dangerous missions she'd sent them on over the years or the desire to repay a debt from her past, she could not say. Perhaps it was simply loyalty to Dubb.

Ember spoke what she believed was the sword's true name, and Lily thought she saw a weak winking of the moons on the cross-guards. The lunamancer placed her finger at the end of the crack nearer the hilt. Dubb walked to the other side of the room, nervously checking the hallway for Tavin.

Suddenly, emanating from where Ember stood, Lily felt a pricking at her senses, and the hairs on her arms rose. Ember had closed her eyes and was making lilting sounds in her throat, not unlike a melody. Dubb came back and peered over her shoulder.

The melody became clearer, and with finger poised on the edge of the crack, Ember hummed, working out something in her mind. Then she spoke a word that Lily had heard many times before: it was *ungelari* the first word of the nonsense poem her mother would say when Lily and Jasper were sick.

She felt the soft pulse of the moon coin, but the translation in her mind sounded like an electric crackle followed by distant thunder. Ember's finger began to slide down the crack. She spoke the second word of the poem, and the moon coin pulsed again. Lily detected a force flowing from Ember. It ignited with her words, growing larger before swirling down a vortex where her fingertip met the blade. Inexplicably, Lily could feel that Ember was now locked to her task—and that she had not expected this.

Ember spoke the third, fourth, and fifth words, each time echoed by the coin like a storm off in the distance. She mispronounced the sixth word, mangling a short syllable. The results were immediate. A spasm of pain gripped her face, and her voice strangled in her throat. Lily felt Ember attempt to slow herself, but what she had started carried her forward relentlessly. She could not turn back. The currents flowing through her had increased. Lily perceived Ember was not just in great pain, but in dire danger as well.

"Ember!" Lily heard Dubb say, but his voice was far away.

Ember did better with the next several words, not stumbling again until the second verse, when she mispronounced another syllable. This time, she fared far worse. She shrieked in pain, trembling all over. Lily felt the flow increase, and she felt a bit of Ember's mind rip loose from its moorings, sucked downward and swallowed by the hungry crack. Her face was drained of color, and for a second, Lily thought Ember would fail, but she rallied, continuing with the second verse of the poem.

Lily couldn't explain the connection she felt to Ember. Somehow she could sense the lunamancer's thoughts. She tried to help Ember focus while also trying to slow her progress. But Ember's fear was mounting. Through some intuition she didn't understand, Lily knew with absolute certainty that Ember might be able to survive one more mistake, but the next would surely end her life. If Lily were to intervene, now was the time. But she could think of no way to help.

Suddenly, Lily felt Ember call up within herself an awesome power, as though preparing for the next time she would fail. Feeling helpless, Lily watched Ember struggle, pausing her finger's march down the crack. She was only a quarter of the way through the poem. Why was she stopping? With a great wrench, Ember turned to Dubb.

"This will not end quietly. You must get to safety. . . . You must take Lily. . . ." Ember's voice sputtered, and her head jerked back to her task. The fight had left her. Ember had used all the power she'd summoned to try and save them—to save *her*.

Knowing that Dubb was a man of action, Lily imagined he would soon scoop her up and run from the room, and Ember would die—her life force and all her knowledge sucked into the crack of this greedy blade. But what to do?

And then it came to her. Without another thought, Lily placed the tip of her index finger on the top of the crack. But when *she* spoke the poem, she spoke it clearly—perfectly—and more quickly. The instant her finger touched the crack, she felt an electric jolt. She became part of the spell, attached to the task as though she had jumped onto an invisible track. In time with every word of the poem, the moon coin pulsed strongly on her chest.

Lily felt Ember attempting to slow her pace again, trying to gather her ebbing strength, but she was failing. They were both speaking the same poem, but in different parts. Worrying that each word Ember spoke could be her last, Lily increased her pace. As she approached the place where Ember had first stumbled, Lily sensed a palpable resistance building against her. Simply continuing took great effort. She summoned her will and leaned into the gale, pressing forward with all her might. Sweat streaked down her face. Ever so slowly, she gained on Ember.

When Lily reached the sixth word, where Ember had made her first mistake, she discerned something like a knot that she knew she must untangle. She passed over the damaged area, shouting out the correct pronunciation of the word that Ember had misspoken. The moon coin thumped upon her chest as she corrected the word, and Lily felt something within the process right itself. Immediately, she felt strength returning to Ember, as though Lily had drawn something back that the crack had taken.

That's one, thought Lily.

Lily dug in for the long fight, and wondered if she'd increased the chances that Ember might survive another mistake. She pushed herself harder. For a short time, the going got easier, until she came to Ember's second—and worse—mistake. Lily prepared herself. She knew the poem perfectly. She knew she would not fail. And yet, at the exact moment Lily attempted the correction, Ember mispronounced another word. In the jolt of confusion, Lily almost stumbled herself. Although it was Ember's fate that tilted in the balance, Lily came to the horrifying realization that continued mistakes could drag them *both* to their doom. But Lily succeeded in saying her word correctly, and Ember, though terribly weakened, held fast.

Lily found it difficult to take her eyes off her own finger after that. She could sense Ember's finger ahead of her, but she was unsure how far. Lily started on the next verse, pronouncing each word loudly and clearly. All the while, her finger inched closer to Ember's: two inches away . . . one inch away . . . and then they were touching.

Now for the hard part, she thought.

Using all her remaining strength, Lily slowly inched her finger onto Ember's, willing Ember not to speak as she herself finished the last verse of the poem. Watching their fingers move as one, as she parceled out the last remaining words, Lily realized that their rate of movement across the crack was somehow related to the length of the poem, and that they would reach the end of the crack just as she spoke the last word.

Which she did.

With an electric shock, Ember lurched backward. Dubb caught her by the shoulders, guiding her to the chair by the fire, where she collapsed.

Lily eyed the blade contemptuously. The hungry crack was unchanged. She felt an inexplicable anger welling up. Wheeling away from the sword, she advanced on Ember.

"Don't *ever* do that again!" Lily spat furiously.

Ember gave Lily a look of bewilderment, but found it too difficult to look directly into her eyes.

"Those words don't belong to you!" Lily heard herself scream.

Ember nodded wearily.

Still seething, Lily examined the pendant, which did not appear any the worse for wear. She thumbed loose the fob, and the moons shimmered silvery white. Lily spun the inner wheel of moons, the now-familiar click sounding as each moon passed the pointer.

"Lily!" said Ember, exhausted. "Where are you going?"

"Home," said Lily. Her anger spent, anxiety crept into her voice.

"When will you come back?"

Lily tried to imagine how her mother and father had been dealing with her long disappearance. No simple trick or fib would get her out of this one. Her parents were no fools. Surely, Jasper would have told them by now about the necklace.

She gave Ember a hard look. "Someone will come, but I doubt it will be me."

Lily spun the ring of glowing circles until Earth was directly underneath the pointer, then snapped the fob closed. A moment later, she was gone.

A Cry in the Night

D UBB stared at the place Lily had been just moments before.

"What do you make of this?" Dubb asked Ember. "Is she safe?"

"For the moment."

Dubb ran his finger over the crack in the moon sword. "Where do you think Lord Autumn could be? Do you think he's alive?"

Ember twisted her hands, which Dubb took as a yes, though she said nothing.

"He's been missing for a very long time," Dubb began delicately. "But you know where he went last, don't you?"

"I need to rest." Ember struggled to stand.

"Wait. There's something else. I probably should have given them to you a long time ago, but I was afraid. You lunamancers are a mysterious lot, but I've made it my business to understand your abilities."

"You mean from a tactical perspective."

"Precisely. Knowledge is power. For example, I'm no master of the two-handed sword. I don't have the wrists for it. You have to be a man half again the size of me to truly master such a weapon. But that doesn't mean I don't know its strengths and weaknesses.

"I understand the knife's edge you walk when you dive deep into your peerins. I've seen what happens when something stored in a peerin for too long goes bad." Ember grimaced. "You know, I didn't *have* to become a Dragondain. It was my right, by blood, but I was not bound to it. I could have chosen the path of the peerin."

"Your father never would have allowed that."

Dubb nodded his head. "And he would have been right to try and stop me. It would have been folly for me not to pursue the blade."

"You would have made a great lunamancer."

"It doesn't matter—I *knew* I would be a greater Dragondain." Dubb paused. "You, Cora, and now her daughters . . . I have watched your progress these years."

"What are you getting at?"

"Do you know what happens to the bearer of a moon sword?"

"The challengers come for you."

"Yes. As they should. If you bear a moon sword, and you want to keep it—"

"You must be the best of the best."

Dubb paused. "There is similar lore for peerins. Is there not?"

Ember looked up quickly. "What have you found?"

Dubb reached once more into the rags that had wrapped the sword, producing a small leather pouch.

"On the day Wrengfoul attacked, after we did what we could to rescue the lower townships from the rising waters, we noticed large band of Wrengfoul's creatures bent on breaching Castle Fendragon.

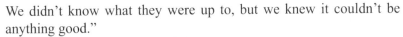

We didn't know what they were up to, but we knew it couldn't be anything good."

"Where were they headed?"

"Down. Down to the burial chambers of the Kings."

"But those chambers are locked by powerful wards. They couldn't have gotten in."

"They had a dwythbane with them, three blackmages, and a dozen other assorted uglies. Tavin and I knew another way to get down there. Tavin has a knack for those passages. He can detect and open secret passages that I can't even see after he's shown me where they are. We put together a small band of our own and went down to intercept them.

"I won't explain it all, but they broke into places we'd never been before. It wasn't difficult to find them, though. They weren't making any effort to be quiet. It was the very first time we'd ever encountered a dwythbane face to face. We lost nearly everyone on that sortie. When it was over, and we started picking up the pieces, Tavin and I came upon two swords. This one here"—Dubb pointed to the moon sword—"and the thing he now carries. We saw them at the same instant, even though they lay a fair way off. We both knew the moon sword on sight, of course; we'd dreamt of them all our young lives. Like little boys, we raced off at once."

Dubb went on. "Tavin was full of tricks, even then."

Ember smirked.

"Well, yes, you would know something of that. I kept a very close eye on him as we ran. I knew it was coming—I could see it in his eye. And he knew I knew. He's like a magician that way. He thrives in chaotic environments: he knows how to create them; he knows how to escalate them." Dubb sat on the edge of the bed, next to the moon sword.

"It was the floor that proved my undoing. He didn't *know* that would be my undoing. In fact, I'm sure Tavin was going to try something else, but he worked to keep my mind and eye distracted. You see, the floor was strewn with bits of bone, shards of rusted metal, all kinds of things, everything covered in cobwebs and dust. I was so concerned with him that I misplaced a step—just one! It wasn't much, really; I would have recovered in a second, but Tavin reacted instantly, making as if to trip me. He could have taken me down, but he correctly judged that I'd've brought him down with me." Dubb laughed. "But it was only a cleverly dealt feint, and so was the next. I lost a little of my balance, then a little more. The next thing I knew I was helpless. Tavin brought me down with a push of two fingers. I tried to take him down, but he'd done his job well and got away free and clear."

"So, Tavin got to the swords first?"

"Yes."

"Then how did you end up with the moon sword?"

Dubb shook his head. "It was the damnedest thing. He picked up the moon sword, leaving the other on the ground, and then . . . he gave it to me—just handed it over. He had that insane grin he gets—"

"I know that grin," said Ember, smiling.

"Then, as I watched, he simply reached down and picked up that wretched blade. It never occurred to me that he would keep it. Next thing I knew, he was unbuckling his old sword—his father's sword—and casting it aside as if it were a piece of junk, buckling on the cursed one in its place. We acted like it was a joke. We laughed a long time over that—too long, what with all that had happened that day. It was two days before we realized the depths of his peril.

"Anyway, there was something else I found that day, something I've never shown to anyone. I thought there would come a time when it would be clear to me who was the greater lunamancer: you or Cora. But then Cora's daughters came along . . ."

"Annora and Bree are uncontrollable. They take too many risks. I fear for their lives."

Dubb smiled. "That's exactly how I felt about you and Cora. When you were Annora and Bree's age," Dubb added quickly.

Ember's gaze drifted to the cracked blade that had nearly killed her. "You're too kind."

Dubb upended the small bag. Four rings fell into Ember's open hand.

"You're going to have to choose which one is the best of you. I can't be the one to decide. I broke them loose from a pair of mummified hands: two on the thumbs, two on the index fingers."

Ember poked at the rings in her palm. "Peerin rings. A full set. Dubb, these must be passed down to work properly. There are things the wearer needs to know. It would be too dangerous to—"

"Look at the runes on them," said Dubb. "There's one on each."

Ember held up one of the rings. "It's not any form of Dainish I'm familiar with."

"They look like trouble to me."

"So why are you giving them to me now, after all these years?"

"Take out Balherk's book." Ember pulled the small volume from her robes. "Turn the spine toward the firelight. Do you see?"

Running down the blue leather spine was a series of small runes embossed in gold. Ember lined up the rings. They matched perfectly.

If it had been anyone but Dubb, Ember would have been amazed that he remembered such a small detail from so long ago.

"They're *Balherk's* peerin rings!"

"You'll find an entire chapter on them in that book. He must have handed them down to someone, who handed them down to someone. Eventually, someone didn't. Instead, they took them to their grave."

Ember gave a weak smile. "I'll show them to Cora. Maybe something in the book will help us make a decision." Then she tilted her head to one side. "Dubb, whatever happened to Tavin's old sword?"

"You mean his father's?"

"Yes."

Dubb grinned grimly. "I couldn't get him to take it back. He meant no disrespect, of course. He just wasn't acting himself. . . . I wasn't sure what to do. So I took it to my father and asked for his thoughts on the matter."

"But didn't your father and Tavin's father—"

"I know, but I didn't know what else to do. He isn't called The

Glaive for nothing. And Tavin *is*, after all, the closest thing he has to a favorite."

"I don't believe that," said Ember. "Tavin was terrified of him. You both were."

"Were?"

"Your father loves you, Dubb. He just doesn't know how to show it."

Dubb unconsciously massaged the scars on the backs of his hands.

"He was far too brutal to the two of you," she added.

Dubb's eyes flashed. "He most certainly was not! We were foolishly talented."

"Those are his words."

"And damned accurate! He was—and remains to this day—the royal master-at-arms. He couldn't have us running around like idiots, doing whatever we pleased."

"He *made* you fear him."

"Everyone fears him. It's *natural* to fear The Glaive. He sees all weaknesses."

Ember folded her arms. "Your Darce doesn't fear him," she said pointedly.

Dubb rolled his eyes. "By the moons, she should."

"It's he who fears her."

Dubb smiled. "Fear would find no life in that man's heart. Darce is still young. Perhaps what you're seeing is respect . . . for what *could* be—nothing more."

"I know fear when I see it. And I tell you, he *fears* her."

Dubb looked down at his hands, as if just noticing the lacework of scars on their backs for the first time.

"I understand he won't cross blades with her anymore," continued Ember, "not even practice ones. He won't even allow her to see his bouts. Why is that?"

"Because—" began Dubb, but he had no answer.

"Because he *fears* she will find his weakness," said Ember.

Dubb's eyes darted about. "The Glaive has no weaknesses," he said as though by rote. "Only traps."

"I tell you she's found one—maybe more."

Dubb snorted, shaking his head as though Ember had suggested something crazy.

"So, what did he say about the sword?" she asked.

"What? Oh, yes. You must understand, he is very traditional about these kinds of things."

"You mean superstitious, don't you?"

"Hm." Dubb's eyes clouded over with memories. "I'm not so sure anymore. The older I get—" Dubb glanced to the door, distractedly, then back to Ember. "He said . . . he said bad things happen when swords fall out of families."

"Do you believe that?"

"All my life I have found it unwise to doubt his knowledge concerning any aspect of the blade. Lore or no."

From down the hallway came the creaking of the door.

"Good, Tavin's back," she said. "I must be going now."

Ember dropped the rings into a pouch at her waist. Quickly pocketing the book, she hastily folded up the rubbings and reached for her traveling cloak.

"You're still too weak to travel alone. Let him take you as far as the rampart. You'll be safe from there on."

Ember looked doubtfully at Dubb. "Couldn't you take me?" she asked.

"I think not."

Tavin entered the room, limping slightly but in a much brighter mood. "I've arranged for the carts and wagons. They'll be ready at sunrise."

"Good work. Now take Ember to the ramparts."

Tavin's face fell. A second later, he noticed the moon sword lying on his bed. "What's been going on? Where's Lily?"

Ember brushed past him as she left the room.

"Lily's gone," said Dubb.

"Gone? Did she say when she'd be back?"

"No. In fact, she said someone else may come in her stead." Dubb nudged Tavin out of the room. "Now go."

Ember was just closing the door behind her, stepping out into the street. Tavin paused in the hallway. "Couldn't you take her?" he asked, avoiding Dubb's eyes.

"Tavin," Dubb began, looking uneasily at the door, "she tried some kind of spell that didn't work. She's very weakened. You know how she is; she's not about to—"

But Tavin had limped out into the street before Dubb could finish his sentence.

Ember was nowhere to be seen. She could have taken any number of routes to the ramparts through the warren of roads and alleys in this quarter. Tavin would need to be lucky to guess which one. Sadly, it's not the lot of the cursed to be lucky.

Tavin had long since grown accustomed to most things in his life going wrong. But he refused to give in. Nothing about his life was simple anymore. Used to failure, he had learned always to prepare a backup plan—a sound philosophy, be the task as deadly as a duel, or as harmless as picking the apple without the worm. Over the years, Tavin had come to think that, occasionally, briefly, he could still will his luck to the good, just as in the days before he met Curse, when his luck had always run high.

Guessing Ember's route correctly, he arrived at her side within moments. Neither spoke a word during the long walk to the ramparts. At different times, though, each stole a lingering glance, though neither realized or would have guessed that the other did so, too.

It was well after midnight when Tavin tossed Dubb's moon sword onto the dresser. Rarely had the friends been more exhausted. During Tavin's walk with Ember, Dubb had decided it would be wise to watch over him this first night back, and had already appropriated half of Ta-

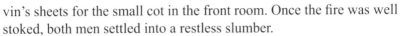
vin's sheets for the small cot in the front room. Once the fire was well stoked, both men settled into a restless slumber.

A clear cold wind descended from the mountaintops. It pushed away the fog and stink that so often hung over the fortress-city, revealing the white-misted moon of Rel' Kah, silently receding. As the night wore on, Taw became the dominant moon, filling the night sky and halting just short of a crossover. Its forests hung dark, green, and lush over the rim of mountains that surrounded Bairne. In time, Taw swung aside, revealing a trailing Darwyth, which soon filled the night with its dead forests and empty seas.

Tavin opened his eyes first.

The fire had burned down to embers, transforming all the room's furniture into dim red shapes, all save the dresser and the hearthstone before the fire. There, two bright shafts of Darwyth's ghostly moonlight shone. The jewels on the moon sword's scabbard cast thin beams onto the ceiling and walls.

And then Tavin heard it clearly: a noise from within the room. He leapt from his bed, dagger at the ready.

"Who goes there?" he shouted.

The noise, a steady metallic whine, grew louder, but he couldn't pinpoint its source.

"Show yourself!" he commanded.

Dubb came flying into the room, his own dagger drawn.

"Is that Curse?" he croaked.

From the bedside chair, Tavin seized his scabbard, holding it to his ear.

"No," he said, belting the sword on over his nightclothes.

The whine increased in volume and pitch.

Instinctively, they moved together, back to back, spinning first to one wall, then another.

Suddenly, beneath the whine, words became audible.

"Tavin, it must be your sword!" protested Dubb.

"No! That's not Curse's voice. Nor its language. I have never heard this tongue, I'm sure of it."

Dubb cocked an ear, listening. "I have," he said. "And just tonight."

The voice rose louder, becoming painful to the ear, like metal being dragged over metal.

Dubb approached the scabbard on the dresser and carefully placed two fingers upon its surface. It was alive with a steady vibration.

He seized the grip in one hand and the scabbard in the other.

"Stand back!" he yelled.

With a yank, he withdrew the moon sword, knelt down, and laid it upon the hearthstones, where the light streaming in from above was its brightest. The moment the blade was free, the metallic whine rose to a tortured scream so painful they had to cover their ears with their hands. And yet they could clearly hear the words of the ancient poem.

Grimacing, both hands pressed tightly to his head, Dubb looked back over his shoulder and caught sight of Tavin staring down at the hearth.

"The blade!" Tavin yelled.

The blade howled like a soul in mortal pain. Shielding their ears did little to diminish the tumult; their heads felt foul and sick. When Dubb turned back to the hearth, he expected to see what he'd feared since the day the crack first surfaced: the blade finally being rent apart, breaking into shards and spilling from its hilt. But instead, he saw the dark crack sealing shut. And as its length shortened, the metallic scream worsened.

The two edges of the crack met. A brilliant flash ignited. A great thunderclap shook the room as though a giant had slammed a tree-sized mace against the outer wall of Tavin's house. They both lost their footing and tumbled to the floor. Then all was silent.

The darkened shapes of the room slowly began to reveal themselves, and the fire, which had looked like ash under the moonlight, slowly regained its red glow. Only now, there was a new light within the room, shining upward from the hearth. Mechanically, both men rolled into squatting positions. Tavin removed a hand from his ear. The only sound in the room came from their breathing.

The new light was coming from the moon sword itself. The runes running the length of the blade shimmered, and an even brighter light shone from the moons on the hilt's cross-guards.

Dubb closed his fingers around the sword's grip and rammed it into its scabbard. The pale light coming from the moons on the hilt extinguished, like the snuffing out of twin candles. He pulled his sword free, just an inch, and the moons rekindled.

"Now, that's new," said Tavin.

Dubb took two quick paces away from the hearth, drawing the blade with a flourish. He quickly traced several complicated patterns in the air at terrific speed.

"It's lighter, faster," he announced.

"By the sound of it, I dare say sharper, too." Tavin pushed a handful of dry twigs into the fireplace's embers, followed by two small logs, then sat down on the edge of the bed. The twigs smoldered before bursting into flame and lighting up the room.

Dubb re-sheathed the sword and sat opposite his old friend.

"Let me guess," said Tavin, "there's some little story or other that goes along with all this that you *somehow* neglected to mention."

Weary, hunched over, the two men stared at each other through the tops of their eyes.

"Yeah, something like that."

"And you had no intention of filling me in?"

"None whatsoever," Dubb confessed, shaking his head wearily.

Staring hard at each other, they slowly dissolved into helpless laughter.

Back Home

L OFTED into total darkness, buffeted by swift currents as thick as water but dry as air, Lily hurtled across distances she couldn't begin to imagine. Not for the first time, she cursed herself for not having brought a flashlight.

This time, she landed bottom first, in her room, in her chair, at her desk, and with a force that rattled her teeth.

The fog in Lily's head dispersed faster this time, but the darkness of the room confused her until, by degrees, her eyes slowly adjusted to the dim moonlight streaming through her window.

Lily pressed her fingertips against the edge of her desk.

Solid. She was back. It was nighttime. She let out a small sigh and flicked on the Christmas lights strung around the front of her bookcase. A rainbow of colors winked to life, illuminating a floor strewn with clothes, books, towels, homework papers, scrunchies, pencils, music CDs, mutilated cat toys, and ribbons. Home. The only bare bits of carpet were narrow paths connecting the more desirable areas: her door, her closet, her bed, her desk.

Her room appeared unchanged, except for the darkened desk lamp, which now rested on its side. Gingerly, she righted the lamp, turning its switch a few times. Nothing.

She drew in a deep breath, held it, and listened to the house's sounds. A breeze stirred through the trees outside her window. The swaying limbs splayed a lacework of shadows across the bedspread. She continued to hold her breath, trying to detect any vibration of activity. But she sensed nothing. If she really wanted to know who was up, she was going to have to investigate.

What if her parents were asleep? Should she wake them? Or wait until morning? They must be crazy with worry—but if they were asleep, wouldn't it be better to wait until morning? She couldn't decide. One thing was certain: she ought to hide as much evidence from her journey as possible *before* seeing them. At least they hadn't been waiting in her room when she returned. Lily stood up, still a bit wobbly, and unfastened her riding cloak.

And then she thought about the door. Once they discovered she was gone, her parents would have used their master key and left the room unlocked—meaning her mother or father could walk in at any moment. She had no idea what story she would eventually come up with, but she knew, from years of experience, that details were best left vague, scant, or missing . . . it just turned out better all round. Just the clothes alone would entail far more explaining than she wanted to do.

In a nervous motion that was becoming a habit, Lily's hand went to the pendant. It felt cool. Had it been this cool when she'd arrived on Barreth or Dain? Eyeing it warily in her palm, she double-checked that the fob was properly clasped.

Suddenly, she thought of the drawing on the desk. It was still there! Why hadn't Jasper hidden it? She knew *she* would have. This meant her parents knew she had Ebb's necklace. Lily wondered how much, if anything, her parents knew about the pendant. How had everything gone so bad so quickly?

Lily fought to bring some order to her thoughts. Could she get away with saying that she'd lost the necklace? Not if they knew she'd used it to get back. She had found it in Uncle Ebb's house; wouldn't that mean he was somewhere on Earth? But why had he left it on the dress mannequin? Had he somehow sent it back while he stayed in the Moon Realm? Why would he do such a thing?

Once again Lily remembered the door—the *unlocked* door. She dashed over to it, but the locking mechanism wouldn't turn. Had her parents broken it trying to get in?

She jiggled the latch. Maybe it was just stuck. And then the answer became clear: she couldn't lock it because it was already locked. But why? Were they preserving her room like a crime scene?

Lily switched into damage-control mode. She needed a plan—a good one. She would face her parents in the morning. They would be apoplectic with rage. How was she going to handle them? Jasper would have told them something, but what? He probably knew less than they did about what was going on.

Still, what would he have told them? They must know about the pendant. Did he tell them about the secret room? She needed answers and she needed them now. Lily sighed. She would have to wake Jasper. That would go badly—he never woke well. But desperate times called for desperate measures. As Uncle Ebb always said, if you want to make good plans, then you have to build them on good information—or, when he was in a hurry—good information, good plans.

Jasper could wait a little longer, though. First, there were tracks to cover. Lily tossed everything she'd brought back from the Moon Realm on the bed: the helmet, greaves, and vambraces. The slim ring, the riding cloak, the strange wooden orb with the carved runes, the beautiful boots. Only the necklace around her neck remained. She eyed the pile. What was she missing? Inspecting the contents of her jeans, she noticed nearly every pocket was bulging with the kinds of things she loved to collect: odd leaves, twigs, moss, pieces of bark, unusual stones. She stared at them, unable to remember picking them up.

"By the moons," she whispered, "I'm a kleptonaturalist."

She folded them all into a purple bandana, hoping that when she catalogued them, she might somehow remember which moons they'd come from.

She stepped out of her dirty jeans, leaving them where they lay, and stripped off her t-shirt. She wanted a shower, but that would mean leaving her room. She wasn't ready to risk that yet. From a pile next to the bed, she plucked out a nightshirt that, compared to her Moon Realm garb, felt and smelled like it had just come out of a field of daisies and honeysuckle.

Lily crawled across the bed, retrieved her laptop, and settled down into the pillows. The screen was bright at first, but once her eyes adjusted, she read the computer's clock: *Mon 3:26 AM.* Monday? But she'd left on Sunday. She knew she'd been gone for a long time . . . but a whole week?

Was there something wrong with her laptop? Lily closed its lid, opened it. She yawned. It still said Monday. She yawned again. She'd spent an awful long time in the saddle since she'd left home, and while saddle time was always exhilarating in the moment, it was also exhausting after the fact.

Lily clicked on the calendar program in the Dock and stared. The highlighted date was the very next day after she'd left . . . making her total time in the Moon Realm a little over six hours. But that wasn't possible. It had been *days*. She had distinct memories, and she had *not* been dreaming. She had brought things back! *They're at my feet, right? You can't do that in dreams!* Slowly, Lily tipped down the screen of her laptop and peered at the pile of clothes and objects she'd brought back from the Moon Realm. They were still there. Good. Not even the most realistic dreams can create piles of clothing. Lily pulled up her browser and googled *time est.* Her first hit was *The official U.S. time clock.* She clicked on it. Its date and time were the same as her computer's: she'd been gone for a little over six hours.

This changed everything. It didn't make any sense, but it changed *everything*. For one, it meant that unless her parents had come to check on her, which was highly unlikely . . . then she was totally free and clear. They wouldn't know she'd gone *anywhere*. They wouldn't know anything! Relief and excitement flooded through her.

What had her last actions been on Earth? She remembered kissing both her parents goodnight. It hadn't been super late. Would they have checked on her? Of course not. There would be no reason for it. And it explained the locked door. Was it possible? Had she *really* gotten away with visiting the Moon Realm?

Lily's mind reeled. New plan! No confession—no difficult explanations. The only lies would be lies of omission—a personal strong suit. She would still need to hide everything, of course, but after that . . . she could even squeeze in a shower. This was just *too* good.

Lily set to work.

The riding cloak, being the largest item, would be the hardest to hide. There wasn't a huge amount of room in the cedar chest at the foot of her bed, but after moving around the winter blankets and fiddling with the sweaters, she was finally able to get the lid closed again. That would buy her the rest of spring and all of summer. She wouldn't need to think about a different hiding place until fall.

Lily walked into her closet, surveying the possibilities. It was so cavernous that she'd wondered, when she was growing up, if it had once been a small bedroom. But on her ninth birthday, as a surprise, her father and uncle had transformed it into a closet paradise: shelves, nooks, pullout drawers, the works. A tall cedar-lined cabinet, with a full-length mirror on the door, held her winter things. A rolling ladder swiveled on a curved rail, giving her full access to all the top shelves. The next year, she had asked for pegs to be attached down its sides. There she hung all manner of beaded necklaces and feathered boas from her dress-up days.

On the longest rod—one of four—hung the bulk of her clothing, compulsively grouped by type of garment and organized within garment type by color: white to black then yellow, orange, red, green, blue, and purple in strict order. Underneath the racks, however, existed a world populated by the once-loved and prematurely mangled. She would yield neither of these to the laundry basket of judgment. If she did, the once-loved would vanish, consigned to the endless hunger of the thrift store donation bag that lurked next to the washing machine. And the prematurely mangled? Lily shuddered to think. This nether area would be the perfect hiding place. Only Tarzanna, the family cat, was brave enough to venture here.

Sad that she wasn't able to recall a prayer for an occasion like this, Lily knelt down and began excavating. The first item she pulled out was a blouse she'd received that Christmas. It had lasted approximately two hours before she tore it nearly in half. If only she hadn't worn it into the barn to show Hello Kitty her new bridle. Freak accident. Or so she would have sworn, although the truth was slightly completely different. She buried her face in the blouse. *Stupid, stupid, stupid.* The second item was a gift from Uncle, a yellow sundress. Smeared across the front was a big dark stain. *I don't deserve nice things. Why do they give me nice things?* The next was a pair of white dress boots her mother had given her for nationals. They were missing a heel and looked like they'd been chewed on by a teething wirtle. *I'm blind! I'm blind!*

Lily concentrated hard after that on seeing objects only for what they were, not how they looked. She dug out a prized jacket (both pieces), a dozen lonely socks, leggings, orphaned halves of outfits, old dress-up clothes. She gasped as a long-lost pair of jeans surfaced. They were unscathed. After hugging them for ten minutes, and crying a little, she decided that maybe, just maybe, she could use a good night's sleep. Ten minutes later, she'd burrowed a narrow passageway stretching all the way to the wall.

Dragging herself to the bed, fighting a wave of exhaustion, she sorted through the remaining items from the Moon Realm. The purple bandana full of stones and plant matter she set aside. Eventually, every seed, stone, and leaf would need to be categorized and filed in one of her museum books, but that could wait until tomorrow. The boots were another thing altogether. The boots would be trouble. She'd want to clean them. She'd want to *wear* them. A good pair of boots should never be wasted, and these were the handsomest pair she'd ever slipped her toe in. If she made a mistake and left them lying around, her mother would grill her. Wistfully, she scooped up everything and deposited it at the mouth of her recent excavation. She removed the purple bandana and pushed the rest of the jumble to the back of the passageway. The entombing took no time. Turned out Lily was a respectable entomber.

She leaned back on her heels. She needed a good place for the necklace. After several minutes, she slid open a drawer and withdrew a pair of *very* old black riding boots. Cracked and worn, and stuffed with purple tissue paper to help them keep their shape, they were much too small now. She'd worn them to her first horse show, and she doubted if she would *ever* be able to throw them away. Lily emptied the stuffing from one, and gently inserted the bandana into the foot, followed by the necklace, followed by all the tissue paper. She placed the boots back in the drawer and admired her handiwork. Her closet looked just as it always had.

Lily surprised herself by deciding not to take a shower, vowing instead to change her bed linens in the morning. The flannel sheets, covered with dancing purple penguins wearing ice skates, were cool as she slipped between them, but warmed up quickly. With the lights out at last, she buried her head in her softest pillow and relished the comfort of her own bed. Outside, the wind picked up and died down. On her dresser, the dim display on her alarm clock read 3:45. Her eyelids dipped. What would she tell Jasper? she wondered.

When she opened her eyes again, the clock read 4:05. Her brain felt sluggish and confused; her memories, suspect. Had she dozed off? *Tomorrow*, she thought. *I was thinking about tomorrow. When I show Jasper the pendant. . . . Tomorrow I'll explain my adventures. He'll listen . . . he'll laugh . . . and then he'll make me give the moon coin to . . . to Dad.*

Lily patted her chest groggily, feeling for the shape of the pendant. It wasn't there. Had she dropped it? She groped about her neck for the chain. Nothing. Her pulse quickened, and the sleepiness that had been weighing her down lifted like a leaf kicked up in a storm wind. She sat bolt upright, surveying her room. Now her heart was pounding. She'd been asleep—had she been dreaming? The room was dark, but there was plenty of moonlight.

Dark outlines of model horses pranced atop her dresser. On the bookcase, more figures balanced, fantastic birthday gifts from Uncle Ebb: a black unicorn; a seahorse dragon; a mermaid with three children; a Dain lunamancer riding a Rinn; Kormor the giantess, complete with hammer and anvil; and her favorite, Faerathil the Faerie Queen, currently posed with her arms reaching upward and her wings fully extended. The wings were like something Da Vinci would have dreamed up. Even after nine years, Faerathil's first flight, with Morgoroth chasing her around the bedposts, remained a vivid, much-loved memory.

Lily gazed uneasily at her closet door. The curtains billowed, and the riding ribbons attached to the tops of her bedposts fluttered, casting their large, twirling shadows against the doors and walls. The aquarium by the window was empty and quiet: no visitors for Hotel Lily tonight. Her room looked exactly the same. Everything was the same. Nothing had changed.

Her breathing was ragged. *Could* she have dreamed it? It wouldn't have been the first time. But no. This time she'd really been there. Nimlinn *was* real—no one would ever convince her otherwise. Lily whipped back the covers and leapt from the bed, yanking open the closet door and retrieving the old riding boot. Just for a moment, she wondered, *wouldn't it be easier if the moon coin wasn't in there?*

Picking her steps carefully, she cradled the boot like a five million dollar Ming vase containing a sleeping Djinn of unknown sympathies. Tree shadows swayed across the room. Sitting at her desk, with the boot upright in her lap, she hesitated. *Just a boot.* She screwed up her courage and tugged out a piece of purple tissue paper, then another, and another until her desk was covered. *Something I should have let go of a long time ago. An old riding boot, too small to fit.*

And those tales? Just stupid bedtime stories told by an uncle with an overactive imagination and way too much time on his hands. . . .

Lily tilted the dark opening of the boot up to her face. It was big and black and seemed surreally larger than it should be. Strange feelings loomed in her mind: the hole was growing larger and larger, threatening to swallow her up, and then she was falling, falling down some endless rabbit's hole. *Just stories?*

Lily ran her index finger around the top of the boot, took a deep breath, and plunged in. The back of her hand brushed worn leather, but her fingers closed around something cold and metallic. She drew out a long gold chain and dangling pendant, fitted with an odd coin: Uncle Ebb's moon coin. Well, at least she hadn't imagined that. Lily lowered the necklace onto her desk. The chain clinked softly as it piled up on itself. *And now*, she thought, *for Wonderland.*

She thrust her hand into the boot and grasped the balled-up bandana. It felt very light in her nervous hands, but when she unfolded it, even in the moonlight, Lily could make out the proof she was looking for: little stones, leaves, and seeds that she had brought back from the Moon Realm. *See all the trouble you started?*

Tomorrow, she thought, Jasper would give the necklace to their father. And what would he do with it?

Her mind raced. What would happen to her new friends in the Moon Realm? What would Nimlinn and Roan do without her? What if her father stored it away for months? Nimlinn and Roan needed help *now*. How would she get back to Barreth? "That option for returning to Barreth is closed to you," Ember had said. "The Blight Marsh is far too dangerous." But cross-overs between Dain and Barreth didn't happen every day, and they were hard to predict. How would she know what time to go back?

Lily thought of her last moments on Barreth, as the moon coin drew her away. Nimlinn knew their time was short. She'd said something: eel, the number eight, and ear. Lily rolled the sounds around inside her brain. Eel couldn't have been right, though she would have been surprised if there weren't lots of eels in the Blight Marsh, along with much worse things. Eight could refer to a particular moon. Could Nimlinn have been refer-ring to the next moon to cross over with Barreth? Ear. Ear? She

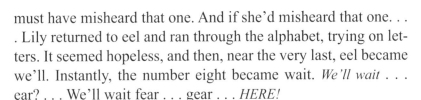
must have misheard that one. And if she'd misheard that one. . . . Lily returned to eel and ran through the alphabet, trying on letters. It seemed hopeless, and then, near the very last, eel became we'll. Instantly, the number eight became wait. *We'll wait* . . . ear? . . . We'll wait fear . . . gear . . . *HERE!*

Nimlinn was waiting!

The Queen of the Rinn was waiting in the Blight Marsh for her return! But how long would Nimlinn wait? And with time flowing differently on Earth and in the Moon Realm, how long had they already waited? Lily furrowed her brow. The fire-breathing dragonflies had originally come from the Blight Marsh. Would they return there out of instinct? How would Nimlinn protect herself? Surely, Aleron would be no match for fire-breathing dragonflies!

Lily flicked open the fob. The moons remained dark. Ember had said it took very little time for the moon coin to replenish on Earth. But how did *she* know that? Had Ember been to Earth, to Ebb's mansion? Had Ember been on the farm, in this house? Did she know Lily's parents? And just what was Ember to Ebb, anyway, if he was showing her how the coin worked and traveling to and from the Moon Realm with her?

Lily pressed the fob closed. If it only took an hour or two to replenish, there would be time for one more trip before sunrise. If it took longer, she would have to wait until tomorrow night. But how would she get Jasper to believe her?

Lily stepped into her bunny slippers, unlocked her bedroom door, and padded down the hall to her brother's room.

He would need clothes. A warm jacket wouldn't hurt, and shoes, and socks . . . and food! Lily ran back to her dresser, grabbing a handful of LUNA Bars and her iPod before returning.

Jasper's door was ajar. The trees outside his window grew closer to the house, making it darker in his room. She could hear the branches scraping against the outside brick. Lily activated her iPod and flashed it into the darkness like a mini flashlight. Tarzanna, curled at the foot of the bed, was not amused. Jasper's dresser creaked noisily each time she opened or closed a drawer. Sadly, there were no actual clothes in *any* of the drawers. "Boys are such heathens," she hissed under her breath.

By the end, she collected all the clothing from his floor, clicking the iPod repeatedly to keep the light going. When she finally found a jacket, she stuffed its pockets with the LUNA Bars, filled the body of it with the rest of the clothes, and rolled the whole thing up like a log.

Even under the best of circumstances, rousing Jasper was not advisable. He was a grumpy waker and generally stayed grumpy for long periods of time afterwards. Staring at his limp form, she realized she had another problem: her brother would remember little to none of what she was going to tell him. She decided to write a note with the key points he'd need to know and put it in his pocket.

Lily shined her iPod at Jasper's desk. Unlike her own, his was neat as a pin. Seizing a pen she quickly jotted down the names of those she thought could be trusted. She made a few calculations and scribbled wild guesses about how long it might take for the moon coin to recharge in the Moon Realm, and then, in big letters, she noted which moons *not* to visit. Lily had to hold the coin in a patch of moonlight in order to copy down the symbols of the safe ones: Earth, Barreth, Dain, Taw. Lastly, she dashed down the coin's basic operation, as she understood it, and explained that time-wise, he couldn't afford going to ANY other moons before coming back to Earth. It was a bit of a jumble, she realized as she re-read the note, but he was smart—he'd figure it out. Lily folded the paper and slipped it in amongst the LUNA Bars. It was time.

Lily took a position at the head of the bed. A simple nudge would be a waste of time. Bears hibernated less soundly. A good shake to the shoulder? Useless. Lily placed a hand on each of her brother's shoulders and shook him so violently his whole body bounced off the bed.

"Wake up!" she hissed. "Wake up!"

After a full minute, he started making groggy sounds. A little while later, words came.

"Stop. Leave . . . me . . . alone. Go away."

Lily did none of these things.

Eventually, Jasper opened his eyes to see who was shaking him.

"Hey. Wha—?"

"Wake up!" said Lily.

Jasper's voice grew louder. "What? What's going on?"

"Listen! I've figured out where Uncle Ebb has been going."

Jasper angled himself up on his elbows and squinted.

"Lily? Is that you?" he asked.

"Yes! It's me, you idiot! Now listen! I've figured out where Uncle Ebb has been going."

"Do you know where he is now?"

"No. Not exactly. But we need to find him. We need to go back."

"Go back? Go back where?"

"That's what I'm trying to tell you. I know what the necklace is for! The bedtime tales—they're real! I've been to the Moon

Realm! Ebb wasn't making it up. You need to go there, too. You need to see it for yourself!"

Jasper blinked his eyes as though he thought that might help. It didn't.

"Lily, you've been dreaming. Go back to bed." He dropped back into his pillows, pulling one up over his ear.

Lily yanked the pillow away and tossed it behind her.

"No!" she said. "You have to listen to me!"

"Go to bed, Lily," said Jasper, sounding grumpier. "Let me sleep. We'll talk about it in the morning."

"No. Morning will be too late. You have to go. You have to go back tonight!"

Jasper flopped onto his stomach.

"The only place I'm going back to is sleep. Get out!"

"No!" pleaded Lily. "Just let me explain."

Jasper swung his legs out of the bed and stood. He clutched the blanket around his shoulders, and an angry look bloomed on his sleepy face.

"Go," he said hoarsely.

Lily backed away quickly, her eyes widening with alarm. She wasn't afraid of being removed, or even of being locked out, for she had long ago secured a key to his room, but Jasper had installed a bolt, and if he woke up enough, he just might think about using it. Then she would have no way of getting in.

"You're right," she said, holding up her hands.

"I am?" said Jasper, looking a bit confused.

"Yes! You're right. Now just sit down for a minute and let me think. Then I'll leave . . . and you can go back to sleep."

"Okay," said Jasper, sitting down and staring at nothing in particular.

A minute passed. Jasper's eyelids drooped.

"Maybe you should lie down," she offered. "You know, I—I always think better that way."

"Right," said Jasper, slumping onto his side. A minute later he began to snore.

So much for the direct approach, Lily thought, removing the moon coin from her own neck and carefully slipping it around his. She wrapped his arms around the log of clothes. Then, leaning over him, she unlocked the coin's fob and spun the inner circle of moons. Dodging the shadows of the swaying tree limbs, Lily struggled to pick out Barreth's little symbol. But Earth, with its tiny satellite moon, was easy to find, and she remembered the moons were in alphabetical order after it. Barreth would be the very first one. She took a long time fussing with the moon coin before snapping the fob closed and backing away.

It was done. When the moon coin reached a full charge, her brother would vanish. Lily stepped backward and sank down into the cushioned chair under the window, drawing up her knees and hugging the pillow she'd yanked away.

The clock on Jasper's desk read 4:25. She'd been back for a whole hour. Time was running short. She just needed to stay awake so that if it got too late, she could call off the mission and set the coin back to Earth. And if she couldn't *show* him the Moon Realm, she'd have to attempt to explain . . . although she knew, deep down, she would have very little chance of convincing him.

Lily glanced around Jasper's darkened room. His tastes were changing faster than hers. He was leaving his childhood behind. His once fanciful drawings were morphing into feasible-looking drafts. All of his picture books were gone. But on his bookcase,

Uncle Ebb's figurines still stood tall: a giant Jasper had named Big Thud; at his feet, the three tiny tinkers, Think, Thank, and Thunk; a Dragondain, Major Combat, riding Rinnjinn; a bird of Taw; Dolf, the merman, on the mighty Kress, his seahorse dragon; and towering over them all, his wings spread wide, Morgoroth the Devourer, Keeper of the Magic Flame, greatest dragon in all the Moon Realm.

A cool draft poured across the windowsill. Lily shivered. She unfolded the blanket draped over the back of the chair and snuggled into it. Maybe if she showed him the things she had brought back. . . . Would he believe her then?

Lily woke with a start, a sound memory rapidly retreating from her consciousness. What had she heard? Tarzanna?

The sunlight streaming through the windows was so blinding she dared not open her eyes more than a crack. A sharp rap sounded on the door. *That was it! That was the sound!*

"Jasper?" came Linnea's muffled voice. "Have you seen your sister?"

"Oh no!" Lily gasped. "Mother."

She forced her eyes open, her gaze darting around the room before finally settling on the bed's rumpled sheets . . . *empty*, rumpled sheets.

"Jasper!" Lily breathed, barely above a whisper. "What have I done?"

The End

TheMoonRealm.com

Return to Barreth

JASPER understood nightmares. Drowning, tumbling about in darkness, not being able to breathe—or just being *afraid* to breathe—these were all fair game in the realm of nightmares. The weirdest thing about this dream, though, was that he *really* thought he was wide awake. Of course, he'd had those dreams before, too: the lucid ones—dreams so real they were *just* like being awake.

And he was pretty sure he was having one of them right now.

Wasn't Lily in this dream earlier? She was going on about something. . . .

With a crash of snapping twigs, Jasper came to rest. He had landed flat on his back, woozy and blinded.

Did I sleepwalk out of my window?

A grayness crept into his vision. Odd, muffled noises like birds and deeper sounds you might expect to hear at a zoo surrounded him. Something was thumping on his chest. In his head, Jasper heard voices.

"It's definitely not she," said an aristocratic voice.

"Are you sure? It looked an awful lot like her to me," came a deeper, rumbling voice.

And there were other voices, in the background, but also inside his head.

"Shorter hair, different clothes. And if I'm not mistaken, this one is a male Dain cub."

"I find it very hard to tell those Dain cubs apart, especially after they change their coats. And we've been in this swamp so long, my nose has become useless."

Blurry, swirling lights appeared on the gray background. Jasper turned onto his side and groped around. *I'm definitely not in the yard*, he thought. He was lying in what felt like a giant bird's nest. His vision cleared a bit more, and he realized that the blurry lights were actually intensely bright stars. The top edge of the nest flickered with the red glow of a nearby fire—a big one, from the sound of it. All of a sudden, an enormous bird's head popped over the rim of the nest and peeked down at him, chattering something . . . *birdish.*

"Are you all right?" he heard in English, followed again with the strange thumping—or was it more like a pulsing?—echoing in time upon his chest.

The huge head pivoted as if to look nearby. "Is it possible it doesn't understand me?" asked the bird.

"Nonsense," said the deep rumbling voice, sounding much closer than it had just a moment before. "Lily understood us just—"

Something leaned over the nest, blotting out the stars. It was a great head—full of teeth and whiskers—wreathed by a blazing mane of fire. Two luminous, amber eyes the size of dinner plates stared down at him.

Jasper fell back and screamed, instinctively raising his arms for protection.

The fiery head retreated quickly, uncloaking the bright stars.

"Oh, I see your point," conceded the deep voice.

. . . to be continued